THE CHRONICLES OF AMBER

VOLUME II

The Chronicles of Amber

VOLUME II

Sign of the Unicorn
The Hand of Oberon
The Courts of Chaos

ROGER ZELAZNY

NELSON DOUBLEDAY, INC.
Garden City, New York

CONTENTS

THE CHRONICLES OF AMBER

VOLUME II

SIGN OF THE UNICORN

*For Jadawin and his Demiurge,
not to forget Kickaha.*

I

I ignored the questions in the eyes of the groom as I lowered the grisly parcel and turned the horse in for care and maintenance. My cloak could not really conceal the nature of its contents as I slung the guts over my shoulder and stamped off toward the rear entrance to the palace. Hell would soon be demanding its paycheck.

I skirted the exercise area and made my way to the trail that led toward the southern end of the palace gardens. Fewer eyes along that route. I would still be spotted, but it would be a lot less awkward than going in the front way, where things are always busy. Damn.

And again, damn. Of troubles I considered myself amply possessed. But those who have do seem to get. Some spiritual form of compound interest, I suppose.

There were a few idlers beside the fountain at the far end of the garden. Also, a couple of guards were passing among the bushes near the trail. The guards saw me coming, held a brief discussion, and looked the other way. Prudent.

Me, back less than a week. Most things, still unresolved. The court of Amber, full of suspicion and unrest. This, now: a death to further jeopardize the brief, unhappy prereign of Corwin I: me.

Time now to do something I should have done right away. But there had been so many things to do, from the very first. It was not as if I had been nodding, as I saw it. I had assigned priorities and acted on them. Now, though . . .

I crossed the garden, out of the shade and into the slanting sunlight. I swung up the wide, curving stair. A guard snapped to attention as I entered the palace. I made for the rear stairway, then up to the second floor. Then the third.

From the right, my brother Random stepped out of his suite and into the hallway.

"Corwin!" he said, studying my face. "What's the matter? I saw you from the balcony and—"

"Inside," I said, gesturing with my eyes. "We are going to have a private conference. Now."

He hesitated, regarding my burden.

"Let's make it two rooms up," he said. "Okay? Vialle's in here."

"All right."

He led the way, opened the door. I entered the small sitting room, sought a likely spot, dropped the body.

Random stared at the bundle.

"What am I supposed to do?" he asked.

"Unwrap the goodies," I said, "and take a look."

He knelt and undid the cloak. He folded it back.

"Dead all right," he observed. "What's the problem?"

"You did not look closely enough," I said. "Peel back an eyelid. Open the mouth and look at the teeth. Feel the spurs on the backs of the hands. Count the joints in the fingers. Then you tell me about the problem."

He began doing these things. As soon as he looked at the hands he stopped and nodded.

"All right," he said. "I remember."

"Remember out loud."

"It was back at Flora's place . . ."

"That was where *I* first saw anyone like this," I said. "They were after you, though. I never did find out why."

"That's right," he said. "I never got a chance to tell you about it. We weren't together all that long. Strange . . . Where did this one come from?"

I hesitated, torn between pushing him for his story and telling him mine. Mine won out because it was mine and very immediate.

I sighed and sank into a chair.

"We've just lost us another brother," I said. "Caine is dead. I got there a bit too late. That thing—person—did it. I wanted it alive, for obvious reasons. But it put up quite a fight. I didn't have much of a choice."

He whistled softly, seated himself in the chair opposite me.

"I see," he said very softly.

I studied his face. Was that the faintest of smiles waiting in the wings to enter and meet my own? Quite possibly.

"No," I said flatly. "If it were otherwise, I would have arranged for a lot less doubt as to my innocence. I'm telling you what really happened."

"All right," he said. "Where is Caine?"

"Under a layer of sod, near the Grove of the Unicorn."

"That looks suspicious right there," he said. "Or will. To the others."

I nodded.

"I know. I had to hide the body and cover it in the meantime, though. I couldn't just bring him back and start parrying questions. Not when there were important facts waiting for me, in your head."

"Okay," he said. "I don't know how important they are, but they're yours. But don't leave me hanging, huh? How did this thing happen?"

"It was right after lunch," I said. "I had eaten down at the harbor with Gérard. Afterward, Benedict brought me topside through his Trump. Back in my rooms, I found a note which apparently had been slipped in under the door. It requested a private meeting, later in the afternoon, at the Grove of the Unicorn. It was signed 'Caine.'"

"Have you still got the note?"

"Yes." I dug it out of my pocket and passed it to him. "Here."

He studied it and shook his head.

"I don't know," he said. "It *could* be his writing—if he were in a hurry—but I don't think it is."

I shrugged. I took the note back, folded it, put it away.

"Whatever, I tried to reach him with his Trump, to save myself the ride. But he wasn't receiving. I guessed it was to maintain secrecy as to his whereabouts, if it was all that important. So I got a horse and rode on down."

"Did you tell anyone where you were going?"

"Not a soul. I did decide to give the horse a workout, though, so I rode along at a pretty good clip. I didn't see it happen, but I saw him lying there as I came into the wood. His throat had been cut, and there was a disturbance off in the bushes some distance away. I rode the guy down, jumped him, fought with him, had to kill him. We didn't engage in any conversation while this was going on."

"You're sure you got the right guy?"

"As sure as you can be under such circumstances. His trail went back to Caine. He had fresh blood on his garments."

"Might have been his own."

"Look again. No wounds. I broke his neck. Of course I remembered where I had seen his like before, so I brought him right to you.

Before you tell me about it, though, there was one more thing—just for a clincher." I withdrew the second note, passed it over. "The creature had this on its person. I presume it had removed it from Caine."

Random read it, nodded, and handed it back.

"From you, to Caine, asking to be met there. Yes, I see. Needless to say . . ."

"Needless to say," I finished. "And it does look a bit like my writing—at first glance, anyway."

"I wonder what would have happened if you had gotten there first?"

"Probably nothing," I said. "Alive and looking bad—that seems how they wanted me. The trick was to get us there in the proper order, and I didn't hurry quite enough to miss what was bound to follow."

He nodded.

"Granting the tight scheduling," he said, "it had to be someone on the scene, here in the palace. Any ideas?"

I chuckled and reached for a cigarette. I lit it and chuckled again.

"I'm just back. You have been here all along," I said. "Which one hates me the most these days?"

"That is an embarrassing question, Corwin," he stated. "Everyone's down on you for something. Ordinarily, I would nominate Julian. Only it doesn't seem to hold up here."

"Why not?"

"He and Caine got along very well. For years now. They had been looking out for each other, hanging around together. Pretty thick. Julian is cold and petty and just as nasty as you remember. But if he liked anybody, he liked Caine. I don't think he'd do it to him, not even to get at you. After all, he probably could have found plenty of other ways if that was all he wanted."

I sighed.

"Who's next?"

"I don't know. I just don't know."

"Okay. How do you read the reactions to this?"

"You're screwed, Corwin. Everyone is going to think you did it, no matter what you say."

I nodded at the corpse. Random shook his head.

"That could easily be some poor clod you dug up out of Shadow to take the blame."

"I know," I said. "Funny, coming back to Amber as I did, I arrived at an ideal time for positioning myself advantageously."

"A perfect time," Random agreed. "You didn't even have to kill Eric to get what you wanted. That was a stroke of luck."

"Yes. Still, it is no secret that that is what I came to do, and it is only a matter of time before my troops—foreign, specially armed, and quartered here—are going to start provoking some very bad feelings. Only the presence of an external threat has saved me from that so far. And then there are the things I am suspected of having done before my return—like murdering Benedict's retainers. Now this . . ."

"Yes," Random said, "I saw it coming as soon as you told me. When you and Bleys attacked years ago, Gérard deployed part of the fleet so that it was out of your way. Caine, on the other hand, engaged you with his vessels and scuttled you. Now that he is gone, I imagine you will put Gérard in command of the entire fleet."

"Who else? He is the only man for the job."

"Nevertheless . . ."

"Nevertheless. Admitted. If I were going to kill any one person to strengthen my position, Caine would be the logical choice. That's the real, damning truth."

"How do you propose handling this?"

"Tell everyone what happened and try to discover who was behind it. Have you any better suggestions?"

"I've been trying to think how I could alibi you. But it does not look promising."

I shook my head.

"You are too close to me. No matter how good we made it sound, it would probably have the opposite effect."

"Have you considered admitting to it?"

"Yes. But self-defense is out. With a cut throat, it had to be a matter of surprise. And I have no stomach for starting off with the alternative: hoke up some evidence that he was up to something rotten and say I did it for the good of Amber. I flatly refuse to take on fake guilt under those terms. I'd wind up with a bad odor that way, too."

"But with a real tough reputation."

"It's the wrong kind of tough for the sort of show I want to run. No, that's out."

"That covers everything, then—just about."

"What do you mean 'just about'?"

He studied his left thumbnail through slitted eyes.

"Well, it occurs to me that if there is anyone else you are anxious to get out of the picture, now is the time to consider that a frame can often be shifted."

I thought about it and finished my cigarette.

"Not bad," I said, "but I can't spare any more brothers at the moment. Not even Julian. Anyhow, he's the least frameable."

"It need not be family," he said. "Plenty of noble Amberites around with possible motives. Take Sir Reginald—"

"Forget it, Random! The reframing is out, too."

"Okay. I've exhausted my little gray cells, then."

"Not the ones in charge of memory, I hope."

"All right."

He sighed. He stretched. He got to his feet, stepped over the room's other occupant, and made his way to the window. Drawing back the drapes, he stared out for a time.

"All right," he repeated. "There's a lot to tell. . . ."

Then he remembered out loud.

II

While sex heads a great number of lists, we all have other things we like to do in between. With me, Corwin, it's drumming, being up in the air, and gambling—in no special order. Well, maybe soaring has a little edge—in gliders, balloons, and certain variations—but mood has a lot to do with that too, you know. I mean, ask me another time and I might say one of the others. Depends on what you want most at the moment.

Anyway, I was here in Amber some years ago. Not doing much of anything. Just visiting and being a nuisance. Dad was still around, and when I noticed that he was getting into one of his grumpy moods, I decided it was time to take a walk. A long one. I had often noticed that his fondness for me tended to increase as an inverse function of my proximity. He gave me a fancy riding crop for a going-away present—to hasten the process of affection, I suppose. Still, it was a very nice crop—silver-chased, beautifully tooled—and I made good use of it. I had decided to go looking for an assemblage of all my simple pleasures in one small nook of Shadow.

It was a long ride—I will not bore you with the details—and it was pretty far from Amber, as such things go. This time, I was not looking for a place where I would be especially important. That can get either boring or difficult fairly quickly, depending on how responsible you want to be. I wanted to be an irresponsible nonentity and just enjoy myself.

Texorami was a wide open port city, with sultry days and long nights, lots of good music, gambling around the clock, duels every morning and in-between mayhem for those who couldn't wait. And the air currents were fabulous. I had a little red sail plane I used to go sky surfing in, every couple of days. It was the good life. I played drums till all hours in a basement spot up the river where the walls sweated almost as much as the customers and the smoke used to wash around the lights like streams of milk. When I was done playing I'd go find some action, women, or cards, usually. And that was it for the rest of the night. Damn Eric, anyway! That reminds me again . . . He once accused me of cheating at cards, did you know that? And that's about the only thing I wouldn't cheat at. I take my card playing seriously. I'm good and I'm also lucky. Eric was neither. The trouble with him was that he was good at so many things he wouldn't admit even to himself that there were some things other people could do better. If you kept beating him at anything you had to be cheating. He started a nasty argument over it one night—could have gotten serious—but Gérard and Caine broke it up. Give Caine that. He took my part that time. Poor guy . . . Hell of a way to go, you know? His throat . . . Well, anyhow, there I was in Texorami, making music and women, winning at cards and jockeying around the sky. Palm trees and night-blooming wallflowers. Lots of good port smells—spices, coffee, tar, salt—you know. Gentlefolk, merchants, and peons—the same straights as in most other places. Sailors and assorted travelers passing in and out. Guys like me living around the edges of things. I spent a little over two years in Texorami, happy. Really. Not much contact with the others. Sort of postcardlike hellos via the Trumps every now and then, and that was about it. Amber was pretty much off my mind. All this changed one night when I was sitting there with a full house and the guy across from me was trying to make up his mind whether or not I was bluffing.

The Jack of Diamonds began talking to me.

Yes, that is how it started. I was in a weird frame of mind anyway. I had just finished a couple hot sets and was still kind of high. Also, I was physically strung out from a long day's gliding and not much sleep the night before. I decided later it must be our mental quirk associated with the Trumps that made me see it that way when someone was trying to reach me and I had cards in my hand—any cards. Ordinarily, of course, we get the message empty-handed, unless we are doing the calling. It could have been that my subconscious—which was kind of footloose at the time—just seized on the available props out of habit. Later, though, I had cause to wonder. Really, I just don't know.

The Jack said, "Random." Then its face blurred and it said, "Help me." I began getting a feel of the personality by then, but it was weak. The whole thing was very weak. Then the face rearranged itself and I saw that I was right. It was Brand. He looked like hell, and he seemed to be chained or tied to something. "Help me," he said again.

"I'm here," I said. "What's the matter?"

". . . prisoner," he said, and something else that I couldn't make out.

"Where?" I asked.

He shook his head at that.

"Can't bring you through," he said. "No Trumps, and I am too weak. You will have to come the long way around. . . ."

I did not ask him how he was managing it without my Trump. Finding out where he was seemed of first importance. I asked him how I could locate him.

"Look very closely," he said. "Remember every feature. I may only be able to show you once. Come armed, too. . . ."

Then I saw the landscape—over his shoulder, out a window, over a battlement. I can't be sure. It was far from Amber, somewhere where the shadows go mad. Farther than I like to go. Stark, with shifting colors. Fiery. Day without a sun in the sky. Rocks that glided like sailboats across the land. Brand there in some sort of tower—a small point of stability in that flowing scene. I remembered it, all right. And I remembered the presence coiled about the base of that tower. Brilliant. Prismatic. Some sort of watch-thing, it seemed —too bright for me to make out its outline, to guess its proper size. Then it all just went away. Instant off. And there I was, staring at the Jack of Diamonds again, with the guy across from me not knowing whether to be mad at my long distraction or concerned that I might be having some sort of sick spell.

I closed up shop with that hand and went home. I lay stretched out on my bed, smoking and thinking. Brand had still been in Amber when I had departed. Later, though, when I had asked after him, no one had any idea as to his whereabouts. He had been having one of his melancholy spells, had snapped out of it one day and ridden off. And that was that. No messages either—either way. He wasn't answering, he wasn't talking.

I tried to figure every angle. He was smart, damn smart. Possibly the best mind in the family. He was in trouble and he had called me. Eric and Gérard were more the heroic types and would probably have welcomed the adventure. Caine would have gone out of curiosity, I think. Julian, to look better than the rest of us and to score points with Dad. Or, easiest of all, Brand could have called Dad himself. Dad would have done something about it. But he had called me. Why?

It occurred to me then that maybe one or more of the others had been responsible for his circumstances. If, say, Dad was beginning to favor him . . . Well. You know. Eliminate the positive. And if he did call Dad, he would look like a weakling.

So I suppressed my impulse to yell for reinforcements. He had called me, and it was quite possible that I would be cutting his throat by letting anyone back in Amber in on the fact that he had gotten the message out. Okay. What was in it for me?

If it involved the succession and he had truly become fairhaired, I figured that I could do a lot worse than give him this to remember me by. And if it did not . . . There were all sorts of other possibilities. Perhaps he had stumbled onto something going on back home, something it would be useful to know about. I was even curious as to the means he had employed for bypassing the Trumps. So it was curiosity, I'd say, that made me decide to go it alone and try to rescue him.

I dusted off my own Trumps and tried reaching him again. As you might expect, there was no response. I got a good night's sleep then and tried one more time in the morning. Again, nothing. Okay, no sense waiting any longer.

I cleaned up my blade, ate a big meal, and got into some rugged clothes. I also picked up a pair of dark, polaroid goggles. Didn't know how they would work there, but that warden-thing had been awfully bright—and it never hurts to try anything extra you can think of. For that matter, I also took a gun. I had a feeling it would be worthless, and I was right. But, like I said, you never know till you try.

The only person I said good-bye to was another drummer, because I stopped to give him my set before I left. I knew he'd take good care of them.

Then I went on down to the hangar, got the sail plane ready, went aloft, and caught a proper current. It seemed a neat way to do it.

I don't know whether you've ever glided through Shadow, but— No? Well, I headed out over the sea till the land was only a dim line to the north. Then I had the waters go cobalt beneath me, rear up and shake sparkly beards. The wind shifted. I turned. I raced the waves shoreward beneath a darkening sky. Texorami was gone when I returned to the rivermouth, replaced by miles of swamp. I rode the currents inward, crossing and recrossing the river at new twists and kinks it had acquired. Gone were the piers, the trails, the traffic. The trees were high.

Clouds massed in the west, pink and pearl and yellow. The sun phased from orange through red to yellow. You shake your head? The sun was the price of the cities, you see. In a hurry, I depopulate —or, rather, go the elemental route. At that altitude artifacts would have been distracting. Shading and texture becomes everything for me. That's what I meant about gliding it being a bit different.

So, I bore to the west till the woods gave way to surface green, which quickly faded, dispersed, broke to brown, tan, yellow. Light and crumbly then, splotched. The price of that was a storm. I rode it out as much as I could, till the lightnings forked nearby and I feared that the gusts were getting to be too much for the little glider. I toned it down fast then, but got more green below as a result. Still, I pulled it out of the storm with a yellow sun firm and bright at my back. After a time, I got it to go desert beneath me again, stark and rolling.

Then the sun shrank and strands of cloud whipped past its face, erasing it bit by bit. That was the shortcut that took me farther from Amber than I had been in a long while.

No sun then, but the light remained, just as bright but eerie now, directionless. It tricked my eyes, it screwed up perspective. I dropped lower, limiting my range of vision. Soon large rocks came into view, and I fought for the shapes I remembered. Gradually, these occurred.

The buckling, flowing effect was easier to achieve under these conditions, but its production was physically disconcerting. It made it even more difficult to judge my effectiveness in guiding the glider. I got lower than I thought I was and almost collided with one of the rocks. Finally, though, the smokes rose and flames danced about as I remembered them—conforming to no particular pattern, just emerging here and there from crevasses, holes, cave mouths. Colors began to misbehave as I recalled from my brief view. Then came the actual motion of the rocks—drifting, sailing, like rudderless boats in a place where they wring out rainbows.

By then, the air currents had gone crazy. One updraft after another, like fountains. I fought them as best I could, but knew I could not hold things together much longer at that altitude. I rose a considerable distance, forgetting everything for a time while trying to stabilize the craft. When I looked down again, it was like viewing a free-form regatta of black icebergs. The rocks were racing around, clashing together, backing off, colliding again, spinning, arcing across the open spaces, passing among one another. Then I was slammed about, forced down, forced up—and I saw a strut give way. I gave the shadows their final nudge, then looked again. The tower had appeared in the distance, something brighter than ice or aluminum stationed at its base.

That final push had done it. I realized that just as I felt the winds start a particularly nasty piece of business. Then several cables snapped and I was on my way down—like riding a waterfall. I got the nose up, brought it in low and wild, saw where we were headed, and jumped at the last moment. The poor gilder was pulverized by one of those peripatetic monoliths. I felt worse about that than I did about the scrapes, rips, and lumps I collected.

Then I had to move quickly, because a hill was racing toward me. We both veered, fortunately in different directions. I hadn't the faintest notion as to their motive force, and at first I could see no pattern to their movements. The ground varied from warm to extremely hot underfoot, and along with the smoke and occasional jets of flame, nasty-smelling gases were escaping from numerous openings in the ground. I hurried toward the tower, following a necessarily irregular course.

It took a long while to cover the distance. Just how long, I was uncertain, as I had no way of keeping track of the time. By then, though, I was beginning to notice some interesting regularities. First, the larger stones moved at a greater velocity than the smaller ones. Second, they seemed to be orbiting one another—cycles within cycles within cycles, larger about smaller, none of them ever still. Perhaps the prime mover was a dust mote or a single molecule— somewhere. I had neither time nor desire to indulge in any attempt to determine the center of the affair. Keeping this in mind, I did manage to observe as I went, though, enough so that I was able to anticipate a number of their collisions well in advance.

So Childe Random to the dark tower came, yeah, gun in one hand, blade in the other. The goggles hung about my neck. With all the smoke and confused lighting, I wasn't about to don them until it became absolutely necessary.

Now, whatever the reason, the rocks avoided the tower. While it seemed to stand on a hill, I realized as I approached that it would be more correct to say that the rocks had scooped out an enormous basin just short of it. I could not tell from my side, however, whether the effect was that of an island or a peninsula.

I dashed through the smoke and rubble, avoiding the jets of flame that leaped from the cracks and holes. Finally I scrambled up the slope, removing myself from the courseway. Then for several moments I clung at a spot just below any line of sight from the tower. I checked my weapons, controlled my breathing, and put on the goggles. Everything set, I went over the top and came up into a crouch.

Yes, the shades worked. And yes, the beast was waiting.

It was a fright all right, because in some ways it was kind of beautiful. It had a snake body as big around as a barrel, with a head sort of like a massive claw hammer, but kind of tapered to the snout end. Eyes of a very pale green. And it was clear as glass, with very faint, fine lines seeming to indicate scales. Whatever flowed in its veins was reasonably clear, also. You could look right into it and see its organs —opaque or cloudy as the case might be. You could almost be distracted by watching the thing function. And it had a dense mane, like bristles of glass, about the head and collaring its gullet. Its movement when it saw me, raised that head and slithered forward, was like flowing water—living water, it seemed, a bedless river without banks. What almost froze me, though, was that I could see into its stomach. There was a partly digested man in it.

I raised the gun, aimed at the nearest eye, and squeezed the trigger.

I already told you it didn't work. So I threw the gun, leaped to my left, and sprang in on its right side, going for its eye with my blade.

You know how hard it can be to kill things built along reptilian lines. I decided immediately to try to blind the thing and hack off its tongue as the first order of business. Then, being more than a little fast on my feet, I might have any number of chances to lay in some good ones about the head until I decapitated it. Then let it tie itself in knots till it stopped. I was hoping, too, that it might be sluggish because it was still digesting someone.

If it was sluggish then, I was glad that I hadn't stopped by earlier. It drew its head out of the path of my blade and snapped down over it while I was still off balance. That snout glanced across my chest, and it did feel as if I had been hit by a massive hammer. It knocked me sprawling.

I kept on rolling to get out of range, coming up short near the edge of the embankment. I recovered my footing there while it unwound itself, dragged a lot of weight in my direction, and then reared up and cocked its head again, about fifteen feet above me.

I know damn well that Gérard would have chosen that moment to attack. The big bastard would have strode forward with that monster blade of his and cut the thing in half. Then it probably would have fallen on him and writhed all over him, and he'd have come away with a few bruises. Maybe a bloody nose. Benedict would not have missed the eye. He would have had one in each pocket by then and be playing football with the head while composing a footnote to Clausewitz. But they are genuine hero types. Me, I just stood there holding the blade point upward, both hands on the hilt, my elbows on my hips, my head as far back out of the way as possible. I would much rather have run and called it a day. Only I knew that if I tried it, that head would drop down and smear me.

Cries from within the tower indicated that I had been spotted, but I was not about to look away to see what was going on. Then I began cursing the thing. I wanted it to strike and get it over with, one way or the other.

When it finally did, I shuffled my feet, twisted my body, and swung the point into line with my target.

My left side was partly numbed by the blow, and I felt as if I had been driven a foot into the ground. Somehow I managed to remain upright. Yes, I had done everything perfectly. The maneuver had gone exactly as I had hoped and planned.

Except for the beast's part. It wasn't cooperating by producing the appropriate death throes.

In fact, it was beginning to rise.

It took my blade with it, too. The hilt protruded from its left eye socket, the point emerged like another bristle amid the mane on the back of its head. I had a feeling that the offensive team had had it.

At that moment, figures began to emerge—slowly, cautiously—from an opening at the base of the tower. They were armed and ugly-looking, and I had a feeling that they were not on my side of the disagreement.

Okay. I know when it is time to fold and hope for a better hand another day.

"Brand!" I shouted. "It's Random! I can't get through! Sorry!"

Then I turned, ran, and leaped back over the edge, down into the place where the rocks did their unsettling things. I wondered whether I had chosen the best time to descend.

Like so many things, the answer was yes and no.

It was not the sort of jump I would make for many reasons other than those which prevailed. I came down alive, but that seemed the most that could be said for it. I was stunned, and for a long while I thought I had broken my ankle.

The thing that got me moving again was a rustling sound from above and the rattle of gravel about me. When I readjusted the goggles and looked up, I saw that the beast had decided to come down and finish the job. It was winding its phantom way down the slope, the area about its head having darkened and opaqued since I had skewered it upstairs.

I sat up. I got to my knees. I tried my ankle, couldn't use it. Nothing around to serve as a crutch, either. Okay. I crawled then. Away. What else was there to do? Gain as much ground as I could and think hard while I was about it.

Salvation was a rock—one of the smaller, slower ones, only about the size of a moving van. When I saw it approaching, it occurred to me that here was transportation if I could make it aboard. Maybe some safety, too. The faster, really massive ones appeared to get the most abuse.

This in mind, I watched the big ones that accompanied my own, estimated their paths and velocities, tried to gauge the movement of the entire system, readied myself for the moment, the effort. I also listened to the approach of the beast, heard the cries of the troops from the edge of the bluff, wondered whether anyone up there was giving odds on me and what they might be if they were.

When the time came, I went. I got past the first big one without any trouble, but had to wait for the next one to go by. I took a chance in crossing the path of the final one. Had to, to make it in time.

I made it to the right spot at the right moment, caught on to the holds I had been eyeing, and was dragged maybe twenty feet before I could pull myself up off the ground. Then I hauled my way to its uncomfortable top, sprawled there, and looked back.

It had been close. Still was, for that matter, as the beast was pacing me, its one good eye following the spinning big ones.

From overhead I heard a disappointed wail. Then the guys started down the slope, shouting what I took to be encouragement to the creature. I commenced massaging my ankle. I tried to relax. The brute crossed over, passing behind the first big rock as it completed another orbit.

How far could I shift through Shadow before it reached me? I wondered. True, there was constant movement, a changing of textures . . .

The thing waited for the second rock, slithered by behind it, paced me again, drew nearer.

Shadow, Shadow, on the wing—

The men were almost to the base of the slope by then. The beast was waiting for its opening—the next time around—past the inner satellite. I knew that it was capable of rearing high enough to snatch me from my perch.

—Come alive and smear that thing!

As I spun and glided I caught hold of the stuff of Shadow, sank into the feel of it, worked with the textures, possible to probable to actual, felt it coming with the finest twist, gave it that necessary fillip at the appropriate moment . . .

It came in from the beast's blind side, of course. A big mother of a rock, careening along like a semi out of control . . .

It would have been more elegant to mash it between two of them. However, I hadn't the time for finesse. I simply ran it over and left it there, thrashing in the granite traffic.

Moments later, however, inexplicably, the mashed and mangled body rose suddenly above the ground and drifted skyward, twisting. It kept going, buffeted by the winds, dwindling, dwindling, gone.

My own rock bore me away, slowly, steadily. The entire pattern was drifting. The guys from the tower then went into a huddle and decided to pursue me. They moved away from the base of the slope, began to make their way across the plain. But this was no real problem, I felt. I would ride my stony mount through Shadow, leaving them worlds away. This was by far the easiest course of action open to me. They would doubtless have been more difficult to take by surprise than the beast. After all, this was their land; they were wary and unmaimed.

I removed the goggles and tested my ankle again. I stood for a moment. It was very sore, but it bore my weight. I reclined once more and turned my thoughts to what had occurred. I had lost my blade and I was now in less than top shape. Rather than go on with the venture under these conditions, I knew that I was doing the safest, wisest thing by getting the hell out. I had gained enough knowl-

edge of the lay-out and the conditions for my chances to be better
next time around. All right . . .

The sky brightened above me, the colors and shadings lost something of their arbitrary, meandering habit. The flames began to subside about me. Good. Clouds started to find their ways across the
sky. Excellent. Soon a localized glow began behind a cloudbank. Su-
perb. When it went away, a sun would hang once again in the
heavens.

I looked back and was surprised to see that I was still being
pursued. However, it could easily be that I had not dealt properly
with their analogues for this slice of Shadow. It is never good to assume that you have taken care of everything when you are in a
hurry. So . . .

I shifted again. The rock gradually altered its course, shifted its
shape, lost its satellites, moved in a straight line toward what was to
become the west. Above me, the clouds dispersed and a pale sun
shone down. We picked up speed. That should have taken care of
everything right there. I had positively come into a different place.

But it had not. When I looked again, they were still coming. True,
I had gained some distance on them. But the party trooped right
along after me.

Well, all right. Things like that can sometimes happen.

There were of course two possibilities. My mind still being more
than a little disturbed from all that had just occurred, I had not performed ideally and had drawn them along with me. Or, I had maintained a constant where I should have suppressed a variable—that is,
shifted into a place and unconsciously required that the pursuit element be present. Different guys then, but still chasing me.

I rubbed my ankle some more. The sun brightened toward orange.
A wind out of the north raised a screen of dust and sand and hung it
at my back, removing the gang from my sight. I raced on into the
west, where a line of mountains had now grown up. Time was in a
distortion phase. My ankle felt a little better.

I rested a while. Mine was reasonably comfortable, as rocks go.
No sense turning it into a hellride when everything seemed to be proceeding smoothly. I stretched out, hands behind my head, and
watched the mountains draw nearer. I thought about Brand and the
tower. That was the place all right. Everything was just as it had
been in the glimpse he had given me. Except for the guards, of
course. I decided that I would cut through the proper piece of

Shadow, recruit a cohort of my own, then go back and give them hell. Yes, then everything would be fine . . . .

After a time, I stretched, rolled over onto my stomach, and looked back. Damned if they weren't still following me! They had even gained some.

Naturally, I got angry. To hell with flight! They were asking for it, and it was time they got it.

I rose to my feet. My ankle was only half sore, a little numb. I raised my arms and looked for the shadows I wanted. I found them.

Slowly the rock swung out from its straight course into an arc, turning off to the right. The curve tightened. I swung through a parabola and headed back toward them, my velocity gradually increasing as I went. No time to raise a storm at my back, though I thought that would have been a nice touch if I could have managed it.

As I swept down upon them—there were maybe two dozen—they pudently began to scatter. A number of them didn't make it, though. I swung through another curve and returned as soon as I could.

I was shaken by the sight of several corpses rising into the air, dripping gore, two of them already high above me.

I was almost upon them on that second pass when I realized that a few of them had jumped aboard as I had gone through. The first one over the edge drew his blade and rushed me. I blocked his arm, took the weapon away from him, and threw him back down. I guess it was then that I became aware of those spurs on the backs of their hands. I had been slashed by his.

By that time I was the target of a number of curiously shaped missiles from below, two more guys were coming over the edge, and it looked as if several more might have made it aboard.

Well, even Benedict sometimes retreats. I had at least given the survivors something to remember.

I let go of the shadows, tore a barbed wheel from my side, another from my thigh, hacked off a guy's swordarm and kicked him in the stomach, dropped to my knees to avoid a wild swing from the next one, and caught him across the legs with my riposte. He went over, too.

There were five more on the way up and we were sailing westward once again, leaving perhaps a dozen live ones to regroup on the sand at my back, a sky full of oozing drifters above them.

I had the advantage with the next fellow because I caught him just partway over the edge. So much for him, and then there were four.

While I had been dealing with him, though, three more had arisen, simultaneously, at three different points.

I rushed the nearest and dispatched him, but the other two made it over and were upon me while I was about it. As I defended myself from their attack, the final one came up and joined them.

They were not all that good, but it was getting crowded and there were a lot of points and sharp edges straying about me. I kept parrying and moving, trying to get them to block one another, get in each other's way. I was partly successful, and when I had the best lineup I thought I was going to get, I rushed them, taking a couple of cuts—I had to lay myself open a bit to do it—but splitting one skull for my pains. He went over the edge and took the second one with him in a tangle of limbs and gear.

Unfortunately, the inconsiderate lout had carried off my blade, snagged in some bony cleft or other he had chosen to interpose when I swung. It was obviously my day for losing blades, and I wondered if my horoscope would have mentioned it if I had thought to look before I'd set out.

Anyhow, I moved quickly to avoid the final guy's swing. In doing so, I slipped on some blood and went skidding toward the front of the rock. If I went down that way, it would plow right over me, leaving a very flat Random there, like an exotic rug, to puzzle and delight future wayfarers.

I clawed for handholds as I slid, and the guy took a couple of quick steps toward me, raising his blade to do unto me as I had his buddy.

I caught hold of his ankle, though, and it did the trick of braking me very nicely—and damned if someone shouldn't choose that moment to try to get hold of me via the Trumps.

"I'm busy!" I shouted. "Call back later!" and my own motion was arrested as the guy toppled, clattered, and went sliding by.

I tried to reach him before he fell to rugdom, but I was not quite quick enough. I had wanted to save him for questioning. Still, my unegged beer was more than satisfactory. I headed back top and center to observe and muse.

The survivors were still following me, but I had a sufficient lead. I did not at the moment have to worry about another boarding party. Good enough. I was headed toward the mountains once again. The sun I had conjured was beginning to bake me. I was soaked with sweat and blood. My wounds were giving me trouble. I was thirsty.

Soon, soon, I decided, it would have to rain. Take care of that before anything else.

So I began the preliminaries to a shift in that direction: clouds massing, building, darkening . . . .

I drifted off somewhere along the line, had a disjointed dream of someone trying to reach me again but not making it. Sweet darkness.

I awakened to the rain, sudden and hard-driving. I could not tell whether the darkness in the sky was from storm, evening, or both. It was cooler, though, and I spread my cloak and just lay there with my mouth open. Periodically I wrung moisture from the cloak. My thirst was eventually slaked and I began feeling clean again. The rock had also become so slick-looking that I was afraid to move about on it. The mountains were much nearer, their peaks limned by frequent lightnings. Things were too dark in the opposite direction for me to tell whether my pursuers were still with me. It would have been pretty rough trekking for them to have kept up, but then it is seldom good policy to rely on assumptions when traveling through strange shadows. I was a bit irritated with myself for going to sleep, but since no harm had come of it I drew my soggy cloak about me and decided to forgive myself. I felt around for some cigarettes I had brought along and found that about half of them had survived. After the eighth try, I juggled shadows enough to get a light. Then I just sat there, smoking and being rained on. It was a good feeling and I didn't move to change anything else, not for hours.

When the storm finally let up and the sky came clear, it was a night full of strange constellations. Beautiful though, the way nights can be on the desert. Much later, I detected a gentle upward sloping and my rock started to slow. Something began happening in terms of whatever physical rules controlled the situation. I mean, the slope itself did not seem so pronounced that it would affect our velocity as radically as it had. I did not want to tamper with Shadow in a direction that would probably take me out of my way. I wanted to get back onto more familiar turf as soon as possible—find my way to a place where my gut anticipations of physical events had more of a chance of being correct.

So I let the rock grind to a halt, climbed down when it did, and continued on up the slope, hiking. As I went, I played the Shadow game we all learned as children. Pass some obstruction—a scrawny tree, a stand of stone—and have the sky be different from one side to the other. Gradually I restored familiar constellations. I knew that I would be climbing down a different mountain from the one I ascended. My wounds still throbbed dully, but my ankle had stopped bothering me except for a little stiffness. I was rested. I knew that I could go for a long while. Everything seemed to be all right again.

It was a long hike, up the gradually steepening way. But I hit a trail eventually, and that made things easier. I trudged steadily upward under the now familiar skies, determined to keep moving and make it across by morning. As I went, my garments altered to fit the shadow—denim trousers and jacket now, my wet cloak a dry serape. I heard an owl nearby, and from a great distance below and behind came what might have been the yipyip-howl of a coyote. These signs of a more familiar place made me feel somewhat secure, exorcised any vestiges of desperation that remained with my flight.

An hour or so later, I yielded to the temptation to play with Shadow just a bit. It was not all that improbable for a stray horse to be wandering in these hills, and of course I found him. After ten or so minutes of becoming friendly, I was mounted bareback and moving toward the top in a more congenial fashion. The wind sowed frost in our path. The moon came and sparked it to life.

To be brief, I rode all night, passing over the crest and commencing my downward passage well before dawn. As I descended, the mountain grew even more vast above me, which of course was the best time for this to occur. Things were green on this side of the range, and divided by neat highways, punctuated by occasional dwellings. Everything therefore was proceeding in accordance with my desire.

Early morning. I was into the foothills and my denim had turned to khaki and a bright shirt. I had a light sport jacket slung before me. At a great height, a jetliner poked holes in the air, moving from horizon to horizon. There were birdsongs about me, and the day was mild, sunny.

It was about then that I heard my name spoken and felt the touch of the Trump once more. I drew up short and responded.

"Yes?"

It was Julian.

"Random, where are you?" he asked.

"Pretty far from Amber," I replied. "Why?"

"Have any of the others been in touch with you?"

"Not recently," I said. "But someone did try to get hold of me yesterday. I was busy though, and couldn't talk."

"That was me," he said. "We have a situation here that you had better know about."

"Where are you?" I asked.

"In Amber. A number of things have happened recently."

"Like what?"

"Dad has been gone now for an unusually long time. No one knows where."

"He's done that before."

"But not without leaving instructions and making delegations. He always provided them in the past."

"True," I said. "But how long is 'Long'?"

"Well over a year. You weren't aware of this at all?"

"I knew that he was gone. Gérard mentioned it some time back."

"Then add more time to that."

"I get the idea. How have you been operating?"

"That is the problem. We have simply been dealing with affairs as they arise. Gérard and Caine had been running the navy anyway, on Dad's orders. Without him, they have been making all their own decisions. I took charge of the patrols in Arden again. There is no central authority though, to arbitrate, to make policy decisions, to speak for all of Amber."

"So we need a regent. We can cut cards for it, I suppose."

"It is not that simple. We think Dad is dead."

"Dead? Why? How?"

"We have tried to raise him on his Trump. We have been trying every day for over half a year now. Nothing. What do you think?"

I nodded.

"He may be dead," I said. "You'd think he would have come across with something. Still, the possibility of his being in some trouble—say, a prisoner somewhere—is not precluded."

"A cell can't stop the Trumps. Nothing can. He would call for help the minute we made contact."

"I can't argue with that," I said. But I thought of Brand as I said it. "Perhaps he is deliberately resisting contact, though."

"What for?"

"I have no idea, but it is possible. You know how secretive he is about some things."

"No," Julian said, "it doesn't hold up. He would have given some operating instructions, somewhere along the line."

"Well, whatever the reasons, whatever the situation, what do you propose doing now?"

"Someone has to occupy the throne," he said.

I had seen it coming throughout the entire dialogue, of course—the opportunity it had long seemed would never come to pass.

"Who?" I asked.

"Eric seems the best choice," he replied. "Actually, he has been acting in that capacity for months now. It simply becomes a matter of formalizing it."

"Not just as regent?"

"Not just as regent."

"I see . . . Yes, I guess that things have been happening in my absence. What about Benedict as a choice?"

"He seems to be happy where he is, off somewhere in Shadow."

"What does he think of the whole idea?"

"He is not entirely in favor of it. But we do not believe he will offer resistance. It would disrupt things too much."

"I see," I said again. "And Bleys?"

"He and Eric had some rather heated discussions of the issue, but the troops do not take their orders from Bleys. He left Amber about three months ago. He could cause some trouble later. But then, we are forewarned."

"Gérard? Caine?"

"They will go along with Eric. I was wondering about yourself."

"What about the girls?"

He shrugged.

"They tend to take things lying down. No problem."

"I don't suppose Corwin . . ."

"Nothing new. He's dead. We all know it. His monument has been gathering dust and ivy for centuries. If not, then he has intentionally divorced himself from Amber forever. Nothing there. Now I am wondering where you stand."

I chuckled.

"I am hardly in a position to possess forceful opinions," I said.

"We need to know now."

I nodded.

"I have always been able to detect the quarter of the wind," I said. "I do not sail against it."

He smiled and returned my nod.

"Very good," he said.

"When is the coronation? I assume that I am invited."

"Of course, of course. But the date has not yet been set. There are still a few minor matters to be dealt with. As soon as the affair is calendared, one of us will contact you again."

"Thank you, Julian."

"Good-bye for now, Random."

And I sat there being troubled for a long while before I started on downward again. How long had Eric spent engineering it? I wondered. Much of the politicking back in Amber could have been done pretty quickly, but the setting up of the situation in the first place seemed the product of long-term thinking and planning. I was naturally suspicious as to his involvement in Brand's predicament. I also could not help but give some thought to the possibility of his having a hand in Dad's disappearance. That would have taken some doing and have required a really foolproof trap. But the more I thought of it, the less I was willing to put it past him. I even dredged up some old speculations as to his part in your own passing, Corwin. But, offhand, I could not think of a single thing to do about any of it. Go along with it, I figured, if that's where the power was. Stay in his good graces.

Still . . . One should always get more than one angle on a story. I tried to make up my mind as to who would give me a good one. While I was thinking along these lines, something caught my eye as I glanced back and up, appreciating anew the heights from which I had not quite descended.

There were a number of riders up near the top. They had apparently traversed the same trail I had taken. I could not get an exact nose count, but it seemed suspiciously close to a dozen—a fairly sizable group to be out riding at just that place and time. As I saw that they were proceeding on down the same way that I had come, I had a prickly feeling along the base of my neck. What if . . . ? What if they were the same guys? Because I felt that they were.

Individually, they were no match for me. Even a couple of them together had not made that great a showing. That was not it. The real chiller was that if that's who it was, then we were not alone in our ability to manipulate Shadow in a very sophisticated fashion. It meant that someone else was capable of a stunt that for all my life I had thought to be the sole property of our family. Add to this the fact that they were Brand's wardens, and their designs on the family

—at least part of it—did not look all that clement. I perspired suddenly at the notion of enemies who could match our greatest power.

Of course, they were too far off for me to really know just then whether that was truly who it was. But you have to explore every contingency if you want to keep winning the survival game. Could Eric have found or trained or created some special beings to serve him in this particular capacity? Along with you and Eric, Brand had one of the firmest claims on the succession . . . . not to take anything away from your case, damn it! Hell! You know what I mean. I have to talk about it to show you how I was thinking at the time. That's all. So, Brand had had the basis for a pretty good claim if he had been in a position to press it. You being out of the picture, he was Eric's chief rival when it came to adding a legal touch to things. Putting that together with his plight and the ability of those guys to traverse Shadow, Eric came to look a lot more sinister to me. I was more scared by that thought than I was by the riders themselves, though they did not exactly fill me with delight. I decided that I had better do several things quickly: talk to someone else in Amber, and have him take me through the Trump.

Okay. I decided quickly. Gérard seemed the safest choice. He is reasonably open, neutral. Honest about most things. And from what Julian had said, Gérard's role in the whole business seemed kind of passive. That is, he was not going to resist Eric's move actively. He would not want to cause a lot of trouble. Didn't mean he approved. He was probably just being safe and conservative old Gérard. That decided, I reached for my deck of Trumps and almost howled. They were gone.

I searched every pocket in every garment about me. I had taken them along when I'd left Texorami. I could have lost them at any point in the previous day's action. I had certainly been battered and thrown about a lot. And it had been a great day for losing things. I composed a complicated litany of curses and dug my heels into the horse's sides. I was going to have to move fast and think faster now. The first thing would be to get into a nice, crowded, civilized place where an assassin of the more primitive sort would be at a disadvantage.

As I hurried downhill, heading for one of the roads, I worked with the stuff of Shadow—quite subtly this time, using every bit of skill I could muster. There were just two things I desired at the moment: a final assault on my possible trackers and a fast path to a place of sanctuary.

The world shimmered and did a final jig, becoming the California I had been seeking. A rasping, growling noise reached my ears, for the final touch I had intended. Looking back, I saw a section of cliff face come loose, almost in slow motion, and slide directly toward the horsemen. A while later, I had dismounted and was walking in the direction of the road, my garments even fresher and of better quality. I was uncertain as to the time of year, and I wondered what the weather was like in New York.

Before very long, the bus that I had anticipated approached and I flagged it down. I located a window seat, smoked for a while, and watched the countryside. After a time, I dozed.

I did not wake until early afternoon, when we pulled into a terminal. I was ravenous by then, and decided I had better have something to eat before getting a cab to the airport. So I bought three cheeseburgers and a couple of malts with a few of my quondam Texorami greenbacks. Getting served and eating took me maybe twenty minutes. Leaving the snack bar, I saw that there were a number of taxis standing idle at the stand out front. Before I picked one up, though, I decided to make an important stop in the men's room.

At the very damnedest moment you can think of, six stalls flew open behind my back and their occupants rushed me. There was no mistaking the spurs on the backs of their hands, the oversized jaws, the smoldering eyes. Not only had they caught up with me, they were now clad in the same acceptable garb as anyone else in the neighborhood. Gone were any remaining doubts as to their power over Shadow.

Fortunately, one of them was faster than the others. Also, perhaps because of my size, they still might not have been fully aware of my strength. I seized that first one high up on the arm, avoiding those hand bayonets he sported, pulled him over in front of me, picked him up, and threw him at the others. Then I just turned and ran. I broke the door on the way out. I didn't even pause to zip up until I was in a taxi and had the driver burning rubber.

Enough. It was no longer simple sanctuary that I had in mind. I wanted to get hold of a set of Trumps and tell someone else in the family about those guys. If they were Eric's creatures, the others ought to be made aware of them. If they were not, then Eric ought to be told, too. If they could make their way through Shadow like that, perhaps others could, also. Whatever they represented might one day constitute a threat to Amber herself. Supposing—just supposing— that no one back home was involved? What if Dad and Brand were the victims of a totally unsuspected enemy? Then there was something big and menacing afoot, and I had stepped right into it. That would be an excellent reason for their hounding me this thoroughly. They would want me pretty badly. My mind ran wild. They might even be harrying me toward some sort of a trap. No need for the visible ones to be the only ones about.

I brought my emotions to heel. One by one, you must deal with those things that come to hand, I told myself. That is all. Divorce the feelings from the speculations, or at least provide for separate maintenance. This is sister Flora's shadow. She lives on the other edge of the continent in a place called Westchester. Get to a phone, get hold of information, and call her. Tell her it is urgent and ask for sanctuary. She can't refuse you that, even if she does hate your guts. Then jump a jet and get the hell over there. Speculate on the way if you want, but keep cool now.

So I telephoned from the airport and you answered it, Corwin. That was the variable that broke all the possible equations I had been juggling—you suddenly showing up at that time, that place, that point in events. I grabbed for it when you offered me protection, and not just because I wanted protection. I could probably have taken those six guys out by myself. But that was no longer it. *I thought they were yours.* I figured you had been lying low all along, waiting for the right moment to move in. Now, I thought, you were ready. This explains everything. You had taken out Brand and you were about to use your Shadow-walking zombies for purposes of going back and catching Eric with his pants down. I wanted to be on your side because I hated Eric and because I knew you were a careful planner and you usually get what you go after. I mentioned the pursuit by guys out of Shadow to see what you would say. The fact that you said nothing didn't really prove anything, though. Either you were being cagey, I figured, or you had no way of knowing where I had been. I also thought of the possibility of walking into a trap of your devising, but I was already in trouble and did not see that I was so important to the balance of power that you would want to dispose of me. Especially if I offered my support, which I was quite willing to do. So I flew on out. And damned if those six didn't board later and follow me. Is he giving me an escort? I wondered. Better not start making more assumptions. I shook them again when we landed, and headed for Flora's place. Then I acted as if none of my guesses had occurred, waiting to see what you would do. When you helped me dispose of the guys, I was really puzzled. Were you genuinely surprised, or was it a put-on, with you sacrificing a few of the troops to keep me ignorant of something? All right, I decided, be ignorant, cooperate, see what he has in mind. I was a perfect setup for that act you pulled to cover the condition of your memory. When I did learn the truth, it was simply too late. We were headed for Rebma and none of this would have meant anything to you. Later, I didn't care to tell Eric anything after his coronation. I was his prisoner then and not exactly kindly disposed toward him. It even occurred to me that my information might be worth something one day —at least, my freedom again—if that threat ever materialized. As for Brand, I doubt anyone would have believed me; and even if someone did, I was the only one who knew how to reach that shadow. Could you see Eric buying that as a reason for releasing me? He would have laughed and told me to come up with a better story. And I never heard from Brand again. None of the others seem to have heard from him either. Odds are he's dead by now—I'd say. And that is the story I never got to tell you. You figure out what it all means.

III

I studied Random, remembering what a great card player he was. By looking at his face, I could no more tell whether he was lying, in whole or in part, than I could learn by scrutinizing the Jack of, say, Diamonds. Nice touch, that part, too. There was enough of that kind of business to his story to give it some feel of verisimilitude.

"To paraphrase Oedipus, Hamlet, Lear, and all those guys," I said, "I wish I had known this some time ago."

"This was the first chance I really had to tell you," he said.

"True," I agreed. "Unfortunately, it not only fails to clarify things, it complicates the puzzle even more. Which is no mean trick. Here we are with a black road running up to the foot of Kolvir. It passes through Shadow, and things have succeeded in traversing it to beset Amber. We do not know the exact nature of the forces behind it, but they are obviously malign and they seem to be growing in strength. I have been feeling guilty about it for some while now, because I see it as being tied in with my curse. Yes, I laid one on us. Curse or no curse, though, everything eventually resolves into some sort of tangibility that can be combatted. Which is exactly what we are going to do. But all week long I have been trying to figure out Dara's part in things. Who is she really? What is she? Why was she so anxious to try the Pattern? How is it that she managed to succeed? And that final threat of hers . . . 'Amber will be destroyed,' she said. It seems more than coincidental that this occurred at the same time as the attack over the black road. I do not see it as a separate thing, but as a part of the same cloth. And it all seems to be tied in with the fact that there is a traitor somewhere here in Amber—Caine's death, the notes . . . Someone here is either abetting an external enemy or is behind the whole thing himself. Now you link it all up with Brand's disappearance, by way of this guy." I nudged the corpse with my foot. "It makes it look as if Dad's death or absence is also a part of it. If that is the case, though, it makes for a major conspiracy—with detail after detail having been carefully worked out over a period of years."

Random explored a cupboard in the corner, produced a bottle and a pair of goblets. He filled them and brought me one, then returned to his chair. We drank a silent toast to futility.

"Well," he said, "plotting is the number-one pastime around here, and everyone *has* had plenty of time, you know. We are both too young to remember brothers Osric and Finndo, who died for the good of Amber. But the impression I get from talking with Benedict —"

"Yes," I said, "—that they had done more than wishful thinking about the throne, and it became necessary that they die bravely for Amber. I've heard that, too. Maybe so, maybe not. We'll never know for sure. Still . . . Yes, the point is well taken, though almost unnecessary. I do not doubt that it has been tried before. I do not put it past a number of us. Who, though? We will be operating under a severe handicap until we find out. Any move that we make externally will probably only be directed against a limb of the beast. Come up with an idea."

"Corwin," he said, "to be frank about it, I could make a case for it being anyone here—even myself, prisoner status and all. In fact, something like that would be a great blind for it. I would have taken genuine delight in looking helpless while actually pulling the strings that made all the others dance. Any of us would, though. We all have our motives, our ambitions. And over the years we all have had time and opportunity to lay a lot of groundwork. No, that is the wrong way to go about it, looking for suspects. Everyone here falls into that category. Let us decide instead what it is that would distinguish such an individual, aside from motives, apart from opportunities. I would say, let's look at the methods involved."

"All right. Then you start."

"Some one of us knows more than the rest of us about the workings of Shadow—the ins and the outs, the whys and the hows. He also has allies, obtained from somewhere fairly far afield. This is the combination he has brought to bear upon Amber. Now, we have no way of looking at a person and telling whether he possesses such special knowledge and skills. But let us consider where he could have obtained them. It could be that he simply learned something off in Shadow somewhere, on his own. Or he could have been studying all along, here, while Dworkin was still alive and willing to give lessons."

I stared down into my glass. Dworkin could *still* be living. He had provided my means of escape from the dungeons of Amber—how long ago? I had told no one this, and was not about to. For one thing, Dworkin was quite mad—which was apparently why Dad had had him locked away. For another, he had demonstrated powers I did not understand, which convinced me he could be quite dangerous. Still, he had been kindly disposed toward me after a minimum of flattery and reminiscence. If he were still around, I suspected that with a bit of patience I might be able to handle him. So I had kept the whole business locked away in my mind as a possible secret weapon. I saw no reason for changing that decision at this point.

"Brand did hang around him a lot," I acknowledged, finally seeing what he was getting at. "He was interested in things of that sort."

"Exactly," Random replied. "And he obviously knew more than the rest of us, to be able to send me that message without a Trump."

"You think he made a deal with outsiders, opened the way for them, then discovered that they no longer needed him when they hung him out to dry?"

"Not necessarily. Though I suppose that is possible, too. My thinking runs more like this—and I don't deny my prejudice in his favor: I think he had learned enough about the subject so that he was able to detect it when someone did something peculiar involving the Trumps, the Pattern, or that area of Shadow most adjacent to Amber. Then he slipped up. Perhaps he underestimated the culprit and confronted him directly, rather than going to Dad or Dworkin. What then? The guilty party subdued him and imprisoned him in that tower. Either he thought enough of him not to want to kill him if he did not have to, or he had some later use of him in mind."

"You make that sound plausible, too," I said, and I would have added, "and it fits your story nicely" and watched his poker face again, except for one thing. Back when I was with Bleys, before our attack on Amber, I had had a momentary contact with Brand while fooling with the Trumps. He had indicated distress, imprisonment, and then the contact had been broken. Random's story did fit, to that extent. So, instead, I said, "If he can point the finger, we have got to get him back and set him to pointing."

"I was hoping you would say that," Random replied. "I hate to leave a bit of business like that unfinished."

I went and fetched the bottle, refilled our glasses. I sipped. I lit another cigarette.

"Before we get into that, though," I said, "I have to decide on the best way of breaking the news about Caine. Where is Flora, anyway?"

"Down in town, I think. She was here this morning. I can find her for you, I'm pretty sure."

"Do it, then. She is the only other one I know of who has seen one of these guys, back when they broke into her place in Westchester. We might as well have her handy for that much corroboration as to their nastiness. Besides, I have some other things I want to ask her."

He swallowed his drink and rose.

"All right. I'll go do that now. Where should I bring her?"

"My quarters. If I'm not there, wait."

He nodded.

I rose and accompanied him into the hall.

"Have you got the key to this room?" I asked.

"It's on a hook inside."

"Better get it and lock up. We wouldn't want a premature unveiling."

He did that and gave me the key. I walked with him as far as the first landing and saw him on his way. Then I headed for my own quarters.

From my safe, I removed the Jewel of Judgment, a ruby pendant which had given Dad and Eric control over the weather in the vicinity of Amber. Before he died, Eric had told me the procedure to be followed in tuning it to my own use. I had not had time to do it, though, and did not really have the time now. But during my conversation with Random I had decided that I was going to have to take the time. I had located Dworkin's notes, beneath a stone near Eric's fireplace. He had given me that much information also, that last time. I would have liked to know where he had come across the notes in the first place, though, for they were incomplete. I fetched them from the rear of the safe and regarded them once again. They did agree with Eric's explanation as to how the attunement was to be managed.

But they also indicated that the stone had other uses, that the control of meteorological phenomena was almost an incidental, though spectacular, demonstration of a complex of principles which underlay the Pattern, the Trumps, and the physical integrity of Amber herself, apart from Shadow. Unfortunately, the details were lacking. Still, the more I searched my memory, the more something along these lines did seem indicated. Only rarely had Dad produced the stone; and though he had spoken of it as a weather changer, the weather had not always been especially altered on those occasions when he had sported it. And he had often taken it along with him on his little trips. So I was ready to believe that there was more to it than that. Eric had probably reasoned the same way, but he had not been able to dope out its other uses either. He had simply taken advantage of its obvious powers when Bleys and I had attacked Amber; and he had used it the same way this past week when the creatures had made their assault from the black road. It had served him well on both occasions, even if it had not been sufficient to save his life. So I had better get hold of its power myself, I decided, now. Any extra edge was important. And it would be good to be seen wearing the thing, too, I judged. Especially now.

I put the notes back into the safe, the jewel in my pocket. I left then and headed downstairs. Again, as before, to walk those halls made me feel as if I had never been away. This was home, this was what I wanted. Now I was its defender. I did not even wear the crown, yet all its problems had become my own. It was ironic. I had come back to claim the crown, to wrest it from Eric, to hold the glory, to reign. Now, suddenly, things were falling apart. It had not taken long to realize that Eric had behaved incorrectly. If he had indeed done Dad in, he had no right to the crown. If he had not, then he had acted prematurely. Either way, the coronation had served only to fatten his already obese ego. Myself, I wanted it and I knew that I could take it. But it would be equally irresponsible to do so with my troops quartered in Amber, suspicion of Caine's murder about to descend upon me, first signs of a fantastic plot suddenly displayed before me, and the continuing possibility that Dad was still alive. On several occasions it seemed we had been in contact, briefly —and at one such time, years ago, that he had okayed my succession. But there was so much deceit and trickery afoot that I did not know what to believe. He had not abdicated. Also, I had had a head injury, and I was well aware of my own desires. The mind is a funny place. I do not even trust my own. Could it be that I had manufactured that whole business? A lot had happened since. The price of being an Amberite, I suppose, is that you cannot even trust yourself. I wondered what Freud would have said. While he had failed to pierce my amnesia, he had come up with some awfully good guesses as to what my father had been like, what our relationship had been, even though I had not realized it at the time. I wished that I could have one more session with him.

I made my way through the marble dining hall and into the dark, narrow corridor that lay behind. I nodded to the guard and walked on back to the door. Through it then, out onto the platform, across and down. The interminable spiral stairway that leads into the guts of Kolvir. Walking. Lights every now and then. Blackness beyond.

It seemed that a balance had shifted somewhere along the way, and that I was no longer acting but being acted upon, being forced to move, to respond. Being herded. And each move led to another. Where had it all begun? Maybe it had been going on for years and I was only just now becoming aware of it. Perhaps we were all victims, in a fashion and to a degree none of us had realized. Great victuals for morbid thought. Sigmund, where are you now? I had wanted to be king— still wanted to be king—more than anything else. Yet the more I learned and the more I thought about what I had learned, the more all of my movements actually seemed to amount to Amber Pawn to King Four. I realized then that this feeling had been present for some time, growing, and I did not like it at all. But nothing that has ever lived has gotten by without making some mistake, I consoled myself. If my feeling represented actuality, my personal Pavlov was getting closer to my fangs with each ringing of the bell. Soon now, soon, I felt that it had to be soon, I would have to see that he came very near. Then it would be mine to see that he neither went away nor ever came again.

Turning, turning, around and down, light here, light there, these my thoughts, like thread on a spool, winding or unwinding, hard to be sure. Below me the sound of metal against stone. A guard's scabbard, the guard rising. A ripple of light from a lantern raised.

"Lord Corwin . . ."

"Jamie."

At bottom, I took a lantern from the shelf. Putting a light to it, I turned and headed toward the tunnel, pushing the darkness on ahead of me, a step at a time.

Eventually the tunnel, and so up it, counting side passages. It was the seventh that I wanted. Echoes and shadows. Must and dust.

Coming to it, then. Turning there. Not too much farther.

Finally, that great, dark, metal-bound door. I unlocked it and pushed hard. It creaked, resisted, finally moved inward.

I set down the lantern, just to the right, inside. I had no further need of it, as the Pattern itself gave off sufficient light for what I had to do.

For a moment I regarded the Pattern—a shining mass of curved lines that tricked the eye as it tried to trace them—imbedded there, huge, in the floor's slick blackness. It had given me power over Shadow, it had restored most of my memory. It would also destroy me in an instant if I were to essay it improperly. What gratitude the prospect did arouse in me was therefore not untinged with fear. It was a splendid and cryptic old family heirloom which belonged right where it was, in the cellar.

I moved off to the corner where the tracery began. There I composed my mind, relaxed my body, and set my left foot upon the Pattern. Without pausing, I strode forward then and felt the current begin. Blue sparks outlined my boots. Another step. There was an audible crackling this time and the beginning of resistance. I took the first curvelength, striving to hurry, wanting to reach the First Veil as quickly as possible. By the time I did, my hair was stirring and the sparks were brighter, longer.

The strain increased. Each step required more effort than the previous one. The crackling grew louder and the current intensified. My hair rose and I shook off sparks. I kept my eyes on the fiery line and did not stop pushing.

Suddenly the pressure abated. I staggered but kept moving. I was through the First Veil and into the feeling of accomplishment that that entailed. I recalled the last time that I had come this way, in Rebma, the city under the sea. The maneuver I had just completed was what had started the return of my memories. Yes. I pushed ahead and the sparks grew and the currents rose once again, setting my flesh to tingling.

The Second Veil . . . The angles . . . It always seemed to tax the strength to its limits, to produce the feeling that one's entire being was transformed into pure Will. It was a driving, relentless sensation. At the moment, the negotiation of the Pattern was the only thing in the world that meant anything to me. I had always been there, striving, never been away, always would be there, contending, my will against the maze of power. Time had vanished. Only the tension held.

The sparks were up to my waist. I entered the Grand Curve and fought my way along it. I was continually destroyed and reborn at every step of its length, baked by the fires of creation, chilled by the cold at entropy's end.

Out and onward, turning. Three more curves, a straight line, a number of arcs. Dizziness, a sensation of fading and intensifying as though I were oscillating into and out of existence. Turn after turn after turn after turn . . . A short, sharp arc . . . The line that led to the Final Veil . . . I imagine I was gasping and drenched with sweat by then. I never seem to remember for sure. I could hardly move my feet. The sparks were up to my shoulders. They came into my eyes and I lost sight of the Pattern itself between blinks. In, out, in, out . . . There it was. I dragged my right foot forward, knowing how Benedict must have felt, his legs snared by the black grass. Right before I rabbit-punched him. I felt bludgeoned myself—all over. Left foot, forward . . . So slowly it was hard to be certain it was actually moving. My hands were blue flames, my legs pillars of fire. Another step. Another. Yet another.

I felt like a slowly animated statue, a thawing snowman, a buckling girder. . . . Two more . . . Three . . . Glacial, my movements, but I who directed them had all of eternity and a perfect constancy of will that would be realized. . . .

I passed through the Veil. A short arc followed. Three steps to cross it into blackness and peace. They were the worst of all.

A coffee break for Sisyphus! That was my first thought as I departed the Pattern. *I've done it again!* was my second. And, *Never again!* was my third.

I allowed myself the luxury of a few deep breaths and a little shaking. Then I unpocketed the jewel and raised it by its chain. I held it before my eye.

Red inside, of course—a deep cherry-red, smoke-shot, fulgent. It seemed to have picked up something extra of light and glitter during the trip through the Pattern. I continued to stare, thinking over the instructions, comparing them with things I already knew.

Once you have walked the Pattern and reached this point, you can cause it to transport you to any place that you can visualize. All that it takes is the desire and an act of will. Such being the case, I was not without a moment's trepidation. If the effect proceeded as it normally did, I could be throwing myself into a peculiar sort of trap. But Eric had succeeded. He had not been locked into the heart of a gem somewhere off in Shadow. The Dworkin who had written those notes had been a great man, and I had trusted him.

Composing my mind, I intensified my scrutiny of the stone's interior.

There was a distorted reflection of the Pattern within it, surrounded by winking points of light, tiny flares and flashes, different curves and paths. I made my decision, I focused my will. . . .

Redness and slow motion. Like sinking into an ocean of high viscosity. Very slowly, at first. Drifting and darkening, all the pretty lights far, far ahead. Faintly, my apparent velocity increased. Flakes of light, distant, intermittent. A trifle faster then, it seemed. No scale. I was a point of consciousness of indeterminate dimensions. Aware of movement, aware of the configuration toward which I advanced, now almost rapidly. The redness was nearly gone, as was the consciousness of any medium. Resistance vanished. I was speeding. All of this, now, seemed to have taken but a single instant, was still taking that same instant. There was a peculiar, timeless quality to the entire affair. My velocity relative to what now seemed my target was enormous. The little, twisted maze was growing, was resolving into what appeared a three-dimensional variation of the Pattern itself. Punctuated by flares of colored light, it grew before me, still reminiscent of a bizarre galaxy half raveled in the middle of the ever-night, haloed with a pale shine of dust, its streamers composed of countless flickering points. And it grew or I shrank, or it advanced or I advanced, and we were near, near together, and it filled all of space now, top to bottom, this way to that, and my personal velocity still seemed, if anything, to be increasing. I was caught, overwhelmed by the blaze, and there was a stray streamer which I knew to be the beginning. I was too close—lost, actually—to apprehend its over-all configuration any longer, but the buckling, the flickering, the weaving of all that I could see of it, everywhere about me, made me wonder whether three dimensions were sufficient to account for the senses-warping complexities with which I was confronted. Rather than my galactic analogy, something in my mind shifted to the other extreme, suggesting the infinitely dimensioned Hilbert space of the subatomic. But then, it was a metaphor of desperation. Truly and simply, I did not understand anything about it. I had only a growing feeling—Pattern-conditioned? Instinctive?—that I had to pass through this maze also to gain the new degree of power that I sought.

Nor was I incorrect. I was swept on into it without any slackening of my apparent velocity. I was spun and whirled along blazing ways, passing through substanceless clouds of glitter and shine. There were no areas of resistance, as in the Pattern itself, my initial impetus seeming sufficient to bear me throughout. A whirlwind tour of the Milky Way? A drowning man swept among canyons of coral? An insomniac sparrow passing over an amusement park of a July Fourth evening? These my thoughts as I recapitulated my recent passage in this transformed fashion.

. . . And out, through, over, and done, in a blaze of ruddy light that found me regarding myself holding the pendant beside the Pattern, then regarding the pendant, Pattern within it, within me, everything within me, me within it, the redness subsiding, down, gone. Then just me, the pendant, the Pattern, alone, subject-object relationships reestablished—only an octave higher, which I feel is about the best way there is to put it. For a certain empathy now existed. It was as though I had acquired an extra sense, and an additional means of expression. It was a peculiar sensation, satisfying.

Anxious to test it, I summoned my resolve once again and commanded the Pattern to transport me elsewhere.

I stood then in the round room, atop the highest tower in Amber. Crossing it, I passed outside, onto a very small balcony. The contrast was powerful, coming so close to the supersensory voyage I had just completed. For several long moments I simply stood there, looking.

The sea was a study in textures, as the sky was partly overcast and getting on toward evening. The clouds themselves showed patterns of soft brightness and rough shading. The wind made its way seaward, so that the salt smell was temporarily denied me. Dark birds dotted the air, swinging and hovering at a great distance out over the water. Below me, the palace yards and the terraces of the city lay spread in enduring elegance out to Kolvir's rim. People were tiny on the thoroughfares, their movements discountable. I felt very alone.

Then I touched the pendant and called for a storm.

IV

Random and Flora were waiting in my quarters when I returned. Random's eyes went first to the pendant, then to my own. I nodded.

I turned toward Flora, bowing slightly.

"Sister," I said, "it has been a while, and then a while."

She looked somewhat frightened, which was all to the good. She smiled and took my hand, though.

"Brother," she said. "I see that you have kept your word."

Pale gold, her hair. She had cut it, but retained the bangs. I could not decide whether I liked it that way or not. She had very lovely hair. Blue eyes, too, and tons of vanity to keep everything in her favorite perspective. At times she seemed to behave quite stupidly, but then at other times I have wondered.

"Excuse me for staring," I said, "but the last time that we met I was unable to see you."

"I am very happy that the situation has been corrected," she said. "It was quite—There was nothing that I could do, you know."

"I know," I said, recalling the occasional lilt of her laughter from the other side of the darkness on one of the anniversaries of the event. "I know."

I moved to the window and opened it, knowing that the rain would not be coming in. I like the smell of a storm.

"Random, did you learn anything of interest with regard to a possible postman?" I asked.

"Not really," he said. "I made some inquiries. No one seems to have seen anyone else in the right place at the right time."

"I see," I said. "Thank you. I may see you again later."

"All right," he said. "I'll be in my quarters all evening, then."

I nodded, turned, leaned back against the sill, watched Flora. Random closed the door quietly as he left. I listened to the rain for half a minute or so.

"What are you going to do with me?" she said finally.

"Do?"

"You are in a position to call for a settlement on old debts. I assume that things are about to begin."

"Perhaps," I said. "Most things depend on other things. This thing is no different."

"What do you mean?"

"Give me what I want, and we'll see. I have even been known to be a nice guy on occasion."

"What is it that you want?"

"The story, Flora. Let's start with that. Of how you came to be my shepherdess there on that shadow, Earth. All pertinent details. What was the arrangement? What was the understanding? Everything. That's all."

She sighed.

"The beginning . . ." she said. "Yes . . . It was in Paris, a party, at a certain Monsieur Focault's. This was about three years before the Terror—"

"Stop," I said. "What were you doing there?"

"I had been in that general area of Shadow for approximately five of their years," she said. "I had been wandering, looking for something novel, something that suited my fancy. I came upon that place at that time in the same way we find anything. I let my desires lead me and I followed my instincts."

"A peculiar coincidence."

"Not in light of all the time involved—and considering the amount of travel in which we indulge. It was, if you like, my Avalon, my Amber surrogate, my home away from home. Call it what you will, I was there, at that party, that October night, when you came in with the little redheaded girl—Jacqueline, I believe, was her name."

That brought it back, from quite a distance, a memory I hadn't called for in a long, long while. I remembered Jacqueline far better than I did Focault's party, but there had been such an occasion.

"Go ahead."

"As I said," she went on, "I was there. You arrived later. You caught my attention immediately, of course. Still, if one exists for a sufficiently long period of time and travels considerably, one does occasionally encounter a person greatly resembling someone else one has known. That was my first thought after the initial excitement faded. Surely it had to be a double. So much time had passed without a whisper. Yet we all have secrets and good reasons for having them.

This could be one of yours. So I saw that we were introduced and then had a devil of a time getting you away from that little redheaded piece for more than a few minutes. And you insisted your name was Fenneval—Cordell Fenneval. I grew uncertain. I could not tell whether it was a double or you playing games. The third possibility did cross my mind, though—that you had dwelled in some adjacent area of Shadow for a sufficient time to cast shadows of yourself. I might have departed still wondering had not Jacqueline later boasted to me concerning your strength. Now this is not the commonest subject of conversation for a woman, and the way in which she said it led me to believe that she had actually been quite impressed by some things you had done. I drew her out a bit and realized that they were all of them feats of which you were capable. That eliminated the notion of it being a double. It had to be either you or your shadow. This in mind, even if Cordell was not Corwin he was a clue, a clue that you were or had been in that shady neighborhood—the first real clue I had come across concerning your whereabouts. I had to pursue it. I began keeping track of you then, checking into your past. The more people I questioned, the more puzzling it became. In fact, after several months I was still unable to decide. There were enough smudgy areas to make it possible. Things were resolved for me the following summer, though, when I revisited Amber for a time. I mentioned the peculiar affair to Eric . . ."

"Yes?"

"Well . . . he was—somewhat—aware—of the possibility."

She paused and rearranged her gloves on the seat beside her.

"Uh-huh," I said. "Just what did he tell you?"

"That it might be the real you," she said. "He told me there had been—an accident."

"Really?"

"Well, no," she admitted. "Not an accident. He said there had been a fight and he had injured you. He thought you were going to die, and he did not want the blame. So he transported you off into Shadow and left you there, in that place. After a long while, he decided that you must be dead, that it was finally all over between you. My news naturally disturbed him. So he swore me to secrecy and sent me back to keep you under surveillance. I had a good excuse for being there, as I had already told everyone how much I liked the place."

"You didn't promise to keep silent for nothing, Flora. What did he give you?"

"He gave me his word that should he ever come into power here in Amber, I would not be forgotten."

"A little risky," I said. "After all, that would still leave you with something on him—knowledge of the whereabouts of a rival claimant, and of his part in putting him there."

"True. But things sort of balanced out, and I would have to admit having become an accomplice in order to talk about it."

I nodded.

"Tight, but not impossible," I agreed. "But did you think he would let me continue living if he ever did get a chance at the throne?"

"That was never discussed. Never."

"It must have crossed your mind, though."

"Yes, later," she said, "and I decided that he would probably do nothing. After all, it was beginning to seem likely that you had been deprived of your memory. There was no reason to do anything to you so long as you were harmless."

"So you stayed on to watch me, to see that I remained harmless?"

"Yes."

"What would you have done had I shown signs of recovering my memory?"

She looked at me, then looked away.

"I would have reported it to Eric."

"And what would he have done then?"

"I don't know."

I laughed a little, and she blushed. I could not remember the last time I had seen Flora blush.

"I will not belabor the obvious," I said. "All right, you stayed on, you watched me. What next? What happened?"

"Nothing special. You just went on leading your life and I went on keeping track of it."

"All of the others knew where you were?"

"Yes. I'd made no secret of my whereabouts. In fact, all of them came around to visit me at one time or another."

"That includes Random?"

She curled her lip.

"Yes, several times," she said.

"Why the sneer?"

"It is too late to start pretending I like him," she said. "You know.

I just don't like the people he associates with—assorted criminals, jazz musicians. . . . I had to show him family courtesy when he was visiting my shadow, but he put a big strain on my nerves, bringing those people around at all hours—jam sessions, poker parties. The place usually reeked for weeks afterward and I was always glad to see him go. Sorry. I know you like him, but you wanted the truth."

"He offended your delicate sensibilities. Okay. I now direct your attention to the brief time when I was your guest. Random joined us rather abruptly. Pursuing him were half a dozen nasty fellows whom we dispatched in your living room."

"I recall the event quite vividly."

"Do you recall the guys responsible—the creatures we had to deal with?"

"Yes."

"Sufficiently well to recognize one if you ever saw another?"

"I think so."

"Good. Had you ever seen one before?"

"No."

"Since?"

"No."

"Had you ever heard them described anywhere?"

"Not that I can remember. Why?"

I shook my head.

"Not yet. This is my inquisition, remember? Now I want you to think back for a time before that evening. Back to the event that put me in Greenwood. Maybe even a little earlier. What happened, and how did you find out about it? What were the circumstances? What was your part in things?"

"Yes," she said, "I knew you would ask me that sooner or later. What happened was that Eric contacted me the day after it occurred —from Amber, via my Trump." She glanced at me again, obviously to see how I was taking it, to study my reactions. I remained expressionless. "He told me you had been in a bad accident the previous evening, and that you were hospitalized. He told me to have you transferred to a private place, one where I could have more say as to the course of your treatment."

"In other words, he wanted me to stay a vegetable."

"He wanted them to keep you sedated."

"Did he or did he not admit to being responsible for the accident?"

"He did not say that he had had someone shoot out your tire, but he did know that that was what had happened. How else could he have known? When I learned later that he was planning to take the throne, I assumed that he had finally decided it was best to remove you entirely. When the attempt failed, it seemed logical that he would do the next most effective thing: see that you were kept out of the way until after the coronation."

"I was not aware that the tire had been shot out," I said.

Her face changed. She recovered.

"You told me that you knew it was not an accident—that someone had tried to kill you. I assumed you were aware of the specifics."

I was treading on slightly mucky ground again for the first time in a long while. I still had a bit of amnesia, and I had decided I probably always would. My memories of the few days prior to the accident were still spotty. The Pattern had restored the lost memories of my entire life up until then, but the trauma appeared to have destroyed recollection of some of the events immediately preceding it. Not an uncommon occurrence. Organic damage rather than simple functional distress, most likely. I was happy enough to have all the rest back, so those did not seem especially lamentable. As to the accident itself, and my feelings that it had been more than an accident, I did recall the gunshots. There had been two of them. I might even have glimpsed the figure with the rifle—fleetingly, too late. Or maybe that was pure fantasy. It seemed that I had, though. I had had something like that in mind when I had headed out for Westchester. Even at this late time, though, when I held the power in Amber, I was loath to admit this single deficiency. I had faked my way with Flora before with a lot less to go on. I decided to stick with a winning combination.

"I was in no position to get out and see what had been hit," I said. "I heard the shots. I lost control. I had assumed that it was a tire, but I never knew for sure. The only reason I raised the question was because I was curious as to how you knew it was a tire."

"I already told you that Eric told me about it."

"It was the way that you said it that bothered me. You made it sound as if you already knew all the details before he contacted you."

She shook her head.

"Then pardon my syntax," she said. "That sometimes happens when you look at things after the fact. I am going to have to deny what you are implying. I had nothing to do with it and I had no prior knowledge that it had occurred."

"Since Eric is no longer around to confirm or deny anything, we will simply have to let it go," I said, "for now," and I said it to make her look even harder to her defense, to direct her attention away from any possible slip, either in word or expression, from which she might infer the small flaw which still existed in my memory. "Did you later become aware of the indentity of the person with the gun?" I asked.

"Never," she said. "Most likely some hired thug. I don't know."

"Have you any idea how long I was unconscious before someone found me, took me to a hospital?"

She shook her head again.

Something was bothering me and I could not quite put my finger on it.

"Did Eric say what time I had been taken into the hospital?"

"No."

"When I was with you, why did you try walking back to Amber rather than using Eric's Trump?"

"I couldn't raise him."

"You could have called someone else to bring you through," I said. "Flora, I think you are lying to me."

It was really only a test, to observe her reaction. Why not?

"About what?" she asked. "I couldn't raise anyone else. They were all otherwise occupied. Is that what you mean?"

She studied me.

I raised my arm and pointed at her and the lightning flashed at my back, just outside the window. I felt a tingle, a mild jolt. The thunderclap was also impressive.

"You sin by omission," I tried.

She covered her face with her hands and began to weep.

"I don't know what you mean!" she said. "I answered all your questions! What do you want? I don't know where you were going or who shot at you or what time it occurred! I just know the facts I've given you, damn it!"

She was either sincere or unbreakable by these means, I decided. Whichever, I was wasting my time and could get nothing more this way. Also, I had better switch us away from the accident before she began thinking too much about its importance to me. If there was something there that I was missing, I wanted to find it first.

"Come with me," I said.

"Where are we going?"

"I have something I want you to identify. I will tell you why after you see it."

She rose and followed me. I took her up the hall to see the body before I gave her the story on Caine. She regarded the corpse quite dispassionately. She nodded.

"Yes," she said, and, "Even if I did not know it I would be glad to say that I did, for you."

I grunted a noncommittal. Family loyalty always touches me, somewhere. I could not tell whether she believed what I had said about Caine. But things sort of equal to equal things sort of being equal to each other, it didn't much seem to matter. I did not tell her anything about Brand and she did not seem to possess any new information concerning him. Her only other comment when everything I'd had to say was said, was, "You wear the jewel well. What about the headpiece?"

"It is too soon to talk of such things," I told her.

"Whatever my support may be worth . . ."

"I know," I said. "I know."

My tomb is a quiet place. It stands alone in a rocky declivity, shielded on three sides against the elements, surrounded by transported soil wherein a pair of scrubby trees, miscellaneous shrubs, weeds, and great ropes of mountain ivy are rooted, about two miles down, in back of the crest of Kolvir. It is a long, low building with two benches in front, and the ivy has contrived to cover it to a great extent, mercifully masking most of a bombastic statement graven on its face beneath my name. It is, understandably, vacant most of the time.

That evening, however, Ganelon and I repaired thither, accompanied by a good supply of wine and some loaves and cold cuts.

"You weren't joking!" he said, having dismounted, crossed over, and parted the ivy, able to read by the moon's light the words that were rendered there.

"Of course not," I said, climbing down and taking charge of the horses. "It's mine all right."

Tethering our mounts to a nearby shrub, I unslung our bags of provisions and carried them to the nearest bench. Ganelon joined me as I opened the first bottle and poured us a dark, deep pair.

"I still don't understand," he said, accepting his.

"What's there to understand? I'm dead and buried there," I said. "It's my cenotaph, is what it is—the monument that gets set up when the body has not been recovered. I only just learned about mine recently. It was raised several centuries ago, when it was decided I wasn't coming back."

"Kind of spooky," he said. "What's inside then?"

"Nothing. Though they did thoughtfully provide a niche and a casket, just in case my remains put in an appearance. You cover both bets that way."

Ganelon made himself a sandwich.

"Whose idea was it?" he asked.

"Random thinks it was Brand's or Eric's. No one remembers for sure. They all seemed to feel it was a good idea at the time."

He chuckled, an evil noise that perfectly suited his creased, scarred, and red-bearded self.

"What's to become of it now?"

I shrugged.

"I suppose some of them think it's a shame to waste it this way and would like to see me fill it. In the meantime, though, it's a good place to come and get drunk. I hadn't really paid my respects yet."

I put together a pair of sandwiches and ate them both. This was the first real breather I had had since my return, and perhaps the last for some time to come. It was impossible to say. But I had not really had a chance to speak with Ganelon at any length during the past week, and he was one of the few persons I trusted. I wanted to tell him everything. I had to. I had to talk with someone who was not a part of it in the same way as the rest of us. So I did.

The moon moved a considerable distance and the shards of broken glass multiplied within my crypt.

"So how did the others take it?" he asked me.

"Predictably," I answered. "I could tell that Julian did not believe a word of it even though he said that he did. He knows how I feel about him, and he is in no position to challenge me. I don't think Benedict believes me either, but he is a lot harder to read. He is biding his time, and I hope giving me the benefit of the doubt while he is about it. As for Gérard, I have the feeling that this was the final weight, and whatever trust he had left for me has just collapsed. Still, he will be returning to Amber early tomorrow, to accompany me to the grove to recover Caine's body. No sense in turning it into a sa-

fari, but I did want another family member present. Deirdre now—
she seemed happy about it. Didn't believe a word, I'm sure. But no
matter. She has always been on my side, and she has never liked
Caine. I'd say she is glad that I seem to be consolidating my position.
I can't really tell whether Llewella believed me or not. She doesn't
much give a damn what the rest of us do to one another, so far as I
can see. As to Fiona, she simply seemed amused at the whole business. But then, she has always had this detached, superior way of regarding things. You can never be certain what represents her real
thinking."

"Did you tell them the business about Brand yet?"

"No. I told them about Caine and I told them I wanted them all to
be in Amber by tomorrow evening. That is when the subject of
Brand will be raised. I've an idea I want to try out."

"You contacted all of them by means of the Trumps?"

"That's right."

"There is something I have been meaning to ask you about that.
Back on the shadow world we visited to obtain the weapons, there
are telephones. . . ."

"Yes?"

"I learned about wiretaps and such while we were there. Is it possible, do you think, that the Trumps could be bugged?"

I began to laugh, then caught myself as some of the implications of
his suggestion sank in. Finally, "I don't really know," I said. "So
much concerning Dworkin's work remains a mystery—the thought
just never occurred to me. I've never tried it myself. I wonder,
though. . . ."

"Do you know how many sets there are?"

"Well, everyone in the family has a pack or two and there were a
dozen or so spares in the library. I don't really know whether there
are any others."

"It seems to me that a lot could be learned just by listening in."

"Yes. Dad's deck, Brand's, my original pack, the one Random lost
—Hell! There are quite a number unaccounted for these days. I
don't know what to do about it. Start an inventory and try some experiments, I guess. Thanks for mentioning it."

He nodded and we both sipped for a while in silence.

Then, "What are you going to do, Corwin?" he asked.

"About what?"

"About everything. What do we attack now, and in what order?"

"My original intention was to begin tracing the black road toward its origin as soon as things were settled here in Amber," I said. "Now, though, I have shifted my priorities. I want Brand returned as soon as possible, if he is still living. If not, I want to find out what happened to him."

"But will the enemy give you the breathing time? He might be preparing a new offensive right now."

"Yes, of course. I have considered that. I feel we have some time, since they were defeated so recently. They will have to pull themselves together again, beef up their forces, reassess the situation in light of our new weapons. What I have in mind for the moment is to establish a series of lookout stations along the road to give us advance warning of any new movements on their part. Benedict has already agreed to take charge of the operation."

"I wonder how much time we have."

I poured him another drink, as it was the only answer I could think of.

"Things were never this complicated back in Avalon—*our* Avalon, I mean."

"True," I said. "You are not the only one who misses those days. At least, they seem simpler now."

He nodded. I offered him a cigarette, but he declined in favor of his pipe. In the flamelight, he studied the Jewel of Judgment which still hung about my neck.

"You say you can really control the weather with that thing?" he asked.

"Yes," I said.

"How do you know?"

"I've tried it. It works."

"What did you do?"

"That storm this afternoon. It was mine."

"I wonder . . ."

"What?"

"I wonder what I would have done with that sort of power. What I would do with it."

"The first thing that crossed my mind," I said, slapping the wall of my tomb, "was to destroy this place by lightning—strike it repeatedly and reduce it to rubble. Leave no doubt in anyone's mind as to my feelings, my power."

"Why didn't you?"

"Got to thinking about it a bit more then. Decided—Hell! They might really have a use for the place before too long, if I'm not smart enough or tough enough or lucky enough. Such being the case, I tried to decide where I would like them to dump my bones. It caught me then that this is really a pretty good spot—up high, clean, where the elements still walk naked. Nothing in sight but rock and sky. Stars, clouds, sun, moon, wind, rain . . . better company than a lot of other stiffs. Don't know why I should have to lie beside anyone I wouldn't want next to me now, and there aren't many."

"You're getting morbid, Corwin. Or drunk. Or both. Bitter, too. You don't need that."

"Who the hell are you to say what I need?"

I felt him stiffen beside me, then relax.

"I don't know," he finally said. "Just saying what I see."

"How are the troops holding up?" I asked.

"I think they are still bewildered, Corwin. They came to fight a holy war on the slopes of heaven. They think that's what the shooting was all about last week. So they are happy on that count, seeing as we won. But now this waiting, in the city . . . They don't understand the place. Some of the ones they thought to be enemies are now friends. They are confused. They know they are being kept ready for combat, but they have no idea against whom, or when. As they have been restricted to the billets the whole time, they have not yet realized the extent to which their presence is resented by the regulars and the population at large. They will probably be catching on fairly soon, though. I had been waiting to raise the subject, but you've been so busy lately. . . ."

I sat smoking for a time.

Then, "I guess I had better have a talk with them," I said. "Won't have a chance tomorrow, though, and something should be done soon. I think they should be moved—to a bivouac area in the Forest of Arden. Tomorrow, yes. I'll locate it for you on the map when we get back. Tell them it is to keep them close to the black road. Tell them that another attack could come that way at any time—which is no less that the truth. Drill them, maintain their fighting edge. I'll come down as soon as I can and talk to them."

"That will leave you without a personal force in Amber."

"True. It may prove a useful risk, though, both as a demonstration of confidence and a gesture of consideration. Yes, I think it will turn out to be a good move. If not . . ." I shrugged.

I poured and tossed another empty into my tomb.

"By the way," I said, "I'm sorry."

"What for?"

"I just noticed that I am morbid and drunk and bitter. I don't need that."

He chuckled and clicked his glass against my own.

"I know," he said. "I know."

So we sat there while the moon fell, till the last bottle was interred among its fellows. We talked for a time of days gone by. At length we fell silent and my eyes drifted to the stars above Amber. It was good that we had come to this place, but now the city was calling me back. Knowing my thoughts, Ganelon rose and stretched, headed for the horses. I relieved myself beside my tomb and followed him.

V

The Grove of the Unicorn lies in Arden to the southwest of Kolvir, near to that jutting place where the land begins its final descent into the valley called Garnath. While Garnath had been cursed, burned, invaded, and fought through in recent years, the adjacent highlands stood unmolested. The grove where Dad claimed to have seen the unicorn ages before and to have experienced the peculiar events which led to his adopting the beast as the patron of Amber and placing it on his coat of arms, was, as near as we could tell, a spot now but slightly screened from the long view across Garnath to the sea—twenty or thirty paces in from the upper edge of things: an asymmetrical glade where a small spring trickled from a mass of rock, formed a clear pool, brimmed into a tiny creek, made its way off toward Garnath and on down.

It was to this place that Gérard and I rode the following day, leaving at an hour that found us halfway down our trail from Kolvir before the sun skipped flakes of light across the ocean, then cast its whole bucketful against the sky. Gérard drew rein as it was doing this. He dismounted then and motioned to me to do the same. I did, leaving Star and the pack horse I was leading there beside his own huge piebald. I followed him off perhaps a dozen paces into a basin half-filled with gravel. He halted and I came up beside him.

"What is it?" I asked.

He turned and faced me and his eyes were narrow and his jaw clamped tight. He unfastened his cloak, folded it, and placed it on the ground. He unclasped his swordbelt and lay it atop the cloak.

"Get rid of your blade and your cloak," he said. "They will only get in the way."

I had an inkling of what was coming, and I decided I had better go along with it. I folded my cloak, placed the Jewel of Judgment beside Grayswandir, and faced him once again. I said only one word.

"Why?"

"It has been a long time," he said, "and you might have forgotten."

He came at me slowly, and I got my arms out in front of me and backed away. He did not swing at me. I used to be faster than he was. We were both crouched, and he was making slow, pawing movements with his left hand, his right hand nearer to his body, twitching slightly.

If I had had to choose a place to fight with Gérard, this would not have been it. He, of course, was aware of this. If I had to fight with Gérard at all, I would not have chosen to do so with my hands. I am better than Gérard with a blade or a quarterstaff. Anything that involved speed and strategy and gave me a chance to hit him occasionally while keeping him at bay would permit me to wear him down eventually and provide openings for heavier and heavier assaults. He, of course, was aware of this also. That is why he had trapped me as he had. I understood Gérard, though, and I had to play by his rules now.

I brushed his hand away a couple of times as he stepped up his movements, pressing nearer to me with every pace. Finally I took a chance, ducked and swung. I landed a fast, hard left just a little above his middle. It would have broken a stout board or ruptured the insides of a lesser mortal. Unfortunately, time had not softened Gérard. I heard him grunt, but he blocked my right, got his right hand under my left arm, and caught my shoulder from behind.

I closed with him fast then, anticipating a shoulder lock I might not be able to break; and, turning, driving forward, catching his left shoulder in a similar fashion, I hooked my right leg behind his knee and was able to cast him backward to the ground.

He maintained his grip, though, and I came down atop him. I released my own hold and was able to drive my right elbow into his left side as we hit. The angle was not ideal and his left hand went up and across, reaching to grasp his right somewhere behind my head.

I was able to duck out of it, but he still had my arm. For a moment I had a clear shot at his groin with my right, but I restrained myself. It is not that I have any qualms about hitting a man below his belt. I knew that if I did it to Gérard just then his reflexes would probably cause him to break my shoulder. Instead, scraping my forearm on the gravel, I managed to twist my left arm up behind his head, while at the same time sliding my right arm between his legs and catching him about the left thigh. I rolled back as I did this, attempting to straighten my legs as soon as my feet were beneath me. I wanted to raise him off the ground and slam him down again, driving my shoulder into his middle for good measure.

But Gérard scissored his legs and rolled to the left, forcing me to somersault across his body. I let go my hold on his head and pulled my left arm free as I went over. I scrambled clockwise then, dragging my right arm away and going for a toehold.

But Gérard would have none of that. He had gotten his arms beneath him by then. With one great heave he tore himself free and twisted his way back to his feet. I straightened myself and leaped backward. He began moving toward me immediately, and I decided that he was going to maul the hell out of me if I just kept grappling with him. I had to take a few chances.

I watched his feet, and at what I judged to be the best moment I dove in beneath his extended arms just as he was shifting his weight forward onto his left foot and raising his right. I was able to catch hold of his right ankle and hoist it about four feet high behind him. He went over and down, forward and to his left.

He scrambled to get to his feet and I caught him on the jaw with a left that knocked him down again. He shook his head and blocked with his arms as he came up once more. I tried to kick him in the stomach, but missed as he pivoted, catching him on the hip. He maintained his balance and advanced again.

I threw jabs at his face and circled. I caught him twice more in the stomach and danced away. He smiled. He knew I was afraid to close with him. I snapped a kick at his stomach and connected. His arms dropped sufficiently for me to chop him alongside the neck, just above the collarbone. At that moment, however, his arms shot forward and locked about my waist. I slammed his jaw with the heel of my hand, but it did not stop him from tightening his grip and raising me above the ground. Too late to hit him again. Those massive arms were already crushing my kidneys. I sought his carotids with my thumbs, squeezed.

But he kept raising me, back, up over his head. My grip loosened, slipped away. Then he slammed me down on my back in the gravel, as peasant women do their laundry on rocks.

There were exploding points of light and the world was a jittering, half-real place as he dragged me to my feet again. I saw his fist—

The sunrise was lovely, but the angle was wrong . . . By about ninety degrees . . .

Suddenly I was assailed by vertigo. It canceled out the beginning awareness of a roadmap of pains that ran along my back and reached the big city somewhere in the vicinity of my chin.

I was hanging high in the air. By turning my head slightly I could see for a very great distance, down.

I felt a set of powerful clamps affixed to my body—shoulder and thigh. When I turned to look at them, I saw that they were hands. Twisting my neck even farther, I saw that they were Gérard's hands. He was holding me at full arm's length above his head. He stood at the very edge of the trail, and I could see Garnath and the terminus of the black road far below. If he let go, part of me might join the bird droppings that smeared the cliff face and the rest would come to resemble washed-up jellyfish I had known on beaches past.

"Yes. Look down, Corwin," he said, feeling me stir, glancing up, meeting my eyes. "All that I need to do is open my hands."

"I hear you," I said softly, trying to figure a way to drag him along with me if he decided to do it.

"I am not a clever man," he said. "But I had a thought—a terrible thought. This is the only way that I know to do something about it. My thought was that you had been away from Amber for an awfully long while. I have no way of knowing whether the story about your losing your memory is entirely true. You have come back and you have taken charge of things, but you do not yet truly rule here. I was troubled by the deaths of Benedict's servants, as I am troubled now by the death of Caine. But Eric has died recently also, and Benedict is maimed. It is not so easy to blame you for this part of things, but it has occurred to me that it might be possible—if it should be that you are secretly allied with our enemies of the black road."

"I am not," I said.

"It does not matter, for what I have to say," he said. "Just hear me out. Things will go the way that they will go. If, during your long absence, you arranged this state of affairs—possibly even removing Dad and Brand as part of your design—then I see you as out to destroy all family resistence to your usurpation."

"Would I have delivered myself to Eric to be blinded and imprisoned if this were the case?"

"Hear me out!" he repeated. "You could easily have made mistakes that led to that. It does not matter now. You may be as innocent as you say or as guilty as possible. Look down, Corwin. That is all. Look down at the black road. Death is the limit of the distance

you travel if that is your doing. I have shown you my strength once
again, lest you have forgotten. I can kill you, Corwin. Do not even
be certain that your blade will protect you, if I can get my hands on
you but once. And I will, to keep my promise. My promise is only
that if you are guilty I will kill you the moment I learn of it. Know
also that my life is insured, Corwin, for it is linked now to your
own."

"What do you mean?"

"All of the others are with us at this moment, via my Trump,
watching, listening. You cannot arrange my removal now without
revealing your intentions to the entire family. That way, if I die for-
sworn, my promise can still be kept."

"I get the point," I said. "And if someone else kills you? They
remove me, also. That leaves Julian, Benedict, Random, and the
girls to man the barricades. Better and better—for whoever it is.
Whose idea was this, really?"

"Mine! Mine alone!" he said, and I felt his grip tighten, his arms
bend and grow tense. "You are just trying to confuse things! Like
you always do!" he groaned. "Things didn't go bad till you came
back! Damn it, Corwin! I think it's your fault!"

Then he hurled me into the air.

"Not guilty, Gérard!" was all I had time to shout.

Then he caught me—a great, shoulder-wrenching grab—and
snatched me back from the precipice. He swung me in and around
and set me on my feet. He walked off immediately, heading back to
the gravelly area where we had fought. I followed him and we
collected our things.

As he was clasping his big belt he looked up at me and looked
away again.

"We'll not talk about it any more," he said.

"All right."

I turned and walked back to the horses. We mounted and continued on down the trail.

The spring made its small music in the grove. Higher now, the sun
strung lines of light through the trees. There was still some dew on
the ground. The sod that I had cut for Caine's grave was moist with
it.

I fetched the spade that I had packed and opened the grave. Without a word, Gérard helped me move the body onto a piece of

sailcloth we had brought for that purpose. We folded it about him and closed it with big, loose stitches.

"Corwin! Look!" It was a whisper, and Gérard's hand closed on my elbow as he spoke.

I followed the direction of his gaze and froze. Neither of us moved as we regarded the apparition: a soft, shimmering white encompassed it, as if it were covered with down rather than fur and maning; its tiny, cloven hooves were golden, as was the delicate, whorled horn that rose from its narrow head. It stood atop one of the lesser rocks, nibbling at the lichen that grew there. Its eyes, when it raised them and looked in our direction, were a bright, emerald green. It joined us in immobility for a pair of instants. Then it made a quick, nervous gesture with its front feet, pawing the air and striking the stone, three times. And then it blurred and vanished like a snowflake, silently, perhaps in the woods to our right.

I rose and crossed to the stone. Gérard followed me. There, in the moss, I traced its tiny hoofmarks.

"Then we really did see it," Gérard said.

I nodded.

"We saw something. Did you ever see it before?"

"No. Did you?"

I shook my head.

"Julian claims he once saw it," he said, "in the distance. Says his hounds refused to give chase."

"It was beautiful. That long, silky tail, those shiny hooves . . ."

"Yes. Dad always took it as a good omen."

"I'd like to myself."

"Strange time for it to appear . . . All these years . . ."

I nodded again.

"Is there a special observance? It being our patron and all . . . is there something we should do?"

"If there is, Dad never told me about it," I said. I patted the rock on which it had appeared. "If you herald some turn in our fortunes, if you bring us some measure of grace—thanks, unicorn," I said. "And even if you do not, thanks for the brightness of your company at a dark time."

We went and drank from the spring then. We secured our grim parcel on the back of the third horse. We led our mounts until we were away from the place, where, save for the water, things had become very still.

VI

Life's incessant ceremonies leap everlasting, humans spring eternal on hope's breast, and frying pans without fires are often far between: the sum of my long life's wisdom that evening, tendered in a spirit of creative anxiety, answered by Random with a nod and a friendly obscenity.

We were in the library, and I was seated on the edge of the big desk. Random occupied a chair to my right. Gérard stood at the other end of the room, inspecting some weapons that hung on the wall. Or maybe it was Rein's etching of the unicorn he was looking at. Whichever, along with ourselves, he was also ignoring Julian, who was slouched in an easy chair beside the display cases, right center, legs extended and crossed at the ankles, arms folded, staring down at his scaley boots. Fiona—five-two, perhaps, in height—green eyes fixed on Flora's own blue as they spoke, there beside the fireplace, hair more than compensating for the vacant hearth, smoldering, reminded me, as always, of something from which the artist had just drawn back, setting aside his tools, questions slowly forming behind his smile. The place at the base of her throat where his thumb had notched the collarbone always drew my eyes as the mark of a master craftsman, especially when she raised her head, quizzical or imperious, to regard us taller others. She smiled faintly, just then, doubtless aware of my gaze, an almost clairvoyant faculty the acceptance of which has never deprived of its ability to disconcert. Llewella, off in a corner, pretending to study a book, had her back to the rest of us, her green tresses bobbed a couple of inches above her dark collar. Whether her withdrawal involved animus, self-consciousness in her alienation, or simple caution, I could never be certain. Probably something of all these. Hers was not that familiar a presence in Amber.

. . . And the fact that we constituted a collection of individuals rather than a group, a family, at a time when I wanted to achieve some over-identity, some will to cooperate, was what led to my observations and Random's acknowledgment.

I felt a familiar presence, heard a "Hello, Corwin" and there was Deirdre, reaching toward me. I extended my hand, clasped her own, raised it. She took a step forward, as if to the first strain of some formal dance, and moved close, facing me. For an instant a grilled window had framed her head and shoulders and a rich tapestry had adorned the wall to her left. Planned and posed, of course. Still, effective. She held my Trump in her left hand. She smiled. The others glanced our way as she appeared and she hit them all with that smile, like the Mona Lisa with a machine gun, turning slowly.

"Corwin," she said, kissing me briefly and withdrawing, "I fear I am early."

"Never," I replied, turning toward Random, who had just risen and who anticipated me by seconds.

"May I fetch you a drink, sister?" he asked, taking her hand and nodding toward the sideboard.

"Why, yes. Thank you," and he led her off and poured her some wine, avoiding or at least postponing, I suppose, her usual clash with Flora. At least, I assumed most of the old frictions were still alive as I remembered them. So if it cost me her company for the moment it also maintained the domestic-tranquility index, which was important to me just then. Random can be good at such things when he wants to.

I drummed the side of the desk with my fingertips, I rubbed my aching shoulder, I uncrossed and recrossed my legs, I debated lighting a cigarette. . . .

Suddenly he was there. At the far end of the room, Gérard had turned to his left, said something, and extended his hand. An instant later, he was clasping the left and only hand of Benedict, the final member of our group.

All right. The fact that Benedict had chosen to come in on Gérard's Trump rather than mine was his way of expressing his feelings toward me. Was it also an indication of an alliance to keep me in check? It was at least calculated to make me wonder. Could it have been Benedict who had put Gérard up to our morning's exercise? Probably.

At that moment Julian rose to his feet, crossed the room, gave Benedict a word and a handclasp. This activity attracted Llewella. She turned, closing her book and laying it aside. Smiling then, she advanced and greeted Benedict, nodded to Julian, said something to Gérard. The impromptu conference warmed, grew animated. All right again, and again.

Four and three. And two in the middle . . .

I waited, staring at the group across the room. We were all present, and I could have asked them for attention and proceeded with what I had in mind. However . . .

It was too tempting. All of us could feel the tension, I knew. It was as if a pair of magnetic poles had suddenly been activated within the room. I was curious to see how all the filings would fall.

Flora gave me one quick glance. I doubted that she had changed her mind overnight—unless, of course, there had been some new development. No, I felt confident that I had anticipated the next move.

Nor was I incorrect. I overheard her mentioning thirst and a glass of wine. She turned partway and made a move in my direction, as if expecting Fiona to accompany her. She hesitated for a moment when this did not occur, suddenly became the focus of the entire company's attention, realized this fact, made a quick decision, smiled, and moved in my direction.

"Corwin," she said, "I believe I would like a glass of wine."

Without turning my head or removing my gaze from the tableau before me, I called back over my shoulder, "Random, pour Flora a glass of wine, would you?"

"But of course," he replied, and I heard the necessary sounds.

Flora nodded, unsmiled, and passed beyond me to the right.

Four and four, leaving dear Fiona burning brightly in the middle of the room. Totally self-conscious and enjoying it, she immediately turned toward the oval mirror with the dark, intricately carved frame, hanging in the space between the two nearest tiers of shelves. She proceeded to adjust a stray strand of hair in the vicinity of her left temple.

Her movement produced a flash of green and silver among the red and gold geometries of the carpet, near to the place where her left foot had rested.

I had simultaneous desires to curse and to smile. The arrant bitch was playing games with us again. Always remarkable, though . . . Nothing had changed. Neither cursing nor smiling, I moved forward, as she had known I would.

But Julian too approached, and a trifle more quickly than I. He had been a bit nearer, may have spotted it a fraction of an instant sooner.

He scooped it up and dangled it gently.

"Your bracelet, sister," he said pleasantly. "It seems to have forsaken your wrist, foolish thing. Here—allow me."

She extended her hand, giving him one of those lowered-eyelash smiles while he refastened her chain of emeralds. Completing the business, he folded her hand within both of his own and began to turn back toward his corner, from whence the others were casting sidelong glances while attempting to seem locally occupied.

"I believe you would be amused by a witticism we are about to share," he began.

Her smile grew even more delightful as she disengaged her hand.

"Thank you, Julian," she replied. "I am certain that when I hear it I will laugh. Last, as usual, I fear." She turned and took my arm. "I find that I feel a greater desire," she said, "for a glass of wine."

So I took her back with me and saw her refreshed. Five and four.

Julian, who dislikes showing strong feelings, reached a decision a few moments later and followed us over. He poured himself a glass, sipped from it, studied me for ten or fifteen seconds, then said, "I believe we are all present now. When do you plan to proceed with whatever you have in mind?"

"I see no reason for further delay," I said, "now that everyone has had his turn." I raised my voice then and directed it across the room. "The time has come. Let us get comfortable."

The others drifted over. Chairs were dragged up and settled into. More wine was poured. A minute later we had an audience.

"Thank you," I said when the final stirrings had subsided. "I have a number of things I would like to say, and some of them might even get said. The course of it all will depend on what goes before, and we will get into that right now. Random, tell them what you told me yesterday."

"All right."

I withdrew to the seat behind the desk and Random moved to occupy the edge of it. I leaned back and listened again to the story of his communication with Brand and his attempt to rescue him. It was a condensed version, bereft of the speculations which had not really strayed from my consciousness since Random had put them there. And despite their ommission, a tacit awareness of the implications was occurring within all the others. I knew that. It was the main reason I had wanted Random to speak first. Had I simply come out with an attempt to make a case for my suspicions, I would almost certainly have been assumed to be engaged in the time-honored practice of directing attention away from myself—an act to be followed immediately by the separate, sharp, metallic clicks of minds snapping shut against me. This way, despite any thoughts that Random would say whatever I wanted him to say, they would hear him out, wondering the while. They would toy with the ideas, attempting to foresee the point of my having called the assembly in the first place. They would allow the time that would permit the premises to take root contingent upon later corroboration. And they would be wondering whether we could produce the evidence. I was wondering that same thing myself.

While I waited and wondered I watched the others, a fruitless yet inevitable exercise. Simple curiosity, more than suspicion even, required that I search these faces for reactions, clues, indications— the faces that I knew better than any others, to the limits of my understanding such things. And of course they told me nothing. Perhaps it is true that you really only look at a person the first time you see him, and after that you do a quick bit of mental shorthand each time you recognize him. My brain is lazy enough to give that its likelihood, using its abstracting powers and a presumption of regularity to avoid work whenever possible. This time I forced myself to see, though, and it still did not help. Julian maintained his slightly bored, slightly amused mask. Gérard appeared alternately surprised, angry, and wistful. Benedict just looked bleak and suspicious. Llewella seemed as sad and inscrutable as ever. Deirdre looked distracted, Flora acquiescent, and Fiona was studying everyone else, myself included, assembling her own catalog of reactions.

The only thing that I could tell, after some time, was that Random was making an impression. While no one betrayed himself, I saw the boredom vanish, the old suspicion abate, the new suspicion come to life. Interest rose among my kin. Fascination, almost. Then everyone had questions. At first a few, then a barrage.

"Wait," I finally interrupted. "Let him finish. The whole thing. Some of these will answer themselves. Get the others afterward."

There were nods and growls, and Random proceeded through to the real end. That is, he carried it on to our fight with the beastmen at Flora's, indicating that they were of the same ilk as the one who had slain Caine. Flora endorsed this part.

Then, when the questions came, I watched them carefully. So long as they dealt with the matter of Random's story, they were all to the good. But I wanted to cut things short of speculation as to the possibility of one of us being behind it all. As soon as that came out, talk of me and the smell of red herring would also drift in. This could lead to ugly words and the emergence of a mood I was not anxious to engender. Better to go for the proof first, save on later recriminations, corner the culprit right now if possible, and consolidate my position on the spot.

So I watched and waited. When I felt that the vital moment had ticked its way too near I stopped the clock.

"None of this discussion, this speculation, would be necessary," I said, "if we had all of the facts right now. And there may be a way to get them—right now. That is why you are here."

That did it. I had them Attentive. Ready. Maybe even willing.

"I propose we attempt to reach Brand and bring him home," I said, "now."

"How?" Benedict asked me.

"The Trumps."

"It has been tried," said Julian. "He cannot be reached that way. No reponse."

"I was not referring to the ordinary usage," I said. "I asked you all to bring full sets of Trumps with you. I trust that you have them?"

There were nods.

"Good," I said. "Let us shuffle out Brand's Trump now. I propose that all nine of us attempt to contact him simultaneously."

"An interesting thought," Benedict said.

"Yes," Julian agreed, producing his deck and riffling through it. "Worth trying, at least. It may generate additional power. I do not really know."

I located Brand's Trump. I waited until all the others had found it. Then, "Let us coordinate things," I said. "Is everyone ready?"

Eight assents were spoken.

"Then go ahead. Try. Now."

I studied my card. Brand's features were similar to my own, but he was shorter and slenderer. His hair was like Fiona's. He wore a green riding suit. He rode a white horse. How long ago? How long ago was that? I wondered. Something of a dreamer, a mystic, a poet, Brand was always disillusioned or elated, cynical or wholly trusting. His feelings never seemed to find a middle ground. Manic-depressive is too facile a term for his complex character, yet it might serve to indicate a direction of departure, multitudes of qualifications lining the roadway thereafter. Pursuant to this state of affairs, I must admit that there were times when I found him so charming, considerate, and loyal that I valued him above all my other kin. Other times, however, he could be so bitter, sarcastic, and downright savage that I tried to avoid his company for fear that I might do him harm. Summing up, the last time I had seen him had been one of the latter occasions, just a bit before Eric and I had had the falling out that led to my exile from Amber.

. . . And those were my thoughts and feelings as I studied his Trump, reaching out to him with my mind, my will, opening the vacant place I sought him to fill. About me, the others shuffled their own memories and did the same.

Slowly the card took on a dream-dust quality and acquired the illusion of depth. There followed that familiar blurring, with the sense of movement which heralds contact with the subject. The Trump grew colder beneath my fingertips, and then things flowed and formed, achieving a sudden verity of vision, persistent, dramatic, full.

He seemed to be in a cell. There was a stone wall behind him. There was straw on the floor. He was manacled, and his chain ran back through a huge ring bolt set in the wall above and behind him. It was a fairly long chain, providing sufficient slack for movement, and at the moment he was taking advantage of this fact, lying sprawled on a heap of straw and rags off in the corner. His hair and beard were quite long, his face thinner than I had ever before seen it. His clothes were tattered and filthy. He seemed to be sleeping. My mind went back to my own imprisonment—the smells, the cold, the wretched fare, the dampness, the loneliness, the madness that came and went. At least he still had his eyes, for they flickered and I saw them when several of us spoke his name; green they were, with a flat, vacant look.

Was he drugged? Or did he believe himself to be hallucinating?

But suddenly his spirit returned. He raised himself. He extended his hand.

"Brothers!" he said. "Sisters . . ."

"I'm coming!" came a shout that shook the room.

Gérard had leaped to his feet, knocking over his chair. He dashed across the room and snatched a great battle ax from its pegs on the wall. He slung it at his wrist, holding the Trump in that same hand. For a moment he froze, studying the card. Then he extended his free hand and suddenly he was there, clasping Brand, who chose that moment to pass out again. The image wavered. The contact was broken.

Cursing, I sought through the pack after Gérard's own Trump. Several of the others seemed to be doing the same thing. Locating it, I moved for contact. Slowly, the melting, the turning, the re-forming occurred. There!

Gérard had drawn the chain taut across the stones of the wall and was attacking it with the ax. It was a heavy thing, however, and resisted his powerful blows for a long while. Eventually several of the links were mashed and scarred, but by then he had been at it for almost two minutes, and the ringing, chopping sounds had alerted the jailers.

For there were noises from the left—a rattling sound, the sliding of bolts, the creaking of hinges. Although my field of perception did not extend that far, it seemed obvious that the cell's door was being opened. Brand raised himself once more. Gérard continued to hack at the chain.

"Gérard! The door!" I shouted.

"I know!" he bellowed, wrapping the chain about his arm and yanking it. It did not yield.

Then he let go of the chain and swung the ax, as one of the horny-handed warriors rushed him, blade upraised. The swordsman fell, to be replaced by another. Then a third and a fourth crowded by them. Others were close on their heels.

There was a blur of movement at that moment and Random knelt within the tableau, his right hand clasped with Brand's, his left holding his chair before him like a shield, its legs pointing outward. He sprang to his feet and rushed the attackers, driving the chair like a battering ram amid them. They fell back. He raised the chair and swung it. One lay dead on the floor, felled by Gérard's ax. Another had drawn off to one side, clutching at the stump of his right arm. Random produced a dagger and left it in a nearby stomach, brained two more with the chair, and drove back the final man. Eerily, while this was going on, the dead man rose above the floor and slowly drifted upward, spilling and dripping the while. The one who had been stabbed collapsed to his knees, clutching at the blade.

In the meantime, Gérard had taken hold of the chain with both hands. He braced one foot against the wall and commenced to pull. His shoulders rose as the great muscles tightened across his back. The chain held. Ten seconds, perhaps. Fifteen . . .

Then, with a snap and a rattle, it parted. Gérard stumbled backward, catching himself with an outflung hand. He glanced back, apparently at Random, who was out of my line of sight at the moment. Seemingly satisfied, he turned away, stooped and raised Brand, who had fallen unconscious again. Holding him in his arms, he turned and extended one hand from beneath the limp form. Random leaped back into sight beside them, *sans* chair, and gestured to us also.

All of us reached for them, and a moment later they stood amid us and we crowded around.

A sort of cheer had gone up as we rushed to touch him, to see him, our brother who had been gone these many years and just now snatched back from his mysterious captors. And at last, hopefully, finally, some answers might also have been liberated. Only he looked so weak, so thin, so pale . . . .

"Get back!" Gérard shouted. "I'm taking him to the couch! Then you can look all you—"

Dead silence. For everyone had backed off, and then turned to stone. This was because there was blood on Brand, and it was dripping. And this was because there was a knife in his left side, to the rear. It had not been there moments before. Some one of us had just tried for his kidney and possibly succeeded. I was not heartened by the fact that the Random-Corwin Conjecture that it was One Of Us Behind It All had just received a significant boost. I had an instant during which to concentrate all my faculties in an attempt to mentally photograph everyone's position. Then the spell was broken. Gérard bore Brand to the couch and we drew aside; and we all knew that we all realized not only what had happened, but what it implied.

Gérard set Brand down in a prone position and tore away his filthy shirt.

"Get me clean water to bathe him," he said. "And towels. Get me saline solution and glucose and something to hang them from. Get me a whole medical kit."

Deirdre and Flora moved toward the door.

"My quarters are closest," said Random. "One of you will find a medical kit there. But the only IV stuff is in the lab on the third floor. I'd better come and help."

They departed together.

We all had had medical training somewhere along the line, both here and abroad. That which we learned in Shadow, though, had to be modified in Amber. Most antibiotics from the shadow worlds, for example, were ineffectual here. On the other hand, our personal immunological processes appear to behave differently from those of any other peoples we have studied, so that it is much more difficult for us to become infected—and if infected we deal with it more expeditiously. Then, too, we possess profound regenerative abilities.

All of which is as it must be, of course, the ideal necessarily being superior to its shadows. And Amberites that we are, and aware of these facts from an early age, all of us obtained medical training relatively early in life. Basically, despite what is often said about being your own physician, it goes back to our not unjustified distrust of virtually everyone, and most particularly of those who might hold our lives in their hands. All of which partly explains why I did not rush to shoulder Gérard aside to undertake Brand's treatment myself, despite the fact that I had been through a med school on the shadow Earth within the past couple of generations. The other part of the explanation is that Gérard was not letting anyone else near Brand. Julian and Fiona had both moved forward, apparently with the same thing in mind, only to encounter Gérard's left arm like a gate at a railway crossing.

"No," he had said. "I know that I did not do it, and that is all that I know. There will be no second chance for anyone else."

With any one of us sustaining that sort of wound while in an otherwise sound condition, I would say that if he made it through the first half hour he would make it. Brand, though. . . The shape he was in . . . There was no telling.

When the others returned with the materials and equipment, Gérard cleaned Brand, sutured the wound, and dressed it. He hooked up the IV, broke off the manacles with a hammer and chisel Random had located, covered Brand with a sheet and a blanket, and took his pulse again.

"How is it?" I asked.

"Weak," he said, and he drew up a chair and seated himself beside the couch. "Someone fetch me my blade—and a glass of wine. I didn't have any. Also, if there is any food left over there, I'm hungry."

Llewella headed for the sideboard and Random got him his blade from the rack behind the door.

"Are you just going to camp there?" Random asked, passing him the weapon.

"I am."

"What about moving Brand to a better bed?"

"He is all right where he is. I will decide when he can be moved. In the meantime, someone get a fire going. Then put out a few of those candles."

Random nodded.

"I'll do it," he said. Then he picked up the knife Gérard had drawn from Brand's side, a thin stiletto, its blade about seven inches in length. He held it across the palm of his hand.

"Does anyone recognize this?" he asked.

"Not I," said Benedict.

"Nor I," said Julian.

"No," I said.

The girls shook their heads.

Random studied it.

"Easily concealed—up a sleeve, in a boot or bodice. It took real nerve to use it that way . . . ."

"Desperation," I said.

". . . And a very accurate anticipation of our mob scene. Inspired, almost."

"Could one of the guards have done it?" Julian asked. "Back in the cell?"

"No," Gérard said. "None of them came near enough."

"It looks to be decently balanced for throwing," Deirdre said.

"It is," said Random, shifting it about his fingertips. "Only none of them had a clear shot or the opportunity. I'm positive."

Llewella returned, bearing a tray containing slabs of meat, half a loaf of bread, a bottle of wine, and a goblet. I cleared a small table and set it beside Gérard's chair. As Llewella deposited the tray, she asked, "But why? That only leaves us. Why would one of us want to do it?"

I sighed.

"Whose prisoner do you think he might have been?" I asked.

"One of us?"

"If he possessed knowledge which someone was willing to go to this length to suppress, what do you think? The same reason also served to put him where he was and keep him there."

Her brows tightened.

"That does not make sense either. Why didn't they just kill him and be done with it?"

I shrugged.

"Must have had some use for him," I said. "But there is really only one person who can answer that question adequately. When you find him, ask him."

"Or her," Julian said. "Sister, you seem possessed of a superabundance of naïveté, suddenly."

Her gaze locked with Julian's own, a pair of icebergs reflecting frigid infinities.

"As I recall," she said, "you rose from your seat when they came through, turned to the left, rounded the desk, and stood slightly to Gérard's right. You leaned pretty far forward. I believe your hands were out of sight, below."

"And as I recall," he said, "you were within striking distance yourself, off to Gérard's left—and leaning forward."

"I would have had to do it with my left hand—and I am right-handed."

"Perhaps he owes what life he still possesses to that fact."

"You seem awfully anxious, Julian, to find that it was someone else."

"All right," I said. "All right! You know this is self-defeating. Only one of us did it, and this is not the way to smoke him out."

"Or her," Julian added.

Gérard rose, towered, glared.

"I will not have you disturbing my patient," he said. "And, Random, you said you were going to see to the fire."

"Right away," Random said, and moved to do it.

"Let us adjourn to the sitting room off the main hall," I said, "downstairs. Gérard, I will post a couple of guards outside the door here."

"No," Gérard said. "I would rather that anyone who wishes to try it get this far. I will hand you his head in the morning."

I nodded.

"Well, you can ring for anything you need—or call one of us on the Trumps. We will fill you in in the morning on anything that we learn."

Gérard seated himself, grunted, and began eating. Random got the fire going and extinguished some lights. Brand's blanket rose and fell, slowly but regularly. We filed quietly from the room and headed for the stairway, leaving them there together with the flare and the crackle, the tubes and the bottles.

VII

Many are the times I have awakened, sometimes shaking, always afraid, from the dream that I occupied my old cell, blind once more, in the dungeons beneath Amber. It is not as if I were unfamiliar with the condition of imprisonment. I have been locked away on a number of occasions, for various periods of time. But solitary, plus blindness with small hope of recovery, made for a big charge to the sensory-deprivation counter in the department store of the mind. That, with the sense of finality to it all, had left its marks. I generally keep these memories safely tucked away during waking hours, but at night, sometimes, they come loose, dance down the aisles and frolic round the notions counter, one, two, three. Seeing Brand there in his cell had brought them out again, along with an unseasonal chill; and that final thrust served to establish a more or less permanent residence for them. Now, among my kin in the shield-hung sitting room, I could not avoid the thought that one or more of them had done unto Brand as Eric had done unto me. While this capacity was in itself hardly a surprising discovery, the matter of occupying the same room with the culprit and having no idea as to his identity was more than a little disturbing. My only consolation was that each of the others, according to his means, must be disturbed also. Including the guilty, now that the existence theorem had shown a positive. I knew then that I had been hoping all along that outsiders were entirely to blame. Now, though . . . On the one hand I felt even more restricted than usual in what I could say. On the other, it seemed a good time to press for information, with everyone in an abnormal state of mind. The desire to cooperate for purposes of dealing with the threat could prove helpful. And even the guilty party would want to behave the same as everyone else. Who knew but that he might slip up while making the effort?

"Well, have you any other interesting little experiments you would care to conduct?" Julian asked me, clasping his hands behind his head and leaning back in my favorite chair.

"Not at the moment, "I said.

"Pity," he replied. "I was hoping you would suggest we go looking for Dad now in the same fashion. Then, if we are lucky, we find him and someone puts him out of the way with more certainty. After that, we could all play Russian roulette with those fine new weapons you've furnished—winner take all."

"Your words are ill-considered," I said.

"Not so. I considered every one of them," he answered. "We spend so much time lying to one another that I decided it might be amusing to say what I really felt. Just to see whether anyone noticed."

"Now you see that we have. We also notice that the real you is no improvement over the old one."

"Whichever you prefer, both of us have been wondering whether you have any idea what you are going to do next."

"I do," I said. "I now intend to obtain answers to a number of questions dealing with everything that is plaguing us. We might as well start with Brand and his troubles." Turning toward Benedict, who was sitting gazing into the fire, I said, "Back in Avalon, Benedict, you told me that Brand was one of the ones who searched for me after my disappearance."

"That is correct," Benedict answered.

"All of us went looking," Julian said.

"Not at first," I replied. "Initially, it was Brand, Gérard, and yourself, Benedict. Isn't that what you told me?"

"Yes," he said. "The others did have a go at it later, though. I told you that, too."

I nodded.

"Did Brand report anything unusual at that time?" I asked.

"Unusual? In what way?" said Benedict.

"I don't know. I am looking for some connection between what happened to him and what happened to me."

"Then you are looking in the wrong place," Benedict said. "He returned and reported no success. And he was around for ages after that, unmolested."

"I gathered that much," I said. "I understand from what Random has told me, though, that his final disappearance occurred approximately a month before my own recovery and return. That almost strikes me as peculiar. If he did not report anything special after his return from the search, did he do so prior to his disappearance? Or in the interim? Anyone? Anything? Say it if you've got it!"

There followed some mutual glancing about. The looks seemed more curious than suspicious or nervous, though.

Finally, then, "Well," Llewella said, "I do not know. Do not know whether it is significant, I mean."

All eyes came to rest upon her. She began to knot and unknot the ends of her belt cord, slowly, as she spoke.

"It was in the interim, and it may have no bearing," she went on. "It is just something that struck me as peculiar. Brand came to Rebma long ago—"

"How long ago?" I asked.

She furrowed her brow.

"Fifty, sixty, seventy years . . . I am not certain."

I tried to summon up the rough conversion factor I had worked out during my long incarceration. A day in Amber, it seemed, constituted a bit over two and a half days on the shadow Earth where I had spent my exile. I wanted to relate events in Amber to my own time-scale whenever possible, just in case any peculiar correspondences turned up. So Brand had gone to Rebma sometime in what was, to me, the nineteenth century.

"Whatever the date," she said, "he came and visited me. Stayed for several weeks." She glanced at Random then. "He was asking about Martin."

Random narrowed his eyes and cocked his head.

"Did he say why?" he asked her.

"Not exactly," she said. "He implied that he had met Martin somewhere in his travels, and he gave the impression that he would like to get in touch with him again. I did not realize until some time after his departure that finding out everything he could concerning Martin was probably the entire reason for his visit. You know how subtle Brand can be, finding out things without seeming to be after them. It was only after I had spoken with a number of others whom he had visited that I began to see what had occurred. I never did find out why, though."

"That is—most peculiar," Random observed. "For it brings to mind something to which I had never attached any significance. He once questioned me at great length concerning my son—and it may well have been at about the same time. He never indicated that he had met him, however—or that he had any desire to do so. It started out as a bit of banter on the subject of bastards. When I took offense he apologized and asked a number of more proper questions about the boy, which I assumed he then put for the sake of politeness—to leave me with a softer remembrance. As you say, though, he had a way of drawing admissions from people. Why is it you never told me of this before?"

She smiled prettily.

"Why should I have?" she said.

Random nodded slowly, his face expressionless.

"Well, what did you tell him?" he said. "What did he learn? What do you know about Martin that I don't?"

She shook her head, her smile fading.

"Nothing—actually," she said. "To my knowledge, no one in Rebma ever heard from Martin after he took the Pattern and vanished. I do not believe that Brand departed knowing any more than he did when he arrived."

"Strange . . ." I said. "Did he approach anyone else on the subject?"

"I don't remember," Julian said.

"Nor I," said Benedict.

The others shook their heads.

"Then let us note it and leave it for now," I said. "There are other things I also need to know. Julian, I understand that you and Gérard attempted to follow the black road a while back, and that Gérard was injured along the way. I believe you both stayed with Benedict for a time after that, while Gérard recuperated. I would like to know about that expedition."

"It seems as if you already do," Julian replied. "You have just stated everything that occurred."

"Where did you learn of this, Corwin," Benedict inquired.

"Back in Avalon," I said.

"From whom?"

"Dara," I said.

He rose to his feet, came over, stood before me, glared down.

"You still persist in that absurd story about the girl!"

I sighed.

"We have been round and round on this too many times," I said. "By now I have told you everything that I know on the subject. Either you accept it or you do not. She is the one who told me, though."

"Apparently, then, there were some things you did not tell me. You never mentioned that part before."

"Is it true or isn't it? About Julian and Gérard."

"It is true," he said.

"Then forget the source for now and let us get on with what happened."

"Agreed," Benedict said. "I may speak candidly, now that the reason for secrecy is no longer with us. Eric, of course. He was unaware of my whereabouts, as were most of the others. Gérard was my main source of news in Amber. Eric grew more and more apprehensive concerning the black road and finally decided to send scouts to trace it through Shadow to its source. Julian and Gérard were selected. They were attacked by a very strong party of its creatures at a point near Avalon. Gérard called to me, via my Trump, for assistance and I went to their aid. The enemy was dispatched. As Gérard had sustained a broken leg in the fighting and Julian was a bit battered himself, I took them both home with me. I broke my silence with Eric at that time, to tell him where they were and what had become of them. He ordered them not to continue their journey, but to return to Amber after they had recovered. They remained with me until they did. Then they went back."

"That is all?"

"That is all."

But it wasn't. Dara had also told me something else. She had mentioned another visitor. I remembered it quite distinctly. That day, beside the stream, a tiny rainbow in the mist above the waterfall, the mill wheel turning round and round, delivering dreams and grinding them, that day we had fenced and talked and walked in Shadow, had passed through a primordial wood, coming to a spot beside a mighty torrent where turned a wheel fit for the granary of the gods, that day we had picnicked, flirted, gossiped, she had told me many things, some of them doubtless false. But she had not lied concerning the journey of Julian and Gérard, and I believed it possible that she had also spoken truly when she said that Brand had visited Benedict in Avalon. "Frequently" was the word she had used.

Now, Benedict made no secret of the fact that he distrusted me. I could see this alone as sufficient reason for his withholding information on anything he judged too sensitive to become my business.

Hell, buying his story, I would not have trusted me either if our situations were reversed. Only a fool would have called him on it at that moment, though. Because of the other possibilities.

It could be that he planned to tell me later, in private, of the circumstances surrounding Brand's visits. They could well have involved something he did not wish to discuss before the group, and especially before Brand's would-be killer.

Or—There was, of course, the possibility that Benedict himself was behind it all. I did not even like to think about the consequences. Having served under Napoleon, Lee, and MacArthur, I appreciated the tactician as well as the strategist. Benedict was both, and he was the best I had ever known. The recent loss of his right arm had in no way diminished him in this, or for that matter impaired his personal fighting skills. Had I not been very lucky recently he could easily have turned me into a pile of scallops over our misunderstanding. No, I did not want it to be Benedict, and I was not about to grope after whatever he had at that moment seen fit to conceal. I only hoped that he was just saving it for later.

So I settled for his, "That is all," and decided to move on to other matters.

"Flora," I said, "back when I first visited you, after my accident, you said something which I still do not quite understand. In that I had ample time relatively soon thereafter in which to review many things, I came across it in my memories and occasionally puzzled over it. I still do not understand it. So would you please tell me what you meant when you said that the shadows contained more horrors than any had thought?"

"Why, I do not properly recall saying it," Flora said. "But I suppose that I must have, if it made such an impression. You know the effect that I was referring to: that Amber seems to act as something of a magnet on adjacent shadows, drawing things across from them; the nearer you get to Amber the easier the road becomes, even for shadow-things. While there always seems to be some exchange of materials among adjacent shadows themselves, the effect is more forceful and also more of a one-way process when it comes to Amber. We have always been alert for peculiar things slipping through. Well, for several years prior to your recovery, more such things than usual seemed to be showing up in the vicinity of Amber. Dangerous things, almost invariably. Many were recognizable creatures from nearby realms. After a time, though, things kept coming

in from farther and farther afield. Eventually, some which were totally unknown made it through. No reason could be found for this
sudden transportation of menaces, although we sought fairly far for
disturbances which might be driving them this way. In other words,
highly improbable penetrations of Shadow were occurring."

"This actually began while Dad was still around?"

"Oh yes. It started several years before your recovery—as I said."

"I see. Did anyone consider the possibility of there being a connection between this state of affairs and Dad's departure?"

"Certainly," Benedict replied. "I still feel that that was the reason
for it. He went off to investigate, or to seek a remedy."

"But that is purely conjecture," Julian said. "You know how he
was. He gave no reasons."

Benedict shrugged.

"It is a resonable inference, though," he said. "I understand that
he had spoken of his concern over the—monster migrations, if you
like—on numerous occasions."

I withdrew my cards from their case, having recently gotten into
the habit of carrying a set of Trumps with me at all times. I raised
Gérard's Trump and regarded it. The others were silent, watching
me as I did this. Moments later, there was contact.

Gérard was still seated in his chair, his blade across his knees. He
was still eating. He swallowed when he felt my presence and said,
"Yes, Corwin? What do you want?"

"How is Brand?"

"Sleeping," he said. "His pulse is a little stronger. His breathing is
the same—regular. It's still too early—"

"I know," I said. "I mainly wanted to check your recollection of
something: Near the end there, did you get the impression from anything he might have said or done that Dad's going away might have
been connected with the increased number of Shadow beings that
were slipping through into Amber?"

"That," said Julian, "is what is known as a leading question."

Gérard wiped his mouth.

"There could have been a connection, yes," he said. "He seemed
disturbed, preoccupied with something. And he did talk about the
creatures. But he never really said that that was his main concern—
or whether it was something entirely different."

"Like what?"

He shook his head.

"Anything. I—yes . . . yes, there is something you probably ought to know, for whatever it is worth. Some time after his disappearance, I did make an effort to find out one thing. That was, whether I was indeed the last person to see him before his departure. I am fairly certain that I was. I had been here in the palace all evening, and I was preparing to return to the flagship. Dad had retired about an hour earlier, but I had stayed on in the guard room, playing draughts with Captain Thoben. As we were sailing the following morning, I decided to take a book with me. So I came up here to the library. Dad was seated at the desk." He gestured with his head. "He was going through some old books, and he had not yet changed his garments. He nodded to me when I entered, and I told him I had just come up for a book. He said, 'You've come to the right place,' and he kept on reading. While I was looking over the shelves, he said something to the effect that he could not sleep. I found a book, told him good night, he said, 'Good sailing,' and I left." He lowered his eyes again. "Now I am positive he was wearing the Jewel of Judgment that night, that I saw it on him then as plainly as I see it on you now. I am equally certain that he had not had it on earlier that evening. For a long while after, I thought that he had taken it along with him, wherever he went. There was no indication in his chambers that he had later changed his clothing. I never saw the stone again until you and Bleys were defeated in your assault on Amber. Then, Eric was wearing it. When I questioned him he claimed that he had found it in Dad's chambers. Lacking evidence to the contrary, I had to accept his story. But I was never happy with it. Your question—and seeing you wearing it—has brought it all back. So I thought you had better know about it."

"Thanks," I said, and another question occurred to me but I decided against asking it at that moment. For the benefit of the others, I closed off by saying, "So do you think he needs any more blankets? Or anything else?"

Gérard raised his glass to me, then took a drink.

"Very good. Keep up the good work," I said, and I passed my hand over his card.

"Brother Brand seems to be doing all right," I said, "and Gérard does not recollect Dad's saying anything that would directly connect Shadow slippage and his departure. I wonder how Brand will recall things, when he comes around?"

"*If* he comes around," Julian said.

"I think that he will," I said. "We have all taken some pretty bad beatings. Our vitality is one of the few things we have come to trust. My guess is that he will be talking by morning."

"What do you propose doing with the guilty party," he asked, "if Brand names him?"

"Question him," I said.

"Then I would like to do the questioning. I am beginning to feel that you may be right this time, Corwin, and that the person who stabbed him may also be responsible for our intermittent state of siege, for Dad's disappearance, and for Caine's killing. So I would enjoy questioning him before we cut his throat, and I would like to volunteer for that last part also."

"We will keep it in mind," I said.

"You are not excluded from the reckoning, Corwin."

"I was aware of that."

"I have something to say," said Benedict, smothering a rejoinder from Julian. "I find myself troubled both by the strength and the apparent objective of the opposition. I have encountered them now on several occasions, and they *are* out for blood. Accepting for the moment your story of the girl Dara, Corwin, her final words do seem to sum up their attitude: 'Amber will be destroyed.' Not conquered, subjugated, or taught a lesson. Destroyed. Julian, you wouldn't mind ruling here, would you?"

Julian smiled.

"Perhaps next year this time," he said. "Not today, thank you."

"What I am getting at is that I could see you—or any of us—employing mercenaries or obtaining allies to effect a takeover. I cannot see you employing a force so powerful that it would represent a grave problem itself afterward. Not a force that seems bent on destruction rather than conquest. I cannot see you, me, Corwin, the others as actually trying to destroy Amber, or willing to gamble with forces that would. That is the part I do not like about Corwin's notion that one of us is behind this."

I had to nod. I was not unaware of the weakness of that link in my chain of speculations. Still, there were so many unknowns. . . . I could offer alternatives, such as Random then did, but guesses prove nothing.

"It may be," Random said, "that one of us made the deal but underestimated his allies. The guilty party may now be sweating this thing as much as the rest of us. He may not be in a position to turn things off now, even if he wants to."

"We could offer him the opportunity," Fiona said, "to betray his allies to us now. If Julian could be persuaded to leave his throat uncut and the rest of us were willing to do the same, he might come around—if Random's guess is correct. He would not claim the throne, but he was obviously not about to have it before. He would have his life and he could save Amber quite a bit of trouble. Is anyone willing to commit himself to a position on this?"

"I am," I said. "I will give him his life if he will come across, with the understanding that it will be spent in exile."

"I will go along with that." Benedict said.

"So will I," said Random.

"On one condition," Julian said. "If he was not personally responsible for Caine's death, I will go along with it. Otherwise, no. And there would have to be evidence."

"Life, in exile," Deirdre said. "All right. I agree."

"So do I," said Flora.

"And I," Llewella followed.

"Gérard will probably agree too," I said. "But I really wonder whether Brand will feel the same as the rest of us. I've a feeling he may not."

"Let us check with Gérard," Benedict said. "If Brand makes it and proves the only holdout, the guilty party will know he has only one enemy to avoid—and they can always work out their own terms on that count."

"All right," I said, smothering a few misgivings, and I recontacted Gérard, who agreed also.

So we rose to our feet and swore that much by the Unicorn of Amber—Julian's oath having an extra clause to it—and swore to enforce exile on any of our own number who violated the oath. Frankly, I did not think it would net us anything, but it is always nice to see families doing things together.

After that, everyone made a point of mentioning that he would be remaining in the palace overnight, presumably to indicate that no one feared anything Brand might have to say in the morning—and especially to indicate that no one had a desire to get out of town, a thing that would not be forgotten, even if Brand gave up the ghost during the night. In that I had no further questions to put to the group and no one had sprung forward to own up to the misdeeds covered by the oath, I leaned back and listened for a time after that. Things came apart, falling into a series of conversations and exchanges, one of the main topics being an attempted reconstruction of the library tableau, each of us in his own place and, invariably, why each of us was in a position to have done it, except for the speaker. I smoked; I said nothing on the subject. Deirdre did spot an interesting possibility, however. Namely, that Gérard could have done the stabbing himself while we were all crowded around, and that his heroic efforts were not prompted by any desire to save Brand's neck, but rather to achieve a position where he could stop his tongue—in which case Brand would never make it through the night. Ingenious, but I just couldn't believe it. No one else bought it either. At least, no one volunteered to go upstairs and throw Gérard out.

After a time Fiona drifted over and sat beside me.

"Well, I've tried the only thing I could think of," she said. "I hope some good comes of it."

"It may," I said.

"I see that you have added a peculiar piece of ornamentation to your wardrobe," she said, raising the Jewel of Judgment between her thumb and forefinger and studying it.

Then she raised her eyes.

"Can you make it do tricks for you?" she asked.

"Some," I said.

"Then you knew how to attune it. It involves the Pattern, doesn't it?"

"Yes. Eric told me how to go about it, right before he died."

"I see."

She released it, settled back into her seat, regarded the flames.

"Did he give you any cautions to go along with it?" she asked.

"No," I said.

"I wonder whether that was a matter of design or circumstance?"

"Well, he was pretty busy dying at the time. That limited our conversation considerably."

"I know. I was wondering whether his hatred for you outweighed his hopes for the realm, or whether he was simply ignorant of some of the principles involved."

"What do you know about it?"

"Think again of Eric's death, Corwin. I was not there when it occurred, but I came in early for the funeral. I was present when his body was bathed, shaved, dressed—and I examined his wounds. I do not believe that any of them were fatal, in themselves. There were three chest wounds, but only one looked as if it might have run into the mediastinal area—"

"One's enough, if—"

"Wait," she said. "It was difficult, but I tried judging the angle of the puncture with a thin glass rod. I wanted to make an incision, but Caine would not permit it. Still, I do not believe that his heart or arteries were damaged. It is still not too late to order an autopsy, if you would like me to check further on this. I am certain that his injuries and the general stress contributed to his death, but I believe it was the jewel that made the difference."

"Why do you think this?"

"Because of some things that Dworkin said when I studied with him—and things that I noticed afterward, because of this. He indicated that while it conferred unusual abilities, it also represented a drain on the vitality of its master. The longer you wear it, the more it somehow takes out of you. I paid attention after that, and I noticed that Dad wore it only seldom and never kept it on for long periods of time."

My thoughts returned to Eric, the day he lay dying on the slopes of Kolvir, the battle raging about him. I remembered my first look at him, his face pale, his breath labored, blood on his chest. . . . And the Jewel of Judgment, there on its chain, was pulsing, heartlike, among the moist folds of his garments. I had never seen it do that before, or since. I recalled that the effect had grown fainter, weaker. And when he died and I folded his hands atop it, the phenomenon had ceased.

"What do you know of its function?" I asked her.

She shook her head.

"Dworkin considered that a state secret. I know the obvious—weather control—and I inferred from some of Dad's remarks that it has something to do with a heightened perception, or a higher perception. Dworkin had mentioned it primarily as an example of the pervasiveness of the Pattern in everything that gives us power—even the Trumps contain the Pattern, if you look closely, look long enough—and he cited it as an instance of a conservation principle: all of our special powers have their price. The greater the power, the larger the investment. The Trumps are a small matter, but there is still an element of fatigue involved in their employment. Walking through Shadow, which is an exercise of the image of the Pattern which exists within us, is an even greater expenditure. To essay the Pattern itself, physically, is a massive drain on one's energies. But the jewel, he said, represents an even higher octave of the same thing, and its cost to its employer is exponentially greater."

Thus, if correct, another ambiguous insight into the character of my late and least favored brother. If he were aware of this phenomenon and had donned the jewel and worn it overlong anyhow, in the defense of Amber, it made him something of a hero. But then, seen in this light, his passing it along to me, without warnings, became a deathbed effort at a final piece of vengeance. But he had exempted me from his curse, he'd said, so as to spend it properly on our enemies in the field. This, of course, only meant that he hated them a little more than he hated me and was deploying his final energies as strategically as possible, for Amber. I thought then of the partial character of Dworkin's notes, as I had recovered them from the hiding place Eric had indicated. Could it be that Eric had acquired them intact and had purposely destroyed that portion containing the cautions so as to damn his successor? That notion did not strike me as quite adequate, for he had had no way of knowing that I would return when I did, as I did, that the course of battle would run as it had, and that I would indeed be his successor. It could just as easily have been one of his favorites that followed him to power, in which case he would certainly not have wanted him to inherit any booby traps. No. As I saw it, either Eric was not really aware of this property of the stone, having acquired only partial instructions for its use, or someone had gotten to those papers before I had and removed sufficient material to leave me with a mortal liability. It may well have been the hand of the real enemy, once again.

"Do you know the safety factor?" I asked.

"No," she said. "I can give you only two pointers, for whatever they may be worth. The first is that I do not recall Dad's ever wearing it for long periods of time. The second, I pieced together from a number of things that he said, beginning with a comment to the effect that 'when people turn into statues you are either in the wrong place or in trouble." I pressed him quite a bit on that, over a long period of time, and I eventually got the impression that the first sign of having worn it too long is some sort of distortion of your time sense. Apparently it begins speeding up the metabolism—everything—with a net effect that the world seems to be slowing down around you. This must take quite a toll on a person. That is everything that I know about it, and I admit that a large part of the last is guesswork. How long have you been wearing it?"

"A while now," I said, taking my mental pulse and glancing about to see whether things seemed to be slowing down any.

I could not really tell, though of course I did not feel in the best of shape. I had assumed it was totally Gérard's doing, though. I was not about to yank it off, however, just because another family member had suggested it, even if it was clever Fiona in one of her friendlier moods. Perversity, cussedness . . . No, independence. That was it. That and purely formal distrust. I had only put it on for the evening a few hours before, anyway. I'd wait.

"Well, you have made your point in wearing it," she was saying. "I simply wanted to advise you against prolonged exposure until you know more about it."

"Thanks, Fi. I'll have it off soon, and I appreciate your telling me. By the way, whatever became of Dworkin?"

She tapped her temple.

"His mind finally went, poor man. I like to think that Dad had him put away in some restful retreat in Shadow."

"I see what you mean," I said. "Yes, let us think that. Poor fellow."

Julian rose to his feet, concluding a conversation with Llewella. He stretched, nodded to her, and strolled over.

"Corwin, have you thought of any more questions for us?" he said.

"None that I'd care to ask just now."

He smiled.

"Anything more that you want to tell us?"

"Not at the moment."

"Any more experiments, demonstrations, charades?"

"No."

"Good. Then I'm going to bed. Good night."

"Night."

He bowed to Fiona, waved to Benedict and Random, nodded to Flora and Deirdre as he passed them on the way to the door. He paused on the threshold, turned back and said, "Now you can all talk about me," and went on out.

"All right," Fiona said. "Let's. I think he's the one."

"Why?" I asked.

"I'll go down the list, subjective, intuitive, and biased as it is. Benedict, in my opinion, is above suspicion. If he wanted the throne, he'd have it by now, by direct, military methods. With all the time he has had, he could have managed an attack that would have succeeded, even against Dad. He is that good, and we all know it. You, on the other hand, have made a number of blunders which you would not have made had you been in full possession of your faculties. That is why I believe your story, amnesia and all. No one gets himself blinded as a piece of strategy. Gérard is well on the way to establishing his own innocence. I almost think he is up there with Brand now more for that reason than from any desire to protect Brand. At any rate, we will know for sure before long—or else have some new suspicions. Random has simply been watched too closely these past years to have had the opportunity to engineer everything that has been happening. So he is out. Of us more delicate sorts, Flora hasn't the brains, Deirdre lacks the guts, Llewella hasn't the motivations, as she is happy elsewhere but never here, and I, of course, am innocent of all but malice. That leaves Julian. Is he capable? Yes. Does he want the throne? Of course. Has he had time and opportunity? Again, yes. He is your man."

"Would he have killed Caine?" I asked. "They were buddies."

She curled her lip.

"Julian has no friends," she said. "That icy personality of his is thawed only by thoughts of himself. Oh, in recent years he *seemed* closer to Caine than to anyone else. But even that . . . even that could have been a part of it. Shamming a friendship long enough to make it seem believable, so that he would not be suspect at this time. I can believe Julian capable of that because I cannot believe him capable of strong emotional attachments."

I shook my head.

"I don't know," I said. "His friendship with Caine is something that occurred during my absence, so everything I know concerning it is secondhand. Still, if Julian were looking for friendship in the form of another personality close to his own, I can see it. They were a lot alike. I tend to think it was real, because I don't think anybody is capable of deceiving someone about his friendship for years. Unless the other party is awfully stupid, which is something Caine was not. And —well, you say your reasoning was subjective, intuitive, and biased. So is mine, on something like this. I just don't like to think anybody is such a miserable wretch that he would use his only friend that way. That's why I think there is something wrong with your list."

She sighed.

"For someone who has been around for as long as you have, Corwin, you say some silly things. Were you changed by your long stay in that funny little place? Years ago you would have seen the obvious, as I do."

"Perhaps I have changed, for such things no longer seem obvious. Or could it be that you have changed, Fiona? A trifle more cynical than the little girl I once knew. It might not have been all that obvious to you, years ago."

She smiled softly.

"Never tell a woman she has changed, Corwin. Except for the better. You used to know that, too. Could it be that you are really only one of Corwin's shadows, sent back to suffer and intimidate here on his behalf? Is the real Corwin somewhere else, laughing at us all?"

"I am here, and I am not laughing," I said.

She laughed.

"Yes, that is it!" she said. "I have just decided that you are not yourself!

"Announcement, everybody!" she cried, springing to her feet. "I have just noticed that this is not really Corwin! It has to be one of his shadows! It has just announced a belief in friendship, dignity, nobility of spirit, and those other things which figure prominently in popular romances! I am obviously onto something!"

The others stared at her. She laughed again, then sat down abruptly.

I heard Flora mutter "drunk" and return to her conversation with Deirdre. Random said, "Let's hear it for shadows," and turned back to a discussion with Benedict and Llewella.

"See?" she said.

"What?"

"Your're insubstantial," she said, patting my knee. "And so am I, now that I think about it. It has been a bad day, Corwin."

"I know. I feel like hell, too. I thought I had such a fine idea for getting Brand back. Not only that, it worked. A lot of good it did him."

"Don't overlook those bits of virtue you've acquired," she said. "You're not to blame for the way it turned out."

"Thanks."

"I believe that Julian might have had the right idea," she said. "I don't feel like staying awake any longer."

I rose with her, walked her to the door.

"I'm all right," she said. "Really."

"Sure?"

She nodded sharply.

"See you in the morning then."

"I hope so," she said. "Now you can talk about me."

She winked and went out.

I turned back, saw that Benedict and Llewella were approaching.

"Turning in?" I asked.

Benedict nodded.

"Might as well," Llewella said, and she kissed me on the cheek.

"What was that for?"

"A number of things," she said. "Good night."

"Good night."

Random was crouched on the hearth, poking at the fire. Deirdre turned to him and said, "Don't throw on more wood just for us. Flora and I are going too."

"Okay." He set the poker aside and rose. "Sleep well," he called after them.

Deirdre gave me a sleepy smile and Flora a nervous one. I added my good night and watched them leave.

"Learn anything new and useful?" Random asked.

I shrugged.

"Did you?"

"Opinions, conjectures. No new facts," he said. "We were trying to decide who might be next on the list."

"And . . . ?"

"Benedict thinks it's a toss-up. You or him. Providing you are not behind it all, of course. He also thinks your buddy Ganelon ought to watch his step."

"Ganelon . . . Yes, that's a thought—and it should have been mine. I think he is right about the toss-up, too. It may even be slightly weighted against him, since they know I'm alert because of the attempted frameup."

"I would say that all of us are now aware that Benedict is alert himself. He managed to mention his opinion to everyone. I believe that he would welcome an attempt."

I chuckled.

"That balances the coin again. I guess it *is* a toss-up."

"He said that, too. Naturally, he knew I would tell you."

"Naturally, I wish he would start talking to me again. Well . . .

not much I can do about it now," I said. "The hell with everything. I'm going to bed."

He nodded.

"Look under it first."

We left the room, headed up the hall.

"Corwin, I wish you'd had the foresight to bring some coffee back with you, along with the guns," he said. "I could use a cup."

"Doesn't it keep you awake?"

"No. I like a couple of cups in the evening."

"I miss it mornings. We'll have to import some when this mess is all settled."

"Small comfort, but a good idea. What got into Fi, anyhow?"

"She thinks Julian is our man."

"She may be right."

"What about Caine?"

"Supposing it was not a single individual," he said as we mounted the stair. "Say it was two, like Julian *and* Caine. They finally had a falling out, Caine lost, Julian disposed of him and used the death to weaken your position as well. Former friends make the worst enemies."

"It's no use," I said. "I get dizzy when I start sorting the possibilities. We are either going to have to wait for something more to happen, or make something happen. Probably the latter. But not tonight—"

"Hey! Wait up!"

"Sorry." I paused at the landing. "Don't know what got into me. Finishing spurt, I guess."

"Nervous energy," he said, coming abreast of me once more. We continued on up, and I made an effort to match his pace, fighting down a desire to hurry.

"Well, sleep well," he said finally.

"Good night, Random."

He continued on up the stair and I headed off along the corridor toward my quarters. I was feeling jittery by then, which must be why I dropped my key.

I reached and plucked it out of the air before it had fallen very far. Simultaneously, I was struck by the impression that its motion was somewhat slower than it should have been. I inserted it in the lock and turned it.

The room was dark, but I decided against lighting a candle or an oil lamp. I had gotten used to the dark a long time ago. I locked and bolted the door. My eyes were already half adjusted to the gloom, from the dim hallway. I turned. There was some starlight leaking in about the drapes, too. I crossed the room, unfastening my collar.

He was waiting in my bed chamber, to the left of the entrance. He was perfectly positioned and he did nothing to give himself away. I walked right into it. He had the ideal station, he held the dagger ready, he had the element of total surprise going for him. By rights I should have died—not in my bed, but just there at its foot.

I caught a glimpse of the movement, realized the presence and its significance as I stepped over the threshold.

I knew that it was too late to avoid the thrust even as I raised my arm to try to block it. But one peculiarity struck me before the blade itself did: my assailant seemed to be moving too slowly. Quick, with all the tension of his wait behind it, that is how it should have been. I should never have known it was occurring until after the act, if then. I should not have had time to turn partway and swing my arm as far as I did. A ruddy haze filled my vision and I felt my forearm strike the side of the outflung arm at about the same moment as the steel touched my belly and bit. Within the redness there seemed a faint tracing of that cosmic version of the Pattern I had followed earlier in the day. As I doubled and fell, unable to think but still for a moment conscious, it came clearer, came nearer, the design. I wanted to flee, but horse my body stumbled. I was thrown.

VIII

Out of every life a little blood must spill. Unfortunately, it was my turn again, and it felt like more than a little. I was lying, doubled up, on my right side, both arms clutching at my middle. I was wet, and every now and then something trickled along the creases of my belly. Front, lower left, just above the beltline, I felt like a casually opened envelope. These were my first sensations as consciousness came around again. And my first thought was, "What is he waiting for?" Obviously, the *coup de grâce* had been withheld. Why?

I opened my eyes. They had taken advantage of whatever time had elapsed to adjust themselves to the darkness. I turned my head. I did not see anyone else in the room with me. But something peculiar had occurred and I could not quite place it. I closed my eyes and let my head fall back to the mattress once more.

Something was wrong, yet at the same time right. . . .

The mattress . . . Yes, I was lying on my bed. I doubted my ability to have gotten there unassisted. But it would be absurd to knife me and then help me to bed.

My bed . . . It was my bed, yet it was not.

I squeezed my eyes tight. I gritted my teeth. I did not understand. I knew that my thinking could not be normal there on the fringes of shock, by blood pooling in my guts and then leaking out. I tried to force myself to think clearly. It was not easy.

My bed. Before you are fully aware of anything else, you are aware whether you are awakening in your own bed. And I was, but—

I fought down an enormous impulse to sneeze, because I felt it would tear me apart. I compressed my nostrils and breathed in short gasps through my mouth. The taste, smell, and feel of dust was all about me.

The nasal assault subsided and I opened my eyes. I knew then where I was. I did not understand the why and how of it, but I had come once more to a place I had never expected to see again.

I lowered my right hand, used it to raise myself.

It was my bedroom in my house. The old one. The place which had been mine back when I was Carl Corey. I had been returned to Shadow, to that world where I had spent the years of my exile. The room was heavy with dust. The bed had not been made up since the last time I had slept in it, over half a decade before. I knew the state of the house fully, having looked in on it only a few weeks earlier.

I pushed myself further, managed to slide my feet out over the edge of the bed and down. Then I doubled up again and sat there. It was bad.

While I felt temporarily safe from further assault, I knew that I required more than safety just then. I had to have help, and I was in no position to help myself. I was not even certain how much longer I might remain conscious. So I had to get down and get out. The phone would be dead, the nearest house was not too close by. I would have to get down to the road, at least. I reflected grimly that one of my reasons for locating where I had was that it was not a well-traveled road. I enjoy my solitude, at least some of the time.

With my right hand I drew up the nearest pillow and slipped off its case. I turned it inside out, tried to fold it, gave up, wadded it, slipped it beneath my shirt, and pressed it against my wound. Then I sat there, just holding it in place. It had been a major exertion and I found it painful to take too deep a breath.

After a time, though, I drew the second pillow to me, held it across my knees and let it slip out of its case. I wanted the pillowslip to wave at a passing motorist, for my garments, as usual, were dark. Before I could draw it through my belt, though, I was confounded by the behavior of the pillow itself. It had not yet reached the floor. I had released it, nothing was supporting it, and it *was* moving. But it was moving quite slowly, descending with a dreamlike deliberation.

I thought of the fall of the key as I had dropped it outside my room. I thought of my unintended quickness on mounting the stair with Random. I thought of Fiona's words, and of the Jewel of Judgment, which still hung about my neck, now pulsating in time with the throbbing of my side. It might have saved my life, at least for the moment; yes, it probably had, if Fiona's notions were correct. It had probably given me a moment or so more than would otherwise have been my due when the assailant struck, letting me turn, letting me swing my arm. It might, somehow, even have been responsible for my sudden transportation. But I would have to think about such things at another time, should I succeed in maintaining a meaningful relationship with the future. For now, the jewel had to go—in case Fiona's fears concerning it were also correct—and I had to get moving.

I tucked away the second pillow cover, then tried to stand, holding on to the footboard. No good! Dizziness and too much pain. I lowered myself to the floor, afraid of passing out on the way down. I made it. I rested. Then I began to move, a slow crawl.

The front door, as I recalled, was now nailed shut. All right. Out the back, then.

I made it to the bedroom door and halted, leaning against its frame. As I rested there I removed the Jewel of Judgment from my neck and wrapped its chain about my wrist. I had to cache it someplace, and the safe in my study was too far out of the way. Besides, I believed that I was leaving a trail of blood. Anyone finding and following it might well be curious enough to investigate and spring the small thing. And I lacked the time and the energy. . . .

I made my way out, around, and through. I had to rise and exert myself to get the back door open. I made the mistake of not resting first.

When I regained consciousness, I was lying across the threshold. The night was raw and clouds filled much of the sky. A mean wind rattled branches above the patio. I felt several drops of moisture on the back of my outflung hand.

I pushed up and crawled out. The snow was about two inches deep. The icy air helped to revive me. With something near panic, I realized just how foggy my mind had been during much of my course from the bedroom. It was possible that I might go under at any time.

I started immediately for the far corner of the house, deviating only to reach the compost heap, tear my way into it, drop the jewel, and reposition the clump of dead grasses I had broken loose. I brushed snow over it and continued on.

Once I made it about the corner, I was shielded from the wind and headed down a slight incline. I reached the front of the house and rested once more. A car had just passed and I watched its taillights dwindle. It was the only vehicle in sight.

Icy crystals stung my face as I moved again. My knees were wet and burning cold. The front yard sloped, gently at first, then dropped sharply toward the road. There was a dip about a hundred yards to the right, where motorists generally hit their brakes. It seemed that this might give me a few moments more in the headlights of anyone coming from that direction—one of those small assurances the mind always seeks when things get serious, an aspirin for the emotions. With three rest stops, I made it down to the roadside, then over to the big rock that bore my house number. I sat on it and leaned back against the icy embankment. I hauled out the second pillow case and draped it across my knees.

I waited. I knew that my mind was fuzzy. I believe that I drifted into and out of consciousness a number of times. Whenever I caught myself at it, I attempted to impose some version of order on my thoughts, to assess what had happened in the light of everything else that had just happened, to seek other safety measures. The former effort proved too much, however. It was simply too difficult to think beyond the level of responding to circumstance. With a sort of numb enlightenment, though, it occurred to me that I was still in possession of my Trumps. I could contact someone in Amber, have him transport me back.

But who? I was not so far gone that I failed to realize I might be contacting the one responsible for my condition. Would it be better to gamble that way, or to take my chances here? Still, Random or Gérard—

I thought that I heard a car. Faint, distant . . . The wind and my pulsebeat were competing with perception, though. I turned my head. I concentrated.

There . . . Again. Yes. It was an engine. I got ready to wave the cloth.

Even then, my mind kept straying. And one thought that flitted through was that I might already be unable to muster sufficient concentration to manipulate the Trumps.

The sound grew louder. I raised the cloth. Moments later, the farthest visible point along the road to my right was touched with light. Shortly after, I saw the car at the top of the rise. I lost sight of it once more as it descended the hill. Then it climbed again and came on, snowflakes flashing through its headbeams.

I began waving as it approached the dip. The lights caught me as it came up out of it, and the driver could not have missed seeing me. He went by, though, a man in a late model sedan, a woman in the passenger seat. The woman turned and looked at me, but the driver did not even slow down.

A couple of minutes later another car came by, a bit older, a woman driving, no visible passengers. It did slow down, but only for a moment. She must not have liked my looks. She stepped on the gas and was gone in an instant.

I sagged back and rested. A prince of Amber can hardly invoke the brotherhood of man for purposes of moral condemnation. At least not with a straight face, and it hurt too much to laugh just then.

Without strength, concentration, and some ability to move, my power over Shadow was useless. I would use it first, I decided, to get to some warm place . . . . I wondered whether I could make it back up the hill, to the compost heap. I had not thought of trying to use the jewel to alter the weather. Probably I was too weak for that too, though. Probably the effort would kill me. Still . . .

I shook my head. I was drifting off, more than half a dream. I had to stay awake. Was that another car? Maybe. I tried to raise the cloth and dropped it. When I leaned forward to retrieve it, I just had to rest my head on my knees for a moment. Deirdre . . . I would call my dear sister. If anyone would help me, Deirdre would. I would get out her Trump and call her. In a minute. If only she weren't my sister . . . I had to rest. I am a knave, not a fool. Perhaps, sometimes, when I rest, I am even sorry for things. Some things. If only it were warmer . . . But it wasn't too bad, bent over this way . . . Was that a car? I wanted to raise my head but found that I could not. It would not make that much difference in being seen, though, I decided.

I felt light on my eyelids and I heard the engine. Now it was neither advancing nor retreating. Just a steady cycling of growls. Then I heard a shout. Then the click-pause-chunk of a car door opening and closing. I felt that I could open my eyes but I did not want to. I was afraid that I would look only on the dark and empty road, that the sounds would resolve into pulsebeats and wind once more. It was better to keep what I had than to gamble.

"Hey! What's the matter? You hurt?"

Footsteps . . . This was real.

I opened my eyes. I forced myself up once again.

"Corey! My God! It's *you!*"

I forced a grin, cut my nod short of a topple.

"It's me, Bill. How've you been?"

"What happened?"

"I'm hurt," I said. "Maybe bad. Need a doctor."

"Can you walk if I help? Or should I carry you?"

"Let's try walking," I said.

He got me to my feet and I leaned on him. We started for his car. I only remember the first few steps.

When that low-swinging sweet chariot turned sour and swung high once more, I tried to raise my arm, realized that it was restrained, settled for a consideration of the tube affixed thereto, and decided that I was going to live. I had sniffed hospital smells and consulted my internal clock. Having made it this far, I felt that I owed it to myself to continue. And I was warm, and as comfortable as recent history allowed. That settled, I closed my eyes, lowered my head, and went back to sleep.

Later, when I came around again, felt more fit and was spotted by a nurse, she told me that it was seven hours since I had been brought in and that a doctor would be by to talk with me shortly. She also got me a glass of water and told me that it had stopped snowing. She was curious as to what had happened to me.

I decided that it was time to start plotting my story. The simpler the better. All right. I was coming home after an extended stay abroad. I had hitchhiked out, gone on in, and been attacked by some vandal or drifter I had surprised inside. I crawled back out and sought help. Finis.

When I told it to the doctor I could not tell at first whether he believed me. He was a heavy man whose face had sagged and set long ago. His name was Bailey, Morris Bailey, and he nodded as I spoke and then asked me, "Did you get a look at the fellow?"

I shook my head.

"It was dark," I said

"Did he rob you too?"

"I don't know."

"Were you carrying a wallet?"

I decided I had better say yes to that one.

"Well, you didn't have it when you came in here, so he must have taken it."

"Must have," I agreed.

"Do you remember me at all?"

"Can't say that I do. Should I?"

"You seemed vaguely familiar to me when they brought you in. That was all, at first . . ."

"And . . . ?" I asked.

"What sort of garments were you wearing? They seemed something like a uniform."

"Latest thing, Over There, these days. You were saying that I looked familiar?"

"Yes," he agreed. "Where is Over There, anyway? Where did you come from? Where have you been?"

"I travel a lot," I said. "You were going to tell me something a moment ago."

"Yes," he said. "We are a small clinic, and some time ago a fast-talking salesman persuaded the directors to invest in a computerized medical-records system. If the area had developed more and we had expanded a lot, it might have been worthwhile. Neither of these things happened, though, and it is an expensive item. It even encouraged a certain laziness among the clerical help. Old files just don't get purged the way they used to, even for the emergency room. Space there for a lot of useless backlog. So, when Mr. Roth gave me your name and I ran a routine check on you, I found something and I realized why you looked familiar. I had been working the emergency room that night too, around seven years ago, when you had your auto accident. I remembered working on you then—and how I thought you weren't going to make it. You surprised me, though, and you still do. I can't even find the scars that *should* be there. You did a nice job of healing up."

"Thanks. A tribute to the physician, I'd say."

"May I have your age, for the record?"

"Thirty-six," I said. That's always safe.

He jotted it somewhere in the folder he held across his knees.

"You know, I would have sworn—once I got to checking you over and remembering—that that's about what you looked the last time I saw you."

"Clean living."

"Do you know about your blood type?"

"It's an exotic. But you can treat it as an AB Positive for all practical purposes. I can take anything, but don't give mine to anybody else."

He nodded.

"The nature of your mishap is going to require a police report, you know."

"I had guessed that."

"Just thought you might want to be thinking about it."

"Thanks," I said. "So you were on duty that night, and you patched me up? Interesting. What else do you recall about it?"

"What do you mean?"

"The circumstances under which I was brought in that time. My own memory is a blank from right before the accident until some time after I had been transferred up to the other place—Greenwood. Do you recall how I arrived?"

He frowned, just when I had decided he had one face for all occasions.

"We sent an ambulance," he said.

"In response to what? Who reported the accident? How?"

"I see what you mean," he said. "It was the State Patrol that called for the ambulance. As I recollect, someone had seen the accident and phoned their headquarters. They then radioed a car in the vicinity. It went to the lake, verified the report, gave you first aid, and called for the ambulance. And that was it."

"Any record of who called in the report in the first place?"

He shrugged.

"That's not the sort of thing we keep track of," he said.

"Didn't your insurance company investigate? Wasn't there a claim? They could probably—"

"I had to leave the country right after I recovered," I said. "I never pursued the matter. I suppose there would have been a police report, though."

"Surely. But I have no idea how long they keep them around." He chuckled. "Unless, of course, that same salesman got to them, too. . . . It is rather late to be talking about that though, isn't it? It seems to me there is a statue of limitations on things of that sort. Your friend Roth will tell you for sure—"

"It isn't a claim that I have in mind," I said. "Just a desire to know what really happened. I have wondered about it on and off for a number of years now. You see, I have this touch of retrograde amnesia going."

"Have you ever talked it over with a psychiatrist?" he said, and there was something about the way he said it that I did not like. Came one of those little flashes of insight then: Could Flora have managed to get me certified insane before my transfer to Green-wood? Was that on my record here? And was I still on escape status from that place? A lot of time had passed and I knew nothing of the legalities involved. If this was indeed the case, however, I imagined they would have no way of knowing whether I had been certified sane again in some other jurisdiction. Prudence, I guess it was, cau-tioned me to lean forward and glance at the doctor's wrist. I seemed possessed of a subliminal memory that he had consulted a calendar watch when taking my pulse. Yes, he had. I squinted. All right. Day and month: November 28. I did a quick calculation with my two-and-a-half-to-one conversion and had the year. It *was* seven, as he had indicated.

"No, I haven't" I said. "I just assumed it was organic rather than functional and wrote the time off as a loss."

"I see," he said. "You use such phrases rather glibly. People who've been in therapy sometimes do that."

"I know," I said. "I've read a lot about it."

He sighed. He stood.

"Look," he said. "I am going to call Mr. Roth and let him know you are awake. It is probably best."

"What do you mean by that?"

"I mean that with your friend being an attorney, there might be things you want to discuss with him before you talk to the police."

He opened the folder wherein he had somewhere jotted my age, raised his pen, furrowed his brow, and said, "What's the date, any-way?"

I wanted my Trumps. I imagined my belongings would be in the drawer of the bedside table, but getting at it involved too much twist-ing and I did not want to put the strain on my sutures. It was not all that urgent, though. Eight hours' sleep in Amber would come to around twenty hours here, so everyone should still have been re-spectably retired back home. I wanted to get hold of Random, though, to come up with some sort of cover story for my not being there in the morning. Later.

I did not want to look suspicious at a time like this. Also, I wanted to know immediately whatever Brand had to say. I wanted to be in a position to act on it. I did a quick bit of mental juggling. If I could do the worst of my recovering here in Shadow, it would mean less wasted time for me back in Amber. I would have to budget my time carefully and avoid complications on this end. I hoped that Bill would arrive soon. I was anxious to know what the picture was in this place.

Bill was a native of the area, had gone to school in Buffalo, come back, married, joined the family firm, and that was that. He had known me as a retired Army officer who sometimes traveled on vague business. We both belonged to the country club, which was where I had met him. I had known him for over a year without our exchanging more than a few words. Then one evening I happened to be next to him in the bar and it had somehow come out that he was hot on military history, particularly the Napoleonic Wars. The next thing we knew, they were closing up the place around us. We were close friends from then on, right up until the time of my difficulties. I had occasionally wondered about him since. In fact, the only thing that had prevented me from seeing him the last time I had passed through was that he would doubtless have had all sorts of questions as to what had become of me, and I had had too many things on my mind to deal with them all that gracefully and still enjoy myself. I had even thought once or twice of coming back and seeing him if I could, when everything was finally settled in Amber. Next to the fact that this was not the case, I regretted not being able to meet him in the club lounge.

He arrived within the hour, short, heavy, ruddy, a bit grayer on the sides, grinning, nodding. I had propped myself up by then, already tried a few deep breaths and decided they were premature. He clasped my hand and took the bedside chair. He had his briefcase with him.

"You scared the hell out of me last night, Carl. Thought I was seeing a ghost," he said.

I nodded.

"A bit later, and I might have been one," I said. "Thanks. How have you been?

Bill sighed.

"Busy. You know. The same old stuff, only more of it."

"And Alice?"

"She's fine. And we've got two new grandsons—Bill Jr.'s—twins. Wait a minute."

He fished out his wallet and located a photo.

"Here."

I studied it, noted the family resemblances.

"Hard to believe," I said.

"You don't look much worse for the years."

I chuckled and patted my abdomen.

"Subtracting that, I mean," he said. "Where have you been?"

"God! Where haven't I been!" I said. "So many places I've lost count."

He remained expressionless, caught my eyes and stared.

"Carl, what kind of trouble are you in?" he asked.

I smiled.

"If you mean am I in trouble with the law, the answer is no. My troubles actually involve another country, and I am going to have to go back there shortly."

His face relaxed again, and there was a small glint behind his bifocals.

"Are you some sort of military adviser in that place?"

I nodded.

"Can you tell me where?"

I shook my head.

"Sorry."

"That I can sort of understand," he said. "Dr. Roth told me what you said had happened last night. Off the record now, was it connected with whatever you have been doing?"

I nodded again.

"That makes things a little clearer," he said. "Not much, but enough. I won't even ask you which agency, or even if there is one. I have always known you to be a gentleman, and a rational one at that. That was why I grew curious at the time of your disappearance and did some investigating. I felt a bit officious and self-conscious about it. But your civil status was quite puzzling, and I wanted to know what had happened. Mainly, because I was concerned about you. I hope that doesn't disturb you."

"Disturb me?" I said. "There aren't that many people who care what happens to me. I'm grateful. Also, curious what you discovered. I never had the time to look into it, you know, to straighten things out. How about telling me what you learned?"

He opened the briefcase and withdrew a manila folder. Spreading it across his knees, he shuffled out several sheets of yellow paper covered with neat handwriting. Raising the first of these, he regarded it a moment, then said, "After you escaped from the hospital in Albany and had your accident, Brandon apparently dropped out of the picture and—"

"Stop!" I said, raising my hand, trying to sit up.

"What?" he asked.

"You have the order wrong, also the place," I said. "First came the accident, and Greenwood is not in Albany."

"I know," he said. "I was referring to the Porter Sanitarium, where you spent two days and then escaped. You had your accident that same day, and you were brought here as a result of it. Then your sister Evelyn entered the picture. She had you transferred to Greenwood, where you spent a couple of weeks before departing on your own motion once again. Right?"

"Partly," I said. "Namely, the last part. As I was telling the doctor earlier, my memory is shot for a couple of days prior to the accident. This business about a place in Albany *does* sort of seem to ring a bell, but only very faintly. Do you have more on it?"

"Oh yes," he said. "It may even have something to do with the state of your memory. You were committed on a bum order—"

"By whom?"

He shook the paper and peered.

" 'Brother, Brandon Corey; attendant physician, Hillary B. Rand, psychiatrist,' " he read. "Hear any more bells?"

"Quite possibly," I said. "Go ahead."

"Well, an order got signed on that basis," he said. "You were duly certified, taken into custody, and transported. Then, concerning your memory . . ."

"Yes?"

"I don't know that much about the practice and its effects on the memory, but you were subjected to electroshock therapy while you were at Porter. Then, as I said, the record indicates that you escaped after the second day. You apparently recovered your car from some unspecified locale and were heading back this way when you had the accident."

"That seems right," I said. "It does." For a moment, when he had begun talking, I had had a wild vision of having been returned to the wrong shadow—one where everything was similar, but not congruent. Now, though, I did not believe this to be the case. I was responding to this story on some level.

"Now, about that order," he said. "It was based on false evidence, but there was no way of the court's knowing it at the time. The real

Dr. Rand was in England when everything happened, and when I
contacted him later he had never heard of you. His office had been
broken into while he was away, though. Also, peculiarly, his middle
initial is not B. He had never heard of Brandon Corey either."

"What did become of Brandon?"

"He simply vanished. Several attempts were made to contact him
at the time of your escape from Porter, but he could not be found.
Then you had the accident, were brought here and treated. At that
time, a woman named Evelyn Flaumel, who represented herself as
your sister, contacted this place, told them you had been probated
and that the family wanted you transferred to Greenwood. In the absence of Brandon, who had been appointed your guardian, her instructions were followed, as the only available next of kin. That was
how it came about that you were sent to the other place. You escaped again, a couple of weeks later, and that is where my chronol-
ogy ends."

"Then what is my legal status right now?" I asked.

"Oh, you've been made whole," he said. "Dr. Rand went down
after I talked with him and gave the court an affidavit reciting these
facts. The order was vacated."

"Then why is the doctor here acting as if I might be a psycho
case?"

"Oh my! That *is* a thought. It hadn't occurred to me. All their records here would show is that one time you apparently were. I had
better see him on the way out. I have a copy of the journal entry in
here, too. I can show it to him."

"How long was it after I left Greenwood that things were set right
with the court?"

"The following month," he said. "It was several weeks before I
could bring myself to get nosy."

"You couldn't know how happy I am that you did," I said. "And
you have given me several pieces of information I think are going to
prove extremely important."

"It is nice to be able to help a friend sometime," he said, closing
the folder and replacing it in his briefcase. "One thing . . . When
this is all over—whatever you are doing—if you are permitted to
talk about it, I would like to hear the story."

"I can't promise," I said.

"I know. Just thought I'd mention it. By the way, what do you
want to do about the house?"

"Mine? Do I still hold title to it?"

"Yes, but it will probably be sold this year for back taxes if you don't do anything about it."

"I'm surprised that hasn't already happened."

"You gave the bank power of attorney for paying your bills."

"I never thought of that. I'd just set it up for utilities and my charge accounts. Stuff like that."

"Well, the account is nearly empty now," he said. "I was talking to McNally over there the other day. That means the house will go next year if you don't do anything."

"I've got no use for it now," I said. "They can do whatever they want with it."

"Then you might as well sell it and realize what you can."

"I won't be around that long."

"I could handle it for you. Send the money wherever you want."

"All right," I said. "I'll sign anything necessary. Pay my hospital bill out of it and keep the rest."

"I couldn't do that."

I shrugged.

"Do whatever you think best, but be sure and take a good fee."

"I'll put the balance in your account."

"All right. Thanks. By the way, before I forget, would you look in the drawer of that table and see if there is a deck of cards there? I can't reach it yet, and I'll be wanting them later."

"Surely."

He reached over, opened it.

"A big brown envelope," he said. "Kind of bulgy. They probably put whatever was in your pockets in it."

"Open it."

"Yes, here's a pack of cards," he said, reaching inside. "Say! That's a beautiful case! May I?"

"I—" What could I say?

He slipped the case.

"Lovely . . ." he murmured. "Some kind of tarots . . . Are they antique?"

"Yes."

"Cold as ice . . . I never saw anything like these. Say, that's you! Dressed up like some kind of knight! What's their purpose?"

"A very complicated game," I said.

"How could that be you if they are antique?"

"I didn't say it was me. You did."

"Yes, so I did. Ancestor?"

"Sort of."

"Now that's a good-looking gal! But so is the redhead. . . ."

"I think . . ."

He squared the deck and replaced it in the case. He passed it to me.

"Nice unicorn, too," he added. "I shouldn't have looked at them, should I?"

"That's all right."

He sighed and leaned back in the chair, clasping his hands behind his head.

"I couldn't help it," he said. "It is just that there is something very strange about you, Carl, beyond any hush-hush work you may be doing—and mysteries intrigue me. I've never been this close to a real puzzler before."

"Because you just slipped yourself a cold deck of tarots?" I asked.

"No, that just adds atmosphere," he said. "While what you have been doing all these years is admittedly none of my business, there is one recent incident I am unable to comprehend."

"What is that?"

"After I brought you here and took Alice home last night, I went back to your place, hoping to get some sort of idea as to what had happened. The snow had let up by then, though it started in again later, and your track was still clearly visible, going around the house and down the front yard."

I nodded.

"But there were no tracks going in—nothing to indicate your arrival. And for that matter, there were no other tracks departing—nothing to show the flight of your assailant."

I chuckled.

"You think the wound was self-inflicted?"

"No, of course not. There wasn't even a weapon in sight. I followed the bloodstains back to the bedroom, to your bed. I had only my flashlight to see by, of course, but what I saw gave me an eerie feeling. It seemed as if you had just suddenly appeared there on the bed, bleeding, and then gotten up and made your way out."

"Impossible, of course."

"I wonder about the lack of tracks, though."

"The wind must have blown snow over them."

"And not the others?" He shook his head. "No, I don't think so. I just want to go on the record as interested in the answer to that one too, if you ever do want to tell me about things."

"I will remember." I said.

"Yes," he said. "But I wonder . . . I've a peculiar feeling that I may never see you again. It is as if I were one of those minor characters in a melodrama who gets shuffled offstage without ever learning how things turn out."

"I can appreciate the feeling," I said. "My own role sometimes makes me want to strangle the author. But look at it this way: inside stories seldom live up to one's expectations. Usually they are grubby little things, reducing down to the basest of motives when all is known. Conjectures and illusions are often the better possessions."

He smiled.

"You talk the same as always," he said, "yet I have known occasions when you have been tempted to virtue. Several of them . . ."

"How did we get from the footprints to me?" I said. "I was about to tell you that I suddenly recalled having approached the house by exactly the same route as I left it. My departure obviously obliterated the signs of my arrival."

"Not bad," he said. "And your attacker followed the same route?"

"Must have."

"Pretty good," he acknowledged. "You know how to raise a reasonable doubt. But I still feel that the preponderance of evidence indicates the weird."

"Weird? No. Peculiar, perhaps. A matter of interpretation."

"Or semantics. Have you read the police report on your accident?"

"No. Have you?"

"Uh-huh. What if *it* was more than peculiar? Then will you grant me my word, as I used it: 'weird'?"

"Very well."

". . . And answer one question?"

"I don't know. . . ."

"A simple yes-or-no question. That's all."

"Okay, it's a deal. What did it say?"

"It said that they received report of the accident and a patrol car proceeded to the scene. There they encountered a strangely garbed man in the process of giving you first aid. He stated that he had pulled you from the wrecked car in the lake. This seemed believable in that he was also soaking wet. Average height, light build, red hair. He had on a green outfit that one of the officers said looked like something out of a Robin Hood movie. He refused to identify himself, to accompany them or to give a statement of any sort. When they insisted that he do so, he whistled and a white horse came trotting up. He leaped onto its back and rode off. He was not seen again."

I laughed. It hurt, but I couldn't help it.

"I'll be damned!" I said. "Things are starting to make sense."

Bill just stared at me for a moment. Then, "Really?" he said.

"Yes, I think so. It may well have been worth getting stabbed and coming back for what I learned today."

"You put the two in peculiar order," he said, massaging his chin.

"Yes, I do. But I am beginning to see some order where I had seen nothing before. This one may have been worth the price of admission, all unintended."

"All because of a guy on a white horse?"

"Partly, partly . . . Bill, I am going to be leaving here soon."

"You are not going anywhere for a while."

"Just the same—those papers you mentioned . . . I think I had better get them signed today."

"All right. I'll get them over this afternoon. But I don't want you doing anything foolish."

"I grow more cautious by the moment," I said, "believe me."

"I hope so," he said, snapping his briefcase shut and rising. "Well, get your rest. I'll clear things up with the doctor and have those papers sent over today."

"Thanks again."

I shook his hand.

"By the way," he said, "you did agree to answer a question."

"I did, didn't I? What is it?"

"Are you human?" he asked, still gripping my hand, no special expression on his face.

I started in on a grin, then threw it away.

"I don't know. I—I like to think so. But I don't really—Of course I am! That's a silly . . . Oh hell! You really mean it, don't you? And I said I'd be honest. . . ." I chewed my lip and thought for a moment. Then, "I don't think so," I said.

"Neither do I," he said, and he smiled. "It doesn't make any real

difference to me, but I thought it might to you—to know that someone knows you are different and doesn't care."

"I'll remember that, too," I said.

"Well . . . see you around."

"Right."

IX

It was just after the state patrolman left . . . Late afternoon. I was lying there feeling better, and feeling better that I felt better. Lying there, reflecting on the hazards involved in living in Amber. Brand and I were both laid up by means of the family's favorite weapon. I wondered who had gotten it worse. Probably he had. It might have reached his kidney, and he was in poor condition to begin with.

I had stumbled across the room and back again twice before Bill's clerk came over with the papers for me to sign. It was necessary that I know my limits. It always is. Since I tended to heal several times faster than those about me in that shadow, I felt that I ought to be able to stand and walk some, to perform in the same fashion as one of these after, say, a day and a half, maybe two. I established that I could. It did hurt, and I was dizzy the first time, less dizzy the second. That was something, anyway. So I lay there feeling better.

I had fanned the Trumps dozens of times, dealt private solitaires, read ambiguous fortunes among familiar faces. And each time I had restrained myself, suppressing my desire to contact Random, to tell him what had happened, to inquire after new developments. Later, I kept telling myself. Each additional hour they sleep is two and a half for you, here. Each two and a half for you, here, is the equivalent of seven or eight for some lesser mortal, here. Abide. Think. Regenerate.

And so it came to pass that a little after dinnertime, just as the sky was darkening again, I was beaten to the punch. I had already told a well-starched young member of the State Patrol everything that I was going to tell him. I have no idea whether he believed me, but he was polite and he did not stay long. In fact, it was only moments after he left that things began to happen.

Lying there, feeling better, I was waiting for Dr. Bailey to stop by and check whether I was still oriented. Lying there, assessing all of the things Bill had told me, trying to fit them together with other things that I knew or had guessed at . . .

Contact! I had been anticipated. Someone in Amber was an early riser.

"Corwin!"

It was Random, agitated.

"Corwin! Get up! Open the door! Brand's come around, and he's asking for you."

"Have you been pounding on that door, trying to get me up?"

"That's right."

"Are you alone?"

"Yes."

"Good. I am not inside. You have reached me in Shadow."

"I do not understand."

"Neither do I. I am hurt, but I will live. I will give you the story later. Tell me about Brand."

"He woke up just a little while ago. Told Gérard he had to talk to you right away. Gérard rang up a servant, sent him to your room. When he couldn't rouse you, he came to me. I just sent him back to tell Gérard I'd be bringing you along shortly."

"I see," I said, stretching slowly and sitting up. "Get in some place where you can't be seen, and I'll come through. I will need a robe or something. I am missing some clothes."

"It would probably be best if I went back to my rooms, then."

"Okay. Go ahead."

"A minute, then."

And silence.

I moved my legs slowly. I sat on the edge of the bed. I gathered up my Trumps and replaced them in their case. I felt it important that I mask my injury back in Amber. Even in normal times one never advertises one's vulnerability.

I took a deep breath and stood, holding on to the bed frame. My practice had paid off. I breathed normally and relaxed my grip. Not bad, if I moved slowly, if I did not exert myself beyond the barest essentials required for appearances' sake . . . I might be able to carry it until my strength really returned.

Just then I heard a footfall, and a friendly nurse was framed in the doorway, crisp, symmetrical, differing from a snowflake mainly in that they are all of them alike.

"Get back in that bed, Mr. Corey! You are not supposed to be up!"

"Madam," I said, "it is quite necessary that I be up. I have to go."

"You could have rung for a pan," she said, entering the room and advancing.

I gave my head a weary shake just as Random's presence reached me once more. I wondered how she would report this one—and if she would mention my prismatic afterimage as I trumped out. Another entry, I suppose, for the growing record of folklore I tend to leave behind.

"Think of it this way, my dear," I told her. "Ours has been a purely physical relationship all along. There will be others . . . many others. *Adieu!*"

I bowed and blew her a kiss as I stepped forward into Amber, leaving her to clutch at rainbows as I caught hold of Random's shoulder and staggered.

"Corwin! What the hell—"

"If blood be the price of admiralty, I've just bought me a naval commission," I said. "Give me something to wear."

He draped a long, heavy cloak about my shoulders and I fumbled to clasp it at my throat.

"All set," I said. "Take me to him."

He led me out the door, into the hall, toward the stair. I leaned on him heavily as we went.

"How bad is it?" he asked me.

"Knife," I said, and laid my hand on the spot. "Someone attacked me in my room last night."

"Who?"

"Well, it couldn't have been you, because I had just left you," I said, "and Gérard was up in the library with Brand. Subtract the three of you from the rest and start guessing. That is the best—"

"Julian," he said.

"His stock is definitely bearish," I said. "Fiona was just running him down for me the other night, and of course it is no secret that he is not my favorite."

"Corwin, he's gone. He cut out during the night. The servant who came to get me told me that Julian had departed. What does that look like to you?"

We reached the stair. I kept one hand on Random and the other on the banister. I called a halt at the first landing and rested there briefly.

"I don't know," I said. "It can sometimes be just as bad to extend the benefit of the doubt too far as not to grant it at all. But it does occur to me that if he thought he had disposed of me, he would look a lot better by staying here and acting surprised to learn of it than by getting the hell out. That *does* look suspicious. I am inclined to think he might have departed because he was afraid of what Brand would have to say when he came around."

"But you lived, Corwin. You got away from whoever attacked you, and he could not be certain that he had done you in. If it were me, I would be worlds away by now."

"There is that," I acknowledged, and we started on down again. "Yes, you might well be right. Let us leave it academic for now. And no one is to know I have been injured."

He nodded.

"As you say. Silence beats a chamber pot in Amber."

"How's that?"

"'Tis gilt, m'lord, like a royal flush."

"Your wit pains both wounded and unwounded parts, Random. Spend some figuring how the assailant entered my room."

"Your panel?"

"It secures from the inside. I keep it that way now. And the door's lock is a new one. Tricky."

"All right, I have it. My answer requires that it be a family member, too."

"Tell me."

"Someone was willing to psyche himself up and tough it through the Pattern again for a shot at you. He went below, walked it, projected himself into your room, and attacked you."

"That would be perfect except for one thing. We all left at pretty much the same time. The attack did not occur later on in the evening. It happened immediately on my entering. I do not believe there was sufficient time for one of us to get down to the chamber, let alone negotiate the Pattern. The attacker was already waiting. So if it was one of us, he had gotten in by some other means."

"Then he picked your lock, tricks and all."

"Possibly," I said as we reached the landing and continued on. "We will rest at the corner so that I can go into the library unassisted."

"Sure thing."

We did that. I composed myself, drew the cloak completely about me, squared my shoulders, advanced, and knocked on the door.

"Just a minute." Gérard's voice.

Footsteps approaching the door . . .

"Who is it?"

"Corwin," I said. "Random's with me."

I heard him call back, "You want Random, too?" and I heard a soft "No" in reply.

The door opened.

"Just you, Corwin," Gérard said.

I nodded and turned to Random.

"Later," I told him.

He returned my nod and headed back in the direction from which we had come. I entered the library.

"Open your cloak, Corwin," Gérard ordered.

"That is not necessary," Brand said, and I looked over and saw that he was propped up by a number of cushions and showing a yellow-toothed smile.

"Sorry, I am not as trusting as Brand," Gérard said, "and I will not have my work wasted. Let's have a look."

"I said that it is not necessary," Brand repeated. "He is not the one who stabbed me."

Gérard turned quickly.

"How do you know he isn't?" he asked.

"Because I know who did, of course. Don't be an ass, Gérard. I wouldn't have asked for him if I had reason to fear him."

"You were unconscious when I brought you through. You couldn't know who did it."

"Are you certain of that?"

"Well . . . Why didn't you tell me, then?"

"I have my reasons, and they are valid ones. I want to speak with Corwin alone now."

Gérard lowered his head.

"You had better not be delirious," he said. He stepped to the door, opened it again. "I'll be within hailing distance," he added, and closed it behind him.

I moved nearer. Brand reached up and I clasped his hand.

"Good to see that you made it back," he said.

"Vice versa," I said, and then I took Gérard's chair, trying not to collapse into it.

"How do you feel now?" I asked.

"Rotten, in one sense. But better than I have in years, in another. It's all relative."

"Most things are."

"Not Amber."

I sighed.

"All right. I wasn't getting technical. What the hell happened?"

His gaze was most intense. He was studying me, looking for something. What? Knowledge, I'd guess. Or, more correctly, ignorance. Negatives being harder to gauge, his mind had to be moving fast, must have been from the moment he had come around. Knowing him, he was more interested in what I did not know than in what I knew. He wasn't going to give away anything if he could help it. He wanted to know the minimum enlightenment he need shed in order to get what he wanted. Not a watt more would he willingly spend. For this was his way, and of course he wanted something. Unless . . . More strongly in recent years than ever before I have tried to convince myself that people do change, that the passage of time does not serve merely to accentuate that which is already there, that qualitative changes do sometimes occur in people because of things they have done, seen, thought, and felt. It would provide some small solace in times such as these when everything else seems to be going wrong, not to mention pepping up my mundane philosophy no end. And Brand had probably been responsible for saving my life and my memory, whatever his reasons. Very well. I resolved to give him the doubt's benefit without exposing my back. A small concession here, my move against the simple psychology of humors which generally governs the openings of our games.

"Things are never what they seem, Corwin," he began. "Your friend today is your enemy tomorrow, and—"

"Cut it out!" I said. "Cards-on-the-table time is here. I do appreciate what Brandon Corey did for me, and it was my idea to try the trick we used to locate you and bring you back."

He nodded.

"I fancy there were good reasons for a recrudescence of fraternal sentiment after all this time."

"I might suppose you had additional reasons for helping me, also."

He smiled again, raised his right hand and lowered it.

"Then we are either even or in each other's debt, depending upon how one looks at these things. As it would seem we now have need of each other, it would be well to regard ourselves in the most flattering light."

"You are stalling, Brand. You are trying to psych me. You are also spoiling my day's effort at idealism. You got me out of bed to tell me something. Be my guest."

"Same old Corwin," he said, chuckling. Then he looked away. "Or are you? I wonder . . . Did it change you, do you think? Living all that while in Shadow? Not knowing who you really were? Being a part of something else?"

"Maybe," I said. "I don't know. Yes, I guess I did. I know that it shortened my temper when it comes to family politics."

"Plain-speaking, blunt, plain-dealing? You miss some of the fun that way. But then there is a value to such novelty. Keep everyone unbalanced with it . . . revert when they least expect it. . . . Yes, it might prove valuable. Refreshing, too. All right! Panic not. Thus end my preliminaries. All pleasantries are now exchanged. I'll bare the basics, bridle the beast Unreason, and wrest from murky mystery the pearl of sweetest sense. But one thing first, if you would. Have you anything smokable with you? It has been a number of years, and I'd like some foul weed or other—to celebrate my homecoming."

I started to say no. But I was sure there were some cigarettes in the desk, left there by me. I did not really want the exercise, but, "Just a minute," I said.

I tried to make my movements look casual rather than stiff as I rose and crossed the room. I attempted to make it seem as if I were resting my hand naturally upon the desktop as I rummaged through it, rather than leaning as heavily as I was. I masked my movements with my body and my cloak as much as possible.

I located the package and returned as I had come, stopping to light a pair at the hearth. Brand was slow in taking his from me.

"Your hand is rather shaky," he said. "What is the matter?"

"Too much partying last night," I said, returning to my chair.

"I hadn't thought of that. I imagine there would have been, wouldn't there? Of course. Everyone together in one room . . . Unexpected success in finding me, bringing me back . . . A desperate move on the part of a very nervous, very guilty person. . . . Half success there. Me injured and mum, but for how long? Then—"

"You said that you knew who did it. Were you kidding?"

"No, I was not."

"Who then?"

"In its place, dear brother. In its place. Sequence and order, time and stress—they are most important in this matter. Allow me to savor the drama of the event in safe retrospect. I see me punctured and all of you gathered round. Ah! what would I not give to witness that tableau! Could you possibly describe for me the expression on each face?"

"I'm afraid their faces were my least concern at the time."

He sighed and blew smoke.

"Ah, that is good," he said. "Never mind, I can see their faces. I've a vivid imagination, you know. Shock, distress, puzzlement—shading over into suspicion, fear. Then all of you departed, I'm told, and gentle Gérard my nursemaid here." He paused, stared into the smoke, and for a moment the note of mockery was absent. "He is the only decent one among us, you know."

"He's high on my list," I said.

"He took good care of me. He's always looked out for the rest of us." He chuckled suddenly. "Frankly, I can't see why he bothers. As I was musing, though—prompted by your recuperating self—you must have adjourned to talk things over. There is another party I'm sad I missed. All those emotions and suspicions and lies bouncing off one another—and no one wanting to be the first to say good night. It must have gotten shrill after a time. Everyone on his own best behavior, with an eye out to blacken the rest. Attempts to intimidate the one guilty person. Perhaps a few stones shied at scapegoats. But, all in all, nothing much really accomplished. Am I right?"

I nodded, appreciative of the way his mind worked, and resigned to letting him tell it his way.

"You know you're right," I said.

He gave me a sharp look at that, then went on. "But everyone did finally go off, to lie awake worrying, or to get together with an accomplice, to scheme. There were hidden turmoils in the night. It is flattering to know that my well-being was on everyone's mind. Some, of course, were for it, others against. And in the midst of it all, I rallied—nay, flourished—not wishing to disappoint my supporters. Gérard spent a long while bringing me up to date on recent history. When I had enough of this, I sent for you."

"In case you haven't noticed, I'm here. What did you want to tell me?"

"Patience, brother! Patience! Consider all the years you spent in Shadow, not even remembering—this." He gestured widely with his cigarette. "Consider all that time you waited, unknowing, until I succeeded in locating you and tried to remedy your plight. Surely a few moments now are not so priceless by contrast."

"I was told that you had sought me," I said. "I wondered at that, for we had not exactly parted on the best of terms the last time we were together."

He nodded.

"I cannot deny it," he said. "But I always get over such things, eventually."

I snorted.

"I have been deciding how much to tell you, and what you would believe," he continued. "I doubted you would accept it if I had simply come out and said that, save for a few small items, my present motives are almost entirely altruistic."

I snorted again.

"But this is true," he went on, "and to lay your suspicions, I add that it is because I have small choice in it. Beginnings are always difficult. Wherever I begin, something preceded it. You were gone for so long. If one must name a single thing, however, then let it be the throne. There. I have said it. We had thought of a way to take it, you see. This was just after your disappearance, and in some ways, I suppose, prompted by it. Dad suspected Eric of having slain you. But there was no evidence. We worked on this feeling, though—a word here and there, every now and then. Years passed, with you unreachable by any means, and it seemed more and more likely that you were indeed dead. Dad looked upon Eric with growing disfavor. Then, one night, pursuant to a discussion I had begun on a totally neutral matter—most of us present at the table—he said that no fratricide would ever take the throne, and he was looking at Eric as he said it. You know how his eyes could get. Eric grew bright as a sunset and could not swallow for a long while. But then Dad took things much further than any of us had anticipated or desired. In fairness to you, I do not know whether he spoke solely to vent his feelings, or whether he actually meant what he said. But he told us that he had more than half decided upon you as his successor, so that he took whatever misadventure had befallen you quite personally. He would not have spoken of it, but that he was convinced as to your passing. In the months that followed, we reared you a cenotaph to give some solid form to this conclusion, and we made certain that no one forgot Dad's feelings toward Eric. All along, after yourself, Eric was the one we felt had to be gotten around to reach the throne."

"We! Who were the others?"

"Patience, Corwin. Sequence and order, time and stress! Accent, emphasis . . . Listen." He took another cigarette, chain-lit it from the butt, stabbed the air with its burning tip.

"The next step required that we get Dad out of Amber. This was the most crucial and dangerous part of it, and it was here that we disagreed. I did not like the idea of an alliance with a power I did not fully understand, especially one that gave them some hold on us. Using shadows is one thing; allowing them to use you is ill-considered, whatever the circumstances. I argued against it, but the majority had it otherwise." He smiled. "Two to one. Yes, there were three of us. We went ahead then. The trap was set and Dad went after the bait—"

"Is he still living?" I asked.

"I do not know," Brand said. "Things went wrong afterward, and then I'd troubles of my own to concern me. After Dad's departure, though, our next move was to consolidate our position while waiting a respectable period of time for a presumption of death to seem warranted. Ideally, all that we required was the cooperation of one person. Either Caine or Julian—it did not matter which. You see, Bleys had already gone off into Shadow and was in the process of putting together a large military force—"

"Bleys! He was one of you?"

"Indeed. We intended him for the throne—with sufficient strings on him, of course, so that it would have amounted to a *de facto* triumvirate. So, he went off to assemble troops, as I was saying. We hoped for a bloodless takeover, but we had to be ready in the event that words proved insufficient to win our case. If Julian gave us the land route in, or Caine the waves, we could have transported the troops with dispatch and held the day by force of arms, should that have proven necessary. Unfortunately, I chose the wrong man. In my estimate, Caine was Julian's superior in matters of corruption. So, with measured delicacy I sounded him on the matter. He seemed willing to go along with things, at first. But he either reconsidered subsequently or deceived me quite skillfully from the beginning. Naturally, I prefer to believe that it was the former. Whatever, at some point he came to the conclusion that he stood to benefit more by supporting a rival claimant. To wit, Eric. Now Eric's hopes had been somewhat dashed by Dad's attitude toward him—but Dad was gone, and our intended move gave Eric the chance to act as defender of the throne. Unfortunately for us, such a position would also put him but a step away from the throne itself. To make matters darker, Julian went along with Caine in pledging the loyalty of his troops to Eric, as defender. Thus was the other trio formed. So Eric took a public oath to defend the throne, and the lines were thereby drawn. I was naturally in a somewhat embarrassing position at this time. I bore the brunt of their animosity, as they did not know who my fellows were. Yet they could not imprison or torture me, for I would immediately be trumped out of their hands. And if they were to kill me, they realized there might well be a reprisal by parties unknown. So it had to stand as a stalemate for a time. They also saw that I could no longer move directly against them. They kept me under heavy surveillance. So a more devious route was charted. Again I disagreed and again I lost, two to one. We were to employ the same forces we had called upon to deal with Dad, this time for purposes of discrediting Eric. If the job of defending Amber, so confidently assumed, were to prove too much for him and Bleys then came onto the scene and handled the situation with dispatch, why Bleys would even have popular support as he moved on to assume the role of defender himself and—after a fit period of time—suffered the thrusting of sovereignty upon him, for the good of Amber."

"Question," I interrupted. "What about Benedict? I know he was off being discontent in his Avalon, but if something really threatened Amber . . ."

"Yes," he said, nodding, "and for that reason, a part of our deal was to involve Benedict with a number of problems of his own."

I thought of the harassment of Benedict's Avalon by the hellmaids. I thought of the stump of his right arm. I opened my mouth to speak again, but Brand raised his hand.

"Let me finish in my own fashion, Corwin. I am not unmindful of your thought processes as you speak. I feel the pain in your side, twin to my own. Yes, I know these things and many more." His eyes burned strangely as he took another cigarette into his hand and it lit of its own accord. He drew heavily upon it and spoke as he exhaled. "I broke with the others over this decision. I saw it as involving too great a peril, as placing Amber herself in jeopardy. Broke with them . . ." He watched the smoke for several moments before he continued. "But things were too far advanced that I might simply walk away. I had to oppose them, in order to defend myself as well as Amber. It was too late to swing over to Eric's side. He would not have protected me if he could have—and besides, I was certain he was going to lose. It was then that I decided to employ certain new abilities I had acquired. I had often wondered at the strange relationship between Eric and Flora, off on that shadow Earth she pretended so to enjoy. I had had a slight suspicion that there was something about that place which concerned him, and that she might be his agent there. While I could not get close enough to him to achieve any satisfaction on this count, I felt confident that it would not take too much in the way of investigation, direct and otherwise, to learn what Flora was about. And so I did. Then suddenly the pace accelerated. My own party was concerned as to my whereabouts. Then when I picked you up and shocked back a few memories, Eric learned from Flora that something was suddenly quite amiss. Consequently, both sides were soon looking for me. I had decided that your return would throw everyone's plans out the window and get me out of the pocket I was in long enough to come up with an alternative to the way things were going. Eric's claim would be clouded once again, you would have had supporters of your own, my party would have lost the purpose for its entire maneuver and I had assumed you would not be ungrateful to me for my part in things. Then you went and escaped from Porter, and things really got complicated. All of us were looking for you, as I later learned, for different reasons. But my former associates had something very extra going for them. They learned what was happening, located you, and got there first. Obviously, there was a very simple way to preserve the status quo, where they would continue to hold the edge. Bleys fired the shots that put you and your car into the lake. I arrived just as this was occurring. He departed almost immediately, for it looked as if he had done a thorough job. I dragged you out, though, and there was enough left to start treating. It was frustrating now that I think back on it, not knowing whether the treatment had really been effective, whether you would awaken as Corwin or Corey. It was frustrating afterward, also, still not knowing . . . . I hellrode out when help arrived. My associates caught up with me somewhat later and put me where you found me. Do you know the rest of the story?"

"Not all of it."

"Then stop me whenever we've caught up on this. I only obtained it later, myself. Eric's crowd learned of the accident, got your location, and had you transferred to a private place, where you could be better protected, and kept you heavily sedated, so that *they* could be protected."

"Why should Eric protect me, especially if my presence was going to wreck his plans?"

"By then seven of us knew you were still living. That was too many. It was simply too late to do what he would have liked to do. He was still trying to live down Dad's words. If anything had happened to you once you were in his power, it would have blocked his movement to the throne. If Benedict ever got word of it, or Gérard . . . No, he'd not have made it. Afterward, yes. Before, no. What happened was that general knowledge of the fact of your existence forced his hand. He scheduled his coronation and resolved to keep you out of the way until it had occurred. An extremely premature bit of business, not that I see he had much of a choice. I guess you know what happened after that, since it happened to you."

"I fell in with Bleys, just as he was making his move. Not too fortunate."

He shrugged.

"Oh, it might have been—if you had won, and if you had been able to do something about Bleys. You hadn't a chance, though, not really. My grasp of their motivations begins to dissolve at this point, but I believe that that entire assault really constituted some sort of feint."

"Why?"

"As I said, I do not know. But they already had Eric just about where they wanted him. It should not have been necessary to call that attack."

I shook my head. Too much, too fast . . . Many of the facts sounded true, once I subtracted the narrator's bias. But still . . .

"I don't know . . ." I began.

"Of course," he said. "But if you ask me I will tell you."

"Who was the third member of your group?"

"The same person who stabbed me, of course. Would you care to venture a guess?"

"Just tell me."

"Fiona. The whole thing was her idea."

"Why didn't you tell me that right away?"

"Because you would not have sat still long enough to hear the rest of what I had to say. You would have dashed off to put her under restraint, discovered that she was gone, roused all the others, started an investigation, and wasted a lot of valuable time. You still may, but it at least provided me with your attention for a sufficient time for me to convince you that I know what I am about. Now, when I tell you that time is essential and that you must hear the rest of what I have to say as soon as possible—if Amber is to have any chance at all—you might listen rather than chase a crazy lady."

I had already half risen from my chair.

"I shouldn't go after her?" I said.

"The hell with her, for now. You've got bigger problems. You had better sit down again."

So I did.

X

A raft of moonbeams . . . the ghostly torchlight, like fires in black-and-white films . . . stars . . . a few fine filaments of mist . . .

I leaned upon the rail, I looked across the world. . . . Utter silence held the night, the dream-drenched city, the entire universe from here. Distant things—the sea, Amber, Arden, Garnath, the Lighthouse of Cabra, the Grove of the Unicorn, my tomb atop Kolvir . . . Silent, far below, yet clear, distinct . . . A god's eye view, I'd say, or that of a soul cut loose and drifting high . . . In the middle of the night . . .

I had come to the place where the ghosts play at being ghosts, where the omens, portents, signs, and animate desires thread the nightly avenues and palace high halls of Amber in the sky, Tir-na Nog'th . . .

Turning, my back to the rail and dayworld's vestiges below, I regarded the avenues and dark terraces, the halls of the lords, the quarters of the low . . . . The moonlight is intense in Tir-na Nog'th, silvers over the facing sides of all our imaged places . . . . Stick in hand, I passed forward, and the strangelings moved about me, appeared at windows, on balconies, on benches, at gates . . . Unseen I passed, for truly put, in this place I was the ghost to whatever their substance . . . .

Silence and silver . . . Only the tapping of my stick, and that mostly muted . . . More mists adrift toward the heart of things . . . The palace a white bonfire of it . . . Dew, like drops of mercury on the finely sanded petals and stems in the gardens by the walks . . . The passing moon as painful to the eye as the sun at midday, the stars outshone, dimmed by it . . . Silver and silence . . . The shine . . .

I had not planned on coming, for its omens—if that they truly be —are deceitful, its similarities to the lives and places below unsettling, its spectacle often disconcerting. Still, I had come. . . . A part of my bargain with time . . .

After I had left Brand to continue his recovery in the keeping of Gérard, I had realized that I required additional rest myself and sought to obtain it without betraying my disability. Fiona was indeed flown, and neither she nor Julian could be reached by means of the Trumps. Had I told Benedict and Gérard what Brand had told me, I was certain that they would have insisted we begin efforts at tracking her down, at tracking both of them. I was equally certain that such efforts would prove useless.

I had sent for Random and Ganelon and retired to my quarters, giving out that I intended to pass the day in rest and quiet thought in anticipation of spending the night in Tir-na Nog'th—reasonable behavior for any Amberite with a serious problem. I did not put much stock in the practice, but most of the others did. As it was the perfect time for me to be about such a thing, I felt that it would make my day's retirement believable. Of course, this obliged me to follow through on it that night. But this, too, was good. It gave me a day, a night, and part of the following day in which to heal sufficiently to carry my wound that much the better. I felt that it would be time well spent.

You've got to tell someone, though. I told Random and I told Ganelon. Propped in my bed, I told them of the plans of Brand, Fiona, and Bleys, and of the Eric-Julian-Caine cabal. I told them what Brand had said concerning my return and his own imprisonment by his fellow conspirators. They saw why the survivors of both factions—Fiona and Julian—had run off: doubtless to marshal their forces, hopefully to expend them on one another, but probably not. Not immediately, anyhow. More likely, one or the other would move to take Amber first.

"They will just have to take numbers and wait their turns, like everyone else," Random had said.

"Not exactly," I remembered saying. "Fiona's allies and the things that have been coming in on the black road are the same guys."

"And the Circle in Lorraine?" Ganelon had asked.

"The same. That was how it manifested itself in that shadow. They came a great distance."

"Ubiquitous bastards," Random had said.

Nodding, I had tried to explain . . .

And so I came to Tir-na Nog'th. When the moon rose and the apparition of Amber came faintly into the heavens, stars showing through it, pale halo about its towers, tiny flecks of movement upon its walls, I waited, waited with Ganelon and Random, waited on the highest crop of Kolvir, there where the three steps are fashioned, roughly, out of the stone. . . .

When the moonlight touched them, the outline of the entire stairway began to take shape, spanning the great gulf to that point above the sea the vision city held. When the moonlight fell full upon it, the stair had taken as much of substance as it would ever possess, and I set my foot on the stone. . . . Random held a full deck of Trumps and I'd mine within my jacket. Grayswandir, forged upon this very stone by moonlight, held power in the city in the sky, and so I bore my blade along. I had rested all day, and I held a staff to lean upon. Illusion of distance and time . . . The stairs through the Corwin-ignoring sky escalate somehow, for it is not a simple arithmetic progression up them once motion has commenced. I was here, I was there, I was a quarter of the way up before my shoulder had forgotten the clasp of Ganelon's hand. . . . If I looked too hard at any portion of the stair, it lost its shimmering opacity and I saw the ocean far below as through a translucent lens. . . . I lost track of time, though it seems it's never long, afterward . . . As far beneath the waves as I'd soon be above them, off to my right, glittering and curling, the outline of Rebma appeared within the sea. I thought of Moire, wondered how she fared. What would become of our deepwater double should Amber ever fall? Would the image remain unshattered in its mirror? Or would building blocks and bones be taken and shaken alike, dice in the deepwater casino canyons our fleets fly over? No answer in the mandrowning, Corwin-confounding waters, though I felt a twinge in my side.

At the head of the stair, I entered, coming into the ghost city as one would enter Amber after mounting the great forestair up Kolvir's seaward face.

I leaned upon the rail, looked across the world.

The black road led off to the south. I could not see it by night. Not that it mattered. I knew now where it led. Or rather where Brand said that it led. As he appeared to have used up a life's worth of reasons for lying, I believed that I knew where it led.

All the way.

From the brightness of Amber and the power and clean-shining splendor of adjacent Shadow, off through the progressively darkening slices of image that lead away in any direction, farther, through the twisted landscapes, and farther still, on through places seen only when drunk, delirious, or dreaming illy, and farther yet again, running beyond the place where I stop. . . . Where *I* stop . . .

How to put simply that which is not a simple thing . . . ? Solipsism, I suppose, is where we have to begin—the notion that nothing exists but the self, or, at least, that we cannot truly be aware of anything but our own existence and experience. I can find, somewhere, off in Shadow, anything I can visualize. Any of us can. This, in good faith, does not transcend the limits of the ego. It may be argued, and in fact has, by most of us, that we create the shadows we visit out of the stuff of our own psyches, that we alone truly exist, that the shadows we traverse are but projections of our own desires. . . . Whatever the merits of this argument, and there are several, it does go far toward explaining much of the family's attitude toward people, places, and things outside of Amber. Namely, we are toymakers and they, our playthings—sometimes dangerously animated, to be sure; but this, too, is part of the game. We are impresarios by temperament, and we treat one another accordingly. While solipsism does tend to leave one slightly embarrassed on questions of etiology, one can easily avoid the embarrassment by refusing to admit the validity of the questions. Most of us are, as I have often observed, almost entirely pragmatic in the conduct of our affairs. Almost . . .

Yet—yet there is a disturbing element in the picture. There is a place where the shadows go mad. . . . When you purposely push yourself through layer after layer of Shadow, surrendering—again, purposely—a piece of your understanding every step of the way, you come at last to a mad place beyond which you cannot go. Why do this? In hope of an insight, I'd say, or a new game . . . But when you come to this place, as we all have, you realize that you have reached the limit of Shadow or the end of yourself—synonymous terms, as we had always thought. Now, though . . .

Now I know that it is not so, now as I stand, waiting, without the Courts of Chaos, telling you what it was like, I know that it is not so. But I knew well enough then, that night, in Tir-na Nog'th, had known earlier, when I had fought the goat-man in the Black Circle of Lorraine, had known that day in the Lighthouse of Cabra, after my escape from the dungeons of Amber, when I had looked upon ruined Garnath. . . . I knew that that was not all there was to it. I knew because I knew that the black road ran beyond that point. It passed through madness into chaos and kept going. The things that traveled across it came from somewhere, but they were not my things. I had somehow helped to grant them this passage, but they did not spring from my version of reality. They were their own, or someone else's—small matter there—and they tore holes in that small metaphysic we had woven over the ages. They had entered our preserve, they were not of it, they threatened it, they threatened us. Fiona and Brand had reached beyond everything and found something, where none of the rest of us had believed anything to exist. The danger released was, on some level, almost worth the evidence obtained: we were not alone, nor were shadows truly our toys. Whatever our relationship with Shadow, I could nevermore regard it in the old light. . . .

All because the black road headed south and ran beyond the end of the world, where I stop.

Silence and silver . . . Walking away from the rail, leaning on my stick, passing through the fog-spun, mist-woven, moonlight-brushed fabric of vision within the troubling city . . . Ghosts . . . Shadows of shadows . . . Images of probability . . . Might-bes and might-have-beens . . . Probability lost . . . Probability regained . . .

Walking, across the promenade now . . . Figures, faces, many of them familiar . . . What are they about? Hard to say . . . Some lips move, some faces show animation. There are no words there for me. I pass among them, unnoted.

There . . . One such figure . . . Alone, but waiting . . . Fingers unknotting minutes, casting them away . . . Face averted, and I wish to see it . . . A sign that I will or should . . . She sits on a stone bench beneath a gnarly tree . . . She gazes in the direction of the palace . . . Her form is quite familiar . . . Approaching, I see that it is Lorraine . . . She continues to regard a point far beyond me, does not hear me say that I have avenged her death.

But mine is the power to be heard here. . . . It hangs in the sheath at my side.

Drawing Grayswandir, I raise my blade overhead where moonlight tricks its patterns into a kind of motion. I place it on the ground between us.

"Corwin!"

Her head snaps back, her hair rusts in the moonlight, her eyes focus.

"Where did you come from? You're early."

"You wait for me?"

"Of course. You told me to—"

"How did you come to this place?"

"This bench . . . ?"

"No. This city."

"Amber? I do not understand. You brought me yourself. I—"

"Are you happy here?"

"You know that I am, so long as I am with you."

I had not forgotten the evenness of her teeth, the hint of freckles beneath the soft light's veil. . . .

"What happened? It is very important. Pretend for a moment that I do not know, and tell me everything that happened to us after the battle of the Black Circle in Lorraine."

She frowned. She stood. She turned away.

"We had that argument," she said. "You followed me, drove away Melkin, and we talked. I saw that I was wrong and I went with you to Avalon. There, your brother Benedict persuaded you to talk with Eric. You were not reconciled, but you agreed to a truce because of something that he told you. He swore not to harm you and you swore to defend Amber, with Benedict to witness both oaths. We remained in Avalon while you obtained chemicals, and we went to another place later, a place where you purchased strange weapons. We won the battle, but Eric lies wounded now." She stood and faced me. "Are you thinking of ending the truce? Is that it, Corwin?"

I shook my head, and though I knew better I reached to embrace her. I wanted to hold her, despite the fact that one of us did not exist, could not exist, when that tiny gap of space between our skins was crossed, to tell her that whatever had happened or would happen—

The shock was not severe, but it caused me to stumble. I lay across Grayswandir. . . . My staff had fallen to the grass several paces away. Rising to my knees, I saw that the color had gone out of her face, her eyes, her hair. Her mouth shaped ghost words as her head turned, searching. Sheathing Grayswandir, recovering my staff, I rose once again. Her seeing passed through me and focused. Her face grew smooth, she smiled, started forward. I moved aside and turned, watching her run toward the man who approached, seeing her clasped in his arms, glimpsing his face as he bent it toward her own, lucky ghost, silver rose at the throat of his garment, kissing her, this man I would never know, silver on silence, and silver. . . .

Walking away . . . Not looking back . . . Crossing the promenade . . .

The voice of Random: "Corwin, are you all right?"

"Yes."

"Anything interesting happening?"

"Later, Random."

"Sorry."

And sudden, the gleaming stair before the palace grounds . . . Up it, and a turn to the right . . . Slow and easy now, into the garden . . . Ghost flowers throb on their stalks all about me, ghost shrubs spill blossoms like frozen firework displays. *Sans* colors, all . . . Only the essentials sketched in, degrees of luminosity in silver the terms of their claim on the eye. Only the essentials here. Is Tir-na Nog'th a special sphere of Shadow in the real world, swayed by the promptings of the id—a full-sized projective test in the sky, perhaps even a therapeutic device? Despite the silver, I'd say, if this is a piece of the soul, the night is very dark. . . . And silent . . .

Walking . . . By fountains, benches, groves, cunning alcoves in mazes of hedging . . . Passing along the walks, up an occasional step, across small bridges . . . Moving past ponds, among trees, by an odd piece of statuary, a boulder, a sundial (moondial, here?), bearing to my right, pressing steadily ahead, rounding, after a time, the northern end of the palace, swinging left then, past a courtyard overhung by balconies, more ghosts here and there upon them, behind them, within . . .

Circling around to the rear, just to see the back gardens this way, again, for they are lovely by normal moonlight in the true Amber.

A few more figures, talking, standing . . . No motion but my own is apparent.

. . . And feel myself drawn to the right. As one should never turn down a free oracle, I go.

. . . Toward a mass of high hedging, a small open area within, if it is not overgrown . . . Long ago there was . . .

Two figures, embracing, within. They part as I begin to turn away. None of my affair, but . . . Deirdre . . . One of them is Deirdre. I know who the man will be before he turns. It is a cruel joke by whatever powers rule that silver, that silence. . . . Back, back, away from that hedge . . . Turning, stumbling, rising again, going, away, now, quickly . . .

The voice of Random: "Corwin? Are you all right?"

"Later! Damn it! Later!"

"It is not too long till sunrise, Corwin. I felt I had better remind you—"

"Consider me reminded!"

Away, now, quickly . . . Time, too, is a dream in Tir-na Nog'th. Small comfort, but better than none. Quickly, now, away, going, again . . .

. . . Toward the palace, bright architecture of the mind or spirit, more clearly standing now than the real ever did . . . To judge perfection is to render a worthless verdict, but I must see what lies within. . . . This must be an end of sorts, for I am driven. I had not paused to recover my staff from where it had fallen this time, among the sparkling grasses. I know where I must go, what I must do. Obvious now, though the logic which has seized me is not that of the waking mind.

Hurrying, climbing, up to the rearward portal . . . The side-biting soreness comes home again . . . Across the threshold, in . . .

Into an absence of starshine and moonlight. The illumination is without direction, seeming almost to drift and to pool, aimlessly. Wherever it misses, the shadows are absolute, occulting large sections of room, hallway, closet, and stair.

Among them, through them, almost running now . . . Monochrome of my home . . . Apprehension overtakes me . . . The black spots seem like holes in this piece of reality now. . . . I fear to pass too near. Fall in and be lost . . .

Turning . . . Crossing . . . Finally . . . Entering . . . The throne room . . . Bushels of blackness stacked where my eyes would drive down lines of seeing to the throne itself . . .

There, though, is movement.

A drifting, to my right, as I advance.

A lifting, with the drifting.

The boots on feet on legs come into view as forward pressing I near the place's base.

Grayswandir comes into my hand, finding its way into a patch of light, renewing its eyetricking, shapeshifting stretch, acquiring a glow of its own . . .

I place my left foot on the step, rest my left hand on my knee. Distracting but bearable, the throb of my healing gut. I wait for the blackness, the emptiness, to be drawn, appropriate curtain for the theatrics with which I am burdened this night.

And it slides aside, revealing a hand, an arm, a shoulder, the arm a glinting, metallic thing, its planes like the facets of a gem, its wrist and elbow wondrous weaves of silver cable, pinned with flecks of fire, the hand, stylized, skeletal, a Swiss toy, a mechanical insect, functional, deadly, beautiful in its way . . .

And it slides aside, revealing the rest of the man. . . .

Benedict stands relaxed beside the throne, his left and human hand laid lightly upon it. He leans toward the throne. His lips are moving.

And it slides aside, revealing the throne's occupant. . . .

"Dara!"

Turned toward her right, she smiles, she nods to Benedict, her lips move. I advance and extend Grayswandir till its point rests lightly in the concavity beneath her sternum. . . .

Slowly, quite slowly, she turns her head and meets my eyes. She takes on color and life. Her lips move again, and this time her words reach me.

"What are you?"

"No. That is my question. You answer it. Now."

"I am Dara. Dara of Amber, Queen Dara. I hold this throne by right of blood and conquest. Who are you?"

"Corwin. Also of Amber. Don't move! I did not ask *who* you are—"

"Corwin is dead these many centuries. I have seen his tomb."

"Empty."

"Not so. His body lies within."

"Give me your lineage!"

Her eyes move to her right, where the shade of Benedict still stands. A blade has appeared in his new hand, seeming almost an extension of it, but he holds it loosely, casually. His left hand now rests on her arm. His eyes seek me in back of Grayswandir's hilt. Failing, they go again to that which is visible—Grayswandir—recognizing its design. . . .

"I am the great-granddaughter of Benedict and the hellmaid Lintra, whom he loved and later slew." Benedict winces at this, but she continues. "I never knew her. My mother and my mother's mother were born in a place where time does not run as in Amber. I am the first of my mother's line to bear all the marks of humanity. And you, Lord Corwin, are but a ghost from a long dead past, albeit a dangerous shade. How you came here, I do not know. But it was wrong of you. Return to your grave. Trouble not the living."

My hand wavers. Grayswandir strays no more than half an inch. Yet that is sufficient.

Benedict's thrust is below my threshold of perception. His new arm drives the new hand that holds the blade that strikes Grayswandir, as his old arm draws his old hand, which has seized upon Dara, back across the arm of the throne. . . . This subliminal impression reaches me moments later, as I fall back, cutting air, recover and strike an *en garde,* reflexively. . . . It is ridiculous for a pair of ghosts to fight. Here, it is uneven. He cannot even reach me, whereas Grayswandir—

But no! His blade changes hands as he releases Dara and pivots, bringing them together, old hand and new. His left wrist rotates as he slides it forward and down, moving into what would be *corps à corps,* were we two facing mortal bodies. For a moment our guards are locked. That moment is enough. . . .

That gleaming, mechanical hand comes forward, a thing of moonlight and fire, blackness and smoothness, all angles, no curves, fingers slightly flexed, palm silver-scribbled with a half-familiar design, comes forward, comes forward and catches at my throat. . . .

Missing the fingers catch my shoulder and the thumb goes hooking —whether for clavicle or larynx, I do not know. I throw one punch with my left, toward his midsection, and there is nothing there. . . .

The voice of Random: "Corwin! The sun is about to rise! You've got to come down now!"

I cannot even answer. A second or two and that hand would tear away whatever it held. That hand . . . Grayswandir and that hand, which strangely resembles it, are the only two things which seem to coexist in my world and the city of ghosts. . . .

"I see it, Corwin! Pull away and reach for me! The Trump—"

I spin Grayswandir out of the bind and bring it around and down in a long, slashing arc. . . .

Only a ghost could have beaten Benedict or Benedict's ghost with that maneuver. We stand too close for him to block my blade, but his countercut, perfectly placed, would have removed my arm, had there been an arm there to meet it. . . .

As there is not, I complete the stroke, delivering the blow with the full force of my right arm, high upon that lethal device of moonlight and fire, blackness and smoothness, near to the point where it is joined with him.

With an evil tearing at my shoulder, the arm comes away from Benedict and grows still. . . . We both fall.

"Get up! By the unicorn, Corwin, get up! The sun is rising! The city will come apart about you!"

The floor beneath me wavers to and from a misty transparency. I glimpse a light-scaled expanse of water. I roll to my feet, barely avoiding the ghost's rush to clutch at the arm he has lost. It clings like a dead parasite and my side is hurting again. . . .

Suddenly I am heavy and the vision of ocean does not fade. I begin to sink through the floor. Color returns to the world, wavering stripes of pink. The Corwin-spurning floor parts and the Corwin-killing gulf is opened. . . .

I fall. . . .

"This way, Corwin! Now!"

Random stands on a mountaintop and reaches for me. I extend my hand. . . .

XI

. . . And frying pans without fires are often far between . . .

We untangled ourselves and rose. I sat down again immediately, on the bottommost stair. I worked the metal hand loose from my shoulder—no blood there, but a promise of bruises to come—then cast it and its arm to the ground. The light of early morning did not detract from its exquisite and menacing appearance.

Ganelon and Random stood beside me.

"You all right, Corwin?"

"Yes. Just let me catch my breath."

"I brought food," Random said. "We could have breakfast right here."

"Good idea."

As Random began unpacking provisions, Ganelon nudged the arm with the toe of his boot.

"What the hell," he asked, "is that?"

I shook my head.

"I lopped it off the ghost of Benedict," I told him. "For reasons I do not understand, it was able to reach me."

He stooped and picked it up, studied it.

"A lot lighter than I thought it would be," he observed. He raked the air with it. "You could do quite a job on someone, with a hand like that."

"I know."

He worked the fingers.

"Maybe the real Benedict could use it."

"Maybe," I said. "My feelings are quite mixed when it comes to offering it to him but, possibly you're right. . . ."

"How's the side?"

I prodded it gently.

"Not especially bad, everything considered. I'll be able to ride after breakfast, so long as we take it nice and easy."

"Good. Say, Corwin, while Random is getting things ready, I have a question that may be out of order, but it has been bothering me all along."

"Ask it."

"Well, let me put it this way: I am all for you, or I would not be here. I will fight for you to have your throne, no matter what. But every time talk of the succession occurs, someone gets angry and breaks it off or the subject gets changed. Like Random did, while you were up there. I suppose that it is not absolutely essential for me to know the basis of your claim to the throne, or that of any of the others, but I cannot help being curious as to the reasons for all the friction."

I sighed, then sat silent for a time.

"All right," I said after a while, and then I chuckled. "All right. If we cannot agree on these things ourselves, I would guess that they must seem pretty confused to an outsider. Benedict is the eldest. His mother was Cymnea. She bore Dad two other sons, also—Osric and Finndo. Then—how does one put these things?—Faiella bore Eric. After that, Dad found some defect in his marriage with Cymnea and had it dissolved—*ab initio*, as they would say in my old shadow—from the beginning. Neat trick, that. But he was the king."

"Didn't that make all of them illegitimate?"

"Well, it left their status less certain. Osric and Finndo were more than a little irritated, as I understand it, but they died shortly thereafter. Benedict was either less irritated or more politic about the entire affair. He never raised a fuss. Dad then married Faiella."

"And that made Eric legitimate?"

"It would have, if he had acknowledged Eric as his son. He treated him as if he were, but he never did anything formal in that regard. It involved the smoothing-over process with Cymnea's family, which had become a bit stronger around that time."

"Still, if he treated him as his own . . ."

"Ah! But he later *did* acknowledge Llewella formally. She was born out of wedlock, but he decided to recognize her, poor girl. All of Eric's supporters hated her for its effect on his status. Anyway, Faiella was later to become my mother. I was born safely in wedlock, making me the first with a clean claim on the throne. Talk to one of the others and you may get a different line of reasoning, but those are the facts it will have to be based on. Somehow it does not seem quite as important as it once did, though, with Eric dead and Benedict not really interested. . . . But that is where I stand."

"I see—sort of," he said. "Just one more thing, then . . ."

"What?"

"Who is next? That is to say, if anything were to happen to you . . . ?"

I shook my head.

"It gets even more complicated there, now. Caine would have been next. With him dead, I see it as swinging over to Clarissa's brood— the redheads. Bleys would have followed, then Brand."

"Clarissa? What become of your mother?"

"She died in childbirth. Deirdre was the child. Dad did not remarry for many years after mother's death. When he did, it was a redheaded wench from a far southern shadow. I never liked her. He began feeling the same way after a time and started fooling around again. They had one reconciliation after Llewella's birth in Rebma, and Brand was the result. When they were finally divorced, he recognized Llewella to spite Clarissa. At least, that is what I think happened."

"So you are not counting the ladies in the succession?"

"No. They are neither interested nor fit. If I were, though, Fiona would precede Bleys and Llewella would follow him. After Clarissa's crowd, it would swing over to Julian, Gérard, and Random, in that order. Excuse me—count Flora before Julian. The marriage data is even more involved, but no one will dispute the final order. Let it go at that."

"Gladly," he said. "So now Brand gets it if you die, right?"

"Well . . . He is a self-confessed traitor and he rubs everybody the wrong way. I do not believe the rest of them would have him, as he stands now. But I do not believe he has by any means given up."

"But the alternative is Julian."

I shrugged.

"The fact that I do not like Julian does not make him unfit. In fact, he might even be a very effective monarch."

"So he knifed you for the chance to prove it," Random called out. "Come on and eat."

"I still don't think so," I said, getting to my feet and heading for the food. "First, I don't see how he could have gotten to me. Second, it would have been too damned obvious. Third, if I die in the near future Benedict will have the real say as to the succession. Everyone knows that. He's got the seniority, he's got the wits, and he's got the power. He could simply say, for example, 'The hell with all this bickering, I am backing Gérard,' and that would be it."

"What if he decided to reinterpret his own status and take it himself?" Ganelon asked.

We seated ourselves on the ground and took the tin dishes Random had filled.

"He could have had it long before this, had he wanted it," I said. "There are several ways of regarding the offspring of a void marriage, and the most favorable one would be the most likely in his case. Osric and Finndo rushed to judgment, taking the worst view. Benedict knew better. He just waited. So . . . It is possible. Unlikely, though, I'd say."

"Then—in the normal course of affairs—if anything happened to you, it could still be very much up in the air?"

"Very much."

"But why was Caine killed?" Random asked. Then, between mouthfuls, he answered his own question. "So that when they got you, it would swing over to Clarissa's kids immediately. It has occurred to me that Bleys is probably still living, and he is next in line. His body was never found. My guess is this: He trumped off to Fiona during your attack and returned to Shadow to rebuild his forces, leaving you to what he hoped would be your death at the hands of Eric. He is finally ready to move again. So they killed Caine and tried for you. If they are really allied with the black-road horde, they could have arranged for another assault from that quarter. Then he could have done the same thing you did—arrive at the last hour, turn back the invaders, and move on in. And there he would be, next in line and first in force. Simple. Except that you survived and Brand has been returned. If we are to believe Brand's accusation of Fiona —and I see no reason why we should not—then it follows from their original program."

I nodded.

"Possibly," I said. "I asked Brand just those things. He admitted their possibility, but he disavowed any knowledge as to whether Bleys was still living. Personally, I think he was lying."

"Why?"

"It is possible that he wishes to combine revenge for his imprisonment and the attempt on his life with the removal of the one impediment, save for myself, to his own succession. I think he feels that

I will be expended in a scheme he is evolving to deal with the black road. The destruction of his own cabal and the removal of the road could make him look pretty decent, especially after all the penance he has had thrust upon him. Then, maybe then, he would have a chance—or thinks that he would."

"Then you think Bleys is still living, too?"

"Just a feeling," I said. "But yes, I do."

"What is their strength, anyway?"

"An endorsement of higher education," I said. "Fiona and Brand paid attention to Dworkin while the rest of us were off indulging our assorted passions in Shadow. Consequently, they seem to have obtained a better grasp of principles than we possess. They know more about Shadow and what lies beyond it, more about the Pattern, more about the Trumps than we do. That is why Brand was able to send you his message."

"An interesting thought . . ." Random mused. "Do you think they might have disposed of Dworkin after they felt they had learned enough from him? It would certainly help to keep things exclusive, if anything happened to Dad."

"That thought had not occurred to me." I said.

And I wondered, could they have done something that had affected his mind? Something that left him as he was when last I had seen him? If so, were they aware that he was possibly still living, somewhere? Or might they have assumed his total destruction?

"Yes, an interesting thought," I said. "I suppose that it is possible."

The sun inched its way upward, and the food restored me. No trace of Tir-na Nog'th remained in the morning's light. My memories of it had already taken on the quality of images in a dim mirror. Ganelon fetched its only other token, the arm, and Random packed it away along with the dishes. By daylight, the first three steps looked less like stairs and more like jumbled rock.

Random gestured with his head.

"Take the same way back?" he asked.

"Yes," I said, and we mounted.

We had come by way of a trail that wound about Kolvir to the south. It was longer but less rugged than the route across the crest. I'd a humor to pamper myself so long as my side protested.

So we bore to the right, moving single file, Random in the lead, Ganelon to the rear. The trail ran gently upward, then cut back down again. The air was cool, and it bore the aromas of verdure and moist earth, a thing quite unusual in that stark place, at that altitude. Straying air currents, I reasoned, from the forest far below.

We let the horses pick their own casual pace down through the dip and up the next rise. As we neared its crest, Random's horse whinnied and began to rear. He controlled it immediately, and I glanced about but saw nothing that might have startled it.

When he reached its summit, Random slowed and called back, "Take a look at that sunrise now, will you?"

It would have been rather difficult to avoid doing so, though I did not remark on the fact. Random was seldom given to sentimentality over vegetation, geology, or illumination.

I almost drew rein myself as I topped the rise, for the sun was a fantastic golden ball. It seemed half again its normal size, and its peculiar coloration was unlike anything I remembered having seen before. It did marvelous things to the band of ocean that had come into view above the next rise, and the tints of cloud and sky were indeed singular. I did not halt, though, for the sudden brightness was almost painful.

"You're right," I called out, following him down into the next declivity. Behind me, Ganelon snorted an appreciative oath.

When I had blinked away the aftereffects of that display I noticed that the vegetation was heavier than I had remembered in this little pocket in the sky. I had thought there were several scrubby trees and some patches of lichen, but there were actually several dozen trees, larger than I recalled, and greener, with a clutch of grasses here and there and a vine or two softening the outlines of the rocks. However, since my return I had only passed this way after dark. And now that I thought of it, it was probably the source of the aromas that had come to me earlier.

Passing through, it seemed that the little hollow was also wider than I recalled it. By the time we had crossed and were ascending once more, I was certain of it.

"Random," I called out, "has this place changed recently?"

"Hard to say," he answered. "Eric didn't let me out much. It seems to have grown up a bit."

"It seems bigger—wider."

"Yes, it does. I had thought that that was just my imagination."

When we reached the next crest I was not dazzled again because the sun was blocked by foliage. The area ahead of us contained many more trees than the one we had just departed—and they were larger and closer together. We drew rein.

"I don't remember this," he said. "Even passing through at night, it would have registered. We must have taken a wrong turn."

"I don't see how. Still, we know about where we are. I would rather go ahead than go back and start again. We should keep aware of conditions around Amber, anyway."

"True."

He headed down toward the wood. We followed.

"It's kind of unusual, at this altitude—a growth like this," he called back.

"There also seems to be a lot more soil than I recall."

"I believe you are right."

The trail curved to the left as we entered among the trees. I could see no reason for this deviation from the direct route. We stayed with it, however, and it added to the illusion of distance. After a few moments it swung suddenly to the right again. The prospect on cutting back was peculiar. The trees seemed even taller and were now so dense as to puzzle the eye that sought their penetration. When it turned once more it broadened, and the way was straight for a great distance ahead. Too great, in fact. Our little dell just wasn't that wide.

Random halted again.

"Damn it, Corwin! This is ridiculous!" he said. "You are not playing games, are you?"

"I couldn't if I would," I said. "I have never been able to manipulate Shadow anywhere on Kolvir. There isn't supposed to be any to work with here."

"That has always been my understanding, too. Amber casts Shadow but is not of it. I don't like this at all. What do you say we turn back?"

"I've a feeling we might not be able to retrace our way," I said. "There has to be a reason for this, and I want to know it."

"It occurs to me that it might be some sort of a trap."

"Even so," I said.

He nodded and we rode on, down that shaded way, under trees now grown more stately. The wood was silent about us. The ground remained level, the trail straight. Half consciously, we pushed the horses to a greater pace.

About five minutes passed before we spoke again. Then Random said, "Corwin, this can't be Shadow."

"Why not?"

"I have been trying to influence it and nothing happens. Have you tried?"

"No."

"Why don't you?"

"All right."

A rock could jut beyond the coming tree, a morning glory twine and bell within that shrubby stand. . . . There ought a patch of sky come clear, a wispy cloud upon it. . . . Then let there be a fallen limb, a stair of fungus up its side. . . . A scummed-over puddle . . . A frog . . . Falling feather, drifting seed . . . A limb that twists just so . . . Another trail upon our way, fresh-cut, deep-marked, past the place the feather should have fallen . . .

"No good," I said.

"If it is not Shadow, what is it?"

"Something else, of course."

He shook his head and checked again to see that his blade was loose in its scabbard. Automatically, I did the same. Moments later, I heard Ganelon's make a small clicking noise behind me.

Ahead, the trail began to narrow, and shortly thereafter it commenced to wander. We were forced to slow our pace once again, and the trees pressed nearer with branches sweeping lower than at any time before. The trail became a path. It jogged, it curved, it gave a final twist and then quit.

Random ducked a limb, then raised his hand and halted. We came up beside him. For as far as I could see ahead there was no indication of the trail's picking up again. Looking back, I failed to locate any sign of it either.

"Suggestions," he said, "are now in order. We do not know where we have been or where we are going, let alone where we are. My suggestion is the hell with curiosity. Let's get out of here the fastest way we know how."

"The Trumps?" Ganelon asked.

"Yes. What do you say, Corwin?"

"Okay. I don't like it either, and I can't think of anything better to try. Go ahead."

"Who should I try for?" he asked, producing his deck and uncasing it. "Gérard?"

"Yes."

He shuffled through his cards, located Gérard's, stared at it. We stared at him. Time went its way.

"I can't seem to reach him," he finally announced.

"Try Benedict."

"Okay."

Repeat performance. No contact.

"Try Deirdre," I said, drawing forth my own deck and searching out her Trump. "I'll join you. We will see whether it makes a difference with two of us trying."

And again. And again.

"Nothing," I said after a long effort.

Random shook his head.

"Did you notice anything unusual about your Trumps?" he asked.

"Yes, but I don't know what it is. They do seem different."

"Mine seem to have lost that quality of coldness they once possessed," he said.

I shuffled mine slowly. I ran my fingertips across them.

"Yes, you are right," I said. "That's it. But let us try again. Say, Flora."

"Okay."

The results were the same. And with Llewella. And Brand.

"Any idea what could be wrong?" Random asked.

"Not the slightest. They couldn't all be blocking us. They couldn't all be dead. . . . Oh, I suppose they could. But it is highly unlikely. Something seems to have affected the Trumps themselves, is what it is. And I never knew of anything that could do that."

"Well, they are not guaranteed one hundred percent," Random said, "according to the manufacturer."

"What do you know that I don't?"

He chuckled.

"You never forget the day you come of age and walk the Pattern," he said. "I remember it as though it were last year. When I had succeeded—all flushed with excitement, with glory—Dworkin presented me with my first set of Trumps and instructed me in their use. I distinctly recall asking him whether they worked everywhere. And I remember his answer: 'No,' he said. 'But they should serve in any place you will ever be.' He never much liked me, you know."

"But did you ask him what he meant by that?"

"Yes, and he said, 'I doubt that you will ever achieve a state where

they will fail to serve you. Why don't you run along now?' And I did.
I was anxious to go play with the Trumps all by myself."

" 'Achieve a state?' He didn't say 'reach a place'?"

"No. I have a very good memory for certain things."

"Peculiar—though not much help that I can see. Smacks of the metaphysical."

"I'd wager Brand would know."

"I've a feeling you're right, for all the good that does us."

"We ought to do something other than discuss metaphysics," Ganelon commented. "If you can't manipulate Shadow and you can't work the Trumps, it would seem that the next thing to do is determine where we are. And then go looking for help."

I nodded.

"Since we are not in Amber, I think it is safe to assume that we are in Shadow—a very special place, quite near to Amber, since the changeover was not abrupt. In that we were transported without active cooperation on our part, there had to be some agency and presumably some intent behind the maneuver. If it is going to attack us, now is as good a time as any. If there is something else it wants, then it is going to have to show us, because we aren't even in a position to make a good guess."

"So you propose we do nothing?"

"I propose we wait. I don't see any value in wandering about, losing ourselves further."

"I seem to remember your once telling me that adjacent shadows tend to be somewhat congruent," Ganelon said.

"Yes, I probably did. So what?"

"Then, if we are as near to Amber as you suppose, we need but ride toward the rising sun to come to a spot that parallels the city itself."

"It is not quite that simple. But supposing it were, what good would it do us?"

"Perhaps the Trumps would function again at the point of maximum congruity."

Random looked at Ganelon, looked at me.

"That may be worth trying," he said. "What have we got to lose?"

"Whatever small orientation we still possess," I said. "Look, it is not a bad idea. If nothing develops here, we will try it. However, looking back, it seems that the road behind us closes in direct proportion to the distance we advance. We are not simply moving in space. Under these circumstances, I am loath to wander until I am satisfied that we have no other option. If someone desires our presence at a particular location, it is up to him now to phrase the invitation a little more legibly. We wait."

They both nodded. Random began to dismount, then froze, one foot in the stirrup, one on the ground.

"After all these years," he said, and, "I never really believed it . . ."

"What is it?" I whispered.

"The option," he said, and he mounted again.

He persuaded his horse to move very slowly forward. I followed, and a moment later I glimpsed it, white as I had seen it in the grove, standing, half hidden, amid a clump of ferns: the unicorn.

It turned as we moved, and seconds later flashed ahead, to stand partly concealed once more by the trunks of several trees.

"I see it!" Ganelon whispered. "To think there really is such a beast . . . Your family's emblem, isn't it?"

"Yes."

"A good sign, I'd say."

I did not answer, but followed, keeping it in sight. That it was meant to be followed I did not doubt.

It had a way of remaining partly concealed the entire while—looking out from behind something, passing from cover to cover, moving with an incredible swiftness when it did move, avoiding open areas, favoring glade and shade. We followed, deeper and deeper into the wood which had given up all semblance of anything to be found on Kolvir's slopes. It resembled Arden now, more than anything else near Amber, as the ground was relatively level and the trees grew more and more stately.

An hour had passed, I guessed, and another had followed it, before we came to a small, clear stream and the unicorn turned and headed up it. As we rode along the bank, Random commented, "This is starting to look sort of familiar."

"Yes," I said, "but only sort of. I can't quite say why."

"Nor I."

We entered upon a slope shortly thereafter, and it grew steeper before very long. The going became more difficult for the horses, but the unicorn adjusted its pace to accommodate them. The ground became rockier, the trees smaller. The stream curved in its splashing course. I lost track of its twists and turns, but we were finally nearing the top of the small mount up which we had been traveling.

We achieved a level area and continued along it toward the wood from which the stream issued. At this point I caught an oblique view —ahead and to the right, through a place where the land fell away— of an icy blue sea, quite far below us.

"We're pretty high up," Ganelon said. "It seemed like lowland, but—"

"The Grove of the Unicorn!" Random interrupted. "That's what it looks like. See!"

Nor was he incorrect. Ahead lay an area strewn with boulders. Amid them a spring uttered the stream we followed. This place was larger and more lush, its situation incorrect in terms of my internal compass. Yet the similarity had to be more than coincidental. The unicorn mounted the rock nearest the spring, looked at us, then turned away. It might have been staring down at the ocean.

Then, as we continued, the grove, the unicorn, the trees about us, the stream beside us took on an unusual clarity, all, as though each were radiating some special illumination, causing it to quiver with the intensity of its color while at the same time wavering, slightly, just at the edges of perception. This produced in me an incipient feeling like the beginning of the emotional accompaniment to a hellride.

Then, then and then, with each stride of my mount, something went out of the world about us. An adjustment in the relationships of objects suddenly occurred, eroding my sense of depth, destroying perspective, rearranging the display of articles within my field of vision, so that everything presented its entire outer surface without simultaneously appearing to occupy an increased area: angles predominated, and relative sizes seemed suddenly ridiculous. Random's horse reared and neighed, massive, apocalpytic, instantly recalling *Guernica* to my mind. And to my distress I saw that we ourselves had not been untouched by the phenomenon—but that Random, struggling with his mount, and Ganelon, still managing to control Firedrake, had, like everything else, been transfigured by this cubist dream of space.

But Star was a veteran of many a hellride; Firedrake, also, had been through a lot. We clung to them and felt the movements that we could not accurately gauge. And Random succeeded, at last, in imposing his will upon his mount, though the prospect continued to alter as we advanced.

Light values shifted next. The sky grew black, not as night, but like a flat, nonreflecting surface. So did certain vacant areas between objects. The only light left in the world seemed to originate from things themselves, and all of it was gradually bleached. Various intensities of white emerged from the planes of existence, and brightest of all, immense, awful, the unicorn suddenly reared, pawing at the air, filling perhaps ninety percent of creation with what became a slow-motion gesture I feared would annihilate us if we advanced another pace.

Then there was only the light.

Then absolute stillness.

Then the light was gone and there was nothing. Not even blackness. A gap in existence, which might have lasted an instant or an eternity . . .

Then the blackness returned, and the light. Only they were reversed. Light filled the interstices, outlining voids that must be objects. The first sound that I heard was the rushing of water, and I knew somehow that we were halted beside the spring. The first thing that I felt was Star's quivering. Then I smelled the sea.

Then the Pattern came into view, or a distorted negative of it. . . .

I leaned forward and more light leaked around the edges of things. I leaned back; it went away. Forward again, this time farther than before . . .

The light spread, introduced various shades of gray into the scheme of things. With my knees then, gently, I suggested that Star advance.

With each pace, something returned to the world. Surfaces, textures, colors . . .

Behind me, I heard the others begin to follow. Below me, the Pattern surrendered nothing of its mystery, but it acquired a context which, by degrees, found its place within the larger reshaping of the world about us.

Continuing downhill, a sense of depth reemerged. The sea, now plainly visible off to the right, underwent a possibly purely optical separation from the sky, with which it seemed momentarily to have been joined in some sort of *Urmeer* of the waters above and the waters below. Unsettling upon reflection, but unnoted while in effect. We were heading down a steep, rocky incline which seemed to have taken its beginning at the rear of the grove to which the unicorn had led us. Perhaps a hundred meters below us was a perfectly level area which appeared to be solid, unfractured rock—roughly oval in shape, a couple of hundred meters along its major axis. The slope down which we rode swung off to the left and returned, describing a vast arc, a parenthesis, half cupping the smooth shelf. Beyond its rightward jutting there was nothing—that is to say the land fell away in steep descent toward that peculiar sea.

And, continuing, all three dimensions seemed to reassert themselves once more. The sun was that great orb of molten gold we had seen earlier. The sky was a deeper blue than that of Amber, and there were no clouds in it. That sea was a matching blue, unspecked by sail or island. I saw no birds, and I heard no sounds other than our own. An enormous silence lay upon this place, this day. In the bowl of my suddenly clear vision, the Pattern at last achieved its disposition upon the surface below. I thought at first that it was inscribed in the rock, but as we drew nearer I saw that it was contained within it—gold-pink swirls, like veining in an exotic marble, natural-seeming despite the obvious purpose to the design.

I drew rein and the others came up beside me, Random to my right, Ganelon to my left.

We regarded it in silence for a long while. A dark, rough-edged smudge had obliterated an area of the section immediately beneath us, running from its outer rim to the center.

"You know," Random finally said, "it is as if someone had shaved the top off Kolvir, cutting at about the level of the dungeons."

"Yes," I said.

"Then—looking for congruence—that would be about where our own Pattern lies."

"Yes," I said again.

"And that blotted area is to the south, from whence comes the black road."

I nodded slowly as the understanding arrived and forged itself into a certainty.

"What does it mean?" he asked. "It seems to correspond to the true state of affairs, but beyond that I do not understand its significance. Why have we been brought here and shown this thing?"

"It does not correspond to the true state of affairs," I said. "It *is* the true state of affairs."

Ganelon turned toward us.

"On that shadow Earth we visited—where you had spent so many years—I heard a poem about two roads that diverged in a wood," he said. "It ends, 'I took the one less traveled by, and that has made all the difference.' When I heard it, I thought of something you had once said—'All roads lead to Amber'—and I wondered then, as I do now, at the difference the choice may make, despite the end's apparent inevitability to those of your blood."

"You know?" I said. "You understand?"

"I think so."

He nodded, then pointed.

"That is the real Amber down there, isn't it?"

"Yes," I said. "Yes, it is."

THE HAND OF OBERON

To Jay Haldeman,
of fellowship and artichokes.

I

A bright flash of insight, to match that peculiar sun . . .

There it was. . . . Displayed within that light, a thing I had only seen self-illuminated in darkness up until then: the Pattern, the great Pattern of Amber cast upon an oval shelf beneath/above a strange sky-sea.

. . . And I knew, perhaps by that within me which bound us, that this had to be the real one. Which meant that the Pattern in Amber was but its first shadow. Which meant—

Which meant that Amber itself was but a shadow, albeit a special one, for the Pattern was not carried over into places beyond the realm of Amber, Rebma, and Tir-na Nog'th. Meaning, then, that this place to which we had come was, by the law of precedence and configuration, the real Amber.

I turned to a smiling Ganelon, his beard and wild hair molten in the merciless light.

"How did you know?" I asked him.

"You know I am a very good guesser, Corwin," he replied, "and I recall everything you ever told me about how things work in Amber: how its shadow and those of your struggles are cast across the worlds. I often wondered, in thinking of the black road, whether anything could have cast such a shadow into Amber itself. And I imagined that such a something would have to be extremely basic, powerful, and secret." He gestured at the scene before us. "Like that."

"Continue," I said.

His expression changed and he shrugged.

"So there had to be a layer of reality deeper than your Amber," he explained, "where the dirty work was done. Your patron beast led us to what seems to be such a place, and that blot on the Pattern looks to be the dirty work. You agreed."

I nodded.

"It was your perceptiveness rather than the conclusion itself which stunned me so," I said.

"You beat me to it," admitted Random, off to my right, "but the feeling has found its way into my intestines—to put it delicately. I do believe that somehow that is the basis of our world down there."

"An outsider can sometimes see things better than one who is part of them," Ganelon offered.

Random glanced at me and returned his attention to the spectacle.

"Do you think things will change any more," he asked, "if we go down for a closer look?"

"Only one way to find out," I said.

"Single file, then," Random agreed. "I'll lead."

"All right."

Random guided his mount to the right, the left, the right, in a long series of switchbacks which zigged us and zagged us across most of the face of the wall. Continuing in the order we had maintained all day, I followed him and Ganelon came last.

"Seems stable enough now," Random called back.

"So far," I said.

"Some sort of opening in the rocks below."

I leaned forward. There was a cave mouth back to the right, on level with the oval plain. Its situation was such that it had been hidden from sight when we had occupied our higher position.

"We pass fairly near it," I said.

"—quickly, cautiously, and silently," Random added, drawing his blade.

I unsheathed Grayswandir, and one turn back above me Ganelon drew his own weapon.

We did not pass the opening, but turned leftward once more before we came to it. We moved within ten or fifteen feet of it, however, and I detected an unpleasant odor which I could not identify. The horses must have done a better job of it, though, or been pessimists by nature, because they flattened their ears, widened their nostrils, and made alarmed noises while turning against the reins. They calmed, however, as soon as we had made the turn and begun moving away once again. They did not suffer a relapse until we reached the end of our descent and moved to approach the damaged Pattern. They refused to go near it.

Random dismounted. He advanced to the edge of the design, paused and stared. After a time, he spoke without looking back.

"It follows that the damage was deliberate," he said, "from everything else that we know."

"It seems to follow," I said.

"It is also obvious that we were brought here for a reason."

"I'd say so."

"Then it does not take too much imagination to conclude that our purpose for being here is to determine how the Pattern was damaged and what might be done to repair it."

"Possibly. What is your diagnosis?"

"Nothing yet."

He moved along the perimeter of the figure, off to the right where the smear-effect began. I resheathed my blade and prepared to dismount. Ganelon reached over and took hold of my shoulder.

"I can make it myself—" I began.

But, "Corwin," he said, ignoring my words, "there does appear to be a small irregularity out toward the middle of the Pattern. It does not look like something that belongs . . ."

"Where?"

He pointed and I followed the gesture.

There was some foreign object near the center. A stick? A stone? A stray bit of paper . . . ? It was impossible to tell from this distance.

"I see it," I said.

We dismounted and headed toward Random, who by then was crouched at the extreme right of the figure, examining the discoloration.

"Ganelon's spotted something out toward the center," I said.

Random nodded.

"I've noticed it," he replied. "I was just trying to decide on the best way to head out for a better look. I do not relish the notion of walking a broken Pattern. On the other hand, I was wondering what I would be laying myself open to if I tried heading in across the blackened area. What do you think?"

"Walking what there is of the Pattern would take some time," I said, "if the resistance is on par with what it is at home. Also, we have been taught that it is death to stray from it—and this setup would force me to leave it when I reach the blot. On the other hand, as you say, I might be alerting our enemies by treading on the black. So—"

"So neither of you is going to do it," Ganelon interrupted. "I am."

Then, without waiting for a reply, he took a running leap into the black sector, raced along it toward the center, paused long enough to pick up some small object, turned and headed back.

Moments later, he stood before us.

"That was a risky thing to do," Random said.

He nodded.

"But you two would still be debating it if I hadn't." He raised his hand and extended it. "Now, what do you make of this?"

He was holding a dagger. Impaled on it was a rectangle of stained pasteboard. I took them from him.

"Looks like a Trump," Random said.

"Yes."

I worked the card loose, smoothed down the torn sections. The man I regarded upon it was half familiar—meaning of course that he was also half strange. Light, straight hair, a trifle sharp-featured, a small smile, somewhat slight of build.

I shook my head.

"I do not know him," I said.

"Let me see."

Random took the card from me, frowned at it.

"No," he said after a time. "I don't either. It almost seems as though I should, but . . . No."

At that moment, the horses renewed their complaints much more forcefully. And we needed but turn part way to learn the cause of their discomfort, in that it had chosen that moment to emerge from the cave.

"Damn," said Random.

I agreed with him.

Ganelon cleared his throat, took forth his blade.

"Anyone know what it is?" he asked quietly.

My first impression of the beast was that it was snakelike, both from its movements and because of the fact that its long thick tail seemed more a continuation of its long thin body than a mere appendage. It moved on four double-jointed legs, however, large-footed and wickedly clawed. Its narrow head was beaked, and it swung from side to side as it advanced, showing us one pale blue eye and then the other. Large wings were folded against its sides, purple and leathery. It possessed neither hair nor feathers, though there were scaled areas across its breast, shoulders, back, and along the length of its tail. From beak-bayonet to twisting tail-tip it seemed a little over three meters. There was a small tinkling sound as it moved, and I caught a flash of something bright at its throat.

"Closest thing I know," said Random, "is a heraldic beast—the griffin. Only this one is bald and purple."

"Definitely not our national bird," I added, drawing Grayswandir and swinging its point into line with the creature's head.

The beast darted a red, forked tongue. It raised its wings a few inches, then let them fall. When its head swung to the right its tail moved to the left, then left and right, right and left—producing a near-hypnotic, flowing effect as it advanced.

It seemed more concerned with the horses than with us, however, for its course was directed well past us toward the spot where our mounts stood quivering and stamping. I moved to interpose myself.

At that point, it reared.

Its wings went up and out, spreading like a pair of slack sails suddenly caught by a gust of wind. It was back on its hind legs and towering above us, seeming to occupy at least four times the space it had previously. And then it shrieked, a god-awful, hunting scream or challenge that left my ears ringing. With that, it snapped those wings downward and sprang, becoming temporarily airborne.

The horses bolted and ran. The beast was beyond our reach. It was only then that I realized what the bright flash and the tinkling had represented. The thing was tethered, by means of a long chain running back into the cave. The exact length of its leash was immediately a question of more than academic interest.

I turned as it passed, hissing, flapping, and falling, beyond us. It had not possessed sufficient momentum to obtain true flight in that brief rush upward. I saw that Star and Firedrake were retreating toward the far end of the oval. Random's mount Iago, on the other hand, had bolted in the direction of the Pattern.

The beast touched ground again, turned as if to pursue Iago, appeared to study us once more, and froze. It was much nearer this time—under four meters—and it cocked its head, showing us its right eye, then opened its beak and made a soft cawing noise.

"What say we rush it now?" said Random.

"No. Wait. There is something peculiar about its behavior."

It had dropped its head while I was speaking, spreading its wings downward. It struck the ground three times with its beak and looked up again. Then it drew its wings part way back toward its body. Its tail twitched once, then swung more vigorously from side to side. It opened its beak and repeated the cawing sound.

At that moment we were distracted.

Iago had entered the Pattern, well to the side of the darkened area. Five or six meters into it, standing obliquely across the lines of power, he was caught near one of the Veil points like an insect on a piece of flypaper. He cried loudly as the sparks came up about him and his mane rose and stood erect.

Immediately, the sky began to darken directly overhead. But it was no cloud of water vapor which had begun to coalesce. Rather, it was a perfectly circular formation which had appeared, red at the center, yellow nearer the edges, turning in a clockwise direction. A sound like a single bell chime followed by the growl of a bull-roarer suddenly came to our ears.

Iago continued his struggles, first freeing his right front foot, then entangling it again as he freed the left, neighing wildly the while. The sparks were up to his shoulders by then, and he shook them like raindrops from his body and neck, his entire form taking on a soft, buttery glow.

The roaring increased in volume and small lightnings began to play at the heart of the red thing above us. A rattling noise caught my attention at that moment, and I glanced downward to discover that the purple griffin had slithered past and moved to interpose itself between us and the loud red phenomenon. It crouched like a gargoyle, facing away from us, watching the spectacle.

Just then, Iago freed both front feet and reared. There was something insubstantial about him by then, what with his brightness and the spark-shot indistinctness of his outline. He might have neighed at that moment, but all other sounds were submerged by the incessant roar from above.

A funnel descended from the noisy formation—bright, flashing, wailing now, and tremendously fast. It touched the rearing horse, and for a moment his outline expanded enormously, becoming increasingly tenuous in direct proportion to this effect. And then he was gone. For a brief interval, the funnel remained stationary, like a perfectly balanced top. Then the sound began to diminish.

The trunk raised itself, slowly, to a point but a small distance—perhaps the height of a man—above the Pattern. Then it snapped upward as quickly as it had descended.

The wailing ceased. The roaring began to subside. The miniature lightnings faded within the circle. The entire formation began to pale and slow. A moment later, it was but a bit of darkness; another moment and it was gone.

No trace of Iago remained anywhere that I could see.

"Don't ask me," I said when Random turned toward me. "I don't know either."

He nodded, then directed his attention toward our purple companion, who was just then rattling his chain.

"What about Charlie here?" he asked, fingering his blade.

"I had the distinct impression he was trying to protect us," I said, taking a step forward. "Cover me. I want to try something."

"You sure you can move fast enough?" he asked. "With that side . . ."

"Don't worry," I said, a trifle more heartily than necessary, and I kept moving.

He was correct about my left side, where the healing knife wound still ached dully and seemed to exercise a drag on my movements. But Grayswandir was still in my right hand and this was one of those occasions when my trust in my instincts was running high. I had relied on this feeling in the past with good results. There are times when such gambles just seem to be in order.

Random moved ahead and to the right. I turned sidewise and extended my left hand as you would in introducing yourself to a strange dog, slowly. Our heraldic companion had risen from its crouch and was turning.

It faced us again and studied Ganelon, off to my left. Then it regarded my hand. It lowered its head and repeated the ground-striking movement, cawed very softly—a small, bubbling sound—raised its head and slowly extended it. It wagged its great tail, touched my fingers with its beak, then repeated the performance. Carefully, I placed my hand on its head. The wagging increased; its head remained motionless. I scratched it gently about the neck and it turned its head slowly then, as if enjoying it. I withdrew my hand and dropped back a pace.

"I think we're friends," I said softly. "Now you try it, Random."

"Are you kidding?"

"No, I'm sure you're safe. Try it."

"What will you do if you are wrong?"

"Apologize."

"Great."

He advanced and offered his hand. The beast remained friendly.

"All right," he said half a minute or so later, still stroking its neck, "what have we proved?"

"That he is a watchdog."

"What is he watching?"

"The Pattern, apparently."

"Offhand then," said Random, moving back, "I would say that his work leaves something to be desired." He gestured at the dark area. "Which is understandable, if he is this friendly to anyone who doesn't eat oats and whinny."

"My guess is that he is quite selective. It is also possible that he was set here after the damage was done, to defend against further unappreciated activity."

"Who set him?"

"I'd like to know myself. Someone on our side, apparently."

"You can now test your theory further by letting Ganelon approach him."

Ganelon did not move.

"It may be you have a family smell about you," he finally said, "and he only favors Amberites. So I will pass, thank you."

"All right. It is not that important. Your guesses have been good so far. How do you interpret events?"

"Of the two factions out for the throne," he said, "that composed of Brand, Fiona, and Bleys was, as you said, more aware of the nature of the forces that play about Amber. Brand did not supply you with particulars—unless you omitted some incidents he might have related—but my guess is that this damage to the Pattern represents the means by which their allies gained access to your realm. One or more of them did that damage, which provided the dark route. If the watchdog here responds to a family smell or some other identifying information you all possess, then he could actually have been here all along and not seen fit to move against the despoilers."

"Possibly," Random observed. "Any idea how it was accomplished?"

"Perhaps," he replied. "I will let you demonstrate it for me, if you are willing."

"What does it involve?"

"Come this way," he said, turning and heading over to the edge of the Pattern.

I followed him. Random did the same. The watchgriffin slunk at my side.

Ganelon turned and extended his hand.

"Corwin, may I trouble you for that dagger I fetched us?"

"Here," I said, drawing it from my belt and passing it over.

"I repeat, what does it involve?" Random inquired.

"The blood of Amber," Ganelon replied.

"I am not so sure I like this idea," Random said.

"All you have to do is prick your finger with it," he said, extending the blade, "and let a drop fall upon the Pattern."

"What will happen?"

"Let's try it and see."

Random looked at me.

"What do you say?" he asked.

"Go ahead. Let's find out. I'm intrigued."

He nodded.

"Okay."

He received the blade from Ganelon and nicked the tip of his left little finger. He squeezed the finger then, holding it above the Pattern. A tiny red bead appeared, grew larger, quivered, fell.

Immediately, a wisp of smoke rose from the spot where it struck, accompanied by a tiny crackling noise.

"I'll be damned!" said Random, apparently fascinated.

A tiny stain had come into being, gradually spreading to about the size of a half dollar.

"There you are," said Ganelon. "That is how it was done."

The stain was indeed a miniature counterpart of the massive blot further to our right. The watchgriffin gave forth a small shriek and drew back, rapidly turning his head from one of us to the other.

"Easy, fellow. Easy," I said, reaching out and calming him once more.

"But what could have caused such a large—" Random began, and then he nodded slowly.

"What indeed?" said Ganelon. "I see no mark to show where your horse was destroyed.

"The blood of Amber," Random said. "You are just full of insights today, aren't you?"

"Ask Corwin to tell you of Lorraine, the place where I dwelled for so long," he said, "the place where the dark circle grew. I am alert to the effects of these powers, though I knew them then only at a dis-

tance. These matters have become clearer to me with each new thing
I have learned from you. Yes, I have insights now that I know more
of these workings. Ask Corwin of the mind of his general."

"Corwin," Random said, "give me the pierced Trump."

I withdrew it from my pocket and smoothed it. The stains seemed
more ominous now. Another thing also struck me. I did not believe
that it had been executed by Dworkin, sage, mage, artist, and one-
time mentor to the children of Oberon. It had not occurred to me
until that moment that anyone else might be capable of producing
one. While the style of this one did seem somehow familiar, it was
not his work. Where had I seen that deliberate line before, less spon-
taneous than the master's, as though every movement had been totally intellectualized before the pen touched the paper? And there
was something else wrong with it—a quality of idealization of a
different order from that of our own Trumps, almost as if the artist
had been working with old memories, glimpses, or descriptions
rather than a living subject.

"The Trump, Corwin. If you please," Random said.

There was that about the way in which he said it to make me hesitate. It gave rise to the feeling that he was somehow a jump ahead of
me on something important, a feeling which I did not like at all.

"I've petted old ugly here for you, and I've just bled for the cause,
Corwin. Now let's have it."

I handed it over, my uneasiness increasing as he held it in his hand
and furrowed his brow. Why was I suddenly the stupid one? Does a
night in Tir-na Nog'th slow cerebration? Why—

Random began to curse, a string of profanities unsurpassed by
anything encountered in my long military career.

Then, "What is it?" I said. "I don't understand."

"The blood of Amber," he finally said. "Whoever did it walked the
Pattern first, you see. Then they stood there at the center and contacted him via this Trump. When he responded and a firm contact
was achieved, they stabbed him. His blood flowed upon the Pattern,
obliterating that part of it, as mine did here."

He was silent for the space of several deep breaths.

"It smacks of a ritual," I said.

"Damn rituals!" he said. "Damn all of them! One of them is going
to die, Corwin. I am going to kill him—or her."

"I still do not—"

"I am a fool," he said, "for not seeing it right away. Look! Look closely!"

He thrust the pierced Trump at me. I stared. I still did not see.

"Now look at me!" he said. "See me!"

I did. Then I looked back at the card.

I realized what he meant.

"I was never anything to him but a whisper of life in the darkness. But they used my son for this," he said. "That has to be a picture of Martin."

II

Standing there beside the broken Pattern, regarding a picture of the man who may or may not have been Random's son, who may or may not have died of a knife wound received from a point within the Pattern, I turned and took a giant step back within my mind for an instant replay of the events which had brought me to this point of peculiar revelation. I had learned so many new things recently that the occurrences of the past few years seemed almost to constitute a different story than they had while I was living them. Now this new possibility and a number of things it implied had just shifted the perspective again.

I had not even been aware of my name when I had awakened in Greenwood, that private hospital in upstate New York where I had spent two totally blank weeks subsequent to my accident. It was only recently that I had been told that the accident itself had been engineered by my brother Bleys, immediately following my escape from the Porter Sanitarium in Albany. I got this story from my brother Brand, who had railroaded me into Porter in the first place, by means of fake psychiatric evidence. At Porter, I had been subjected to electroshock therapy over the span of several days, results ambiguous but presumably involving the return of a few memories. Apparently, this was what had scared Bleys into making the attempt on my life at the time of my escape, shooting out a couple of my tires on a curve above a lake. This doubtless would have resulted in my death, had Brand not been a step behind Bleys and out to protect his insurance investment, me. He said he had gotten word to the cops, dragged me out of the lake, and administered first aid until help arrived. Shortly after that, he was captured by his former partners—Bleys and our sister Fiona—who confined him in a guarded tower in a distant place in Shadow.

There had been two cabals, plotting and counterplotting after the throne, treading on one another's heels, breathing down one another's necks, and doing anything else to one another that might suggest itself at that range. Our brother Eric, backed by brothers Julian and Caine, had been preparing to take the throne, long left vacant by the unexplained absence of our father, Oberon. Unexplained to Eric, Julian, and Caine, that is. To the other group, consisting of Bleys, Fiona, and—formerly—Brand, it was not unexplained because they were responsible for it. They had arranged for this state of affairs to come into being in order to open the way for Bleys's accession to the throne. But Brand had committed a tactical error in attempting to obtain Caine's assistance in their play for the throne, in that Caine decided a better deal obtained in upholding Eric's part. This left Brand under close scrutiny, but did not immediately result in the betrayal of his partners' identities. At about that time, Bleys and Fiona decided to employ their secret allies against Eric. Brand had demurred in this, fearing the strength of those forces, and as a result had been rejected by Bleys and Fiona. With everyone on his back then, he had sought to upset the balance of powers completely by journeying to the shadow Earth where Eric had left me to die centuries before. It was only later that Eric had learned that I had not died but was possessed of total amnesia, which was almost as good, but set sister Flora to watch over my exile, and hoped that that was the last of it. Brand later told me he had gotten me committed to Porter in a desperate move to restore my memory as a preliminary to my return to Amber.

While Fiona and Bleys had been dealing with Brand, Eric had been in touch with Flora. She had arranged for my transfer to Greenwood from the clinic to which the police had taken me, with instructions to keep me narcotized, while Eric began arrangements for his coronation in Amber. Shortly thereafter, our brother Random's idyllic existence in Texorami was broken when Brand managed to send him a message outside the normal family channels— i.e., the Trumps—requesting deliverance. While Random, who was blissfully nonpartisan in the power struggle, was about this business, I managed to deliver myself from Greenwood, still relatively unmemoried. Having obtained Flora's address from Greenwood's frightened director, I betook myself to her place in Westchester, engaged in some elaborate bluffing, and moved in as a house guest. Random, in the meantime, had been less than successful in his attempt to rescue Brand. Slaying the snaky warden of the tower, he had had to flee its inner guards, utilizing one of the region's strangely mobile rocks. The guards, a hardy band of not quite human guys, had succeeded in pursuing him through Shadow, however, a feat normally impossible for most non-Amberites. Random had fled then to the shadow Earth where I was guiding Flora along the paths of misunderstanding while attempting to locate the proper route to enlightenment as to my own circumstances. Crossing the continent in response to my assurance that he would be under my protection, Random had come believing that his pursuers were my own creatures. When I helped him destroy them he was puzzled but unwilling to raise the issue while I seemed engaged in some private maneuver throneward. In fact, he had easily been tricked into conveying me back to Amber through Shadow.

This venture had proved beneficial in some respects while much less satisfactory in others. When I had finally revealed the true state of my personal situation, Random and our sister Deirdre, whom we had encountered along the way, conducted me to Amber's mirror-city within the sea, Rebma. There I had walked the image of the Pattern and recovered the bulk of my memories as a result—thereby also settling the issue as to whether I was the real Corwin or merely one of his shadows. From Rebma I had traveled into Amber, utilizing the power of the Pattern to effect an instantaneous journey home. After fighting an inconclusive duel with Eric, I had fled via the Trumps into the keeping of my beloved brother and would-be assassin, Bleys.

I joined with Bleys in an attack on Amber, a mismanaged affair which we had lost. Bleys vanished during the final engagement, under circumstances which looked likely to prove fatal but, the more that I learned and thought about it, probably had not. This left me to become Eric's prisoner and an unwilling party to his coronation, after which he had had me blinded and locked away. A few years in the dungeons of Amber had seen a regeneration of my eyes, in direct proportion to the deterioration of my state of mind. It was only the accidental appearance of Dad's old adviser Dworkin, worse off mentally than myself, which had led to a way of escape.

After that, I set about recovering and I resolved to be more prudent the next time I went after Eric. I journeyed through Shadow toward an old land where I had once reigned—Avalon—with plans to obtain there a substance of which I alone among Amberites was aware, a chemical unique in its ability to undergo detonation in Amber. En route, I had passed through the land of Lorraine, there encountering my old exiled Avalonian general Ganelon, or someone very much like him. I remained because of a wounded knight, a girl, and a local menace peculiarly similar to a thing occurring in the vicinity of Amber herself—a growing black circle somehow related to the black road our enemies traveled, a thing for which I held myself partly responsible because of a curse I had pronounced at the time of my blinding. I won the battle, lost the girl, and traveled on to Avalon with Ganelon.

The Avalon we reached, we quickly learned, was under the protection of my brother Benedict, who had been having troubles of his own with a situation possibly akin to the black circle/black road menaces. Benedict had lost his right arm in the final engagement, but had been victorious in his battle with the hellmaids. He had warned me to keep my intentions toward Amber and Eric pure, and had then allowed us the hospitality of his manor while he remained for a few days more in the field. It was at his place that I met Dara.

Dara told me she was Benedict's great-granddaughter, whose existence had been kept secret from Amber. She drew me out as far as she could on Amber, the Pattern, the Trumps, and our ability to walk in Shadow. She was also an extremely skilled fencer. We indulged in a bit of casual lovemaking on my return from a hellride to a place where I obtained a sufficient quantity of rough diamonds to pay for the things I was going to need for my assault on Amber. The following day, Ganelon and I picked up our supply of the necessary chemicals and departed for the shadow Earth where I had spent my exile, there to obtain automatic weapons and ammunition manufactured to my specifications.

En route, we had some difficulties along the black road, which seemed to have extended its scope of influence among the worlds of Shadow. We were equal to the troubles it presented, but I almost perished in a duel with Benedict, who had pursued as through a wild hellride. Too angry for argument, he had fought me through a small wood—still a better man than I, even wielding his blade lefthanded. I had only managed to best him by means of a trick involving a property of the black road of which he was unaware. I had been convinced that he wanted my blood because of the affair with Dara. But no. In the few words that passed between us he denied any knowledge of the existence of such a person. Instead, he had come after us convinced that I had murdered his servants. Now, Ganelon had indeed located some fresh corpses in the wood at Benedict's place, but we had agreed to forget about them, having no idea as to their identities and no desire to complicate our existence any further.

Leaving Benedict in the care of brother Gérard, whom I had summoned via his Trump from Amber, Ganelon and I proceeded to the shadow Earth, armed ourselves, recruited a strike force in Shadow, and headed off to attack Amber. But upon our arrival we discovered that Amber was already under attack by creatures which had come in along the black road. My new weapons quickly turned the tide in Amber's favor, and my brother Eric died in that battle, leaving me his problems, his ill will, and the Jewel of Judgment—a weather-controlling weapon he had used against me when Bleys and I had attacked Amber.

At that point, Dara showed up, swept on by us, rode into Amber, found her way to the Pattern, and proceeded to walk it—prima-facie evidence that we were indeed somehow related. During the course of this ordeal, however, she had exhibited what appeared to be peculiar physical transformations. Upon completion of the Pattern, she announced that Amber would be destroyed. Then she had vanished.

About a week later, brother Caine was murdered, under conditions arranged to show me as the culprit. The fact that I had slain his slayer was hardly satisfactory evidence of my innocence, in that the guy was necessarily in no condition to talk about it. Realizing, however, that I had seen his like before, in the persons of those creatures who had pursued Random into Flora's home, I finally found time to sit down with Random and hear the story of his unsuccessful attempt to rescue Brand from his tower.

Random, subsequent to my leaving him in Rebma years before, when I had journeyed to Amber to fight my duel with Eric, had been forced by Rebma's queen, Moire, to marry a woman of her court: Vialle, a lovely blind girl. This was partly intended as a punishment for Random, who years before had left Moire's late daughter Morganthe pregnant with Martin, the apparent subject of the damaged Trump Random now held in his hands. Strangely, for Random, he appeared to have fallen in love with Vialle, and he now resided with her in Amber.

After I left Random, I fetched the Jewel of Judgment and took it down to the chamber of the Pattern. There, I followed the partial instructions I had received for purposes of attuning it to my use. I underwent some unusual sensations during the process and was successful in obtaining control of its most obvious function: the ability to direct meteorological phenomena. After that, I questioned Flora concerning my exile. Her story seemed reasonable and jibed with those facts I did possess, although I had the feeling she was holding back somewhat on events at the time of my accident. She did promise to identify Caine's slayer as one of the same sort as those individuals Random and I had fought at her home in Westchester, however, and she assured me of her support in anything I might currently be about.

At the time I had heard Random's story, I was still unaware of the two factions and their machinations. I decided then that if Brand were still living, his rescue was of first importance, if for no other reason than the fact that he obviously possessed information that someone did not want circulated. I hit on a scheme for achieving this, the trial of which was only postponed for the time required by Gérard and myself for returning Caine's body to Amber. Part of this time, however, was appropriated by Gérard for purposes of beating me unconscious, just in case I had forgotten he was capable of the feat, to add weight to his words when he informed me that he would personally kill me should it turn out that I was the author of Amber's present woes. It was the most exclusive closed circuit fight I knew of, viewed by the family via Gérard's Trump—an act of insurance should I actually be the culprit and have a mind to erase his name from the list of the living because of his threat. We journeyed on to the Grove of the Unicorn then and exhumed Caine. At that time, we actually caught a brief glimpse of the legendary unicorn of Amber.

That evening we met in the library of the palace in Amber—we being Random, Gérard, Benedict, Julian, Deirdre, Fiona, Flora, Llewella, and myself. There we tested my idea for finding Brand. It amounted to all nine of us simultaneously attempting to reach him via his Trump. And we succeeded.

We contacted him and were successful in transporting him back to Amber. In the midst of the excitement, however, with all of us crowded about as Gérard bore him through, someone planted a dagger in Brand's side. Gérard immediately elected himself attending physician and cleared the room.

The rest of us moved to a downstairs sitting room, there to backbite and discuss events. During this time, Fiona advised me that the Jewel of Judgment might represent a hazard in situations of prolonged exposure, suggesting the possibility that it, rather than his wounds, might have been the cause of Eric's death. One of the first signs, she believed, was a distortion of one's time-sense—an apparent slowdown of temporal sequence, actually representing a speed-up of physiological events. I resolved to be more cautious with it, in that she was more conversant with these matters than the rest of us, having once been an advanced pupil of Dworkin's.

And perhaps she was correct. Perhaps there was such an effect in operation later that evening when I returned to my own quarters. At least, it seemed as if the person who attempted to kill me was moving a trifle more slowly than I would have myself under similar circumstances. At that, the stroke was almost successful. The blade caught me in the side and the world went away.

Leaking life, I awoke in my old bed in my old home on the shadow Earth where I had dwelled for so long as Carl Corey. How I had been returned, I had no idea. I crawled outside and into a blizzard. Clinging precariously to consciousness, I cached the Jewel of Judgment in my old compost heap, for the world did indeed seem to be slowing down about me. Then I made it to the road, to try flagging down a passing motorist.

It was a friend and former neighbor, Bill Roth, who found me there and drove me to the nearest clinic. There, I was treated by the same doctor who had attended me years before, at the time of my accident. He suspected I might be a psychiatric case, as the old record did reflect that faked state of affairs.

Bill showed up later, however, and set a number of things right. An attorney, he had grown curious at the time of my disappearance and done some investigating. He had learned about my fake certification and my successive escapes. He even possessed details on these matters and on the accident itself. He still felt there was something strange about me, but it did not really bother him that much.

Later, Random contacted me via my Trump and advised me that Brand had come around and was asking for me. With Random's assistance, I returned to Amber. I went to see Brand. It was then that I learned of the nature of the power struggle which had been going on about me, and the identities of the participants. His story, together with what Bill had told me back on the shadow Earth, finally brought some sense and coherence to occurrences of the past several years. He also told me more concerning the nature of the danger we currently faced.

I did nothing the following day, ostensibly for purposes of preparing myself for a visit to Tir-na Nog'th, actually to buy additional time in which to recover from my injury. This commitment made, however, it had to be kept. I did journey to the city in the sky that night, encountering a confusing collection of signs and portents, signifying perhaps nothing, and collecting a peculiar mechanical arm from the ghost of my brother Benedict while I was about it.

Returned from this excursion on high, I breakfasted with Random and Ganelon before setting out across Kolvir to return home. Slowly, bewilderingly, the trail began to change about us. It was as though we were walking in Shadow, a well-nigh impossible feat this near to Amber. When we reached this conclusion, we tried to alter our course, but neither Random nor I were able to affect the changing scene. About that time, the unicorn put in an appearance. It seemed to want us to follow it. We did.

It had led us through a kaleidoscopic series of changes, until finally we arrived at this place, where it abandoned us to our present devices. Now, with this entire sequence of events tumbling through my head, my mind moved about the peripheries, pushed its way forward, returned to the words Random had just spoken. I felt that I was slightly ahead of him once more. For how long this state of affairs might last, I did not know, but I realized where I had seen work by the same hand which had executed the pierced Trump.

Brand had often painted when he was entering one of his melancholy periods, and his favorite techniques came to mind as I recalled canvas after canvas he had brightened or darkened. Add to this his campaign of years before to obtain recollections and descriptions from everyone who had known Martin. While Random had not recognized his style, I wondered how long it might be before he began thinking as I just had about the possible ends of Brand's information gathering. Even if his hand had not actually propelled the blade, Brand was party to the act by providing the means. I knew Random well enough to know that he meant what he had said. He would try to kill Brand as soon as he saw the connection. This was going to be more than awkward.

It had nothing to do with the fact that Brand had probably saved my life. I figured I had squared accounts with him by getting him out of that damned tower. No. It was neither indebtedness nor sentiment that caused me to cast about for ways to mislead Random or slow him down. It was the naked, frigid fact that I needed Brand. He had seen to that. My reason for saving him was no more altruistic than his had been in dragging me out of the lake. He possessed something

I needed now: information. He had realized this immediately and he was rationing it—his life's union dues.

"I do see the resemblance," I said to Random, "and you may well be right about what happened."

"Of course I am right."

"It is the card that was pierced," I said.

"Obviously. I don't—"

"He was not brought through on the Trump, then. The person who did it therefore made contact, but was unable to persuade him to come across."

"So? The contact had progressed to a point of sufficient solidity and proximity that he was able to stab him anyway. He was probably even able to achieve a mental lock and hold him where he was while he bled. The kid probably hadn't had much experience with the Trumps."

"Maybe yes, maybe no," I said. "Llewella or Moire might be able to tell us how much he knew about the Trumps, But what I was getting at was the possibility that contact could have been broken before death. If he inherited your regenerative abilities he might have survived."

"Might have? I don't want guesses! I want answers!"

I commenced a balancing act within my mind. I believed I knew something that he did not, but then my source was not the best. Also, I wanted to keep quiet about the possibility because I had not had a chance to discuss it with Benedict. On the other hand, Martin was Random's son, and I did want to direct his attention away from Brand.

"Random, I may have something," I said.

"What?"

"Right after Brand was stabbed," I said, "when we were talking together in the sitting room, do you remember when the conversation turned to the subject of Martin?"

"Yes. Nothing new came up."

"I had something I might have added at that time, but I restrained myself because everyone was there. Also, because I wanted to pursue it in private with the party concerned."

"Who?"

"Benedict."

"Benedict? What has he to do with Martin?"

"I do not know. That is why I wanted to keep it quiet until I found out. And my source of information was a touchy one, at that."

"Go ahead."

"Dara. Benedict gets mad as hell whenever I mention her name, but so far a number of things she told me have proved correct—things like the journey of Julian and Gérard along the black road, their injury, their stay in Avalon. Benedict admitted these things had happened."

"What did she say about Martin?"

Indeed. How to phrase it without giving away the show on Brand . . . ? Dara had said that Brand had visited Benedict a number of times in Avalon, over a span of years. The time differential between Amber and Avalon is such that it seemed likely now that I thought about it, that the visits fell into the period when Brand was so actively seeking information on Martin. I had wondered what kept drawing him back there, since he and Benedict had never been especially chummy.

"Only that Benedict had had a visitor named Martin, whom she thought was from Amber," I lied.

"When?"

"Some while back. I'm not sure."

"Why didn't you tell me this before?"

"It is not really very much—and besides, you had never seemed especially interested in Martin."

Random shifted his gaze to the griffin, crouched and gurgling on my right, then nodded.

"I am now," he said. "Things change. If he is still alive, I would like to get to know him. If he is not . . ."

"Okay," I said. "The best way to be about either one is to start figuring a way to get home. I believe we have seen what we were supposed to see and I would like to clear out."

"I was thinking about that," he said, "and it occurred to me that we could probably use this Pattern for that purpose. Just head out to the center and transfer back."

"Going in along the dark area?" I asked.

"Why not? Ganelon has already tried it and he's okay."

"A moment," said Ganelon. "I did not say that it was easy, and I am positive you could not get the horses to go that route."

"What do you mean?" I said.

"Do you remember that place where we crossed the black road—back when we were fleeing Avalon?"

"Of course."

"Well, the sensations I experienced in retrieving the card and the dagger were not unlike the upset that came over us at that time. It is one of the reasons I was running so fast. I would favor trying the Trumps again first, under the theory that this point is congruent with Amber."

I nodded.

"All right. We might as well try making it as easy as we can. Let's collect the horses first."

We did this, learning the length of the griffin's leash while we were about it. He was drawn up short about thirty meters from the cave mouth, and immediately set up a bleating complaint. This did not make the job of pacifying the horses any easier, but it did give rise to a peculiar notion which I decided to keep to myself.

Once we had things under control, Random located his Trumps and I brought out my own.

"Let's try for Benedict," he said.

"All right. Any time now."

I noticed immediately that the cards felt cold again, a good sign. I shuffled out Benedict's and began the preliminaries. Beside me, Random did the same.

Contact came almost at once.

"What is the occasion?" Benedict asked, his eyes moving over Random, Ganelon, and the horses, then meeting with my own.

"Will you bring us through?" I said.

"Horses, too?"

"The works."

"Come ahead."

He extended his hand and I touched it. We all moved toward him. Moments later, we stood with him in a high, rocky place, a chill wind ruffling our garments, the sun of Amber past midday in a sky full of clouds. Benedict wore a stiff leather jacket and buckskin leggings. His shirt was a faded yellow. An orange cloak concealed the stump of his right arm. He tightened his long jaw and peered down at me.

"Interesting spot you hie from," he said. "I glimpsed something of the background."

I nodded.

"Interesting view from this height, also," I said, noting the spyglass at his belt at the same time that I realized we stood on the wide ledge of rock from which Eric had commanded battle on the day of his death and my return. I moved to regard the dark swath through Garnath, far below and stretching off to the horizon.

"Yes," he said. "The black road appears to have stabilized its boundaries at most points. At a few others though, it is still widening. It is almost as if it is nearing a final conformity with some—pattern. . . . Now tell me, from what point have you journeyed?"

"I spent last night in Tir-na Nog'th," I said, "and this morning we went astray in crossing Kolvir."

"Not an easy thing to do," he said. "Getting lost on your own mountain. You keep heading east, you know. That is the direction from which the sun has been known to take its course."

I felt my face flush.

"There was an accident," I said, looking away. "We lost a horse."

"What sort of accident?"

"A serious one—for the horse."

"Benedict," said Random, suddenly looking up from what I realized to be the pierced Trump, "what can you tell me concerning my son Martin?"

Benedict studied him for several moments before he spoke. Then, "Why the sudden interest?" he asked.

"Because I have reason to believe he may be dead," he said. "If that is the case, I want to avenge it. If it is not the case—well, the thought that it might be has caused me some upset. If he is still living, I would like to meet him and talk with him."

"What makes you think he might be dead?"

Random glanced at me. I nodded.

"Start with breakfast," I said.

"While he is doing that, I'll find us lunch," said Ganelon, rummaging in one of the bags.

"The unicorn showed us the way . . ." Random began.

III

We sat in silence. Random had finished speaking and Benedict was staring skyward over Garnath. His face betrayed nothing. I had long ago learned to respect his silence.

At length, he nodded, once, sharply, and turned to regard Random.

"I have long suspected something of this order," he stated, "from things that Dad and Dworkin left fall over the years. I had the impression there was a primal Pattern which they had either located or created, situating our Amber but a shadow away to draw upon its forces. I never obtained any notion as to how one might travel to that place, however." He turned back toward Garnath, gesturing with his chin. "And that, you tell me, corresponds to what was done there?"

"It seems to," Random replied.

". . . Brought about by the shedding of Martin's blood?"

"I think so."

Benedict raised the Trump Random had passed him during his narration. At that time, Benedict had made no comment.

"Yes," he said now, "this is Martin. He came to me after he departed Rebma. He stayed with me a long while."

"Why did he go to you?" Random asked.

Benedict smiled faintly.

"He had to go somewhere, you know," he said. "He was sick of his position in Rebma, ambivalent toward Amber, young, free, and just come into his power through the Pattern. He wanted to get away, see new things, travel in Shadow—as we all did. I had taken him to Avalon once when he was a small boy, to let him walk on dry land of a summer, to teach him to ride a horse, to have him see a crop harvested. When he was suddenly in a position to go anywhere he would in an instant, his choices were still restricted to the few places of which he had knowledge. True, he might have dreamed up a place in that instant and gone there—creating it, as it were. But he was also aware that he still had many things to learn, to ensure his safety in Shadow. So he elected to come to me, to ask me to teach him. And I did. He spent the better part of a year at my place. I taught him to fight, taught him of the ways of the Trumps and of Shadow, instructed him in those things an Amberite must know if he is to survive."

"Why did you do all these things?" Random asked.

"Someone had to. It was me that he came to, so it was mine to do," Benedict replied. "It was not as if I were not very fond of the boy, though," he added.

Random nodded.

"You say that he was with you for almost a year. What became of him after that?"

"That wanderlust you know as well as I. Once he had obtained some confidence in his abilities, he wanted to exercise them. In the course of instructing him, I had taken him on journeys in Shadow myself, had introduced him to people of my acquaintance at various places. But there came a time when he wanted to make his own way. One day then, he bade me good-by and fared forth."

"Have you seen him since?" Random asked.

"Yes. He returned periodically, staying with me for a time, to tell me of his adventures, his discoveries. It was always clear that it was just a visit. After a time, he would get restless and depart again."

"When was the last time you saw him?"

"Several years ago, Avalon time, under the usual circumstances. He showed up one morning, stayed for perhaps two weeks, told me of the things he had seen and done, talked of the many things he wanted to do. Later, he set off once more."

"And you never heard from him again?"

"On the contrary. There were messages left with mutual friends when he would pass their way. Occasionally, he would even contact me via my Trump—"

"He had a set of the Trumps?" I broke in.

"Yes, I made him a gift of one of my extra decks."

"Did you have a Trump for him?"

He shook his head.

"I was not even aware that such a Trump existed, until I saw this one," he said, raising the card, glancing at it, and passing it back to Random. "I haven't the art to prepare one. Random, have you tried reaching him with this Trump?"

"Yes, any number of times since we came across it. Just a few minutes ago, as a matter of fact. Nothing."

"Of course that proves nothing. If everything occurred as you guessed and he did survive it, he may have resolved to block any future attempts at contact. He does know how to do that."

"Did it occur as I guessed? Do you know more about it?"

"I have an idea," Benedict said. "You see, he did show up injured at a friend's place—off in Shadow—some years ago. It was a body wound, caused by the thrust of a blade. They said he came to them in very bad shape and did not go into details as to what had occurred. He remained for a few days—until he was able to get around again—and departed before he was really fully recovered. That was the last they heard of him. The last that I did, also."

"Weren't you curious?" Random asked. "Didn't you go looking for him?"

"Of course I was curious. I still am. But a man should have the right to lead his own life without the meddling of relatives, no matter how well-intentioned. He had pulled through the crisis and he did not attempt to contact me. He apparently knew what he wanted to do. He did leave a message for me with the Tecys, saying that when I learned of what had happened I was not to worry, that he knew what he was about."

"The Tecys?" I said.

"That's right. Friends of mine off in Shadow."

I refrained from saying the things that I might. I had thought them just another part of Dara's story, for she had so twisted the truth in other areas. She had mentioned the Tecys to me as if she knew them, as if she had stayed with them—all with Benedict's knowledge. The moment did not seem appropriate, however, to tell him of my previous night's vision in Tir-na Nog'th and the things it had indicated concerning his relationship to the girl. I had not yet had sufficient time to ponder the matter and all that it implied.

Random stood, paced, paused near the ledge, his back to us, fingers knotted behind him. After a moment, he turned and stalked back.

"How can we get in touch with the Tecys?" he asked Benedict.

"No way," said Benedict, "except to go and see them."

Random turned to me.

"Corwin, I need a horse. You say that Star's been through a number of hellrides . . ."

"He's had a busy morning."

"It wasn't that strenuous. It was mostly fright, and he seems okay now. May I borrow him?"

Before I could answer, he turned toward Benedict.

"You'll take me, won't you?" he said.

Benedict hesitated.

"I do not know what more there is to learn—" he began.

"Anything! Anything at all they might remember—possibly something that did not really seem important at the time but is now, knowing what we know."

Benedict looked to me. I nodded.

"He can ride Star, if you are willing to take him."

"All right," Benedict said, getting to his feet. "I'll fetch my mount."

He turned and headed off toward the place where the great striped beast was tethered.

"Thanks, Corwin," Random said.

"I'll let you do me a favor in return."

"What?"

"Let me borrow Martin's Trump."

"What for?"

"An idea just hit me. It is too complicated to get into if you want to get moving. No harm should come of it, though."

He chewed his lip.

"Okay. I want it back when you are done with it."

"Of course."

"Will it help find him?"

"Maybe."

He passed me the card.

"You heading back to the palace now?" he asked.

"Yes."

"Would you tell Vialle what has happened and where I have gone? She worries."

"Sure. I'll do that."

"I'll take good care of Star."

"I know that. Good luck."

"Thanks."

I rode Firedrake. Ganelon walked. He had insisted. We followed the route I had taken in pursuing Dara on the day of the battle. Along with recent developments, that is probably what made me think of her again. I dusted off my feelings and examined them carefully. I realized then that despite the games she had played with me, the killings she had doubtless been privy or party to, and her stated designs upon the realm, I was still attracted to her by something more than curiosity. I was not really surprised to discover this. Things had looked pretty much the same the last time I had pulled a surprise inspection in the emotional barracks. I wondered then how much of truth there might have been to my final vision of the previous night, wherein her possible line of descent from Benedict had been stated. There was indeed a physical resemblance, and I was more than half convinced. In the ghost city, of course, the shade of Benedict had conceded as much, raising his new, strange arm in her defense . . .

"What's funny?" Ganelon asked, from where he strode to my left.

"The arm," I said, "that came to me from Tir-na Nog'th—I had worried over some hidden import, some unforeseen force of destiny to the thing, coming as it had into our world from that place of mystery and dream. Yet it did not even last the day. Nothing remained when the Pattern destroyed Iago. The entire evening's visions come to nothing."

Ganelon cleared his throat.

"Well, it wasn't exactly the way you seem to think," he said.

"What do you mean?"

"That arm device was not in Iago's saddlebag. Random stowed it your bag. That's where the food was, and after we had eaten he returned the utensils to where they had been in his own bag, but not the arm. There was no space."

"Oh," I said. "Then—"

Ganelon nodded.

"—So he has it with him now," he finished.

"The arm and Benedict both. Damn! I've small liking for that thing. It tried to kill me. No one has ever been attacked in Tir-na Nog'th before."

"But Benedict, Benedict's okay. He's on our side, even if you have some differences at the moment. Right?"

I did not answer him.

He reached up and took Firedrake's reins, drawing him to a halt. He stared up then, studying my face.

"Corwin, what happened up there, anyway? What did you learn?"

I hesitated. In truth, what had I learned in the city in the sky? No one was certain as to the mechanism behind the visions of Tir-na Nog'th. It could well be, as we have sometimes suspected, that the place simply served to objectify one's unspoken fears and desires, mixing them perhaps with unconscious guesswork. Sharing conclusions and reasonably based conjectures was one thing. Suspicions engendered by something unknown were likely better retained than given currency. Still, that arm was solid enough . . .

"I told you," I said, "that I had knocked that arm off the ghost of Benedict. Obviously, we were fighting."

"You see it then as an omen that you and Benedict will eventually be in conflict?"

"Perhaps."

"You were shown a reason for it, weren't you?"

"Okay," I said, finding a sigh without trying. "Yes. It was indicated that Dara was indeed related to Benedict—a thing which may well be correct. It is also quite possible, if it is true, that he is unaware of it. Therefore, we keep quiet about it until we can verify it or discount it. Understood?"

"Of course. But how could this thing be?"

"Just as she said."

"Great-granddaughter?"

I nodded.

"By whom?"

"The hellmaid we knew only by reputation—Lintra, the lady who cost him his arm."

"But that battle was only a recent thing."

"Time flows differently in different realms of Shadow, Ganelon. In the farther reaches—It would not be impossible."

He shook his head and relaxed his grip on the reins.

"Corwin, I really think Benedict should know about this," he said. "If it is true, you ought to give him a chance to prepare himself rather than let him discover it of a sudden. You people are such an infertile lot that paternity seems to hit you harder than it does others.

Look at Random. For years, he had disowned his son, and now—I've a feeling he'd risk his life for him."

"So do I," I said. "Now forget the first part but carry the second one a step further in the case of Benedict."

"You think he would take Dara's side against Amber?"

"I would rather avoid presenting him with the choice by not letting him know that it exists—if it exists."

"I think you do him a disservice. He is hardly an emotional infant. Get hold of him on the Trump and tell him your suspicions. That way, at least, he can be thinking about it, rather than have him risk some sudden confrontation unprepared."

"He would not believe me. You have seen how he gets whenever I mention Dara."

"That in itself may say something. Possibly he suspects what might have happened and rejects it so vehemently because he would have it otherwise."

"Right now it would just widen a rift I am trying to heal."

"Your holding back on him now may serve to rupture it completely when he finds out."

"No. I believe I know my brother better than you do."

He released the reins.

"Very well," he said. "I hope you are right."

I did not answer, but started Firedrake to moving once more. There was an unspoken understanding between us that Ganelon could ask me anything he wanted, and it also went without saying that I would listen to any advice he had to offer me. This was partly because his position was unique. We were not related. He was no Amberite. The struggles and problems of Amber were his only by choice. We had been friends and then enemies long ago, and finally, more recently, friends again and allies in a battle in his adopted land. That matter concluded, he had asked to come with me, to help me deal with my own affairs and those of Amber. As I saw it, he owed me nothing now, nor I him—if one keeps a scoreboard tally on such matters. Therefore, it was friendship alone that bound us, a stronger thing than bygone debts and points of honor: in other words, a thing which gave him the right to bug me on matters such as this, where I might have told even Random to go to hell once I had made up my mind. I realized I should not be irritated when everything that he said was tendered in good faith. Most likely it was an old military feeling, going back to our earliest relationship as well as being tied in with the present state of affairs: I do not like having my decisions and orders questioned. Probably, I decided, I was irritated even more by the fact that he had made some shrewd guesses of late, and some fairly sound suggestions based upon them—things I felt I ought to have caught myself. No one likes to admit to a resentment based on something like that. Still . . . was that all? A simple projection of dissatisfaction over a few instances of personal inadequacy? An old army reflex as to the sanctity of my decisions? Or was it something deeper that had been bothering me and was just now coming to the surface?

"Corwin," Ganelon said, "I've been doing some thinking . . ."

I sighed.

"Yes?"

". . . about Random's son. The way your crowd heals, I suppose it is possible that he might have survived and still be about."

"I would like to think so."

"Do not be too hasty."

"What do you mean?"

"I gather he had very little contact with Amber and the rest of the family, growing up in Rebma the way that he did."

"That is the way I understand it, too."

"In fact, outside of Benedict—and Llewella, back in Rebma—the only other one he apparently had contact with would have been the one who stabbed him—Bleys, Brand, or Fiona. It has occurred to me that he probably has a pretty distorted view of the family."

"Distorted," I said, "but maybe not unwarranted, if I see what you are getting at."

"I think you do. It seems conceivable that he is not only afraid of the family, but may have it in for the lot of you."

"It is possible," I said.

"Do you think he could have thrown in with the enemy?"

I shook my head.

"Not if he knows they are the tools of the crowd that tried to kill him."

"But are they? I wonder . . . ? You say Brand got scared and tried to back out of whatever arrangement they had with the black road gang. If they are that strong, I wonder whether Fiona and Bleys might not have become *their* tools? If this were the case, I could see Martin angling for something which gave him power over them."

"Too elaborate a structure of guesses," I said.

"The enemy seems to know a lot about you."

"True, but they had a couple traitors to give them lessons."

"Could they have given them everything you say Dara knew?"

"That is a good point," I said, "but it is hard to say." Except for the business about the Tecys, which occurred to me immediately. I decided to keep that to myself for the moment though, to find out what he was leading up to, rather than going off on a tangent. So, "Martin was hardly in a position to tell them much about Amber," I said.

Ganelon was silent for a moment. Then, "Have you had a chance to check on the business I asked you about that night at your tomb?" he said.

"What business?"

"Whether the Trumps could be bugged," he said. "Now that we know Martin had a deck . . ."

It was my turn to be silent while a small family of moments crossed my path, single file, from the left, sticking their tongues out at me.

"No," I said then. "I haven't had a chance."

We proceeded on for quite a distance before he said, "Corwin, the night you brought Brand back . . . ?"

"Yes?"

"You say you accounted for everyone later, in trying to figure out who it was that stabbed you, and that any of them would have been hard put to pull the stunt in the time involved."

"Oh," I said, "and oh."

He nodded.

"Now you have another relative to think about. He may lack the family finesse only because he is young and unpracticed."

Sitting there in my mind, I gestured back at the silent parade of moments that crossed between Amber and then.

IV

She asked who it was when I knocked and I told her.

"Just a moment."

I heard her footsteps and then the door swung in. Vialle is only a little over five feet tall and quite slim. Brunette, fine featured, very soft-spoken. She was wearing red. Her sightless eyes looked through me, reminding me of darkness past, of pain.

"Random," I said, "asked me to tell you that he would be delayed a little longer, but that there was nothing to worry about."

"Please come in," she said, stepping aside and drawing the door the rest of the way open.

I did. I did not want to, but I did. I had not intended to take Random's request literally—that I tell her what had happened and where he had gone. I had meant simply to tell her what I had already said, nothing more. It was not until we had ridden our separate ways that I realized exactly what Random's request had amounted to: He had just asked me to go tell his wife, to whom I had never spoken more than half a dozen words, that he had taken off to go looking for his illegitimate son—the lad whose mother, Morganthe, had committed suicide, a thing for which Random had been punished by being forced to marry Vialle. The fact that the marriage had somehow worked beautifully was something which still amazed me. I had no desire to dispense a load of awkward tidings, and as I moved into the room I sought alternatives.

I passed a bust of Random set on a high shelf on the wall to my left. I had actually gone by before it registered that my brother was indeed the subject. Across the room, I saw her workbench. Turning back, I studied the bust.

"I did not realize that you sculpted," I said.

"Yes."

Casting my gaze about the apartment, I quickly located other examples of her work.

"Quite good," I said.

"Thank you. Won't you sit down?"

I lowered myself into a large, high-armed chair, which proved more comfortable than it had looked. She seated herself on a low divan to my right, curling her legs beneath her.

"May I get you something to eat, or to drink?"

"No thanks. I can only stay a short while. What it is, is that Random, Ganelon, and I had gotten a bit sidetracked on the way home, and after that delay we met with Benedict for a time. The upshot of it was that Random and Benedict had to make another small journey."

"How long will be be away?"

"Probably overnight. Maybe a bit longer. If he is going to be much longer he will probably call back on someone's Trump, and we'll let you know."

My side began to throb and I rested my hand upon it, massaging it gently.

"Random has told me many things about you," she said.

I chuckled.

"Are you certain you would not care for something to eat? It would be no trouble."

"Did he tell you that I am always hungry?"

She laughed.

"No. But if you have been as active as you say, I would guess that you did not take time for lunch."

"In that you would be only half-correct. All right. If you've a spare piece of bread lying about it might do me some good to gnaw on it."

"Fine. Just a moment."

She rose and departed into the next room. I took the opportunity to scratch heartily all about my wound where it was suddenly itching fit to kill. I had accepted her hospitality partly for this reason and partly because of the realization that I actually was hungry. Only a little later it struck me that she could not have seen me attacking my side as I was. Her sure movements, her confident manner, had relaxed my awareness of her blindness. Good. It pleased me that she was able to carry it so well.

I heard her humming a tune: "The Ballad of the Water Crossers," the song of Amber's great merchant navy. Amber is not noted for manufacture, and agriculture has never been our forte. But our ships sail the shadows, plying between anywhere and anywhere, dealing in anything. Just about every male Amberite, noble or otherwise, spends some time in the fleet. Those of the blood laid down the trade routes long ago that other vessels might follow, the seas of a double dozen worlds in every captain's head. I had assisted in this in times gone by, and though my involvement had never been so deep as Gérard's or Caine's, I had been mightily moved by the forces of the deep and the spirit of the men who crossed it.

After a while, Vialle came in bearing a tray heavy with bread, meat, cheese, fruit, and a flask of wine. She set it upon a table near at hand.

"You mean to feed a regiment?" I asked.

"Best to be safe."

"Thanks. Won't you join me?"

"A piece of fruit, perhaps," she said.

Her fingers sought for a second, located an apple. She returned to the divan.

"Random tells me you wrote that song," she said.

"That was a very long time ago, Vialle."

"Have you composed any recently?"

I began to shake my head, caught myself, said, "No. That part of me is . . . resting."

"Pity. It is lovely."

"Random is the real musician in the family."

"Yes, he is very good. But performance and composition are two different things."

"True. One day when things have eased up . . . Tell me, are you happy here in Amber? Is everything to your liking? Is there anything that you need?"

She smiled.

"All that I need is Random. He is a good man."

I was strangely moved to hear her speak of him in this fashion.

"Then I am happy for you," I said. And, "Younger, smaller . . . he might have had it a bit rougher than the rest of us," I went on. "Nothing quite as useless as another prince when there is already a crowd of them about. I was as guilty as the rest. Bleys and I once stranded him for two days on an islet to the south of here . . ."

". . . And Gérard went and got him when he learned of it," she said. "Yes, he told me. It must bother you if you remember it after all this time."

"It must have made an impression on him, too."

"No, he forgave you long ago. He told it as a joke. Also, he drove a spike through the heel of your boot—pierced your foot when you put it on."

"Then it *was* Random! I'll be damned! I had always blamed Julian for that one."

"That one bothers Random."

"How long ago all of this was . . ." I said.

I shook my head and continued eating. Hunger seized me and she gave me several minutes of silence in which to get the upper hand on it. When I had, I felt compelled to say something.

"That is better. Much better," I began. "It was a peculiar and trying night that I spent in the sky-city."

"Did you receive omens of a useful nature?"

"I do not know how useful they might prove. On the other hand, I suppose I'd rather have had them than not. Have there been any interesting happenings hereabouts?"

"A servant tells me your brother Brand continues to rally. He ate well this morning, which is encouraging."

"True," I said. "True. It would seem he is out of danger."

"Likely. It—it is a terrible series of happenings to which you have all been subjected. I am sorry. I was hoping you might obtain some indication of an upturn in your affairs during the night you spent in Tir-na Nog'th."

"It does not matter," I said. "I am not that sure of the value of the thing."

"Then why—Oh."

I studied her with renewed interest. Her face still betrayed nothing, but her right hand twitched, tapping and plucking at the material of the divan. Then, as with a sudden awareness of its eloquence, she stilled it. She was obviously a person who had answered her own question and wished now she had done it in silence.

"Yes," I said, "I was stalling. You are aware of my injury."

She nodded.

"I am not angry with Random for having told you," I said. "His judgment has always been acute and geared to defense. I see no reason not to rely on it myself. I must inquire as to how much he has told you, however, both for your own safety and my peace of mind. For there are things I suspect but have not yet spoken."

"I understand. It is difficult to assess a negative—the things he might have left out, I mean—but he tells me most things. I know your story and most of the others'. He keeps me aware of events, suspicions, conjectures."

"Thank you," I said, taking a sip of the wine. "It makes it easier for me to speak then, seeing how things are with you. I am going to tell you everything that happened from breakfast till now . . ."

So I did.

She smiled occasionally as I spoke, but she did not interrupt. When I had finished, she asked, "You thought that mention of Martin would upset me?"

"It seemed possible," I told her.

"No," she said. "You see, I knew Martin in Rebma, when he was but a small boy. I was there while he was growing up. I liked him then. Even if he were not Random's son he would still be dear to me. I can only be pleased with Random's concern and hope that it has come in time to benefit them both."

I shook my head.

"I do not meet people like you too often," I said. "I am glad that I finally have."

She laughed, then said, "You were without sight for a long while."

"Yes."

"It can embitter a person, or it can give him a greater joy in those things which he does have."

I did not have to think back over my feelings from those days of blindness to know that I was a person of the first sort, even discounting the circumstances under which I had suffered it. I am sorry, but that is the way that I am, and I am sorry.

"True," I said. "You are fortunate."

"It is really only a state of mind—a thing a Lord of Shadow can easily appreciate."

She rose.

"I have always wondered as to your appearance," she said. "Random has described you, but that is different. May I?"

"Of course."

She approached and placed her finger tips upon my face. Delicately, she traced my features.

"Yes," she said, "you are much as I had thought you would be. And I feel the tension in you. It has been there for a long while, has it not?"

"In some form or other, I suppose, ever since my return to Amber."

"I wonder," she said. "whether you might have been happier before you regained your memory."

"It is one of those impossible questions," I said. "I might also be dead if I had not. But putting that part aside for a moment, in those times there was still a thing that drove me, that troubled me every day. I was constantly looking for ways to discover who I really was, what I was."

"But were you happier, or less happy, than you are now?"

"Neither," I said. "Things balance out. It is, as you suggested, a state of mind. And even if it were not so, I could never go back to that other life, now that I know who I am, now that I have found Amber."

"Why not?"

"Why do you ask me these things?"

"I want to understand you," she said. "Ever since I first heard of you back in Rebma, even before Random told me stories, I wondered what it was that drove you. Now I've the opportunity—no right, of course, just the opportunity—I felt it worth speaking out of turn and order beyond my station simply to ask you."

A half-chuckle caught me.

"Fairly taken," I said. "I will see whether I can be honest. Hatred drove me at first—hatred for my brother Eric—and my desire for the throne. Had you asked me on my return which was the stronger, I would have said that it was the summons of the throne. Now, though . . . now I would have to admit that it was actually the other way around. I had not realized it until this moment, but it is true. But Eric is dead and there is nothing left of what I felt then. The throne remains, but now I find that my feelings toward it are mixed. There is a possibility that none of us has a right to it under present circumstances, and even if all family objections were removed I would not take it at this time. I would have to see stability restored to the realm and a number of questions answered first."

"Even if these things showed that you may not have the throne?"

"Even so."

"Then I begin to understand."

"What? What is there to understand?"

"Lord Corwin, my knowledge of the philosophical bases of these things is limited, but it is my understanding that you are able to find anything you wish within Shadow. This has troubled me for a long while, and I never fully understood Random's explanations. If you wished, could not each of you walk in Shadow and find yourself another Amber—like this one in all respects, save that you ruled there or enjoyed whatever other status you might desire?"

"Yes, we can locate such places," I said.

"Then why is this not done, to have an end of strife?"

"It is because a place could be found which *seemed* to be the same —but that would be all. We are a part of this Amber as surely as it is a part of us. Any shadow of Amber would have to be populated with shadows of ourselves to seem worth while. We could even except the shadow of our own person should we choose to move into a ready realm. However, the shadow folk would not be exactly like the other people here. A shadow is never precisely like that which casts it. These little differences add up. They are actually worse than major ones. It would amount to entering a nation of strangers. The best mundane comparison which occurs to me is an encounter with a person who strongly resembles another person you know. You keep expecting him to act like your acquaintance; worse yet, you have a tendency to act toward him as you would toward that other. You face him with a certain mask and his responses are not appropriate. It is an uncomfortable feeling. I never enjoy meeting people who remind me of other people. Personality is the one thing we cannot control in our manipulations of Shadow. In fact, it is the means by which we can tell one another from shadows of ourselves. This is why Flora could not decide about me for so long, back on the shadow Earth: my new personality was sufficiently different."

"I begin to understand," she said. "It is not just Amber for you. It is the place plus everything else."

"The place plus everything else . . . *That* is Amber," I agreed.

"You say that your hate died with Eric and your desire for the throne has been tempered by the consideration of new things you have learned."

"That is so."

"Then I think I do understand what it is that moves you."

"The desire for stability moves me," I said, "and something of curiosity—and revenge on our enemies . . ."

"Duty," she said. "Of course."

I snorted.

"It would be comforting to put such a face on it," I said. "As it is, however, I will not be a hypocrite. I am hardly a dutiful son of Amber or of Oberon."

"Your voice makes it plain that you do not wish to be considered one."

I closed my eyes, closed them to join her in darkness, to recall for a brief while the world where other messages than light waves took precedence. I knew then that she had been right about my voice. Why had I trodden so heavily on the idea of duty as soon as it was suggested? I like credit for being good and clean and noble and high-minded when I have it coming, even sometimes when I do not—the same as the next person. What bothered me about the notion of duty to Amber? Nothing. What was it then?

Dad.

I no longer owed him anything, least of all duty. Ultimately, he was responsible for the present state of affairs. He had fathered a great brood of us without providing for a proper succession, he had been less than kind to all of our mothers and he then expected our devotion and support. He played favorites and, in fact, it even seemed he played us off against one another. He then got suckered into something he could not handle and left the kingdom in a mess. Sigmund Freud had long ago anesthetized me to any normal, generalized feelings of resentment which might operate within the family unit. I have no quarrel on those grounds. Facts are another matter. I did not dislike my father simply because he had given me no reason to like him; in truth, it seemed that he had labored in the other direction. Enough. I realized what it was that bothered me about the notion of duty: its object.

"You are right," I said, opening my eyes, regarding her, "and I am glad that you told me of it."

I rose.

"Give me your hand," I said.

She extended her right hand and I raised it to my lips.

"Thank you," I said. "It was a good lunch."

I turned and made my way to the door. When I looked back she had blushed and was smiling, her hand still partly raised, and I began to understand the change in Random.

"Good luck to you," she said, the moment my footsteps ceased.

" . . . And you," I said, and went out quickly.

I had been planning to see Brand next, but just could not bring myself to do it. For one thing, I did not want to encounter him with my wits dulled by fatigue. For another, talking with Vialle was the first pleasant thing which had happened to me in some time, and just this once I was going to quit while I was ahead.

I mounted the stairs and walked the corridor to my room, thinking, of course, of the night of the knifings as I fitted my new key to my new lock. In my bedchamber, I drew the drapes against the afternoon's light, undressed, and got into bed. As on other occasions of rest after stress with more stress pending, sleep eluded me for a time. For a long while I tossed and twisted, reliving events of the past several days and some from even farther back. When finally I slept, my dreams were an amalgam of the same material, including a spell in my old cell, scraping away at the door.

It was dark when I awoke and I actually felt rested. The tension gone out of me, my reverie was much more peaceful. In fact, there was a tiny charge of pleasant excitement dancing through the back of my head. It was a tip-of-the-tongue imperative, a buried notion that—

Yes!

I sat up. I reached for my clothes, began to dress. I buckled on Grayswandir. I folded a blanket and tucked it under my arm. Of course . . .

My mind felt clear and my side had stopped throbbing. I had no idea how long I had slept, and it was hardly worth checking at this point. I had something far more important to look into, something which should have occurred to me a long while ago—had occurred, as a matter of fact. I had actually been staring right at it once, but the crush of time and events had ground it from my mind. Until now.

I locked my room behind me and headed for the stairs. Candles flickered, and the faded stag who had been dying for centuries on the tapestry to my right looked back on the faded dogs who had been pursuing him for approximately as long. Sometimes my sympathies are with the stag; usually though, I am all dog. Have to have the thing restored one of these days.

The stairs and down. No sounds from below. Late, then. Good. Another day and we're still alive. Maybe even a trifle wiser. Wise enough to realize there are many more things we still need to know. Hope, though. There's that. A thing I lacked when I squatted in that damned cell, hands pressed against my ruined eyes, howling. Vialle . . . I wish I could have spoken with you for a few moments in those days. But I learned what I learned in a nasty school, and even a milder curriculum would probably not have given me your grace. Still . . . hard to say. I have always felt I am more dog than stag, more hunter than victim. You might have taught me something that would have blunted the bitterness, tempered the hate. But would that have been for the best? The hate died with its object and the bitterness, too, has passed—but looking back, I wonder whether I would have made it without them to sustain me. I am not at all certain that I would have survived my internment without my ugly companions to drag me back to life and sanity time and again. Now I can afford the luxury of an occasional stag-thought, but then it might have been fatal. I do not truly know, kind lady, and I doubt that I ever will.

Stillness on the second floor. A few noises from below. Sleep well, lady. Around, and down again. I wondered whether Random had uncovered anything of great moment. Probably not, or he or Benedict should have contacted me by now. Unless there was trouble. But no. It is ridiculous to shop for worries. The real thing makes itself felt in due course, and I'd more than enough to go around.

The ground floor.

"Will," I said, and, "Rolf."

"Lord Corwin."

The two guards had assumed professional stances on hearing my footsteps. Their faces told me that all was well, but I asked for the sake of form.

"Quiet, Lord. Quiet," replied the senior.

"Very good," I said, and I continued on, entering and crossing the marble dining hall.

It would work, I was sure of that, if time and moisture had not totally effaced it. And then . . .

I entered the long corridor, where the dusty walls pressed close on either side. Darkness, shadows, my footsteps . . .

I came to the door at the end, opened it, stepped out onto the platform. Then down once more, that spiraling way, a light here, a light there, into the caverns of Kolvir. Random had been right, I decided then. If you had gouged out everything, down to the level of that distant floor, there would be a close correspondence between what was left and the place of that primal Pattern we had visited this morning.

. . . On down. Twisting and winding through the gloom. The torch and lantern-lit guard station was theatrically stark within it. I reached the floor and headed that way.

"Good evening, Lord Corwin," said the lean, cadaverous figure who rested against a storage rack, smoking his pipe, grinning around it.

"Good evening, Roger. How are things in the nether world?"

"A rat, a bat, a spider. Nothing much else astir. Peaceful."

"You enjoy this duty?"

He nodded.

"I am writing a philosophical romance shot through with elements of horror and morbidity. I work on those parts down here."

"Fitting, fitting," I said. "I'll be needing a lantern."

He took one from the rack, brought it to flame from his candle.

"Will it have a happy ending?" I inquired.

He shrugged.

"I'll be happy."

"I mean, does good triumph and hero bed heroine? Or do you kill everybody off?"

"That's hardly fair," he said.

"Never mind. Maybe I'll read it one day."

"Maybe," he said.

I took the lantern and turned away, heading in a direction I had not taken in a long while. I discovered that I could still measure the echoes in my mind.

Before too long, I neared the wall, sighted the proper corridor, entered it. It was simply a matter of counting my paces then. My feet knew the way.

The door to my old cell stood partly ajar. I set down the lantern and used both hands to open it fully. It gave way grudgingly, moaning as it moved. Then I raised the lantern, held it high, and entered.

My flesh tingled and my stomach clenched itself within me. I began to shiver. I had to fight down a strong impulse to bolt and run. I had not anticipated such a reaction. I did not want to step away from that heavy brassbound door for fear that it would be slammed and bolted behind me. It was an instant close to pure terror that the small dirty cell had aroused in me. I forced myself to dwell on particulars—the hole which had been my latrine, the blackened spot where I had built my fire on that final day. I ran my left hand over the inner surface of the door, finding and tracing there the grooves I had worn while scraping away with my spoon. I remembered what the activity had done to my hands. I stooped to examine the gouging. Not nearly so deep as it had seemed at the time, not when compared to the total thickness of the door. I realized how much I had exaggerated the effects of that feeble effort toward freedom. I stepped past it and regarded the wall.

Faint. Dust and moisture had worked to undo it. But I could still discern the outlines of the lighthouse of Cabra, bordered by four slashes of my old spoon handle. The magic was still there, that force which had finally transported me to freedom. I felt it without calling upon it.

I turned and faced the other wall.

The sketch which I now regarded had fared less well than that of the lighthouse, but then it had been executed with extreme haste by the light of my last few matches. I could not even make out all of the details, though my memory furnished a few of those which were hidden: It was a view of a den or library, bookshelves lining the walls, a desk in the foreground, a globe beside the desk. I wondered whether I should risk wiping it clean.

I set my lantern on the floor, returned to the sketch on the other wall. With a corner of my blanket, I gently wiped some dust from a point near the base of the lighthouse. The line grew clearer. I wiped it again, exerting a little more pressure. Unfortunate. I destroyed an inch or so of outline.

I stepped back and tore a wide strip from the edge of the blanket. I folded what remained into a pad and seated myself on it. Slowly, carefully then, I set to work on the light-house. I had to get an exact feeling for the work before I tried cleaning the other one.

Half an hour later I stood up and stretched, bent and massaged life back into my legs. What remained of the lighthouse was clean. Unfortunately, I had destroyed about 20 per cent of the sketch before I developed a sense of the wall's texture and an appropriate stroke across it. I doubted that I was going to improve any further.

The lantern sputtered as I moved it. I unfolded the blanket, shook it out, tore off a fresh strip. Making up a new pad, I knelt before the other sketch and set to work.

A while later I had uncovered what remained of it. I had forgotten the skull on the desk until a careful stroke revealed it once again— and the angle of the far wall, and a tall candlestick. . . . I drew back. It would be risky to do any more rubbing. Probably unnecessary, also. It seemed about as entire as it had been.

The lantern was flickering once again. Cursing Roger for not checking the kerosene level, I stood and held the light at shoulder level off to my left. I put everything from my mind but the scene before me.

It gained something of perspective as I stared. A moment later and it was totally three-dimensional and had expanded to fill my entire field of vision. I stepped forward then and rested the lantern on the edge of the desk.

I cast my eyes about the place. There were bookshelves on all four walls. No windows. Two doors at the far end of the room, right and left, across from one another, one closed, the other partly ajar. There was a long, low table covered with books and papers beside the opened door. Bizarre curios occupied open spaces on the shelves and odd niches and recesses in the walls—bones, stones, pottery, inscribed tablets, lenses, wands, instruments of unknown function. The huge rug resembled an Ardebil. I took a step toward that end of the room and the lantern sputtered again. I turned and reached for it. At that moment, it failed.

I growled an obscenity and lowered my hand. Then I turned, slowly, to check for any possible light sources. Something resembling a branch of coral shone faintly on a shelf across the room and a pale line of illumination occurred at the base of the closed door. I abandoned the lantern and crossed the room.

I opened the door as quietly as I could. The room it let upon was deserted, a small, windowless living place faintly lit by the still smoldering embers in its single, recessed hearth. The room's walls were of stone and they arched above me. The fireplace was a possibly natural niche in the wall to my left. A large, armored door was set in the far wall, a big key partly turned in its lock.

I entered, taking a candle from a nearby table, and moved toward the fireplace to give it a light. As I knelt and sought a flame among the embers, I heard a soft footfall in the vicinity of the doorway.

Turning, I saw him just beyond the threshold. About five feet in height, hunchbacked. His hair and beard were even longer than I remembered. Dworkin wore a nightshirt which reached to his ankles. He carried an oil lamp, his dark eyes peering across its sooty chimney.

"Oberon," he said, "is it finally time?"

"What time is that?" I asked softly.

He chuckled.

"What other? Time to destroy the world, of course!"

V

I kept the light away from my face, kept my voice low.

"Not quite," I said. "Not quite."

He sighed.

"You remain unconvinced."

He looked forward and cocked his head, peering down at me.

"Why must you spoil things?" he said.

"I've spoiled nothing."

He lowered the lamp. I turned my head again, but he finally got a good look at my face. He laughed.

"Funny. Funny, funny, funny," he said. "You come as the young Lord Corwin, thinking to sway me with family sentiment. Why did you not choose Brand or Bleys? It was Clarissa's lot served us best."

I shrugged and stood.

"Yes and no," I said, determined now to feed him ambiguities for so long as he'd accept them and respond. Something of value might emerge, and it seemed an easy way to keep him in a good humor. "And yourself?" I continued. "What face would you put on things?"

"Why, to win your good will I'll match you," he said, and then he began to laugh.

He threw his head back, and as his laughter rang about me a change came over him. His stature seemed to increase, and his face luffed like a sail cut too close to the wind. The hump on his back was diminished as he straightened and stood taller. His features rearranged themselves and his beard darkened. By then it was obvious that he was somehow redistributing his body mass, for the nightshirt which had reached his ankles was now midway up his shins. He breathed deeply and his shoulders widened. His arms lengthened, his bulging abdomen narrowed, tapered. He reached shoulder height on me, then higher. He looked me in the eye. His garment reached only to his knees. His hump was totally resorbed. His face gave a final twist, his features steadied, were reset. His laughter fell to a chuckle, faded, closed with a smirk.

I regarded a slightly slimmer version of myself.

"Sufficient?" he inquired.

"Not half bad," I said. "Wait till I toss a couple logs on the fire."

"I will help you."

"That's all right."

I drew some wood from a rack to the right. Any stall served me somewhat, buying reactions for my study. As I was about the work, he crossed to a chair and seated himself. When I glanced at him I saw that he was not looking at me, but staring into the shadows. I drew out the fire-building, hoping that he would say something, anything. Eventually, he did.

"Whatever became of the grand design?" he asked.

I did not know whether he was speaking of the Pattern or of some master plan of Dad's to which he had been privy. So, "You tell me," I said.

He chuckled again.

"Why not? You changed your mind, that is what happened," he said.

"From what to what—as you see it?"

"Don't mock me. Even you have no right to mock me," he said. "Least of all, you."

I got to my feet.

"I was not mocking you," I said.

I crossed the room to another chair and carried it over to a position near the fire, across from Dworkin. I seated myself.

"How did you recognize me?" I asked.

"My whereabouts are hardly common knowledge."

"That is true."

"Do many in Amber think me dead?"

"Yes, and others suppose you might be traveling off in Shadow."

"I see."

"How have you been—feeling?"

He gave me an evil grin.

"Do you mean am I still mad?"

"You put it more bluntly than I care to."

"There is a fading, there is an intensifying," he said. "It comes to me and it departs again. For the moment I am almost myself—

almost, I say. The shock of your visit, perhaps . . . Something is
broken in my mind. You know that. It cannot be otherwise, though.
You know that, too."

"I suppose that I do," I said. "Why don't you tell me all about it,
all over again? Just the business of talking might make you feel
better, might give me something I've missed. Tell me a story."

Another laugh.

"Anything you like. Have you any preferences? My flight from
Chaos to this small sudden island in the sea of night? My meditations
upon the abyss? The revelation of the Pattern in a jewel hung around
the neck of a unicorn? My transcription of the design by lightning,
blood, and lyre while our fathers raged baffled, too late come to call
me back while the poem of fire ran that first route in my brain, in-
fecting me with the will to form? Too late! Too late . . . Possessed
of the abominations born of the disease, beyond their aid, their
power, I planned and built, captive of my new self. Is that the tale
you'd hear again? Or rather I tell you of its cure?"

My mind spun at the implications he had just scattered by the
fistful. I could not tell whether he spoke literally or metaphorically or
was simply sharing paranoid delusions, but the things that I wanted
to hear, had to hear, were things closer to the moment. So, regarding
the shadowy image of myself from which that ancient voice emerged,
"Tell me of its cure," I said.

He braced his finger tips together and spoke through them.

"I am the Pattern," he said, "in a very real sense. In passing
through my mind to achieve the form it now holds, the foundation of
Amber, it marked me as surely as I marked it. I realized one day that
I am both the Pattern and myself, and it was forced to become
Dworkin in the process of becoming itself. There were mutual
modifications in the birthing of this place and this time, and therein
lay our weakness as well as our strength. For it occurred to me that
damage to the Pattern would be damage to myself, and damage to
myself would be reflected within the Pattern. Yet I could not be truly
harmed because the Pattern protects me, and who but I could harm
the Pattern? A beautiful closed system, it seemed, its weakness totally shielded by its strength."

He fell silent. I listened to the fire. I do not know what he listened
to.

Then, "I was wrong," he said. "Such a simple matter, too . . . My
blood, with which I drew it, could deface it. But it took me ages to

realize that the blood of my blood could also do this thing. You could use it, you could also change it—yea, unto the third generation."

It did not come to me as a surprise, learning that he was grandsire to us all. Somehow, it seemed that I had known all along, had known but never voiced it. Yet . . . if anything, this raised more questions than it answered. *Collect one generation of ancestry. Proceed to confusion.* I had less idea now than ever before as to what Dworkin really was. Add to this the fact which even he acknowledged: It was a tale told by a madman.

"But to repair it . . . ?" I said.

He smirked, my own face twisting before me.

"Have you lost your taste to be a lord of the living void, a king of chaos?" he asked.

"Mayhap," I replied.

"By the Unicorn, thy mother, I knew it would come to this! The Pattern is as strong in you as is the greater realm. What then is your desire?"

"To preserve the realm."

He shook his/my head.

" 'Twould be simpler to destroy everything and try a new start—as I have told you so often before."

"I'm stubborn. So tell me again," I said, attempting to simulate Dad's gruffness.

He shrugged.

"Destroy the Pattern and we destroy Amber—and all of the shadows in polar array about it. Give me leave to destroy myself in the midst of the Pattern and we will obliterate it. Give me leave by giving me your word that you will then take the Jewel which contains the essence of order and use it to create a new Pattern, bright and pure, untainted, drawing upon the stuff of your own being while the legions of chaos attempt to distract you on every side. Promise me that and let me end it, for broken as I am, I would rather die for order than live for it. What say you now?"

"Would it not be better to try mending the one we've got than to undo the work of eons?"

"Coward!" he cried, leaping to his feet. "I knew you would say that again!"

"Well, wouldn't it?"

He began to pace.

"How many times have we been through this?" he asked.

"Nothing has changed! You are afraid to try it!"

"Perhaps," I said. "But do you not feel that something for which you have given so much is worth some effort—some additional sacrifice—if there is even a possibility of saving it?"

"You still do not understand," he said. "I cannot but think that a damaged thing should be destroyed—and hopefully replaced. The nature of my personal injury is such that I cannot envision repair. I am damaged in just this fashion. My feelings are foreordained."

"If the Jewel can create a new Pattern, why will it not serve to repair the old one, end our troubles, heal your spirit?"

He approached and stood before me.

"Where is your memory?" he said. "You know that it would be infinitely more difficult to repair the damage than it would be to start over again. Even the Jewel could more easily destroy it than repair it. Have your forgotten what it is like out there?" He gestured toward the wall behind him. "Do you want to go and look at it again?"

"Yes," I said. "I would like that. Let's go."

I rose and looked down at him. His control over his form had begun slipping when he had grown angry. He had already lost three or four inches in height, the image of my face was melting back into his own gnomelike features, and a noticeable bulge was growing between his shoulders, had already been visible when he had gestured.

His eyes widened and he studied my face.

"You really mean it," he said after a moment. "All right, then. Let us go."

He turned and moved toward the big metal door. I followed him. He used both hands to turn the key. Then he threw his weight against it. I moved to help him, but he brushed me aside with extraordinary strength before giving the door a final shove. It made a grating noise and moved outward into a fully opened position. I was immediately struck by a strange, somehow familiar odor.

Dworkin stepped through and paused. He located what looked to be a long staff leaning against the wall off to his right. He struck it several times against the ground and its upper end began to glow. It lit up the area fairly well, revealing a narrow tunnel into which he now advanced. I followed him and it widened before too long, so that I was able to come abreast of him. The odor grew stronger, and I could almost place it. It had been something fairly recent . . .

It was close to eighty paces before our way took a turn to the left and upward. We passed then through a little appendixlike area. It was strewn with broken bones, and a large metal ring was set in the rock a couple of feet above the floor. Affixed thereto was a glittering chain, which fell to the floor and trailed on ahead like a line of molten droplets cooling in the gloom.

Our way narrowed again after that and Dworkin took the lead once more. After a brief time, he turned an abrupt corner and I heard him muttering. I nearly ran into him when I made the turn myself. He was crouched down and groping with his left hand inside a shadowy cleft. When I heard the soft cawing noise and saw that the chain vanished into the opening I realized what it was and where we were.

"Good Wixer," I heard him say. "I am not going far. It is all right, good Wixer. Here is something to chew on."

From where he had fetched whatever he tossed the beast, I do not know. But the purple griffin, which I had now advanced far enough to glimpse as it stirred within its lair, accepted the offering with a toss of its head and a series of crunching noises.

Dworkin grinned up at me.

"Surprised?" he asked.

"At what?"

"You thought I was afraid of him. You thought I would never make friends with him. You set him out here to keep me in there— away from the Pattern."

"Did I ever say that?"

"You did not have to. I am not a fool."

"Have it your way," I said.

He chuckled, rose, and continued on along the passageway.

I followed and it grew level underfoot once again. The ceiling rose and the way widened. At length, we came to the cave mouth. Dworkin stood for a moment silhouetted, staff raised before him. It was night outside, and a clean salt smell swept the musk from my nostrils.

Another moment, and he moved forward once more, passing into a world of sky-candles and blue velours. Continuing after him, I had gasped briefly at that amazing view. It was not simply that the stars in the moonless, cloudless sky blazed with a preternatural brilliance, nor that the distinction between sky and sea had once again been totally obliterated. It was that the Pattern glowed an almost acetylene blue by that sky-sea, and all of the stars above, beside, and below were arrayed with a geometric precision, forming a fantastic, oblique latticework which, more than anything else, gave the impression that we hung in the midst of a cosmic web where the Pattern was the true center, the rest of the radiant meshwork a precise consequence of its existence, configuration, position.

Dworkin continued on down to the Pattern, right up to the edge beside the darkened area. He waved his staff over it and turned to look at me just as I came near.

"There you are," he announced, "the hole in my mind. I can no longer think through it, only around it. I no longer know what must be done to repair something I now lack. If you think that you can do it, you must be willing to lay yourself open to instant destruction each time you depart the Pattern to cross the break. Not destruction by the dark portion. Destruction by the Pattern itself when you break the circuit. The Jewel may or may not sustain you. I do not know. But it will not grow easier. It will become more difficult with each circuit, and your strength will be lessening all the while. The last time we discussed it you were afraid. Do you mean to say you have grown bolder since then?"

"Perhaps," I said. "You see no other way?"

"I know it can be done starting with a clean slate, because once I did it so. Beyond that, I see no other way. The longer you wait the more the situation worsens. Why not fetch the Jewel and lend me your blade, son? I see no better way."

"No," I said. "I must know more. Tell me again how the damage was done."

"I still do not know which of your children shed our blood on this spot, if this is what you mean. It was done. Let it go at that. Our darker natures came forth strongly in them. It must be that they are too close to the chaos from which we sprang, growing without the exercises of will we endured in defeating it. I had thought that the ritual of traveling the Pattern might suffice for them. I could think of nothing stronger. Yet it failed. They strike out against everything. They seek to destroy the Pattern itself."

"If we succeed in making a fresh start, might not these events simply repeat themselves?"

"I do not know. But what choice have we other than failure and a return to chaos?"

"What will become of them if we try for a new beginning?"

He was silent for a long while. Then he shrugged.

"I cannot tell."

"What would another generation have been like?"

He chuckled.

"How can such a question be answered? I have no idea."

I withdrew the mutilated Trump and passed it to him. He regarded it near the blaze of his staff.

"I believe it is Random's son Martin," I said, "He whose blood was spilled here. I have no idea whether he still lives. What do you think he might have amounted to?"

He looked back out over the Pattern.

"So this is the object which decorated it," he said. "How did you fetch it forth?"

"It was gotten," I said. "It is not your work, is it?"

"Of course not. I have never set eyes on the boy. But this answers your question, does it not? If there is another generation, your children will destroy it."

"As we would destroy them?"

He met my eyes and peered.

"Is it that you are suddenly becoming a doting father?" he asked.

"If you did not prepare that Trump, who did?"

He glanced down and flicked it with his fingernail.

"My best pupil. Your son Brand. That is his style. See what they do as soon as they gain a little power? Would any of them offer their lives to preserve the realm, to restore the Pattern?"

"Probably," I said. "Probably Benedict, Gérard, Random, Corwin . . ."

"Benedict has the mark of doom upon him, Gérard possesses the will but not the wit, Random lacks courage and determination. Corwin . . . Is he not out of favor and out of sight?"

My thoughts returned to our last meeting, when he had helped me to escape from my cell to Cabra. It occurred to me that he might have had second thoughts concerning that, not having been aware of the circumstances which had put me there.

"Is that why you have taken his form?" he went on. "Is this some manner of rebuke? Are you testing me again?"

"He is neither out of favor nor sight," I said, "though he has enemies among the family and elsewhere. He would attempt anything to preserve the realm. How do you see his chances?"

"Has he not been away for a long while?"

"Yes."

"Then he might have changed. I do not know."

"I believe he is changed. I know that he is willing to try."

He stared at me again, and he kept staring.

"You are not Oberon," he said at length.

"No."

"You are he whom I see before me."

"No more, no less."

"I see . . . . I did not realize that you knew of this place."

"I didn't, until recently. The first time that I came here I was led by the unicorn."

His eyes widened.

"That is—very—interesting," he said. "It has been so long . . ."

"What of my question?"

"Eh? Question? What question?"

"My chances. Do you think I might be able to repair the Pattern?"

He advanced slowly, and reaching up, placed his right hand on my shoulder. The staff tilted in his other hand as he did so; its blue light flared within a foot of my face, but I felt no heat. He looked into my eyes.

"You have changed," he said, after a time.

"Enough," I asked, "to do the job?"

He looked away.

"Perhaps enough to make it worth trying," he said, "even if we are foredoomed to failure."

"Will you help me?"

"I do not know," he said, "that I will be able. This thing with my moods, my thoughts—it comes and it goes. Even now, I feel some of my control slipping away. The excitement, perhaps. . . . We had best get back inside."

I heard a clinking noise at my back. When I turned, the griffin was there, his head swinging slowly from left to right, his tail from right to left, his tongue darting. He began to circle us, halting when he came to a position between Dworkin and the Pattern.

"He knows," Dworkin said. "He can sense it when I begin to change. He will not let me near the Pattern then. . . . Good Wixer. We are returning now. It is all right. . . . Come, Corwin."

We headed back toward the cave mouth and Wixer followed, a clink for every pace

"The Jewel," I said, "the Jewel of Judgment . . . you say that it is necessary for the repair of the Pattern?"

"Yes," he said. "It would have to be borne the entire distance through the Pattern, reinscribing the original design in the places where it has been broken. This could only be done by one who is attuned to the Jewel, though."

"I am attuned to the Jewel," I said.

"How?" he asked, halting.

Wixer made a cackling noise behind us, and we resumed walking.

"I followed your written instructions—and Eric's verbal ones," I said. "I took it with me to the center of the Pattern and projected myself through it."

"I see," he said. "How did you obtain it?"

"From Eric, on his deathbed."

We entered the cave.

"You have it now?"

"I was forced to cache it in a place off in Shadow."

"I would suggest you retrieve it quickly and bring it here or take it back to the palace. It is best kept near the center of things."

"Why is that?"

"It tends to have a distorting effect on shadows if it lies too long among them."

"Distorting? In what fashion?"

"There is no way to tell, in advance. It depends entirely upon the locale."

We rounded a corner, continued on back through the gloom.

"What does it mean," I said, "when you are wearing the Jewel and everything begins to slow down about you? Fiona warned me that this was dangerous, but she was not certain why."

"It means that you have reached the bounds of your own existence, that your energies will shortly be exhausted, that you will die unless you do something quickly."

"What is that?"

"Begin to draw power from the Pattern itself—the primal Pattern within the Jewel."

"How is this achieved?"

"You must surrender to it, release yourself, blot out your identity, erase the bounds which separate you from everything else."

"It sounds easier said that done."

"But it can be done, and it is the only way."

I shook my head. We moved on, coming at last to the big door. Dworkin extinguished the staff and leaned it against the wall. We entered and he secured the door. Wixer had stationed himself just outside.

"You will have to leave now," Dworkin said.

"But there are many more things that I must ask you, and some that I would like to tell you."

"My thoughts grow meaningless, and your words would be wasted. Tomorrow night, or the next, or the next. Hurry! Go!"

"Why the rush?"

"I may harm you when the change comes over me. I am holding it back by main will now. Depart!"

"I do not know how. I know how to get here, but—"

"There are all manner of special Trumps in the desk in the next room. Take the light! Go anywhere! Get out of here!"

I was about to protest that I hardly feared any physical violence he could muster, when his features began to flow like melting wax and he somehow seemed much larger and longer-limbed than he had been. Seizing the light, I fled the room, a sudden chill upon me.

. . . To the desk. I tore open the drawer and snatched at some Trumps which lay scattered within it. I heard footsteps then, of something entering the room behind me, coming from the chamber I had just departed. They did not seem like the footsteps of a man. I did not look back. Instead, I raised the cards before me and regarded the one on top. It was an unfamiliar scene, but I opened my mind immediately and reached for it. A mountain crag, something indistinct beyond it, a strangely stippled sky, a scattering of stars to the left . . . The card was alternately hot and cold to my touch, and a heavy wind seemed to come blowing through it as I stared, somehow rearranging the prospect.

From right behind me then, the heavily altered but still recognizable voice of Dworkin spoke: "Fool! You have chosen the land of your doom!"

A great clawlike hand—black, leathery, gnarled—reached over my shoulder, as if to snatch the card away. But the vision seemed ready, and I rushed forward into it, turning the card from me as soon as I realized I had made my escape. Then I halted and stood stock-still, to let my senses adjust to the new locale.

I knew. From snatches of legend, bits of family gossip, and from a general feeling which came over me, I knew the place to which I had come. It was with full certainty as to identity that I raised my eyes to look upon the Courts of Chaos.

VI

Where? The senses are such uncertain things, and now mine were strained beyond their limits. The rock on which I stood . . . If I attempted to fix my gaze upon it, it took on the aspect of a pavement on a hot afternoon. It seemed to shift and waver, though my footing was undisturbed. And it was undecided as to the portion of the spectrum it might call home. It pulsated and flashed like the skin of an iguana. Looking upward, I beheld a sky such as I had never before set eyes upon. At the moment, it was split down the middle—half of it of deepest night-black, and the stars danced within it. When I say danced, I do not mean twinkled; they cavorted and they shifted magnitudes; they darted and they circled; they flared to nova brilliance, then faded to nothing. It was a frightening spectacle to behold, and my stomach tightened within me as I experienced a profound acrophobia. Yet, shifting my gaze did little to improve the situation. The other half of the sky was like a bottle of colored sands, continuously shaken; belts of orange, yellow, red, blue, brown, and purple turned and twisted; patches of green, mauve, gray, and dead white came and went, sometimes snaking into belthood, replacing or joining the other writhing entities. And these, too, shimmered and wavered, creating impossible sensations of distance and nearness. At times, some or all seemed literally sky-high, and then again they came to fill the air before me, gauzy, transparent mists, translucent swaths or solid tentacles of color. It was not until later that I realized that the line which separated the black from the color was advancing slowly from my right while retreating to my left. It was as if the entire celestial mandala were rotating about a point directly overhead. As to the light source of the brighter half, it simply could not be determined. Standing there, I looked down upon what at first seemed a valley filled with countless explosions of color; but when the advancing darkness faced this display away the stars danced and burned within its depths as well as above, giving then the impression of a bottomless chasm. It was as if I stood at the end of the world, the end of the universe, the end of everything. But far, far out from where I stood, something hovered on a mount of sheerest black—a blackness itself, but edged and tempered with barely perceptible flashes of light. I could not guess at its size, for distance, depth, perspective, were absent here. A single edifice? A group? A city? Or simply a place? The outline varied each time that it fell upon my retina. Now faint and misty sheets drifted slowly between us, twisting, as if long strands of gauze were buoyed by heated air. The mandala ceased its turning when it had exactly reversed itself. The colors were behind me now, and imperceptible unless I turned my head, an action I had no desire to take. It was pleasant standing there, staring at the formlessness from which all things eventually emerged. . . . Before the Pattern, even, this thing was. I knew this, dimly but surely, at the very center of my consciousness. I knew this, because I was certain that I had been here before. Child of the man I had become, it seemed that I had been brought here in some distant day—whether by Dad or Dworkin, I could not now recall—and had stood or been held in this place or one very near to it, looking out upon the same scene with, I am certain, a similar lack of comprehension, a similar sense of apprehension. My pleasure was tinged with a nervous excitement, a sense of the forbidden, a feeling of dubious anticipation. Peculiarly, at that moment, there rose in me a longing for the Jewel I had had to abandon in my compost heap on the shadow Earth, the thing Dworkin had made so much of. Could it be that some part of me sought a defense or at least a symbol of resistance against whatever was out there? Probably.

As I continued to stare, fascinated, across the chasm, it was as if my eyes adjusted or the prospect shifted once again, subtly. For now I discerned tiny, ghostly forms moving within that place, like slow-motion meteors along the gauzy strands. I waited, regarding them carefully, courting some small understanding of the actions in which they were engaged. At length, one of the strands drifted very near. Shortly thereafter I had my answer.

There was a movement. One of the rushing forms grew larger, and I realized that it was following the twisting way that led toward me. In only a few moments, it took on the proportions of a horseman. As it came on, it assumed a semblance of solidity without losing that ghostly quality which seemed to cling to everything which lay before me. A moment later, I beheld a naked rider on a hairless horse, both deathly pale, rushing in my direction. The rider brandished a bone-white blade; his eyes and the eyes of the horse both flashed red. I did not really know whether he saw me, whether we existed on the same plane of reality, so unnatural was his mien. Yet I unsheathed Grayswandir and took a step backward as he approached.

His long white hair shed tiny sparkling motes, and when he turned his head I knew that he was coming for me, for then I felt his gaze like a cold pressure across the front of my body. I turned sidewise and raised my blade to guard.

He continued, and I realized that both he and the horse were big, bigger even than I had thought. They came on. When they reached the point nearest me—some ten meters, perhaps—the horse reared as the rider drew it to a halt. They regarded me then, bobbing and swaying as if on a raft in a gently swelling sea.

"Your name!" the rider demanded. "Give me your name, who comes to this place!"

His voice produced a crackling sensation in my ears. It was all of one sound level, loud and without inflection.

I shook my head.

"I give my name when I choose, not when I am ordered to," I said. "Who are you?"

He gave three short barks, which I took to be a laugh.

"I will hale you down and about, where you will cry it out forever."

I pointed Grayswandir at his eyes.

"Talk is cheap," I said. "Whisky costs money."

I felt a faint cool sensation just then, as if someone were toying with my Trump, thinking of me. But it was dim, weak, and I had no attention to spare, for the rider had passed some signal to his mount and the beast reared. The distance is too great, I decided. But this thought belonged to another shadow. The beast plunged ahead toward me, departing the tenuous roadway that had been its course.

Its leap bore it to a point far short of my position. But it did not fall from there and vanish, as I had hoped. It resumed the motions of galloping, and although its progress was not fully commensurate with the action, it continued to advance across the abyss at about half-speed.

While this was occurring, I saw that in the distance from which it had come another figure appeared to be headed my way. Nothing to do but stand my ground, fight, and hope that I could dispatch this attacker before the other was upon me.

As the rider advanced, his ruddy gaze flicked over my person and halted when it fell upon Grayswandir. Whatever the nature of the mad illumination at my back, it had tricked the delicate tracery on my blade to life once more, so that that portion of the Pattern it bore swam and sparkled along its length. The horseman was very near by then, but he drew back on the reins and his eyes leaped upward, meeting my own. His nasty grin vanished.

"I know you!" he said. "You are the one called Corwin!"

But we had him, me and my ally momentum.

His mount's front hoofs fell upon the ledge and I rushed forward. The beast's reflexes caused it to seek equal footing for its hind legs despite the drawn reins. The rider swung his blade into a guard position as I came on, but I cross-stepped and attacked from his left. As he moved his blade cross-body, I was already lunging. Grayswandir sheared through his pale hide, entering beneath the sternum and above the guts.

I wrenched my blade free and gouts of fire poured like blood from his wound. His sword arm sagged and his mount uttered a shriek that was almost a whistle as the blazing stream fell upon its neck. I danced back as the rider slumped forward and the beast, now fully footed, plunged on toward me, kicking. I cut again, reflexively, defensively. My blade nicked its left foreleg, and it, too, began to burn.

I side-stepped once again as it turned and made for me a second time. At that moment, the rider erupted into a pillar of light. The beast bellowed, wheeled, and rushed away. Without pausing, it plunged over the edge and vanished into the abyss, leaving me with the memory of the smoldering head of a cat which had addressed me long ago and the chill which always accompanied the recollection.

I was backed against rock, panting. The wispy road had drifted nearer—ten feet, perhaps, from the ledge. I had developed a cramp in my left side. The second rider was rapidly approaching. He was not pale like the first. His hair was dark and there was color in his face. His mount was a properly maned sorrel. He bore a cocked and bolted crossbow. I glanced behind me and there was no retreat, no crevice into which I might back.

I wiped my palm on my trousers and gripped Grayswandir by the forte of the blade. I turned sideways, so as to present the narrowest target possible. I raised my blade between us, hilt level with my head, point toward the ground, the only shield I possessed.

The rider came abreast of me and halted at the nearest point on the gauzy strip. He raised the crossbow slowly, knowing that if he did not drop me instantly with his single shot, I might be able to hurl my blade like a spear. Our eyes met.

He was beardless, slim. Possibly light-eyed within the squint of his aim. He managed his mount well, with just the pressure of his legs. His hands were big, steady. Capable. A peculiar feeling passed over me as I beheld him.

The moment stretched beyond the point of action. He rocked backward and lowered the weapon slightly, though none of the tenion left his stance.

"You," he called out. "Is that the blade Grayswandir?"

"Yes," I answered, "It is."

He continued his appraisal, and something within me looked for words to wear, failed, ran naked away through the night.

"What do you want here?" he asked.

"To depart," I said.

There was a *chish-chá,* as his bolt struck the rock far ahead and to the left of me.

"Go then," he said. "This is a dangerous place for you."

He turned his mount back in the direction from which he had come.

I lowered Grayswandir.

"I won't forget you," I said.

"No," he answered. "Do not."

Then he galloped away, and moments later the gauze drifted off also.

I resheathed Grayswandir and took a step forward. The world was beginning to turn about me again, the light advancing on my right, the dark retreating to my left. I looked about for some way to scale the rocky prominence at my back. It seemed to rise only thirty or forty feet higher, and I wanted the view that might be available from its summit. My ledge extended to both my right and my left. On inspection, the way to the right narrowed quickly, however, without affording a suitable ascent. I turned and made my way to the left.

I came upon a rougher spot in a narrow place beyond a rocky shoulder. Running my gaze up its height, an ascent seemed possible. I checked behind me after the approach of additional threats. The ghostly roadway had drifted farther away; no new riders advanced. I commenced climbing.

The going was not difficult, though the height proved greater than it had seemed from below. Likely a symptom of the spatial distortion which seemed to have affected my sight of so much else in this place. After a time, I hauled myself up and stood erect at a point which afforded a better view in the direction opposite the abyss.

Once again, I beheld the chaotic colors. From my right, the darkness herded them. The land they danced above was rock-cropped and cratered, no sign of any life within it. Passing through its midst, however, from the far horizon to a point in the mountains somewhere to the right, inky and serpentine, ran what could only be the black road.

Another ten minutes of climbing and maneuvering, and I had positioned myself to view its terminus. It swept through a broad pass in the mountains and ran right to the very edge of the abyss. There, its blackness merged with that which filled the place, noticeable now only by virtue of the fact that no stars shone through it. Using this occlusion to gauge it, I obtained the impression that it continued on to the dark eminence about which the misty strips drifted.

I stretched out on my belly, so as to disturb the outline of the low crest as little as possible to whatever unseen eyes might flick across it. Lying there, I thought upon the opening of this way. The damage to the Pattern had laid Amber open to this access, and I believed that my curse had provided the precipitating element. I felt now that it would have come to pass without me, but I was certain that I had done my part. The guilt was still partly mine though no longer entirely so, as I had once believed. I thought then of Eric, as he lay dying on Kolvir. He had said that as much as he hated me, he was saving his dying curse for the enemies of Amber. In other words, this, and these. Ironic. My efforts were now entirely directed toward making good on my least-liked brother's dying wish. His curse to cancel my curse, me as the agent. Fitting though, perhaps, in some larger sense.

I sought, and was pleased not to discover, ranks of glowing riders setting forth or assembling upon that road. Unless another raiding party was already under way Amber was still temporarily safe. A number of things immediately troubled me, however. Mainly, if time did indeed behave as peculiarly in that place as Dara's possible origin indicated, then why had there not been another attack? They had certainly had ample time in which to recover and prepare for another assault. Had something occurred recently, by Amber's time, that is, to alter the nature of their strategy? If so, what? My weapons? Brand's recovery? Or something else? I wondered, too, how far Benedict's outposts reached. Certainly not this far, or I should have been informed. Had he ever been to this place? Had any of the others, within recent memory, stood where I had just stood, looking upon the Courts of Chaos, knowing something that I did not know? I resolved to question Brand and Benedict in this regard as soon as I returned.

All of which led me to wonder how time was behaving with me, at that moment. Better not to spend any more time here than I had to, I decided. I scanned the other Trumps I had removed from Dworkin's desk. While they were all of them interesting, I was familiar with none of the scenes depicted. I slipped my own case then and riffled through to Random's Trump. Perhaps he was the one who had tried to contact me earlier. I raised his card and regarded it.

Shortly, it swam before my eyes and I looked upon a blurred kaleidoscope of images, the impression of Random in their midst. Motion, and twisting perspectives . . .

"Random," I said. "This is Corwin."

I felt his mind, but there was no response from it. It struck me then that he was in the middle of a hellride, all his concentration bent on warping the stuff of Shadow about him. He could not respond wthout losing control. I blocked the Trump with my hand, breaking the contact.

I cut to Gérard's card. Moments later, there was contact. I stood.

"Corwin, where are you?" he inquired.

"At the end of the world," I said. "I want to come home."

"Come ahead."

He extended his hand. I reached out and clasped it, stepped forward.

We were on the ground floor of the palace in Amber, in the sitting room to which we had all adjourned on the night of Brand's return. It seemed to be early morning. There was a fire going on the grate. No one else was present.

"I tried to reach you earlier," he said. "I think Brand did, too. But I can't be sure."

"How long have I been away?"

"Eight days," he said.

"Glad I hurried. What's happening?"

"Nothing untoward," he said. "I do not know what Brand wants. He kept asking for you, and I could not reach you. Finally, I gave him a deck and told him to see whether he could do any better. Apparently, he could not."

"I was distracted," I said, "and the time-flow differential was bad."

He nodded.

"I have been avoiding him now that he is out of danger. He is in one of his black moods again, and he insists he can take care of himself. He is right, in that, and it is just as well."

"Where is he now?"

"Back in his own quarters, and he was still there as of perhaps an hour ago—brooding."

"Has he been out at all?"

"A few brief walks. But not for the past several days."

"I guess I had best go see him then. Any word on Random?"

"Yes," he said. "Benedict returned several days ago. He said they had found a number of leads concerning Random's son. He helped him check on a couple of them. One led further, but Benedict felt he had best not be away from Amber for too long, things being as uncertain as they are. So he left Random to continue the search on his own. He gained something in the venture, though. He came back sporting an artificial arm—a beautiful piece of work. He can do anything with it that he could before."

"Really?" I said. "It sounds strangely familiar."

He smiled, nodded.

"He told me you had brought it back for him from Tir-na Nog'th. In fact, he wants to speak with you about it as soon as possible."

"I'll bet," I said. "Where is he now?"

"At one of the outposts he has established along the black road. You would have to reach him by Trump."

"Thanks," I said. "Anything further on Julian or Fiona?"

He shook his head.

"All right," I said, turning toward the door. "I guess I will go see Brand first."

"I am curious to know what it is that he wants," he said.

"I will remember that," I told him.

I left the room and headed for the stairs.

VII

I rapped on Brand's door.

"Come in, Corwin," he said.

I did, deciding as I crossed the threshold that I would not ask him how he had known who it was. His room was a gloomy place, candles burning despite the fact that it was daytime and he had four windows. The shutters were closed on three of them. The fourth was only part way open. Brand stood beside this one, staring out toward the sea. He was dressed all in black velvet with a silver chain about his neck. His belt was also of silver—a fine, linked affair. He played with a small dagger, and did not look at me as I entered. He was still pale, but his beard was neatly trimmed and he looked well scrubbed and a bit heavier than he had when last I had seen him.

"You are looking better," I said. "How are you feeling?"

He turned and regarded me, expressionless, his eyes half-closed.

"Where the hell have you been?" he said.

"Hither and yon. What did you want to see me about?"

"I asked you where you've been."

"And I heard you," I said, reopening the door behind me. "Now I am going to go out and come back in. Supposing we start this conversation over again?"

He sighed.

"Wait a minute. I am sorry," he said. "Why are we all so thin-skinned? I do not know. . . . All right. It may be better if I do start over again."

He sheathed his dagger and crossed to sit in a heavy chair of black wood and leather.

"I got to worrying about all the things we had discussed," he said, "and some that we had not. I waited what seemed an appropriate time for you to have concluded your business in Tir-na Nog'th and returned. I then inquired after you and was told you had not yet come back. I waited longer. First I was impatient, and then I grew concerned that you might have been ambushed by our enemies. When I inquired again later, I learned that you had been back only long enough to speak with Random's wife—it must have been a conversation of great moment—and then to take a nap. You then departed once more. I was irritated that you had not seen fit to keep me posted as to events, but I resolved to wait a bit longer. Finally, I asked Gérard to get hold of you with your Trump. When he failed, I was quite concerned. I tried it myself then, and while it seemed that I touched you on several occasions I could not get through. I feared for you, and now I see that I had nothing to fear all along. Hence, I was abrupt."

"I see," I said, taking a seat off to his right. "Actually, time was running faster for me than it was for you, so from where I am sitting I have hardly been away. You are probably further recuperated from your puncture than I am from mine."

He smiled faintly and nodded.

"That is something, anyway," he said, "For my pains."

"I have had a few pains myself," I said, "So don't give me any more. You wanted me for something. Let's have it."

"Something is bothering you," he said. "Perhaps we ought to discuss that first."

"All right," I said. "Let's."

I turned and looked at the painting on the wall beside the door. An oil, a rather somber rendering of the well at Mirata, two men standing beside their horses nearby, talking.

"You've a distinctive style," I said.

"In all things," he replied.

"You stole my next sentence," I said, locating Martin's Trump and passing it to him.

He remained expressionless as he examined it, gave me one brief, sidelong look and then nodded.

"I cannot deny my hand," he said.

"It executed more than that card, your hand. Didn't it?"

He traced his upper lip with the tip of his tongue.

"Where did you find it?" he asked.

"Right where you left it, at the heart of things—in the real Amber."

"So . . ." he said, rising from the chair and returning to the window, holding up the card as if to study it in a better light. "So," he repeated, "you are aware of more than I had guessed. How did you learn of the primal Pattern?"

I shook my head.

"You answer my question first: Did you stab Martin?"

He turned toward me once again, stared a moment, then nodded sharply. His eyes continued to search my face.

"Why?" I asked.

"Someone had to," he explained, "to open the way for the powers we needed. We drew straws."

"And you won."

"Won? Lost?" He shrugged. "What does any of this matter now? Things did not come about as we had intended. I am a different person now than I was then."

"Did you kill him?"

"What?"

"Martin, Random's son. Did he die as a result of the wound you inflicted?"

He turned his hands palms upward.

"I do not know," he said. "If he did not, it was not because I did not try. You need look no further. You have found your guilty party. Now that you have, what are you going to do?"

I shook my head.

"I? Nothing. For all I know, the lad may still be living."

"Then let us move on to matters of greater moment. For how long have you known of the existence of the true Pattern?"

"Long enough," I said. "Its origin, its functions, the effect of the blood of Amber upon it—long enough. I paid more attention to Dworkin than you might have thought. I saw no gain to be had in damaging the fabric of existence, though. So I let Rover lie sleeping for a long, long while. It did not even occur to me until I spoke with you recently that the black road might have been connected with such foolishness. When I went to inspect the Pattern I found Martin's Trump and all the rest."

"I was not aware that you were acquainted with Martin."

"I have never set eyes on him."

"Then how were you aware he was the subject of the Trump?"

"I was not alone in that place."

"Who was with you?"

I smiled.

"No, Brand. It is still your turn. You told me when last we talked that the enemies of Amber hied all the way from the Courts of Chaos, that they have access to the realm via the black road because of something you and Bleys and Fiona had done back when you were of one mind as to the best way to take the throne. Now I know what it is that you did. Yet Benedict has been watching the black road and I have just looked upon the Courts of Chaos. There is no new massing of forces, no movement toward us upon that road. I know that time flows differently in that place. They should have had more than enough time to ready a new assault. I want to know what is holding them back. Why have they not moved? What are they waiting for, Brand?"

"You credit me with more knowledge than I possess."

"I don't think so. You are the resident expert on the subject. You have dealt with them. That Trump is evidence that you have been holding back on other matters. Don't weasel, just talk."

"The Courts . . ." he said. "You have been busy. Eric was a fool not to have killed you immediately—if he was aware you had knowledge of these things."

"Eric was a fool," I acknowledged. "You are not. Now talk."

"But I am a fool," he said, "a sentimental one, at that. Do you recall the day of our last argument, here in Amber, so long ago?"

"Somewhat."

"I was sitting on the edge of my bed. You were standing by my writing desk. As you turned away and headed toward the door, I resolved to kill you. I reached beneath my bed, where I keep a cocked crossbow with a bolt in it. I actually had my hand on it and was about to raise it when I realized something which stopped me."

He paused.

"What was that?" I asked.

"Look over there by the door."

I looked, I saw nothing special. I began to shake my head, just as he said, "On the floor."

Then I realized what it was—russet and olive and brown and green, with a small geometric pattern.

He nodded.

"You were standing on my favorite rug. I did not want to get blood on it. Later, my anger passed. So I, too, am a victim of emotion and circumstance."

"Lovely story—" I began.

"—but now you want me to stop stalling. I was not stalling, however. I was attempting to make a point. We are all of us alive by one another's sufferance and an occasional fortunate accident. I am going to propose suspending that sufferance and eliminating the possibility of accident in a couple of very important cases. First though, to answer your question, while I do not know for certain what is holding them back, I can venture a very good guess. Bleys has assembled a large strike force for an attack on Amber. It will be nowhere near the scale of the one on which you accompanied him, however. You see, he will be counting on the memory of that last attack to have conditioned the response to this one. It will probably also be preceded by attempts to assassinate Benedict and yourself. The entire affair will be a feint, though. I would guess that Fiona has contacted the Courts of Chaos—may even be there right now—and has prepared them for the real attack, which might be expected any time after Bleys's diversionary foray. Therefore—"

"You say this is a very good guess," I interrupted. "But we do not even know for certain that Bleys is still living."

"Bleys is alive," he said. "I was able to ascertain his existence via his Trump—even a brief assessment of his current activities—before he became aware of my presence and blocked me out. He is very sensitive to such surveillance. I found him in the field with troops he intends to employ against Amber."

"And Fiona?"

"No," he said, "I did no experimenting with her Trump, and I would advise you not to either. She is extremely dangerous, and I did not want to lay myself open to her influence. My estimate of her current situation is based on deduction rather than direct knowledge. I would be willing to rely on it, though."

"I see," I said.

"I have a plan."

"Go ahead."

"The manner in which you retrieved me from durance was quite inspired, combining the forces of everyone's concentration as you did. The same principle could be utilized again, to a different end. A force such as that would break through a person's defense fairly easily—even someone like Fiona, if the effort is properly directed."

"That is to say, directed by yourself?"

"Of course. I propose that we assemble the family and force our way through to Bleys and Fiona, wherever they may be. We hold them, locked in the full, in the flesh, just for a moment or so. Just long enough for me to strike."

"As you did Martin?"

"Better, I trust. Martin was able to break free at the last moment. That should not occur this time, with all of you helping. Even three or four would probably be sufficient."

"You really think you can pull it off that easily?"

"I know we had better try. Time is running. You will be one of the ones executed when they take Amber. So will I. What do you say?"

"If I become convinced that it is necessary. Then I would have no choice but to go along with it."

"It is necessary, believe me. The next thing is that I will need the Jewel of Judgment."

"What for?"

"If Fiona is truly in the Courts of Chaos, the Trump alone will probably be insufficient to reach her and hold her—even with all of us behind it. In her case, I will require the Jewel to focus our energies."

"I suppose that could be arranged."

"Then the sooner we are about it the better. Can you set things up for tonight? I am sufficiently recovered to handle my end of it."

"Hell, no," I said, standing.

"What do you mean?" He clenched the arms of the chair, half-rising. "Why not?"

"I said I would go along with it if I became convinced that it was necessary. You have admitted that a lot of this is conjecture. That alone is sufficient to keep me from being convinced."

"Forget about being convinced then. Can you afford to take the chance? The next attack is going to be a lot stronger than the last, Corwin. They are aware of your new weapons. They are going to allow for this in their planning."

"Even if I agreed with you, Brand, I am certain I could not convince the others that the executions are necessary."

"Convince them? Just tell them! You've got them all by the throat, Corwin! You are on top right now. You want to stay there, don't you?"

I smiled and moved toward the door.

"I will, too," I said, "by doing things my way. I will keep your suggestion on file."

"Your way is going to get you dead. Sooner than you think."

"I am standing on your rug again," I said.

He laughed.

"Very good. But I was not threatening you. You know what I meant. You are responsible for all of Amber now. You have to do the right thing."

"And you know what I meant. I am not going to kill a couple more of us because of your suspicions. I would need more than that."

"When you get it, it may be too late."

I shrugged.

"We'll see."

I reached toward the door.

"What are you going to do now?"

I shook my head.

"I don't tell anybody everything that I know, Brand. It is a kind of insurance."

"I can appreciate that. I only hope that you know enough."

"Or perhaps you fear that I know too much," I said.

For a moment a wary look danced on the muscles beneath his eyes. Then he smiled.

"I am not afraid of you, brother," he said.

"It is good to have nothing to fear," I said.

I opened the door.

"Wait," he said.

"Yes?"

"You neglected to tell me who was with you when you discovered Martin's Trump, in the place where I had left it."

"Why, it was Random," I said.

"Oh. Is he aware of the particulars?"

"If you mean, does he know that you stabbed his son," I said, "the answer is no, not yet."

"I see. And of Benedict's new arm? I understand that you somehow got it for him in Tir-na Nog'th. I would like to know more about this."

"Not now," I said. "Let's save something for our next get-together. It won't be all that long."

I went on out and closed the door, my silent regards to the rug.

VIII

After visiting the kitchens, compiling an enormous meal and demolishing it, I headed for the stables, where I located a handsome young sorrel which had once belonged to Eric. I made friends with him in spite of this, and a short while later we were moving toward the trail down Kolvir which would take us to the camp of my Shadow forces. As I rode and digested, I tried to sort out the events and revelations of what, to me, had been the past few hours. If Amber had indeed arisen as the result of Dworkin's act of rebellion within the Courts of Chaos, then it followed that we were all of us related to the very forces which now threatened us. It was, of course, difficult to decide how far anything Dworkin said might now be trusted. Yet, the black road did run to the Courts of Chaos, apparently as a direct result of Brand's ritual, a thing which he had based on principles learned from Dworkin. Fortunately, for now, the parts of Dworkin's narrative which required the greatest credulity were those things which were not of any great moment, from an immediate, practical standpoint. Still, I had mixed feelings about being descended from a unicorn—

"Corwin!"

I drew rein. I opened my mind to the sending and the image of Ganelon appeared.

"I am here," I said. "Where did you get hold of a set of Trumps? And learn how to use them?"

"I picked up a pack from the case in the library a while back. Thought it a good idea to have a way of getting in touch with you in a hurry. As for using them, I just did what you and the others seem to do—study the Trump, think about it, concentrate on getting in touch with the person."

"I should have gotten you a pack long ago," I said. "It was an oversight on my part which I am glad you've remedied. Are you just testing them now, or did something come up?"

"Something," he said. "Where are you?"

"As chance would have it, I am on my way down to see you."

"You are all right?"

"Yes."

"Fine. Come ahead then. I'd rather not try bringing you through this thing, the way you people do. It is not that urgent. I will see you by and by."

"Yes."

He broke the contact and I rustled the reins and continued on. For a moment, I had been irritated that he had not simply asked me for a deck. Then I recalled that I had been away for over a week, by Amber's time. He had probably been getting worried, didn't trust any of the others to do it for him. Perhaps rightly so.

The descent went quickly, as did the balance of the journey to the camp. The horse—whose name, by the way, was Drum—seemed happy to be going somewhere and had a tendency to pull away at the least excuse. I gave him his head at one point to tire him a bit, and it was not too long afterward that I sighted the camp. I realized at about that time that I missed Star.

I was the subject of stares and salutes as I rode into camp. A silence followed me and all activity ceased as I passed. I wondered whether they believed I had come to deliver a battle order.

Ganelon emerged from his tent before I had dismounted.

"Fast," he observed, clasping my hand as I came down. "Pretty horse, that."

"Yes," I agreed, turning the reins over to his orderly. "What news have you?"

"Well . . ." he said. "I've been talking to Benedict . . ."

"Something stirring on the black road?"

"No, no. Nothing like that. He came to see me after he returned from those friends of his—the Tecys—to tell me that Random was all right, that he was following a lead as to Martin's whereabouts. We got to talking of other matters after that, and finally he asked me to tell him everything I knew about Dara. Random had told him about her walking the Pattern, and he had decided then that too many people other than yourself were aware of her existence."

"So what did you tell him?"

"Everything."

"Including the guesswork, the speculation—after Tir-na Nog'th?"

"Just so."

"I see. How did he take this?"

"He seemed excited about it. Happy, I'd even say. Come talk with him yourself."

I nodded and he turned toward his tent. He pushed back the flap and stepped aside. I entered.

Benedict was seated on a low stool beside a foot locker atop which a map had been spread. He was tracing something on the map with the long metal finger of the glinting, skeletal hand attached to the deadly, silver-cabled, firepinned mechanical arm I had brought back from the city in the sky, the entire device now attached to the stump of his right arm a little below the point where the sleeve had been cut away from his brown shirt, a transformation which halted me with a momentary shudder, so much did he resemble the ghost I had encountered. His eyes rose to meet my own and he raised the hand in greeting, a casual, perfectly executed gesture, and he smiled the broadest smile I had ever seen crease his face.

"Corwin!" he said, and then he rose and extended that hand.

I had to force myself to clasp the device which had almost killed me. But Benedict looked more kindly disposed toward me than he had in a long while. I shook the new hand and its pressures were perfect. I tried to disregard its coldness and angularity and almost succeeded, in my amazement at the control he had acquired over it in such a brief time.

"I owe you an apology," he said. "I have wronged you. I am very sorry."

"It's all right," I said. "I understand."

He clasped me for a moment, and my belief that things had apparently been set right between us was darkened only by the grip of those precise and deadly fingers on my shoulder.

Ganelon chuckled and brought up another stool, which he set at the other end of the locker. My irritation at his having aired the subject I had not wanted mentioned, whatever the circumstances, was submerged by the sight of its effects: I could not remember having seen Benedict in better spirits; Ganelon was obviously pleased at having effected the resolution of our differences.

I smiled myself and accepted a seat, unbuckling my sword belt and hanging Grayswandir on the tent pole. Ganelon produced three glasses and a bottle of wine. As he set the glasses before us and poured, he remarked, "To return the hospitality of your tent, that night, back in Avalon."

Benedict took up his glass with but the faintest of clicks.

"There is more ease in this tent," he said. "Is that not so, Corwin?"

I nodded and raised my glass.

"To that ease. May it always prevail."

"I have had my first opportunity in a long while," he said, "to talk with Random at some length. He has changed quite a bit."

"Yes," I agreed.

"I am more inclined to trust him now than I was in days gone by. We had the time to talk after we left the Tecys."

"Where were you headed?"

"Some comments Martin had made to his host seemed to indicate that he was going to a place I knew of further off in Shadow—the block city of Heerat. We journeyed there and found this to be correct. He had passed that way."

"I am not familiar with Heerat," I said.

"A place of adobe and stone—a commercial center at the junction of several trade routes. There, Random found news which took him eastward and probably deeper into Shadow. We parted company at Heerat, for I did not want to be away from Amber overlong. Also, there was a personal matter I was anxious to pursue. He told me how he had seen Dara walk the Pattern on the day of the battle."

"That's right," I said. "She did. I was there, too."

He nodded.

"As I said, Random had impressed me. I was inclined to believe he was telling the truth. If this were so, then it was possible that you were also. Granting this, I had to pursue the matter of the girl's allegations. You were not available, so I came to Ganelon—this was several days ago—and had him tell me everything he knew about Dara."

I glanced at Ganelon, who inclined his head slightly.

"So you now believe you have uncovered a new relative." I said, "a mendacious one, to be sure, and quite possibly an enemy—but a relative, nevertheless. What is your next move?"

He took a sip of wine.

"I would like to believe in the relationship," he said. "The notion somehow pleases me. So I would like to establish it or negate it to a certainty. If it turns out that we are indeed related, then I would like to understand the motives behind her actions. And I would like to learn why she never made her existence known to me directly." He put down his glass, raised his new hand and flexed the fingers. "So I would like to begin," he continued, "by learning of those things you experienced in Tir-na Nog'th which apply to me and to Dara. I am also extremely curious about this hand, which behaves as if it were made for me. I have never heard of a physical object being obtained in the city in the sky." He made a fist, unclenched it, rotated the wrist, extended the arm, raised it, lowered it gently to his knee. "Random performed a very effective piece of surgery, don't you think?" he concluded.

"Very," I agreed.

"So, will you tell me the story?"

I nodded and took a sip of my wine.

"It was in the palace in the sky that it occurred," I said. "The place was filled with inky, shifting shadows. I felt impelled to visit the throne room. I did this, and when the shadows moved aside, I saw you standing to the right of the throne, wearing that arm. When things cleared further, I saw Dara seated upon the throne. I advanced and touched her with Grayswandir, which made me visible to her. She declared me dead these several centuries and bade me return to my grave. When I demanded her lineage, she said she was descended of you and of the hellmaid Lintra."

Benedict drew a deep breath but said nothing. I continued:

"Time, she said, moved at such a different rate in the place of her birth, that several generations had passed there. She was the first of them possessed of regular human attributes. She again bade me depart. During this time, you had been studying Grayswandir. You struck then to remove her from danger, and we fought. My blade could reach you and your hand could reach me. That was all. Otherwise, it was a confrontation of ghosts. As the sun began to rise and the city to fade, you had me in a grip with that hand. I struck it free of the arm with Grayswandir and escaped. It was returned with me because it was still clasping my shoulder."

"Curious," Benedict said. "I have known that place to render false prophecies—the fears and hidden desires of the visitor, rather than a true picture of what is to be. But then, it often reveals unknown truths as well. And as in most other things, it is difficult to separate the valid from the spurious. How did you read it?"

"Benedict," I said. "I am inclined to believe the story of her origin. You have never seen her, but I have. She does resemble you in some ways. As for the rest . . . it is doubtless as you said—that which is left after the truth has been separated out."

He nodded slowly, and I could tell that he was not convinced but did not want to push the matter. He knew as well as I did what the rest implied. If he were to pursue his claim to the throne and succeed in achieving it, it was possible that he might one day step aside in favor of his only descendant.

"What are you going to do?" I asked him.

"Do?" he said. "What is Random now doing about Martin? I shall seek her, find her, have the story from her own lips, and then decide for myself. This will have to wait, however, until the matter of the black road is settled. That is another matter I wish to discuss with you."

"Yes?"

"If time moves so differently in their stronghold, they have had more than they need in which to mount another attack. I do not want to keep waiting to meet them in indecisive encounters. I am contemplating following the black road back to its source and attacking them on their home ground. I would like to do it with your concurrence."

"Benedict," I said, "have you ever looked upon the Courts of Chaos?"

He raised his head and stared at the blank wall of the tent.

"Ages ago, when I was young," he said, "I hellrode as far as I might go, to the end of everything. There, beneath a divided sky, I looked upon an awesome abyss. I do not know if the place lies there or if the road runs that far, but I am prepared to take that way again, if such is the case."

"Such is the case," I said.

"How can you be certain?"

"I am just returned from that land. A dark citadel hovers within it. The road goes to it."

"How difficult was the way?"

"Here," I said, taking out the Trump and passing it to him. "This was Dworkin's. I found it among his things. I only just tried it. It took me there. Time is already rapid at that point. I was attacked by a rider on a drifting roadway, of a sort not shown on the card. Trump contact is difficult there, perhaps because of the time differential. Gérard brought me back."

He studied the card.

"It seems the place I saw that time," he said at length. "This solves our logistics problems. With one of us on either end of a Trump connection we can transport the troops right through, as we did that day from Kolvir to Garnath."

I nodded.

"That is one of the reasons I showed it to you, to indicate my good faith. There may be another way, involving less risk than running our forces into the unknown. I want you to hold off on this venture until I have explored my way further."

"I will have to hold off in any event, to obtain some intelligence concerning that place. We do not even know whether your automatic weapons will function there, do we?"

"No, I did not have one along to test."

He pursed his lips.

"You really should have thought to take one and try it."

"The circumstances of my departure did not permit this."

"Circumstances?"

"Another time. It is not relevant here. You spoke of following the black road to its source . . ."

"Yes?"

"That is not its true source. Its real source lies in the true Amber, in the defect in the primal Pattern."

"Yes, I understand that. Both Random and Ganelon have described your journey to the place of the true Pattern, and the damage you discovered there. I see the analogy, the possible connection—"

"Do you recall my flight from Avalon, and your pursuit?"

In answer, he only smiled faintly.

"There was a point where we crossed the black road," I said. "Do you recall it?"

He narrowed his eyes.

"Yes," he said. "You cut a path through it. The world had returned to normal at that point. I had forgotten."

"It was an effect of the Pattern upon it," I said, "one which I believe can be employed upon a much larger scale."

"How much larger?"

"To wipe out the entire thing."

He leaned back and studied my face.

"Then why are you not about it?"

"There are a few preliminaries I must undertake."

"How much time will they involve?"

"Not too much. Possibly as little as a few days. Perhaps a few weeks."

"Why didn't you mention all of this sooner?"

"I only learned how to go about it recently."

"How *do* you go about it?"

"Basically, it amounts to repairing the Pattern."

"All right," he said. "Say you succeed. The enemy will still be out there." He gestured toward Garnath and the black road. "Someone gave them passage once."

"The enemy has always been out there," I said. "And it will be up to us to see that they are not given passage again —by dealing properly with those who provided it in the first place."

"I go along with you on that," he said, "but that is not what I meant. They require a lesson, Corwin. I want to teach them a proper respect for Amber, such a respect that even if the way is opened again they will fear to use it. That is what I meant. It is necessary."

"You do not know what it would be like to carry a battle to that place, Benedict. It is—literally—indescribable."

He smiled and stood.

"Then I guess I had best go see for myself," he said. "I will keep this card for a time, if you don't mind."

"I don't mind."

"Good. Then you be on with your business about the Pattern, Corwin, and I will be about my own. This will take me some time, too. I must go give my commanders orders concerning my absence now. Let us agree that neither of us commence anything of a final nature without checking first with the other."

"Agreed," I said.

We finished our wine.

"I will be under way myself, very soon now," I said. "So, good luck."

"To you also." He smiled again. "Things are better," he said, and he clasped my shoulder as he passed to the entrance.

We followed him outside.

"Bring Benedict's horse," Ganelon directed the orderly who stood beneath a nearby tree; and turning, he offered Benedict his hand. "I, too, want to wish you luck," he said.

Benedict nodded and shook his hand.

"Thank you, Ganelon. For many things."

Benedict withdrew his Trumps.

"I can bring Gérard up to date," he said, "before my horse arrives."

He riffled through them, withdrew one, studied it.

"How do you go about repairing the Pattern?" Ganelon asked me.

"I have to get hold of the Jewel of Judgment again," I said. "With it, I can reinscribe the damaged area."

"Is this dangerous?"

"Yes."

"Where is the Jewel?"

"Back on the shadow Earth, where I left it."

"Why did you abandon it?"

"I feared that it was killing me."

He contorted his features into a near-impossible grimace.

"I don't like the sound of this, Corwin. There must be another way."

"If I knew a better way, I'd take it."

"Supposing you just followed Benedict's plan and took them all on? You said yourself that he could raise infinite legions in Shadow. You also said that he is the best man there is in the field."

"Yet the damage would remain in the Pattern, and something else would come to fill it. Always. The enemy of the moment is not as important as our own inner weakness. If this is not mended we are already defeated, though no foreign conqueror stands within our walls."

He turned away.

"I cannot argue with you. You know your own realm," he said. "But I still feel you may be making a grave mistake by risking yourself on what may prove unnecessary at a time when you are very much needed."

I chuckled, for it was Vialle's word and I had not wanted to call it my own when she had said it.

"It is my duty," I told him.

He did not reply.

Benedict, a dozen paces away, had apparently reached Gérard, for he would mutter something, then pause and listen. We stood there, waiting for him to conclude his conversation so that we could see him off.

". . . Yes, he is here now," I heard him say. "No, I doubt that very much. But—"

Benedict glanced at me several times and shook his head.

"No, I do not think so," he said. Then, "All right, come ahead."

He extended his new hand, and Gérard stepped into being, clasping it. Gérard turned his head, saw me, and immediately moved in my direction.

He ran his eyes up and down and back and forth across my entire person, as if searching for something.

"What is the matter?" I said.

"Brand," he replied. "He is no longer in his quarters. At least, most of him isn't. He left some blood behind. The place is also broken up enough to show there had been a fight."

I glanced down at my shirt front and trousers.

"And you are looking for bloodstains? As you can see, these are the same things I had on earlier. They may be dirty and wrinkled, but that's all."

"That does not really prove anything," he said.

"It was your idea to look. Not mine. What makes you think I—"

"You were the last one to see him," he said.

"Except for the person he had a fight with—if he really did."

"What do you mean by that?"

"You know his temper, his moods. We had a small argument. He might have started breaking things up after I left, maybe cut himself, gotten disgusted, trumped out for a change of scene—Wait! His rug! Was there any blood on that small, fancy rug before his door?"

"I am not sure—no, I don't think so. Why?"

"Circumstantial evidence that he did it himself. He was very fond of that rug. He avoided messing it."

"I don't buy it," Gérard said, "and Caine's death still looks peculiar—and Benedict's servants, who could have found out you wanted gunpowder. Now Brand—"

"This could well be another attempt to frame me," I said, "and Benedict and I have come to better terms."

He turned toward Benedict, who had not moved from where he stood a dozen paces away, regarding us without expression, listening.

"Has he explained away those deaths?" Gérard asked him.

"Not directly," Benedict answered, "but much of the rest of the story now stands in a better light. So much so, that I am inclined to believe all of it."

Gérard shook his head and glared down at me again.

"Still unsettled," he said. "What were you and Brand arguing about?"

"Gérard," I said, "that is our business, till Brand and I decide otherwise."

"I dragged him back to life and watched over him, Corwin. I didn't do it just to see him killed in a squabble."

"Use your brains," I told him. "Whose idea was it to search for him the way that we did? To bring him back?"

"You wanted something from him," he said. "You finally got it. Then he became an impediment."

"No. But even if that were the case, do you think I would be so damned obvious about it? If he has been killed, then it is on the same order as Caine's death—an attempt to frame me."

"You used the obviousness excuse with Caine, too. It seems to me it could be a kind of subtlety—a thing you are good at."

"We have been through this before, Gérard . . ."

". . . And you know what I told you then."

"It would be difficult to have forgotten."

He reached forward and seized my right shoulder. I immediately drove my left hand into his stomach and pulled away. It occurred to me then that perhaps I should have told him what Brand and I had been talking about. But I didn't like the way he had asked me.

He came at me again. I side-stepped and caught him with a light left near the right eye. I kept jabbing after that, mainly to keep his head back. I was in no real shape to fight him again, and Grayswandir was back in the tent. I had no other weapon with me.

I kept circling him. My side hurt if I kicked with my left leg. I caught him once on the thigh with my right, but I was slow and off-balance and could not really follow through. I continued to jab.

Finally, he blocked my left and managed to drop his hand on my biceps. I should have pulled away then, but he was open. I stepped in with a heavy right to his stomach, all of my strength behind it. It bent him forward with a gasp, but his grip tightened on my arm. He blocked my attempted uppercut with his left, continuing its forward motion until the heel of his hand slammed against my chest, at the same time jerking my left arm backward and to the side with such force that I was thrown to the ground. If he came down on me, that was it.

He dropped to one knee and reached for my throat.

IX

I moved to block his hand, but it halted in midreach. Turning my head, I saw that another hand had fallen upon Gérard's arm, was now grasping it, was holding it back.

I rolled away. When I looked up again, I saw that Ganelon had caught hold of him. Gérard jerked his arm forward, but it did not come free.

"Stay out of this, Ganelon," he said.

"Get going, Corwin!" Ganelon said. "Get the Jewel!"

Even as he called out, Gérard was beginning to rise. Ganelon crossed with his left and connected with Gérard's jaw. Gérard sprawled at his feet. Ganelon moved in and swung a kick toward his kidney, but Gérard caught his foot and heaved him over backward. I scrambled back into a crouch, supporting myself with one hand.

Gérard came up off the ground and rushed Ganelon, who was just recovering his feet. As he was almost upon him, Ganelon came up with a double-fisted blow to Gérard's midsection, which halted him in his tracks. Instantly, Ganelon's fists were moving like pistons against Gérard's abdomen. For several moments, Gérard seemed too dazed to protect himself, and when he finally bent and brought his arms in, Ganelon caught him with a right to the jaw that staggered him backward. Ganelon immediately rushed forward, throwing his arms about Gérard as he slammed into him and hooking his right leg behind Gérard's own. Gérard toppled and Ganelon fell upon him. He straddled Gérard then and drove his right fist against his jaw. When Gérard's head rolled back, Ganelon crossed with his left.

Benedict suddenly moved to intervene, but Ganelon chose that moment to rise to his feet. Gérard lay unconscious, bleeding from his mouth and nose.

I got shakily to my own feet, dusted myself off.

Ganelon grinned at me.

"Don't stay around," he said. "I don't know how I would do in a rematch. Go find the trinket."

I glanced at Benedict and he nodded. I returned to the tent for Grayswandir. When I emerged, Gérard still had not moved, but Benedict stood before me.

"Remember," he said, "you've my Trump and I've yours. Nothing final without a conference."

I nodded. I was going to ask him why he had seemed willing to help Gérard, but not me. But second thoughts had me and I decided against spoiling our fresh-minted amity.

"Okay."

I headed toward the horses. Ganelon clapped me on the shoulder as I came up to him.

"Good luck," he said. "I'd go with you, but I am needed here—especially with Benedict trumping off to Chaos."

"Good show," I said. "I shouldn't have any trouble. Don't worry."

I went off to the paddock. Shortly, I was mounted and moving. Ganelon threw me a salute as I passed and I returned it. Benedict was kneeling beside Gérard.

I headed for the nearest trail into Arden. The sea lay at my back, Garnath and the black road to the left, Kolvir to my right. I had to gain some distance before I could work with the stuff of Shadow. The day lay clean once Garnath was lost to sight, several rises and dips later. I struck the trail and followed its long curve into the wood, where moist shadows and distant bird songs reminded me of the long periods of peace we had known of old and the silken, gleaming presence of the maternal unicorn.

My aches faded into the rhythm of the ride, and I thought once again of the encounter I had departed. It was not difficult to understand Gérard's attitude, since he had already told me of his suspicions and issued me a warning. Still, it was such bad timing for whatever had happened with Brand that I could not but see it as another action intended either to slow me or to stop me entirely. It was fortunate that Ganelon had been on hand, in good shape, and able to put his fists in the right places at the proper times. I wondered what Benedict would have done if there had only been the three of us present. I'd a feeling he would have waited and intervened only at the very last moment, to stop Gérard from killing me. I was still not happy with our accord, though it was certainly an improvement over the previous state of affairs.

All of which made me wonder again what had become of Brand. Had Fiona or Bleys finally gotten to him? Had he attempted his proposed assassinations singlehanded and been met with a counterthrust, then dragged through his intended victim's Trump? Had his old allies from the Courts of Chaos somehow gotten through to him? Had one of his horny-handed guardians from the tower finally been able to reach him? Or had it been as I had suggested to Gérard —an accidental self-injury in a fit of rage, followed by an ill-tempered flight from Amber to do his brooding and plotting elsewhere?

When that many questions arise from a single event the answer is seldom obtainable by pure logic. I had to sort out the possibilities though, to have something to reach for when more facts did turn up. In the meantime, I thought carefully over everything he had told me, regarding his allegations in light of those things which I now knew. With one exception, I did not doubt most of the facts. He had built too cleverly to have the edifice simply toppled—but then, he had had a lot of time to think these things over. No, it was in his manner of presenting events that something had been hidden by misdirection. His recent proposal practically assured me of that.

The old trail twisted, widened, narrowed again, swung to the northwest and downward, into the thickening wood. The forest had changed very little. It seemed almost the same trail a young man had ridden centuries before, riding for the sheer pleasure of it, riding to explore that vast green realm which extended over most of the continent, if he did not stray into Shadow. It would be good to be doing it again for no reason other than this.

After perhaps an hour, I had worked my way well back into the forest, where the trees were great dark towers, what sunlight I glimpsed caught like phoenix nests in their highest branches, an always moist, twilight softness smoothing the outlines of stumps and boles, logs and mossy rocks. A deer bounded across my path, not trusting to the excellent concealment of a thicket at the right of the trail. Bird notes sounded about me, never too near. Occasionally, I crossed the tracks of other horsemen. Some of these were quite fresh, but they did not stay long with the trail. Kolvir was well out of sight, had been for some time.

The trail rose again, and I knew that I would shortly reach the top of a small ridge, pass among rocks, and head downward once more. The trees thinned somewhat as we climbed, until finally I was afforded a partial view of the sky. It was enlarged as I continued, and when I came to the summit I heard the distant cry of a hunting bird.

Glancing upward, I saw a great dark shape, circling and circling, high above me. I hurried past the boulders and shook the reins for a burst of speed as soon as the way was clear. We plunged downward, racing to get under cover of the larger trees once again.

The bird cried out as we did this, but we won to the shade, to the dimness, without incident. I slowed gradually after that and continued to listen, but there were no untoward sounds on the air. This part of the forest was pretty much the same as that we had left beyond the ridge, save for a small stream we picked up and paralleled for a time, finally crossing it at a shallow ford. Beyond, the trail widened and a little more light leaked through and flowed with us for half a league. We had almost come a sufficient distance for me to begin those small manipulations of Shadow which would bear me to the pathway back to the shadow Earth of my former exile. Yet, it would be difficult to begin here, easier farther along. I resolved to save the strain on myself and my mount by continuing to a better beginning. Nothing of a threatening nature had really occurred. The bird could be a wild hunter, probably was.

Only one thought nagged at me as I rode.

Julian . . .

Arden was Julian's preserve, patrolled by his rangers, sheltering several encampments of his troops at all times—Amber's inland border guard, both against incursions natural and against those things which might appear at the boundaries of Shadow.

Where did Julian go when he had departed the palace so suddenly on the night of Brand's stabbing? If he wished simply to hide, there was no necessity for him to flee farther than this. Here he was strong, backed by his own men, moving in a realm he knew far better than the rest of us. It was quite possible that he was not, right now, too far away. Also, he liked to hunt. He had his hellhounds, he had his birds . . .

A half mile, a mile . . .

Just then, I heard the sound that I feared most. Piercing the green and the shade, there came the notes of a hunting horn. They came from some distance behind me, and I think from the left of the trail.

I urged my mount to a gallop and the trees rushed to a blur on either side. The trail was straight and level here. We took advantage of this.

Then from behind, I heard a roar—a kind of deep-chested coughing, growling sound backed by a lot of resonant lung space. I did not know what it was that had uttered it, but it was no dog. Not even a hellhound sounded like that. I glanced back, but there was no pursuit in sight. So I kept low and talked to Drum a bit.

After a time, I heard a crashing noise in the woods off to my right, but the roar was not repeated just then. I looked again, several times, but I was unable to make out what it was that was causing the disturbance. Shortly thereafter, I heard the horn once more, much nearer, and this time it was answered by the barks and the baying which I could not mistake. The hellhounds were coming—swift, powerful, vicious beasts Julian had found in some shadow and trained to the hunt.

It was time, I decided, to begin the shift. Amber was still strong about me, but I laid hold of Shadow as best I could and started the movement.

The trail began to curve to the left, and as we raced along it the trees at either hand diminished in size, fell back. Another curve, and the trail led us through a clearing, perhaps two hundred meters across. I glanced up then and saw that that damned bird was still circling, much nearer now, close enough to be dragged with me through Shadow.

This was more complicated than I had intended. I wanted an open space in which to wheel my mount and swing a blade freely if it came to that. The occurrence of such a place, however, revealed my position quite clearly to the bird, whom it was proving difficult to lose.

All right. We came to a low hill, mounted it, started downward, passing a lone, lightning-blasted tree as we did. On its nearest branch sat a hawk of gray and silver and black. I whistled to it as we passed, and it leaped into the air, shrieking a savage battle cry.

Hurrying on, I heard the individual voices of the dogs clearly now, and the thud of the horses' hoofs. Mixed in with these sounds there was something else, more a vibration, a shuddering of the ground. I looked back again, but none of my pursuit had yet topped the hill. I bent my mind toward the way away and clouds occluded the sun. Strange flowers appeared along the trail—green and yellow and purple—and there came a rumble of distant thunders. The clearing widened, lengthened. It became completely level.

I heard once again the sound of the horn. I turned for another look.

It bounded into view then, and I realized at that instant that I was not the object of the hunt, that the riders, the dogs, the bird, were pursuing the thing that ran behind me. Of course, this was a rather academic distinction, in that I was in front, and quite possibly the object of *its* hunt. I leaned forward, shouting to Drum and digging in with my knees, realizing even as I did that the abomination was moving faster than we could. It was a panic reaction.

I was being pursued by a manticora.

The last time I had seen its like was on the day before the battle in which Eric died. As I had led my troops up the rearward slopes of Kolvir, it had appeared to tear a man named Rall in half. We had dispatched it with automatic weapons. The thing proved twelve feet in length, and like this one it had worn a human face on the head and shoulders of a lion; it, too, had had a pair of eaglelike wings folded against its sides and the long pointed tail of a scorpion curving in the air above it. A number of them had somehow wandered in from Shadow to devil our steps as we headed for that battle. There was no reason to believe all of them had been accounted for, save that none had been reported since that time and no evidence of their continued existence in the vicinity of Amber had come to light. Apparently, this one had wandered down into Arden and been living in the forest since that time.

A final glance showed me that I might be pulled down in moments if I did not make a stand. It also showed me a dark avalanche of dogs rushing down the hill.

I did not know the intelligence or psychology of the manticora. Most fleeing beasts will not stop to attack something which is not bothering them. Self-preservation is generally foremost in their minds. On the other hand, I was not certain that the manticora even realized that it was being pursued. It might have started out on my trail and only had its own picked up afterward. It might have only the one thing on its mind. It was hardly a time to pause and reflect on all the possibilities.

I drew Grayswandir and turned my mount to the left, pulling back on the reins immediately as he made the turn.

Drum screamed and rose high onto his hind legs. I felt myself sliding backward, so I jumped to the ground and leaped to the side.

But I had, for the moment, forgotten the speed of the storm-hounds, had also forgotten how easily they had once overtaken Random and myself in Flora's Mercedes, had also forgotten that unlike ordinary dogs chasing cars, they had begun tearing the vehicle apart.

Suddenly, they were all over the manticora, a dozen or more dogs, leaping and biting. The beast threw back its head and uttered another cry as they struck at it. It swept that vicious tail through them, sending one flying, stunning or killing two others. It reared then and turned, striking out with its forelegs as it descended.

But even as it did this, a hound attached itself to its left foreleg, two more were at its haunches and one had scrambled onto its back, biting at its shoulder and neck. The others were circling it now. As soon as it would go after one, the others would dart in and slash at it.

It finally caught the one on its back with its scorpion sting and disembowled the one gnawing at its leg. However, it was running blood from a double dozen wounds by then. Shortly, it became apparent that the leg was giving it trouble, both for striking purposes and for bearing its weight when it struck with the others. In the meantime, another dog had mounted its back and was tearing at its neck. It seemed to be having a more difficult time getting at this one. Another came in from its right and shredded its ear. Two more plied its haunches, and when it reared again one rushed in and tore at its belly. Their barks and growls also seemed to be confusing it somewhat, and it began striking wildly at the ever-moving gray shapes.

I had caught hold of Drum's bridle and was trying to calm him sufficiently to remount and get the hell out of there. He kept trying to rear and pull away, and it took considerable persuasion even to hold him in place.

In the meantime, the manticora let out a bitter, wailing cry. It had struck wildly at the dog on its back and driven its sting into its own shoulder. The dogs took advantage of this distraction and rushed in wherever there was an opening, snapping and tearing.

I am certain the dogs would have finished it, but at that moment the riders topped the hill and descended. There were five of them, Julian in the lead. He had on his scaled white armor and his hunting horn hung about his neck. He rode his gigantic steed Morgenstern, a beast which has always hated me. He raised the long lance that he bore and saluted with it in my direction. Then he lowered it and shouted orders to the dogs. Grudgingly, they dropped away from the prey. Even the dog on the manticora's back loosened its grip and leaped to the ground. All of them drew back as Julian couched the lance and touched his spurs to Morgenstern's sides.

The beast turned toward him, gave a final cry of defiance, and leaped ahead, fangs bared. They came together, and for a moment my view was blocked by Morgenstern's shoulder. Another moment, however, and I knew from the horse's behavior that the blow had been a true one.

A turning, and I saw the beast stretched out, great gouts of blood upon its breast, flowering about the dark stem of the lance.

Julian dismounted. He said something to the other riders which I did not overhear. They remained mounted. He regarded the still-twitching manticora, then looked at me and smiled. He crossed and placed his foot upon the beast, seized the lance with one hand, and wrenched it from the carcass. Then he drove it into the ground and tethered Morgenstern to its shaft. He reached up and patted the horse's shoulder, looked back at me, turned, and headed in my direction.

When he came up before me he said, "I wish you hadn't killed Bela."

"Bela?" I repeated.

He glanced at the sky. I followed his gaze. Neither bird was now in sight.

"He was one of my favorites."

"I am sorry," I said. "I misunderstood what was going on."

He nodded.

"All right. I've done something for you. Now you can tell me what happened after I left the palace. Did Brand make it?"

"Yes," I said, "and you're off the hook on that. He claimed Fiona stabbed him. And she was not around to question either. She departed during the night, also. It's a wonder you didn't bump into one another."

He smiled.

"I'd have guessed as much," he said.

"Why did you flee under such suspicious circumstances?" I asked. "It made it look bad for you."

He shrugged.

"It would not be the first time I've been falsely accused, suspected. And for that matter, if intent counts for anything, I am as guilty as our little sister. I'd have done it myself if I could. In fact, I'd a blade ready the night we fetched him back. Only, I was crowded aside."

"But why?" I asked.

He laughed.

"Why? I am afraid of the bastard, that's why. For a long while, I had thought he was dead, and certainly hoped so—finally claimed by the dark powers he dealt with. How much do you really know about him, Corwin?"

"We had a long talk."

"And . . . ?"

"He admitted that he and Bleys and Fiona had formed a plan to claim the throne. They would see Bleys crowned, but each would share the real power. They had used the forces you referred to, to assure Dad's absence. Brand said that he had attempted to win Caine to their cause, but that Caine had instead gone to you and to Eric. The three of you then formed a similar cabal to seize power before they could, by placing Eric on the throne."

He nodded.

"The events are in order, but the reason is not. We did not want the throne, at least not that abruptly, nor at that time. We formed our group to oppose their group, because it had to be opposed to protect the throne. At first, the most we could persuade Eric to do was to assume a Protectorship. He was afraid he would quickly turn up dead if he saw himself crowned under those conditions. Then you turned up, with your very legitimate claim. We could not afford to let you press it at that time, because Brand's crowd was threatening out-and-out war. We felt they would be less inclined to make this move if the throne were already occupied. We could not have seated you, because you would have refused to be a puppet, a role you would have had to play since the game was already in progress and you were ignorant on too many fronts. So we persuaded Eric to take the risk and be crowned. That was how it happened."

"So when I did arrive he put out my eyes and threw me in the dungeon for laughs."

Julian turned away and looked back at the dead manticora.

"You are a fool," he finally said. "You were a tool from the very beginning. They used you to force our hand and either way you lost. If that half-assed attack of Bleys's had somehow succeeded, you wouldn't have lasted long enough to draw a deep breath. If it failed, as it did, Bleys disappeared, as he did, leaving you with your life forfeit for attempted usurpation. You had served your purpose and you had to die. They left us small choice in the matter. By rights, we should have killed you—and you know it."

I bit my lip. There were many things I might say. But if he was telling something approximating the truth, he did have a point. And I did want to hear more.

"Eric," he said, "figured that your eyesight might eventually be restored—knowing the way we regenerate—given time. It was a very delicate situation. If Dad were to return, Eric could step down and justify all of his actions to anyone's satisfaction—except for killing you. That would have been too patent a move to ensure his own continued reign beyond the troubles of the moment. And I will tell you frankly that he simply wanted to imprison you and forget you."

"Then whose idea was the blinding?"

He was silent again for a long while. Then he spoke very softly, almost a whisper: "Hear me out, please. It was mine, and it may have saved your life. Any action taken against you had to be tantamount to death, or their faction would have tried for the real thing. You were no longer of any use to them, but alive and about you possessed the potentiality of becoming a danger at some future time. They could have used your Trump to contact you and kill you, or they could have used it to free you in order to sacrifice you in yet another move against Eric. Blinded, however, there was no need to slay you and you were of no use for anything else they might have in mind. It saved you by taking you out of the picture for a time, and it saved us from a more egregious act which might one day be held against us. As we saw it, there was no choice. It was the only thing we could do. There could be no show of leniency either, or we might be suspected of having some use for you ourselves. The moment you assumed any such semblance of value you would have been a dead man. The most we could do was look the other way whenever Lord Rein contrived to comfort you. That was all that could be done."

"I see," I said.

"Yes," he agreed, "You saw too soon. No one had guessed you would recover your sight that quickly, nor that you would be able to escape once you did. How did you manage it?"

"Does Macy's tell Gimbel's?" I said.

"Beg pardon?"

"I said—never mind. What do you know of Brand's imprisonment, then?"

He regarded me once more.

"All I know is that there was some sort of falling out within his group. I lack the particulars. For some reason, Bleys and Fiona were afraid to kill him and afraid to let him run loose. When we freed him from their compromise—imprisonment—Fiona was apparently more afraid of having him free."

"And you said you feared him enough to have made ready to kill him. Why now, after all this time, when all of this is history and the power has shifted again? He was weak, virtually helpless. What harm could he do now?"

He sighed.

"I do not understand the power that he possesses," he said, "but it is considerable. I know that he can travel through Shadow with his mind, that he can sit in a chair, locate what he seeks in Shadow, and then bring it to him by an act of will without moving from the chair; and he can travel through Shadow physically in a somewhat similar fashion. He lays his mind upon the place he would visit, forms a kind of mental doorway, and simply steps through. For that matter, I believe he can sometimes tell what people are thinking. It is almost as if he has himself become some sort of living Trump. I know these things because I have seen him do them. Near the end, when we had him under surveillance in the palace he had eluded us once in this fashion. This was the time he traveled to the shadow Earth and had you placed in Bedlam. After his recapture, one of us remained with him at all times. We did not yet know that he could summon things through Shadow, however. When he became aware that you had escaped your confinement, he summoned a horrid beast which attacked Caine, who was then his bodyguard. Then he went to you once again. Bleys and Fiona apparently got hold of him shortly after that, before we could, and I did not see him again until that night in the library when we brought him back. I fear him because he has deadly powers which I do not understand."

"In such a case, I wonder how they managed to confine him at all?"

"Fiona has similar strengths, and I believe Bleys did also. Between the two of them, they could apparently annul most of Brand's power while they created a place where it would be inoperative."

"Not totally," I said. "He got a message to Random. In fact, he reached me once, weakly."

"Obviously not totally, then," he said. "Sufficiently, however. Until we broke through the defenses."

"What do you know of all their byplay with me—confining me, trying to kill me, saving me."

"That I do not understand," he said, "except that it was part of the power struggle within their own group. They had had a falling out amongst themselves, and one side or the other had some use for you. So, naturally, one side was trying to kill you while the other fought to preserve you. Ultimately, of course, Bleys got the most mileage out of you, in that attack he launched."

"But he was the one who tried to kill me, back on the shadow Earth," I said. "He was the one who shot out my tires."

"Oh?"

"Well, that is what Brand told me, but it jibes with all sorts of secondary evidence."

He shrugged.

"I cannot help you on that," he said. "I simply do not know what was going on among them at that time."

"Yet you countenance Fiona in Amber," I said. "In fact, you are more than a little cordial to her whenever she is about."

"Of course," he said, smiling. "I have always been very fond of Fiona. She is certainly the loveliest, most civilized of us all. Pity Dad was always so dead-set against brother-sister marriages, as well you know. It bothered me that we had to be adversaries for so long as we were. Things returned pretty much to normal after Bleys's death, your imprisonment, and Eric's coronation, though. She accepted their defeat gracefully, and that was that. She was obviously as frightened at the prospect of Brand's return as I was."

"Brand told things differently," I said, "but then, of course, he would. For one thing, he claims that Bleys is still living, that he hunted him down with his Trump and knows that he is off in Shadow, training another force for another strike at Amber."

"I suppose this is possible," Julian said. "But we are more than adequately prepared, are we not?"

"He claims further that the strike will be a feint," I continued, "and that the real attack will then come direct from the Courts of Chaos, over the black road. He says that Fiona is off preparing the way for this right now."

He scowled.

"I hope he was simply lying," he said. "I would hate to see their group resurrected and at us again, this time with help from the dark direction. And I would hate to see Fiona involved."

"Brand claimed he was out of it himself, that he had seen the error of his ways—and suchlike penitent noises."

"Ha! I'd sooner trust that beast I just slew than take Brand at his word. I hope you've had the sense to keep him well guarded—though this might not be of much avail if he has his old powers back."

"But what game could he be playing now?"

"Either he has revived the old triumvirate, a thought I like not at all, or he has a new plan all his own. But mark me, he has a plan. He has never been satisfied to be a mere spectator at anything. He is always scheming. I'd take an oath he even plots in his sleep."

"Perhaps you are right," I said. "You see, there has been a new development, whether for good or ill, I cannot yet tell. I just had a fight with Gérard. He thinks I have done Brand some mischief. This is not the case, but I was in no position to prove my innocence. I was the last person I know of to see Brand, earlier today. Gérard visited his quarters a short time ago. He says the place is broken up, there are blood smears here and there, and Brand is missing. I don't know what to make of it."

"Neither do I. But I hope it means someone has done the job properly this time."

"Lord," I said, "it's tangled. I wish I had known all of these things before."

"There was never a proper time to tell you," he said, "until now. Certainly not when you were a prisoner and could still be reached, and after that you were gone for a long while. When you returned with your troops and your new weapons, I was uncertain as to your full intentions. Then things happened quickly and Brand was back again. It was too late. I had to get out to save my skin. I am strong here in Arden. Here, I can take anything he can throw at me. I have been maintaining the patrols at full battle force and awaiting word of Brand's death. I wanted to inquire of one of you whether he was still around. But I could not decide whom to ask, thinking myself still suspect should he have died. As soon as I did get word, though, should it prove he was still living, I was resolved to have a try at him myself. Now this . . . state of affairs . . . What are you going to do now, Corwin?"

"I am off to fetch the Jewel of Judgement from a place where I cached it in Shadow. There is a way it can be used to destroy the black road. I intend to try it."

"How can this be done?"

"That is too long a story, for a horrible thought has just occurred to me."

"What is that?"

"Brand wants the Jewel. He was asking about it, and now —This power of his to find things in Shadow and fetch them back. How good is it?"

Julian looked thoughtful.

"He is hardly omniscient, if that is what you mean. You can find anything you want in Shadow the normal way we go about it—by traveling to it. According to Fiona, he just cuts out the footwork. It is therefore *an* object, not a particular object that he summons. Besides, that Jewel is a very strange item from everything Eric told me about it. I think Brand would have to go after it in person, once he finds out where it is."

"Then I must get on with my hellride. I have to beat him to it."

"I see you are riding Drum," Julian observed. "He is a good beast, a sturdy fellow. Been through many a hellride."

"Glad to hear that," I said. "What are *you* going to do now?"

"Get in touch with someone in Amber and get up to date on everything we haven't had a chance to talk about—Benedict, probably."

"No good," I said. "You will not be able to reach him. He is off to the Courts of Chaos. Try Gérard, and convince him I am an honorable man while you are about it."

"The redheads are the only magicians in this family, but I will try. . . . You *did* say the Courts of Chaos?"

"Yes, but again, the time is too valuable now."

"Of course. Get you gone. We will have our leisure later—I trust."

He reached out and clasped my arm. I glanced at the manticora, at the dogs seated in a circle about it.

"Thanks, Julian. I— You are a difficult man to understand."

"Not so. I think the Corwin I hated must have died centuries ago. Ride now, man! If Brand shows up around here, I'll nail his hide to a tree!"

He shouted an order to his dogs as I mounted, and they fell upon the carcass of the manticora, lapping at its blood and tearing out huge chunks and strips of flesh. As I rode past that strange, massive, manlike face, I saw that its eyes were still open, though glazed. They were blue, and death had not robbed them of a certain preternatural innocence. Either that, or the look was death's final gift—a senseless way of passing out ironies, if it was.

I took Drum back to the trail and began my hellride.

X

Moving along the trail at a gentle pace, clouds darkening the sky and Drum's whinny of memory or anticipation. . . . A turn to the left, and uphill. . . . The ground is brown, yellow, back to brown again. . . . The trees squat down, draw apart. . . . Grasses wave between them in the cool and rising breeze. . . . A quick fire in the sky. . . . A rumble shakes loose raindrops. . . .

Steep and rocky now. . . . The wind tugs at my cloak. . . . Up. . . . Up to where the rocks are streaked with silver and the trees have drawn their line. . . . The grasses, green fires, die down in the rain. . . . Up, to the craggy, sparkling, rain-washed heights, where the clouds rush and boil like a mud-gorged river at flood crest. . . . The rain stings like buckshot and the wind clears its throat to sing. . . . We rise and rise and the crest comes into view, like the head of a startled bull, horns guarding the trail. . . . Lightnings twist about their tips, dance between them. . . . The smell of ozone as we reach that place and rush on through, the rain suddenly blocked, the wind shunted away. . . .

Emerging on the farther side. . . . There is no rain, the air is still, the sky smoothed and darkened to a proper starfilled black. . . . Meteors cut and burn, cut and burn, cauterizing to afterimage scars, fading, fading. . . . Moons, cast like a handful of coins. . . . Three bright dimes, a dull quarter, a pair of pennies, one of them tarnished and scarred. . . . Down then, that long, winding way. . . . Hoof clops clear and metallic in the night air. . . . Somewhere, a cat-like cough. . . . A dark shape crossing a lesser moon, ragged and swift. . . .

Downward. . . . The land drops away at either hand. . . . Darkness below. . . . Moving along the top of an infinitely high, curved wall, the way itself bright with moonlight. . . . The trail buckles, folds, grows transparent. . . . Soon it drifts, gauzy, filamentous, stars beneath as well as above. . . . Stars below on either side. . . .

There is no land. . . . There is only the night, night and the thin, translucent trail I had to try to ride, to learn how it felt, against some future use. . . .

It is absolutely silent now, and the illusion of slowness attaches to every movement. . . . Shortly, the trail falls away, and we move as if swimming underwater at some enormous depth, the stars bright fish. . . . It is freedom, it is the power of the hellride that brings an elation, like yet unlike the recklessness that sometimes comes in battle, the boldness of a risky feat well learned, the rush of rightness following the finding of the poem's proper word. . . . It is these and the prospect itself, riding, riding, riding, from nowhere to nowhere perhaps, across and among the minerals and fires of the void, free of earth and air and water. . . .

We race a great meteor, we touch upon its bulk. . . . Speeding across its pitted surface, down, around, then up again. . . . It stretches into a great plain, it lightens, it yellows. . . .

It is sand, sand now beneath our movement. . . . The stars fade out as the darkness is diluted to a morning of sunrise. . . . Swaths of shade ahead, desert trees within them. . . . Ride for the dark. . . . Crashing through. . . . Bright birds burst forth, complain, resettle. . . .

Among the thickening trees. . . . Darker the ground, narrower the way. . . . Palm fronds shrink to hand size, barks darken. . . . A twist to the right, a widening of the way. . . . Our hoofs striking sparks from cobblestones. . . . The lane enlarges, becomes a tree-lined street. . . . Tiny row houses flash by. . . Bright shutters, marble steps, painted screens, set back beyond flagged walks. . . . Passing, a horse-drawn cart, loaded with fresh vegetables. . . . Human pedestrians turning to stare. . . . A small buzz of voices. . . .

On. . . . Passing beneath a bridge. . . . Coursing the stream till it widens to river, taking it down to the sea. . . .

Thudding along the beach beneath a lemon sky, blue clouds scudding. . . . The salt, the wrack, the shells, the smooth anatomy of driftwood. . . . White spray off the lime-colored sea. . . .

Racing, to where the place of waters ends at a terrace. . . . Mounting, each step crumbling and roaring down behind, losing its identity, joined with the boom of the surf. . . . Up, up to the flat-topped, tree-grown plain, a golden city shimmering, miragelike, at its end. . . .

The city grows, darkens beneath a shadowy umbrella, its gray towers stretch upward, glass and metal flashing light through the murk. . . . The towers begin to sway. . . .

The city falls in upon itself, soundlessly, as we pass. . . . Towers topple, dust boils, rises, is pinked by some lower glow. . . . A gentle noise, as of a snuffed candle, drifting by. . . .

A dust storm, quickly falling, giving place to fog. . . . Through it, the sounds of automobile horns. . . . A drift, a brief lift, a break in the gray-white, pearl-white, shifting. . . . Our hoofprints on a shoulder of highway. . . . To the right, endless rows of unmoving vehicles. . . . Pearl-white, gray-white, drifting again. . . .

Directionless shrieks and wailings. . . . Random flashes of light. . . .

Rising once more. . . . The fogs lower and ebb. . . . Grass, grass, grass. . . . Clear now the sky, and delicate blue. . . . A sun racing to set. . . . . Birds. . . . A cow in the field chewing, staring and chewing. . . .

Leaping a wooden fence to ride a country road. . . . A sudden chill beyond the hill. . . . The grasses are dry and snow's on the ground. . . . Tin-roofed farmhouse atop a rise, curl of smoke above it. . . .

On. . . . The hills grow up, the sun rolls down, darkness dragged behind. . . . A sprinkle of stars. . . . Here a house, set far back. . . . There another, long driveway wound among old trees. . . . Headlights. . . .

Off to the side of the road. . . . Draw rein and let it pass. . . .

I wiped my brow, dusted my shirt front and sleeves. I patted Drum's neck. The oncoming vehicle slowed as it neared me, and I could see the driver staring. I gave the reins a gentle movement and Drum began walking. The car braked to a halt and the driver called something after me, but I kept going. Moments later, I heard him drive off.

It was country road for a time after that. I traveled at an easy pace, passing familiar landmarks, recalling other times. A few miles later and I came to another road, wider and better. I turned there, staying off on the shoulder to the right. The temperature continued to drop, but the cold air had a good clean taste to it. A sliced moon shone above the hills to my left. There were a few small clouds passing overhead, touched to the moon's quarter with a soft, dusty light.

There was very little wind; an occasional stirring of branches, no more. After a time, I came to a series of dips in the road, telling me I was almost there.

A curve and a couple more dips. . . . I saw the boulder beside the driveway, I read my address upon it.

I drew rein then and looked up the hill. There was a station wagon in the driveway and a light on inside the house. I guided Drum off the road and across a field into a stand of trees. I tethered him behind a pair of evergreens, rubbed his neck, and told him I would not be long.

I returned to the road. No cars in sight. I crossed over and walked up the far side of the driveway, passing behind the station wagon. The only light in the house was in the living room, off to the right. I made my way around the left side of the house to the rear.

I halted when I reached the patio, looking around. Something was wrong.

The back yard was changed. A pair of decaying lawn chairs which had been leaning against a dilapidated chicken coop I had never bothered to remove were gone. So, for that matter, was the chicken coop. They had been present the last time I had passed this way. All of the dead tree limbs which had previously been strewn about, as well as a rotting mass of them I had long ago heaped to cut for firewood, were also gone.

The compost heap was missing.

I moved to the space where it had been. All that was there was an irregular patch of bare earth of the approximate shape of the heap itself.

But I had discovered in attuning myself to the Jewel that I could make myself feel its presence. I closed my eyes for a moment and tried to do so.

Nothing.

I looked again, searching carefully. but there was no tell-tale glitter anywhere in sight. Not that I had really expected to see anything, not if I could not feel it nearby.

There had been no curtains in the lighted room. Studying the house now, I saw that none of the windows had curtains, shades, shutters, or blinds. Therefore . . .

I passed around the other end of the house. Approaching the first lighted window, I glanced in quickly. Dropcloths covered much of the floor. A man in cap and coveralls was painting the far wall.

Of course.

I had asked Bill to sell the place. I had signed the necessary papers while a patient in the local clinic, when I had been projected back to my old home—probably by some action of the Jewel—on the occasion of my stabbing. That would have been several weeks ago, local time, using the Amber to shadow Earth conversion factor of approximately two and a half to one and allowing for the eight days the Courts of Chaos had cost me in Amber. Bill, of course, had gone ahead on my request. But the place had been in bad shape, abandoned as it had been for a number of years, vandalized. . . . It needed some new windowpanes, some roofing work, new guttering, painting, sanding, buffing. And there had been a lot of trash to haul away, outside as well as inside. . . .

I turned away and walked down the front slope to the road, recalling my last passage this way, half-delirious, on my hands and knees, blood leaking from my side. It had been much colder that night and there had been snow on the ground and in the air. I passed near the spot where I'd sat, trying to flag down a car with a pillow case. The memory was slightly blurred, but I still recalled the ones that had passed me by.

I crossed the road, made my way through the field to the trees. Unhitching Drum, I mounted.

"We've some more riding ahead," I told him. "Not too far this time."

We headed back to the road and started along it, continuing on past my house. If I had not told Bill to go ahead and sell the place, the compost heap would still have been there, the Jewel would still have been there. I could be on my way back to Amber with the ruddy stone hung about my neck, ready to have a try at what had to be done. Now, now I had to go looking for it, when I'd a feeling time was beginning to press once again. At least, I had a favorable ratio here with respect to its passage in Amber. I clucked at Drum and shook the reins. No sense wasting it, even so.

A half hour, and I was into town, riding down a quiet street in a residential area, houses all about me. The lights were on at Bill's place. I turned up his driveway. I left Drum in his back yard.

Alice answered my knock, stared a moment, then said, "My God! Carl!"

Minutes later, I was seated in the living room with Bill, a drink on the table to my right. Alice was out in the kitchen, having made the mistake of asking me whether I wanted something to eat.

Bill studied me as he lit his pipe.

"Your ways of coming and going still tend to be colorful," he said.

I smiled.

"Expediency is all," I said.

"That nurse at the clinic . . . scarcely anyone believed her story."

"Scarcely anyone?"

"The minority I refer to is, of course, myself."

"What was her story?"

"She claimed that you walked to the center of the room, became two-dimensional, and just faded away, like the old soldier that you are, with a rainbowlike accompaniment."

"Glaucoma can cause the rainbow symptom. She ought to have her eyes checked."

"She did," he said. "Nothing wrong."

"Oh. Too bad. The next thing that comes to mind is neurological."

"Come on, Carl. She's all right. You know that."

I smiled and took a sip of my drink.

"And you," he said, "you look like a certain playing card I once commented on. Complete with sword. What's going on, Carl?"

"It's still complicated," I said. "Even more than the last time we talked."

"Which means you can't give me that explanation yet?"

I shook my head.

"You have won an all-expense tour of my homeland, when this is over," I said, "if I still have a homeland then. Right now, time is doing terrible things."

"What can I do to help you?"

"Information, please. My old house. Who is the guy you have fixing the place up?"

"Ed Wellen. Local contractor. You know him, I think. Didn't he put in a shower for you, or something?"

"Yes, yes he did. . . . I remember."

"He's expanded quite a bit. Bought some heavy equipment. Has a number of fellows working for him now. I handled his incorporation."

"Do you know who he's got working at my place—now?"

"Offhand, no. But I can find out in just a minute." He moved his hand to rest on the telephone on the side table. "Shall I give him a ring?"

"Yes," I said, "but there is a little more to it than that. There is only one thing in which I am really interested. There was a compost heap in the back yard. It was there the last time I passed this way. It is gone now. I have to find out what became of it."

He cocked his head to the right and grinned around his pipe.

"You serious?" he finally said.

"Sure as death," I said. "I hid something in that heap when I crawled by, decorating the snow with my precious bodily fluids. I've got to have it back now."

"Just what is it?"

"A ruby pendant."

"Priceless, I suppose."

"You're right."

He nodded, slowly.

"If it were anyone else, I would suspect a practical joke," he said. "A treasure in a compost heap. . . . Family heirloom?"

"Yes. Forty or fifty carats. Simple setting. Heavy chain."

He removed his pipe and whistled softly.

"Mind if I ask why you put it there?"

"I'd be dead now if I hadn't."

"Pretty good reason."

He reached for the phone again.

"We've had some action on the house already," he remarked. "Pretty good, since I haven't advertised yet. Fellow'd heard from someone who'd heard from someone else. I took him over this morning. He's thinking about it. We may move it pretty quick."

He began to dial.

"Wait," I said. "Tell me about him."

He cradled the phone, looked up.

"Thin guy," he said. "Redhead. Had a beard. Said he was an artist. Wants a place in the country."

"Son of a bitch!" I said, just as Alice came into the room with a tray.

She made a *tsking* sound and smiled as she delivered it to me.

"Just a couple hamburgers and some leftover salad," she said. "Nothing to get excited about."

"Thank you. I was getting ready to eat my horse. I'd have felt bad afterward."

"I don't imagine he'd have been too happy about it himself. Enjoy," she said, and returned to the kitchen.

"Was the compost heap still there when you took him over?" I asked.

He closed his eyes and furrowed his brow.

"No," he said after a moment. "The yard was already clear."

"That's something, anyway," I said, and I began eating.

He made the call, and he talked for several minutes. I got the drift of things from his end of the conversation, but I listened to the entire thing after he had hung up, while I finished the food and washed it down with what was left in my glass.

"He hated to see good compost go to waste," Bill said. "So he pitched the heap into his pickup just the other day and took it out to his farm. He dumped it next to a plot he intends to cultivate, and he has not had a chance to spread it yet. Says he did not notice any jewelry, but then he could easily have missed it."

I nodded.

"If I can borrow a flashlight, I had better get moving."

"Sure. I will drive you out," he said.

"I do not want to be parted from my horse at this point."

"Well, you will probably want a rake, and a shovel or a pitchfork. I can drive them out and meet you there, if you know where the place is."

"I know where Ed's place is. He must have tools, though."

Bill shrugged and smiled.

"All right," I said. "Let me use your bathroom, and then we had better get moving."

"You seemed as if you knew the prospective buyer."

I put the tray aside and rose to my feet.

"You heard of him last as Brandon Corey."

"The guy who pretended to be your brother and got you committed?"

" 'Pretended' hell! He is my brother. No fault of mine, though. Excuse me."

"He was there."

"Where?"

"Ed's place, this afternoon. At least a bearded redhead was."

"Doing what?"

"Said he was an artist. Said he wanted permission to set up his easel and paint in one of the fields."

"And Ed let him?"

"Yes, of course. Thought it was a great idea. That is why he told me about it. Wanted to brag."

"Get the stuff. I will meet you there."

"Right."

The second thing I took out in the bathroom was my Trumps. I had to reach someone in Amber soonest, someone strong enough to stop him. But who? Benedict was on his way to the Courts at Chaos, Random was off looking for his son, I had just parted with Gérard on somewhat less than amicable terms. I wished that I had a Trump for Ganelon.

I decided that I would have to try Gérard.

I drew forth his card, performed the proper mental maneuvers. Moments later, I had contact.

"Corwin!"

"Just listen, Gérard! Brand is alive, if that is any consolation. I'm damn sure of that. This is important. Life and death. You've got to do something—fast!"

His expressions had changed rapidly while I had spoken—anger, surprise, interest . . .

"Go ahead," he said.

"Brand could be coming back very soon. In fact, he may already be in Amber. You haven't seen him yet, have you?"

"No."

"He must be stopped from walking the Pattern."

"I do not understand. But I can post a guard outside the chamber of the Pattern."

"Put the guard inside the chamber. He has strange ways of coming and going now. Terrible things may happen if he walks the Pattern."

"I will watch it personally then. What is happening?"

"No time now. Here is the next thing: Is Llewella back in Rebma?"

"Yes, she is."

"Get hold of her with her Trump. She's got to warn Moire that the Pattern in Rebma has to be guarded also."

"How serious is this, Corwin?"

"It could be the end of everything," I said. "I have to go now."

I broke the contact and headed for the kitchen and the back door, stopping only long enough to thank Alice and say good night. If

Brand had got hold of the Jewel and attuned himself to it, I was not certain what he would do, but I had a pretty strong hunch.

I mounted Drum and turned him toward the road. Bill was already backing out of the driveway.

XI

I cut through fields in many places where Bill had to follow the roads, so I was not all that far behind him. When I drew up, he was talking with Ed, who was gesturing toward the southwest.

As I dismounted, Ed was studying Drum.

"Nice horse, that," he said.

"Thanks."

"You've been away."

"Yes."

We shook hands.

"Good to see you again. I was just telling Bill that I don't really know how long that artist stayed around. I just figured he would go away when it got dark, and I didn't pay too much attention. Now, if he was really looking for something of yours and knew about the compost heap, he could still be out there for all I know. I'll get my shotgun, if you like, and go with you."

"No," I said, "thanks. I think I know who it was. The gun will not be necessary. We'll just walk over and do a little poking around."

"Okay," he said. "Let me come along and give you a hand."

"You don't have to do that," I said.

"How about your horse, then? What say I give him a drink and something to eat, clean him up a bit?"

"I'm sure he'd be grateful. I know I would."

"What's his name?"

"Drum."

He approached Drum and began making friends with him.

"Okay," he said. "I'll be back in the barn for a while. If you need me for anything, just holler."

"Thanks."

I got the tools out of Bill's car and he carried the electric lantern, leading me off to the southwest where Ed had been pointing earlier.

As we crossed the field, I followed the beam of Bill's light, searching for the heap. When I saw what might be the remains of one, I drew a deep breath, involuntarily. Someone must have been at it, the way the clods were strewn about. The mass would not have been dumped from a truck to fall in such a dispersed fashion.

Still . . . the fact that someone had looked did not mean he had located what he had been seeking.

"What do you think?" Bill siad.

"I don't know," I told him, lowering the tools to the ground and approaching the largest aggregate in sight. "Give me some light here."

I scanned what remained of the heap, then fetched a rake and began taking it apart. I broke each clod and spread it upon the ground, running the tines through it. After a time, Bill set the lantern at a good angle and moved to help me.

"I've got a funny feeling . . ." he said.

"So do I."

". . . that we may be too late."

We kept pulverizing and spreading, pulverizing and spreading. . . .

I felt the tingle of a familiar presence. I straightened and waited. Contact came moments later.

"Corwin!"

"Here, Gérard."

"What'd you say?" said Bill.

I raised my hand to silence him and gave my attention to Gérard. He stood in shadow at the bright beginning of the Pattern, leaning upon his great blade.

"You were right," he said. "Brand did show up here, just a moment ago. I am not sure how he got in. He stepped out of the shadows off to the left, there." He gestured. "He looked at me for a moment, then turned around and walked back. He did not answer when I hailed him. So I turned up the lantern, but he was nowhere in sight. He just disappeared. What do you want me to do now?"

"Was he wearing the Jewel of Judgment?"

"I could not tell. I only had sight of him for a moment, in this bad light."

"Are they watching the Pattern in Rebma now?"

"Yes. Llewella's alerted them."

"Good. Stay on guard, then. I will be in touch again."

"All right. Corwin—about what happened earlier . . ."

"Forget it."

"Thanks. That Ganelon is one tough fellow."

"Indeed," I said. "Stay awake."

His image faded as I released the contact, but a strange thing happened then. The sense of contact, the path, remained with me, objectless, open, like a switched-on radio not tuned to anything.

Bill was looking at me peculiarly.

"Carl, what is happening?"

"I don't know. Wait a minute."

Suddenly, there was contact again, though not with Gérard. She must have been trying to reach me while my attention was diverted.

"Corwin, it is important . . ."

"Go ahead, Fi."

"You will not find what you are looking for there. Brand has it."

"I was beginning to suspect as much."

"We have to stop him. I do not know how much you know—"

"Neither do I any more," I said, "but I have the Pattern in Amber and the one in Rebma under guard. Gérard just told me that Brand appeared at the one in Amber, but was scared off."

She nodded her small, fine-featured face. Her red tresses were unusually disarrayed. She looked tired.

"I am aware of this," she said. "I have him under surveillance. But you have forgotten another possibility."

"No." I said. "According to my calculations, Tir-na Nog'th should not be attainable yet—"

"That is not what I was referring to. He is headed for the primal Pattern itself."

"To attune the Jewel?"

"The first time through," she said.

"To walk it, he would have to pass through the damaged area. I gather that is more than a little difficult."

"So you do know about it," she said. "Good. That saves time. The dark area would not trouble him the way it would another of us. He has come to terms with that darkness. We must stop him, now."

"Do you know any short cuts to that place?"

"Yes. Come to me. I will take you there."

"Just a minute. I want Drum with me."

"What for?"

"No telling. That is why I want him."

"Very well. Then bring me through. We can as easily depart from there as from here."

I extended my hand. In a moment, I held hers. She stepped forward.

"Lord!" said Bill, drawing back. "You were giving me doubts about your sanity, Carl. Now it's mine I wonder about. She—she's on one of the cards, too, isn't she?"

"Yes. Bill, this is my sister Fiona. Fiona, this is Bill Roth, a very good friend."

Fi extended her hand and smiled, and I left them there while I went back to fetch Drum. A few minutes later, I led him forth.

"Bill," I said, "I am sorry to have wasted your time. My brother has the thing. We are going after him now. Thanks for helping me."

I shook his hand. He said, "Corwin." I smiled.

"Yes, that is my name."

"We have been talking, your sister and I. Not much I could learn in a few minutes, but I know it is dangerous. So good luck. I still want the whole story one day."

"Thanks," I said. "I will try to see that you get it."

I mounted, leaned down, and drew Fiona up before me.

"Good night, Mr. Roth," she said. Then, to me, "Start riding, slowly, across the field."

I did.

"Brand says you are the one who stabbed him," I said, as soon as we had gone far enough to feel alone.

"That's right."

"Why?"

"To avoid all this."

"I talked with him for a long while. He claimed it was originally you, Bleys, and himself, together in a scheme to seize power."

"That is correct."

"He told me he had approached Caine, trying to win him to your side, but that Caine would have none of it, that Caine had passed the word along to Eric and Julian. And this led to their forming their own group, to block your way to the throne."

"That is basically correct. Caine had ambitions of his own—long-term ones—but ambitions nevertheless. He was in no position to pursue them, however. So he decided that if his lot was to be a lesser one, he would rather serve it under Eric than under Bleys. I can see his point, too."

"He also claimed that the three of you had a deal going with the powers at the end of the black road, in the Courts of Chaos."

"Yes," she said, "we did."

"You use the past tense."

"For myself and for Bleys, yes."

"That is not the way Brand tells it."

"He wouldn't."

"He said you and Bleys wanted to continue exploiting that alliance, but that he had had a change of heart. Because of this, he claims you turned on him and imprisoned him in that tower."

"Why didn't we just kill him?"

"I give up. Tell me."

"He was too dangerous to be allowed his freedom, but we could not kill him either because he held something, vital."

"What?"

"With Dworkin gone, Brand was the only one who knew how to undo the damage he had done to the primal Pattern."

"You had a long time to get that information out of him."

"He possesses unbelievable resources."

"Then why did you stab him?"

"I repeat, to avoid all this. If it became a question of his freedom or his death, it were better he died. We would have to take our chances on figuring the method of repairing the Pattern."

"This being the case, why did you consent to co-operate in bringing him back?"

"First, I was not co-operating, I was trying to impede the attempt. But there were too many trying too hard. You got through to him in spite of me. Second, I had to be on hand to try to kill him in the event you succeeded. Too bad things worked out the way they did."

"You say that you and Bleys had second thoughts about the alliance, but that Brand did not?"

"Yes."

"How did your second thoughts affect your desire for the throne?"

"We thought we could manage it without any additional outside help."

"I see."

"Do you believe me?"

"I'm afraid that I am beginning to."

"Turn here."

I entered a cleft in a hillside. The way was narrow and very dark, with only a small band of stars above us. Fiona had been manipulating Shadow while we had talked, leading us from Ed's field downward, into a misty, moorlike place, then up again, to clear and rocky trail among mountains. Now, as we moved through the dark defile, I felt her working with Shadow again. The air was cool but not cold. The blackness to our left and our right was absolute, giving the illusion of enormous depths, rather than nearby rock cloaked in shadow. This impression was reinforced, I suddenly realized, by the fact that Drum's hoofbeats were not producing any echoes, aftersounds, overtones.

"What can I do to gain your trust?" she said.

"That's asking quite a bit."

She laughed.

"Let me rephrase it. What can I do to convince you I am telling the truth?"

"Just answer one question."

"What?"

"Who shot out my tires?"

She laughed again.

"You've figured it out, haven't you?"

"Maybe. You tell me."

"Brand," she said. "He had failed in his effort to destroy your memory, so he decided he had better do a more thorough job."

"The version I had of the story was that Bleys had done the shooting and left me in the lake, that Brand had arrived in time to drag me out and save my life. In fact, the police report seemed to indicate something to that effect."

"Who called the police?" she asked.

"They had it listed as an anonymous call, but—"

"Bleys called them. He couldn't reach you in time to save you, once he realized what was happening. He hoped that they could. Fortunately, they did."

"What do you mean?"

"Brand did not drag you out of the wreck. You did it yourself. He waited around to be certain you were dead, and you surfaced and pulled yourself ashore. He went down and was checking you over, to decide whether you would die if he just left you there or whether he should throw you back in again. The police arrived about then and he had to clear out. We caught up with him shortly afterward and were able to subdue him and imprison him in the tower. That took a lot of doing. Later, I contacted Eric and told him what had happened. He then ordered Flora to put you in the other place and see that you were held until after his coronation."

"It fits," I said. "Thanks."

"What does it fit?"

"I was only a small-town GP in simpler times than these, and I never had much to do with psychiatric cases. But I do know that you don't give a person electroshock therapy to restore memories. EST generally does just the opposite. It destroys some of the short-term ones. My suspicions began to stir when I learned that that was what Brand had had done to me. So I came up with my own hypothesis. The auto wreck did not restore my memories, and neither did the EST. I had finally begun recovering them naturally, not as the result of any particular trauma. I must have done something or said something to indicate that this was occurring. Word of it somehow got to Brand and he decided that this would not be a good thing to have happen at that time. So he journeyed to my shadow and managed to get me committed and subjected to treatment which he hoped would wipe out those things I had recently recovered. This was just partly successful, in that its only lasting effect was to fuzz me up for the few days surrounding the sessions. The accident may have contributed, too. But when I escaped from Porter and lived through his attempt to kill me, the process of recovery continued after I regained consciousness in Greenwood and left the place. I was remembering more and more when I was staying at Flora's. The recovery was accelerated by Random's taking me to Rebma, where I walked the Pattern. If this had not occurred, however, I am convinced now that it would all have come back, anyway. It might have taken somewhat longer, but I had broken through and the remembering was an ongoing process, coming faster and faster near the end. So I concluded that Brand was trying to sabotage me, and that is what fits the things you just told me."

The band of stars had narrowed, and it finally vanished above us. We advanced through what seemed a totally black tunnel now, with perhaps the tiniest flickering of light a great distance ahead of us.

"Yes," she said in the darkness before me, "you guessed correctly. Brand was afraid of you. He claimed he had seen your return one night in Tir-na Nog'th, to the undoing of all our plans. I paid him no heed at the time, for I was not even aware you still lived. It must have been then that he set out to find you. Whether he divined your whereabouts by some arcane means or simply saw it in Eric's mind, I do not know. Probably the latter. He is occasionally capable of such a feat. However he located you, you now know the rest."

"It was Flora's presence in that place and her strange liaison with Eric that first made him suspicious. Or so he said. Not that it matters, now. What do you propose doing with him if we get our hands on him?"

She chuckled.

"You are wearing your blade," she said.

"Brand told me, not all that long ago, that Bleys is still alive. Is this true?"

"Yes."

"Then why am I here, rather than Bleys?"

"Bleys is not attuned to the Jewel. You are. You interact with it at near distances, and it will attempt to preserve your life if you are in imminent danger of losing it. The risk, therefore, is not as great," she said. Then, moments later, "Don't take it for granted, though. A swift stroke can still beat its reaction. You can die in its presence."

The light ahead grew larger, brighter, but there were no drafts, sounds, or smells from that direction. Advancing, I thought of the layers upon layers of explanations I had received since my return, each with its own complex of motivations, justifications for what had happened while I was away, for what had happened since, for what was happening now. The emotions, the plans, the feelings, the objectives I had seen swirled like floodwater through the city of facts I was slowly erecting on the grave of my other self, and though an act is an act, in the best Steinian tradition, each wave of interpretation that broke upon me shifted the position of one or more things I had thought safely anchored, and by this brought about an alteration of the whole, to the extent that all of life seemed almost a shifting interplay of Shadow about the Amber of some never to be attained truth. Still, I could not deny that I knew more now than I had several years earlier, that I was closer to the heart of matters than I had been before, that the entire action in which I had been caught up upon my return seemed not to be sweeping toward some final resolution. And what did I want? A chance to find out what was right and a chance to act on it! I laughed. Who is ever granted the first, let alone the second of these? A workable approximation of truth, then. That would be enough. . . . And a chance to swing my blade a few times in the right direction: The highest compensation I could receive from a one o'clock world for the changes wrought since noon. I laughed again and made sure my blade was loose in the sheath.

"Brand said that Bleys had raised another army—" I began.

"Later," she said, "later. There is no more time."

And she was right. The light had grown large, become a circular opening. It had approached at a rate out of proportion to our advance, as though the tunnel itself were contracting. It seemed to be daylight that was rushing in through what I chose to regard as the cave mouth.

"All right," I said, and moments later we reached the opening and passed through it.

I blinked my eyes as we emerged. To my left was the sea, which seemed to merge with the same-colored sky. The golden sun which floated/hung above/within it, bounced beams of brilliance from all directions. Behind me, now, there was nothing but rock. Our passage to this place had vanished without a sign. Not too far below and before me—perhaps a hundred feet distant—lay the primal Pattern. A figure was negotiating the second of its outer arcs, his attention so confined by this activity that he had apparently not yet noted our presence. A flash of red as he took a turn: the Jewel, hanging now from his neck as it had hung from mine, from Eric's, from Dad's. The figure, of course, was Brand's.

I dismounted. I looked up at Fiona, small and distraught, and I placed Drum's reins in her hand.

"Any advice, other than to go after him?" I whispered.

She shook her head.

Turning then, I drew Grayswandir and strode forward.

"Good luck," she said softly.

As I walked toward the Pattern, I saw the long chain leading from the cave mouth to the now still form of the griffin Wixer. Wixer's head lay on the ground several paces to the left of his body. Body and head both leaked a normal-colored blood upon the stone.

As I approached the beginning of the Pattern, I did a quick calculation. Brand had already taken several turns about the general spiral of the design. He was approximately two and a half laps into it. If we were only separated by one winding, I could reach him with my blade once I achieved a position paralleling his own. The going, however, got rougher the further one penetrated the design. Consequently, Brand was moving at a steadily decreasing pace. So it would be close. I did not have to catch him. I just had to pick up a lap and a half and obtain a position across from him.

I placed my foot upon the Pattern and moved forward, as fast as I was able. The blue sparks began about my feet as I rushed through the first curve against the rising resistance. The sparks grew quickly. My hair was beginning to rise when I hit the First Veil, and the crackling of the sparks was quite audible now. I pushed on against the pressure of the Veil, wondering whether Brand had noticed me yet, unable to afford the distraction of a glance in his direction just then. I met the resistance with increased force, and several steps later I was through the Veil and moving more easily again.

I looked up. Brand was just emerging from the terrible Second Veil, blue sparks as high as his waist. He was grinning a grin of resolve and triumph as he pulled free and took a clear step forward. Then he saw me.

The grin went away and he hesitated, a point in my favor. You never stop on the Pattern if you can help it. If you do, it costs a lot of extra energy to get moving again.

"You are too late!" he called out.

I did not answer him. I just kept going. Blue fires fell from the Pattern tracery along Grayswandir's length.

"You will not make it through the black," he said.

I kept going. The dark area was just ahead of me now. I was glad that it had not occurred over one of the more difficult portions of the Pattern this time around. Brand moved forward and slowly began his movement toward the Grand Curve. If I could catch him there, it would be no contest. He would not have the strength or the speed to defend himself.

As I approached the damaged portion of the Pattern, I recalled the means by which Ganelon and I had cut the black road on our flight from Avalon. I had succeeded in breaking the power of the road by holding the image of the Pattern in my mind as we had gone across. Now, of course, I had the Pattern itself all around me, and the distance was not nearly so great. While my first thought had been that Brand was simply trying to rattle me with his threat, it occurred to me that the force of the dark place might well be much stronger here at its source. As I came up to it, Grayswandir blazed with a sudden intensity which outshone its previous light. On an impulse, I touched its point to the edge of the blackness, at the place where the Pattern ended.

Grayswandir clove to the blackness and could not be raised above it. I continued forward, and my blade sliced the area before me, sliding ahead in what seemed an aproximation of the original tracery. I followed. The sun seemed to darken as I trod the dark ground. I was suddenly conscious of my heartbeat, and perspiration formed on my brow. A grayish cast fell over everything. The world seemed to dim, the Pattern to fade. It seemed it would be easy to step amiss in this place, and I was not certain whether the result would be the same as a misstep within the intact portions of the Pattern. I did not want to find out.

I kept my eyes low, following the line Grayswandir was inscribing before me, the blade's blue fire now the only thing of color left to the world. Right foot, left foot . . .

Then suddenly I was out of it and Grayswandir swung free in my hand once again, the fires partly diminished, whether by contrast with the reilluminated prospect or for some other reasons I did not know.

Looking about, I saw that Brand was approaching the Grand Curve. As for me, I was working my way toward the Second Veil. We would both be involved in the strenuous efforts these entailed in a few more minutes. The Grand Curve is more difficult, more prolonged than the Second Veil, however. I should be free and moving more quickly again before he worked his way through his barrier. Then I would have to cross the damaged area another time. He might be free by then, but he would be moving more slowly than I would, for he would be into the area where the going becomes even more difficult.

A steady static arose with each step that I took, and a tingling sensation permeated my entire body. The sparks rose to midthigh as I moved. It was like striding through a field of electric wheat. My hair was at least partly risen by then. I could feel its stirring. I glanced back once to see Fiona, still mounted, unmoving, watching.

I pressed ahead to the Second Veil.

Angles . . . short, sharp turns. . . . The force rose and rose against me, so that all of my attention, all of my strength, was now occupied in striving against it. There came again that familiar sense of timelessness, as though this was all I had ever done, all that I ever would do. And will . . . a focusing of desire to such an intensity that everything else was excluded . . . Brand, Fiona, Amber, my own identity. . . . The sparks rose to even greater heights as I struggled, turned, labored, each step requiring more effort than the previous one.

I pushed through. Right into the black area again.

Reflexively, I moved Grayswandir down and ahead once more. Again, the grayness, the monochrome fog, cut by the blue of my blade opening the way before me like a surgical incision.

When I emerged into normal light, I sought Brand. He was still in the western quadrant, struggling with the Grand Curve, about two thirds of the way through it. If I pushed hard, I might be able to catch him just as he was coming out of it. I threw all of my strength into moving as quickly as possible.

As I made it to the north end of the Pattern and into the curve leading back, it struck me suddenly what I was about to do.

I was rushing to spill more blood upon the Pattern.

If it came to a simple choice between further damage to the Pattern and Brand's destroying it utterly, then I knew what I had to do. Yet, I felt there had to be another way. Yes . . .

I slowed my pace just a trifle. It was going to be a matter of timing. His passage was a lot rougher than mine just then, so I had an edge in that respect. My entire new strategy involved arranging our encounter at just the right point. Ironically, at that moment, I recalled Brand's concern for his rug. The problem of keeping this place clean was a lot trickier, though.

He was nearing the end of the Grand Curve, and I paced him while calculating the distance to the blackness. I had decided to let him do his bleeding over the area which had already been damaged. The only disadvantage I seemed to possess was that I would be situated to Brand's right. To minimize the benefit this would give him when we crossed blades, I would have to remain somewhat to the rear.

Brand struggled and advanced, all of his movements in slow motion. I struggled too, but not as hard. I kept the pace. I wondered as I went, about the Jewel, about the affinity we had shared since the attunement. I could feel its presence, there to my left and ahead, even though I could not see it now upon Brand's breast. Would it really act to save me across that distance should Brand gain the upper hand in our coming conflict? Feeling its presence, I could almost believe that it would. It had torn me from one assailant and found, somehow, within my mind, a traditional place of safety—my own bed— and had transported me there. Feeling it now, almost seeing the way before Brand through it, I felt some assurance that it would attempt to function on my behalf once again. Recalling Fiona's words, however, I was determined not to rely on it. Still, I considered its other functions, speculated upon my ability to operate it without contact . . .

Brand had almost completed the Grand Curve. I reached out from some level of my being and made contact with the Jewel. Laying my will upon it, I called for a storm of the red tornado variety which had destroyed Iago. I did not know whether I could control that particular phenomenon in this particular place, but I called for it nevertheless and directed it toward Brand. Nothing happened immediately, though I felt the Jewel functioning to achieve something. Brand came to the end, offered a final exertion, and passed from the Grand Curve.

I was right there behind him.

He knew it, too—somehow. His blade was out the instant the pressure was off, he gained a couple feet faster than I thought he could, got his left foot ahead of him, turned his body, and met my gaze over the lines of our blades.

"Damned if you didn't make it," he said, touching the tip of my blade with his own. "You would never have gotten here this soon if it weren't for the bitch on the horse, though."

"Nice way to talk about our sister," I said, feinting and watching him move to parry.

We were hampered, in that neither of us could lunge without departing the Pattern. I was further hampered in not wanting to make him bleed, yet. I faked a stop thrust and he drew back, sliding his left foot along the design to his rear. He withdrew his right then, stamped it, and tried a head cut without preliminaries. Damn it! I parried and then riposted by pure reflex. I did not want to catch him with the chest cut I had thrown back at him, but the tip of Grayswandir traced an arc beneath his sternum. I heard a humming in the air above us. I could not afford to take my eyes off Brand, though. He glanced downward and backed some more. Good. A red line now decorated his shirt front where my cut had taken him. So far, the material seemed to be absorbing it. I stamped, feinted, thrust, parried, stop thrust, bound, and unbound—everything I could think of to keep him retreating. I had the psychological edge on him in that I had the greater reach and we both knew I could do more things with it, more quickly. Brand was nearing the dark area. Just a few more paces. . . . I heard a sound like a single bell chime, followed by a great roaring. A shadow suddenly fell upon us, as though a cloud had just occluded the sun.

Brand glanced up. I think I could have gotten him just then, but he was still a couple of feet too far from the target area.

He recovered immediately and glared at me.

"Damn you, Corwin! That's yours, isn't it?" he cried, and then he attacked, discarding what caution he still possessed.

Unfortunately, I was in a bad position, as I had been edging up on him, preparing to press him the rest of the way back. I was exposed and slightly off-balance. Even as I parried, I realized it would not be sufficient, and I twisted and fell back.

I struggled to keep my feet in place as I went down. I caught myself with my right elbow and my left hand. I cursed, as the pain was too much and my elbow slid to the side, dropping me to my right shoulder.

But Brand's thrust had gone by me, and within blue halos my feet still touched the line. I was out of Brand's reach for a death thrust, though he could still hamstring me.

I raised my right arm, still clutching Grayswandir, before me. I began to sit up. As I did, I saw that the red formation, yellow about the edges, was now spinning directly above Brand, crackling with sparks and small lightnings, its roar now changed to a wailing.

Brand took hold of his blade by the forte and raised it above his shoulder like a spear, pointed in my direction. I knew that I could not parry it, that I could not dodge it.

With my mind, I reached out to the Jewel and up to the formation in the sky . . .

There came a bright flash as a small finger of lightning reached down and touched his blade . . .

The weapon fell from his hand and his hand flew to his mouth. With his left hand, he clutched at the Jewel of Judgment, as if he realized what I was doing and sought to nullify it by covering the stone. Sucking his fingers, he looked upward, all of the anger draining from his face to be replaced by a look of fear verging on terror. The cone was beginning to descend.

Turning then, he stepped onto the blackened area, faced south, raised both his arms and cried out something I could not hear above the wailing.

The cone fell toward him, but he seemed to grow two-dimensional as it approached. His outline wavered. He began to shrink—but it did not seem a function of actual size, so much as an effect of distancing. He dwindled, dwindled, was gone, a bare instant before the cone licked across the area he had occupied.

With him went the Jewel, so that I was left with no way of controlling the thing above me. I did not know whether it was better to maintain a low profile or to resume a normal stance on the Pattern. I decided on the latter, because the whirlwind seemed to go for things which broke the normal sequence. I got back into a sitting position and edged over to the line. Then I leaned forward into a crouch, by which time the cone began to rise. The wailing retreated down the scale as it withdrew. The blue fires about my boots had subsided completely. I turned and looked at Fiona. She motioned me to get up and go on.

So I rose slowly, seeing that the vortex above me continued to dissipate as I moved. Advancing upon the area where Brand had so recently stood, I once again used Grayswandir to guide me through. The twisted remains of Brand's blade lay near the far edge of the dim place.

I wished there were some easy way out of the Pattern. It seemed pointless to complete it now. But there is no turning back once you have set foot upon it, and I was extremely leery of trying the dark route out. So I headed on toward the Grand Curve. To what place, I wondered, had Brand taken himself? If I knew, I could command the Pattern to send me after him, once I reached the center. Perhaps Fiona had an idea. Still, he would probably head for a place where he had allies. It would be senseless to pursue him alone.

At least I had stopped the attunement, I consoled myself.

Then I entered the Grand Curve. The sparks shot up about me.

XII

Late afternoon on a mountain: the westering sun shone full on the rocks to my left, tailored long shadows for those to the right; it filtered through the foliage about my tomb; it countered to some extent the chill winds of Kolvir. I released Random's hand and turned to regard the man who sat on the bench before the mausoleum.

It was the face of the youth on the pierced Trump, lines now drawn above the mouth, brow heavier, a general weariness in eye movement and set of jaw which had not been apparent on the card.

So I knew it before Random said, "This is my son Martin."

Martin rose as I approached him, clasped my hand, said, "Uncle Corwin." His expression changed but slightly as he said it. He scrutinized me.

He was several inches taller than Random, but of the same light build. His chin and cheekbones had the same general cut to them, his hair was of a similar texture.

I smiled.

"You have been away a long while," I said. "So was I."

He nodded.

"But I have never really been in Amber proper," he said. "I grew up in Rebma—and other places."

"Then let me welcome you, nephew. You come at an interesting time. Random must have told you about it."

"Yes," he said. "That is why I asked to meet you here, rather than there."

I glanced at Random.

"The last uncle he met was Brand," Random said, "and under very nasty circumstances. Do you blame him?"

"Hardly. I ran into him myself a bit earlier. Can't say it was the most rewarding encounter."

"Ran into him?" said Random. "You've lost me."

"He has left Amber and he has the Jewel of Judgment with him. If

I had known earlier what I know now, he would still be in the tower. He is our man, and he is very dangerous."

Random nodded.

"I know," he said. "Martin confirmed all our suspicions on the stabbing—and it was Brand. But what is this about the Jewel?"

"He beat me to the place where I had left it on the shadow Earth. He has to walk the Pattern with it and project himself through it, though, to attune it to his use. I just stopped him from doing that on the primal Pattern in the real Amber. He escaped, however. I was just over the hill with Gérard, sending a squad of guards through to Fiona in that place, to prevent his returning and trying again. Our own Pattern and that in Rebma are also under guard because of him."

"Why does he want so badly to attune it? So he can raise a few storms? Hell, he could take a walk in Shadow and make all the weather he wants.'"

"A person attuned to the Jewel could use it to erase the Pattern."

"Oh? What happens then?"

"The world as we know it comes to an end."

"Oh," Random said again. Then, "How the hell do you know?"

"It is a long story and I haven't the time, but I had it from Dworkin and I believe that much of what he said."

"He's still around?"

"Later," I said.

"Okay. But Brand would have to be mad to do something like that."

I nodded.

"I believe he thinks he could then cast a new Pattern, redesign the universe with himself as chief executive."

"Could this be done?"

"Theoretically, perhaps. But even Dworkin has certain doubts that the feat could be repeated effectively now. The combination of factors was unique. . . . Yes, I believe Brand is somewhat mad. Looking back over the years, recalling his personality changes, his cycles of moods, it seems there was something of a schizoid pattern there. I do not know whether the deal he made with the enemy pushed him over the edge or not. It does not really matter. I wish he were back in his tower. I wish Gérard were a worse physician."

"Do you know who stabbed him?"

"Fiona. You can get the story from her, though."

He leaned against my epitaph and shook his head.

"Brand," he said. "Damn him. Any one of us might have killed him on a number of occasions—in the old days. Just when he would get you mad enough, though, he would change. After a while, you would get to thinking he wasn't such a bad guy after all. Too bad he didn't push one of us just a little harder at the wrong time . . ."

"Then I take it he is now fair game?" said Martin.

I looked at him. The muscles in his jaws had tightened and his eyes narrowed. For a moment, all of our faces fled across his, like a riffling of the family cards. All of our egoism, hatred, envy, pride, and abuse seemed to flow by in that instant—and he had not even set foot in Amber yet. Something snapped inside me and I reached out and seized him by the shoulders.

"You have good reason to hate him," I said, "and the answer to your question is 'yes.' The hunting season is open. I see no way to deal with him other than to destroy him. I hated him myself for so long as he remained an abstraction. But—now—it is different. Yes, he must be killed. But do not let that hatred be your baptism into our company. There has been too much of it among us. I look at your face—I don't know. . . . I am sorry, Martin. Too much is going on right now. You are young. I have seen more things. Some of them bother me—differently. That's all."

I released my grip and stepped back.

"Tell me about yourself," I said.

"I was afraid of Amber for a long while," he began, "and I guess that I still am. Ever since he attacked me, I have been wondering whether Brand might catch up with me again. I have been looking over my shoulder for years. I have been afraid of all of you, I suppose. I knew most of you as pictures on cards—with bad reputations attached. I told Random—Dad—that I did not want to meet you all at once, and he suggested that I see you first. Neither of us realized at the time that you would be particularly interested in certain things that I know. After I mentioned them though, Dad said I had to see you as soon as possible. He has been telling me all about what has been going on and—you see, I know something about it."

"I had a feeling that you might—when a certain name cropped up not too long ago."

"The Tecys?" Random said.

"The same."

"It is difficult, deciding where to start . . ." Martin said.

"I know that you grew up in Rebma, walked the Pattern, and then used your power over Shadow to visit Benedict in Avalon," I said. "Benedict told you more about Amber and Shadow, taught you the use of the Trumps, coached you in weaponry. Later, you departed to walk in Shadow by yourself. And I know what Brand did to you. That is the sum of my knowledge."

He nodded, stared off into the west.

"After I left Benedict's, I traveled for years in Shadow," he said. "Those were the happiest times I have known. Adventure, excitement, new things to see, to do. . . . In the back of my mind, I always had it that one day when I was smarter and tougher—more experienced—I would journey to Amber and meet my other relatives. Then Brand caught up with me. I was camped on a little hillside, just resting from a long ride and taking my lunch, on my way to visit my friends the Tecys. Brand contacted me then. I had reached Benedict with his Trump, when he was teaching me how to use them, and other times when I had traveled. He had even transported me through occasionally, so I knew what it felt like, knew what it was all about. This felt the same way, and for a moment I thought that somehow it was Benedict calling me. But no. It was Brand—I recognized him from his picture in the deck. He was standing in the midst of what seemed to be the Pattern. I was curious. I did not know how he had reached me. So far as I knew, there was no Trump for me. He talked for a minute—I forget what he said—and when everything was firm and clear, he—he stabbed me. I pushed him and pulled away then. He held the contact somehow. It was hard for me to break it—and when I did, he tried to reach me again. But I was able to block him. Benedict had taught me that. He tried again, several times, but I kept blocking. Finally, he stopped. I was near to the Tecys. I managed to get onto my horse and make it to their place. I thought I was going to die, because I had never been hurt that badly before. But after a time, I began to recover. Then I grew afraid once again, afraid that Brand would find me and finish what he had begun."

"Why didn't you contact Benedict," I asked him, "and tell him what had happened, tell him of your fears?"

"I thought of that," he said, "and I also thought of the possibility that Brand believed he had succeeded, that I was indeed dead. I did not know what sort of power struggle was going on in Amber, but I decided that the attempt on my life was probably part of such a thing. Benedict had told me enough about the family that this was one of the first things to come to mind. So I decided that perhaps it would be better to remain dead. I left the Tecys before I was completely recovered and rode off to lose myself in Shadow.

"I happened upon a strange thing then," he continued, "a thing I had never before encountered, but which now seemed virtually omnipresent: In nearly all of the shadows through which I passed, there was a peculiar black road existing in some form or other. I did not understand it, but since it was the only thing I had come across which seemed to traverse Shadow itself, my curiosity was aroused. I resolved to follow it and learn more about it. It was dangerous. I learned very quickly not to tread the thing. Strange shapes seemed to travel it at night. Natural creatures which ventured upon it sickened and died. So I was careful. I went no nearer than was necessary to keep it in sight. I followed it through many places. I quickly learned that everywhere it ran there was death, desolation, or trouble nearby. I did not know what to make of it.

"I was still weak from my wound," he went on, "and I made the mistake of pressing myself, of riding too far, too fast, in a day's time. That evening, I fell ill and I lay shivering in my blanket through the night and much of the next day. I was into and out of delirium during this time, so I do not know exactly when she appeared. She seemed like part of my dream much of the while. A young girl. Pretty. She took care of me while I recovered. Her name was Dara. We talked interminably. It was very pleasant. Having someone to talk with like that . . . I must have told her my whole life story. Then she told me something of herself. She was not a native of the area in which I had collapsed. She said that she had traveled there through Shadow. She could not yet walk through it as we do, though she felt she could learn to do this, as she claimed descent from the House of Amber through Benedict. In fact, she wanted very badly to learn how it was done. Her means of travel then was the black road itself. She was immune to its noxious effects, she said, because she was also related to the dwellers at its farther end, in the Courts of Chaos. She wanted to learn our ways though, so I did my best to instruct her in those things that I did know. I told her of the Pattern, even sketched it for her. I showed her my Trumps—Benedict had given me a deck—to show her the appearance of her other relatives. She was particularly interested in yours."

"I begin to understand," I said. "Go on."

"She told me that Amber, in the fullness of its corruption and presumption, had upset a kind of metaphysical balance between itself and the Courts of Chaos. Her people now had the job of redressing the matter by laying waste to Amber. Their own place is not a shadow of Amber, but a solid entity in its own right. In the meantime, all of the intervening shadows are suffering because of the black road. My knowledge of Amber being what it was, I could only listen. At first, I accepted everything that she said. Brand, to me, certainly fit her description of evil in Amber. But when I mentioned him, she said no. He was some sort of hero back where she hied from. She was uncertain as to the particulars, but it did not trouble her all that much. It was then that I realized how oversure she seemed about everything—there was a ring of the fanatic when she talked. Almost unwillingly, I found myself trying to defend Amber. I thought of Llewella and of Benedict—and of Gérard, whom I had met a few times. She was eager to learn of Benedict, I discovered. That proved the soft spot in her armor. Here I could speak with some knowledge, and here she was willing to believe the good things I had to say. So, I do not know what the ultimate effect of all this talk was, except that she seemed somewhat less sure of herself near the end . . ."

"The end?" I said. "What do you mean? How long was she with you?"

"Almost a week," he replied. "She had said she would take care of me until I was recovered, and she did. Actually, she remained several days longer. She said that was just to be sure, but I think it was really that she wanted to continue our conversations. Finally though, she said that she had to be moving on. I asked her to stay with me, but she said no. I offered to go with her, but she said no to that, too. She must have realized that I planned to follow her then, because she slipped away during the night. I could not ride the black road, and I had no idea what shadow she would travel to next on her way to Amber. When I awoke in the morning and realized she had gone, I thought for a time of visiting Amber myself. But I was still afraid. Perhaps some of the things she had said had reinforced my own fears. Whatever, I decided to remain in Shadow. And so I traveled on, seeing things, trying to learn things—until Random found me and told me he wanted me to come home. He brought me here first though, to meet you, because he wanted you to hear my story before any of the others. He said that you knew Dara, that you wanted to learn more about her. I hope I have helped."

"Yes," I said. "Thank you."

"I understand that she did finally walk the Pattern."

"Yes, she succeeded in that."

"And afterward declared herself an enemy of Amber."

"That, too."

"I hope," he said, "that she comes to no harm from all this. She was kind to me."

"She seems quite able to take care of herself," I said. "But . . . yes, she is a likable girl. I cannot promise you anything concerning her safety, because I still know so little about her, so little of her part in everything that is going on. Yet, what you have told me has been helpful. It makes her someone I would still like to grant doubt's benefit, as far as I can."

He smiled.

"I am glad to hear that."

I shrugged.

"What are you going to do now?" I asked.

"I am taking him to see Vialle," Random said, "and then to meet the others, as time and opportunity permit. Unless, of course, something new has developed and you need me now."

"There have been new developments," I said, "but I do not really need you now. I had better bring you up to date, though. I still have a little time."

As I filled Random in on events since his departure, I thought about Martin. He was still an unknown quantity so far as I was concerned. His story might be perfectly true. In fact, I felt that it was. On the other hand, I had a feeling that it was not complete, that he was intentionally leaving something out. Maybe something harmless. Then again, maybe not. He had no real reason to love us. Quite the contrary. And Random could be bringing home a Trojan Horse. Probably though, it was nothing like that. It is just that I never trust anyone if there is an alternative available.

Still, nothing that I was telling Random could really be used against us, and I strongly doubted that Martin could do us much damage if that was his intention. No, more likely he was being as cagey as the rest of us, and for pretty much the same reasons: fear and self-preservation. On a sudden inspiration, I asked him, "Did you ever run into Dara again after that?"

He flushed.

"No," he said, too quickly. "Just that time. That's all."

"I see," I said, and Random was too good a poker player not to have noticed; so I had just bought us a piece of instant insurance at the small price of putting a father on guard against his long-lost son.

I quickly shifted our talk back to Brand. It was while we were comparing notes on psychopathology that I felt the tiny tingle and the sense of presence which heralds a Trump contact. I raised my hand and turned aside.

In a moment the contact was clear and Ganelon and I regarded one another.

"Corwin," he said, "I decided it was time to check. By now, you have the Jewel, Brand has the Jewel, or you are both still looking. Which one is it?"

"Brand has the Jewel," I said.

"More's the pity," he said. "Tell me about it."

So I did.

"Then Gérard had the story right," he said.

"He's already told you all this?"

"Not in such detail," Ganelon replied, "and I wanted to be sure I was getting it straight. I just finished speaking with him." He glanced upward. "It would seem you had best be moving then, if my memories of moonrise serve me right."

I nodded.

"Yes, I will be heading for the stairway shortly. It is not all that far from here."

"Good. Now here is what you must be ready to do—"

"I know what I have to do," I said. "I have to get up to Tir-na Nog'th before Brand does and block his way to the Pattern. Failing that, I have to chase him through it again."

"That is not the way to go about it," he said.

"You have a better idea?"

"Yes, I do. You have your Trumps with you?"

"Yes."

"Good. First, you would not be able to get up there in time to block his way to the Pattern—"

"Why not?"

"You have to make the ascension, then you have to walk to the palace and make your way down to the Pattern. That takes time, even in Tir-na Nog'th—especially in Tir-na Nog'th, where time tends to play tricks anyway. For all you know, you may have a hidden death wish slowing you down. I don't know. Whatever the case, he would have commenced walking the Pattern by the time you arrived. It may well be that he would be too far into it for you to reach him this time."

"He will probably be tired. That should slow him some.'

"No. Put yourself in his place. If you were Brand, wouldn't you have headed for some shadow where the time flow was different? Instead of an afternoon, he could well have taken several days to rest up for this evening's ordeal. It is safest to assume that he will be in good shape."

"You are right," I said. "I can't count on it. Okay. An alternative I had entertained but would rather not try if it could be avoided, would be to kill him at a distance. Take along a crossbow or one of our rifles and simply shoot him in the midst of the Pattern. The thing that bothers me about it is the effect of our blood on the Pattern. It may be that it is only the primal Pattern that suffers from it, but I don't know."

"That's right. You do not know," he said. "Also, I would not want you to rely on normal weapons up there. That is a peculiar place. You said yourself it is like a strange piece of Shadow drifting in the sky. While you figured how to make a rifle fire in Amber, the same rules may not apply up there."

"It is a risk," I acknowledged.

"As for the crossbow—supposing a sudden gust of wind deflected the bolt each time you shot one?"

"I am afraid I do not follow you."

"The Jewel. He walked it part way through the primal Pattern, and he has had some time to experiment with it since then. Do you think it possible that he is partly attuned to it now?"

"I do not know. I am not at all that sure how the process works."

"I just wanted to point out that if it does work that way, he may be able to use it to defend himself. The Jewel may even have other properties you are not aware of. So what I am saying is that I would not want you to count on being able to kill him at a distance. And I would not even want you to rely on being able to pull the trick you did with the Jewel again—not if he may have gained some measure of control over it."

"You do make things look a little bleaker than I had them."

"But possibly more realistic," he said.

"Conceded. Go on. You said you had a plan."

"That is correct. My thinking is that Brand must not be allowed to reach the Pattern at all, that once he sets foot upon it the probability of disaster goes way up."

"And you do not think I can get there in time to block him?"

"Not if he can really transport himself around almost instantaneously while you have to take a long walk. My bet is that he is just waiting for moonrise, and as soon as the city takes form he will be inside, right next to the Pattern."

"I see the point, but not the answer."

"The answer is that you are not going to set foot in Tir-na Nog'th tonight."

"Hold on a minute!"

"Hold on, hell! You imported a master strategist, you'd better listen to what he has to say."

"Okay, I am listening."

"You have agreed that you probably cannot reach the place in time. But someone else can."

"Who and how?"

"All right. I have been in touch with Benedict. He has returned. At this moment, he is in Amber, down in the chamber of the Pattern. By now, he should have finished walking it and be standing there at its center, waiting. You proceed to the foot of the stairs to the sky-city. There you await the rising of the moon. As soon as Tir-na Nog'th takes form, you will contact Benedict via his Trump. You tell him that all is ready, and he will use the power of the Pattern in Amber to transport himself to the place of the Pattern in Tir-na Nog'th. No matter how fast Brand travels, he cannot gain much on that."

"I see the advantages," I said. "That is the fastest way to get a man up there and Benedict is certainly a good man. He should have no trouble dealing with Brand."

"Do you really think Brand will make no other preparations?" Ganelon said. "From everything I've heard about the man, he's smart even if he is daft. He just may anticipate something like this."

"Possibly. Any idea what he might do?"

He made a sweeping gesture with one hand, slapped his neck and smiled.

"A bug," he said. "Pardon me. Pesky little things."

"You still think—"

"I think you had better remain in contact with Benedict the entire time he is up there, that is what I think. If Brand gets the upper hand, you may need to pull Benedict back immediately to save his life."

"Of course. But then—"

"But then we would have lost a round. Admitted. But not the game. Even with the Jewel fully attuned, he would have to get to the primal Pattern to do his real damage with it—and you have that under guard."

"Yes," I said. "You seem to have everything figured. You surprised me, moving so fast."

"I've had a lot of time on my hands recently, which can be a bad thing unless you use it for thinking. So I did. What I think now is that you had best move fast. The day isn't getting any longer."

"Agreed," I said. "Thanks for the good counsel."

"Save your thanks till we see what comes of it," he said, and then he broke the contact.

"That one sounded important," Random said. "What's up?"

"Appropriate question," I answered, "but I am all out of time now. You will have to wait till morning for the story."

"Is there anything I can do to help?"

"As a matter of fact," I said, "yes, if you'll either ride double or go back to Amber on a Trump. I need Star."

"Sure," Random said. "No trouble. Is that all?"

"Yes. Haste is all."

We moved toward the horses.

I patted Star a few times and then mounted.

"We'll see you in Amber," Random said. "Good luck."

"In Amber," I said. "Thanks."

I turned and headed toward the place of the stairway, treading my tomb's lengthening shadow eastward.

XIII

On the highest ridge of Kolvir there is a formation which resembles three steps. I sat on the lowest of these and waited for more to occur above me. I takes night and moonlight to do this, so half of the requirements had been met.

There were clouds to the west and northeast. I was leery of those clouds. If they massed sufficiently to block all moonlight, Tir-na Nog'th faded back to nothingness. This was one reason why it was always advisable to have a backup man on the ground, to Trump you to safety should the city vanish about you.

The sky overhead was clear, however, and filled with familiar stars. When the moon came up and its light fell upon the stone at which I rested, the stairway in the sky would come into being, sweeping upward to a great height, taking its way to Tir-na Nog'th, the image of Amber that rode the night's middle air.

I was weary. Too much had occurred in too brief a time. Suddenly to be at rest, to remove my boots and rub my feet, to lean back and rest my head, even against stone, was a luxury, a pure animal pleasure. I drew my cloak together before me against the growing chill. A hot bath, a full meal, a bed would be very good things. But these assumed an almost mythic quality from that vantage. It was more than sufficient simply to rest as I was, to let my thoughts move more slowly, drifting, spectatorlike, back over the day's happenings.

So much . . . but now, at least, I had some answers to some of my questions. Not all of them, certainly. But enough to slake my mind's thirst for the moment. . . . I now had some idea as to what had been going on during my absence, a better understanding of what was happening now, a knowledge of some of the things that had to be done, of what *I* had to do. . . . And I felt, somehow, that I knew more than I realized, consciously, that I already possessed pieces that would fit the growing picture before me, if I were only to jiggle them, flip them, rotate them properly. The pace of recent events, particularly today's, had not allowed me a moment's reflection. Now, though, some of the pieces seemed to be turning at odd angles. . . .

I was distracted by a stirring above my shoulder, a tiny effect of brightening in the higher air. Turning, then standing, I regarded the horizon. A preliminary glow had occurred out over the sea at the point where the moon would ascend. As I watched, a minute arc of light came into view. The clouds had shifted slightly also, though not enough to cause concern. I glanced up then, but the overhead phenomenon had not yet begun. I withdrew my Trumps, however, riffled them, and cut out Benedict's.

Lethargy forgotten, I stared, watching the moon expand above the water, casting a trail of light over the waves. A faint form was suddenly hovering on the threshold of visibility high overhead. As the light grew, a spark limned it here and there. The first lines, faint as spider webbing, appeared above the rock. I studied Benedict's card, I reached for contact. . . .

His cold image came alive. I saw him in the chamber of the Pattern, standing at the design's center. A lighted lantern glowed beside his left foot. He became aware of my presence.

"Corwin," he said, "is it time?"

"Not quite," I told him. "The moon is rising. The city is just beginning to take form. So it will only be a little longer. I wanted to be certain you were ready."

"I am ready," he said.

"It is good that you came back when you did. Did you learn anything of interest?"

"Ganelon called me back," he said, "as soon as he learned what had happened. His plan seemed a good one, which is why I am here. As for the Courts of Chaos, yes. I believe I have learned a few things—"

"A moment," I said.

The moonbeam strands had assumed a more tangible appearance. The city overhead was now clear in outline. The stairway was visible in its entirety, though fainter in some places than in others. I stretched forth my hand, above the second stair, the third . . .

Cool, soft, I encountered the fourth stair. It seemed to give somewhat beneath my push, however.

"Almost," I said to Benedict. "I am going to try the stairs. Be ready."

He nodded.

I mounted the stone stairs, one, two, three. I raised my foot then and lowered it upon the fourth, ghostly one. It yielded gently to my weight. I was afraid to raise my other foot, so I waited, watching the moon. I breathed the cool air as the brightness increased, as the path in the waters widened. Glancing upward, I saw Tir-na Nog'th lose something of its transparency. The stars behind it grew dimmer. As this occurred, the stair became firmer beneath my foot. All resiliency went out of it. I felt that it might bear my full weight. Casting my eyes along its length, I now saw it in its entirety, here translucent, there transparent, sparkling, but continuous all the way up to the silent city that drifted above the sea. I raised my other foot and stood on the fourth stair. If I'd the mind, a few more steps would send me along that celestial escalator into the place of dreams made real, walking neuroses and dubious prophecy, into a moonlit city of ambiguous wish fulfillment, twisted time, and pallid beauty. I stepped back down and glanced at the moon, now balanced on the world's wet rim. I regarded Benedict's Trump in its silvery glow.

"The stair is solid, the moon is up," I said.

"All right. I am going."

I watched him there at the center of the Pattern. He raised the lantern in his left hand and for a moment stood unmoving. An instant later he was gone, and so was the Pattern. Another instant, and he stood within a similar chamber, this time outside the Pattern, next to the point where it begins. He raised the lantern high and looked all around the room. He was alone.

He turned, walked to the wall, set the lantern beside it. His shadow stretched toward the Pattern, changed shape as he turned on his heel, moved back to his first position.

This Pattern, I noted, glowed with a paler light than the one in Amber—silvery white, without the hint of blue with which I was familiar. Its configuration was the same, but the ghost city played strange tricks with perspective. There were distortions—narrowings, widenings—which seemed to shift for no particular reason across its surface, as though I viewed the entire tableau through an irregular lens rather than Benedict's Trump.

I retreated down the stairs, settled once again on the lowest step. I continued to observe.

Benedict loosened his blade in its scabbard.

"You know about the possible effect of blood on the Pattern?" I asked.

"Yes. Ganelon told me."

"Did you ever suspect—any of this?"

"I never trusted Brand," he told me.

"What of your journey to the Courts of Chaos? What did you learn?"

"Later, Corwin. He could come any time now."

"I hope no distracting visions show up," I said, recalling my own journey to Tir-na Nog'th and his own part in my final adventure there.

He shrugged.

"One gives them power by paying them heed. My attention is reserved for one matter tonight."

He turned through a full circle, regarding every part of the chamber, halted when he had finished.

"I wonder if he knows you are there?" I said.

"Perhaps. It does not matter."

I nodded. If Brand did not show up, we had gained a day. The guards would ward the other Patterns, Fiona would have a chance to demonstrate her own skill in matters arcane by locating Brand for us. We would then pursue him. She and Bleys had been able to stop him once before. Could she do it alone now? Or would we have to find Bleys and try to convince him to help? Had Brand found Bleys? What the hell did Brand want that kind of power for anyhow? A desire for the throne I could understand. Yet . . . The man was mad, leave it at that. Too bad, but that's the way it was. Heredity or environment? I wondered wryly. We were all of us, to some degree, mad after his fashion. To be honest, it had to be a form of madness, to have so much and to strive so bitterly for just a little more, for a bit of an edge over the others. He carried this tendency to its extreme, that is all. He was a caricature of this mania in all of us. In this sense, did it really matter which of us was the traitor?

Yes, it did. He was the one who had acted. Mad or not, he had gone too far. He had done things Eric, Julian, and I would not have done. Bleys and Fiona had finally backed away from his thickening plot. Gérard and Benedict were a notch above the rest of us—moral, mature, whatever—for they had exempted themselves from the zero-sum power game. Random had changed, quite a bit, in recent years. Could it be that the children of the unicorn took ages in which to mature, that it was slowly happening to the rest of us but had somehow passed Brand by? Or could it be that by his actions Brand was causing it in the rest of us? Like most such questions, the benefit of these was in the asking, not the answering. We were enough like Brand that I knew a particular species of fear nothing else could so provoke. But yes, it did matter. Whatever the reason, he was the one who had acted.

The moon was higher now, its vision superimposed upon my inward viewing of the chamber of the Pattern. The clouds continued to shift, to boil nearer the moon. I thought of advising Benedict, but it would serve no other end than distraction. Above me, Tir-na Nog'th rode like some supernatural ark upon the seas of night.

. . . And suddenly Brand was there.

Reflexively, my hand went to Grayswandir's hilt, despite the fact that a part of me realized from the very first that he stood across the Pattern from Benedict in a dark chamber high in the sky.

My hand fell again. Benedict had become aware of the intruding presence immediately, and he turned to face him. He made no move toward his weapon, but simply stared across the Pattern at our brother.

My earliest fear had been that Brand would contrive to arrive directly behind Benedict and stab him in the back. I would not have tried that though, because even in death Benedict's reflexes might have been sufficient to dispatch his assailant. Apparently, Brand wasn't that crazy either.

Brand smiled.

"Benedict," he said. "Fancy . . . You . . . Here."

The Jewel of Judgment hung fiery upon his breast.

"Brand," Benedict said, "don't try it."

Still smiling, Brand unclasped his sword belt and let his weapon fall to the floor. When the echoes died, he said, "I am not a fool, Benedict. The man hasn't been born who can go up against you with a blade."

"I don't need the blade, Brand."

Brand began walking, slowly, about the edge of the Pattern.

"Yet you wear it as a servant of the throne, when you could have been king."

"That has never been high on my list of ambitions."

"That is right." He paused, only part way about the Pattern. "Loyal, self-effacing. You have not changed at all. Pity Dad conditioned you so well. You could have gone so much further."

"I have everything that I want," Benedict said.

". . . To have been stifled, cut off, so early."

"You cannot talk your way past me either, Brand. Do not make me hurt you."

The smile still on his face, Brand began moving again, slowly. What was it he was trying to do? I could not figure his strategy.

"You know I can do certain things the others cannot," Brand said. "If there is anything at all that you want and think that you cannot have, now is your chance to name it and learn how wrong you were. I have learned things you would scarcely believe."

Benedict smiled one of his rare smiles.

"You have chosen the wrong line," he said. "I can walk to anything that I want."

"Shadows!" Brand snorted, halting again. "Any of the others can clutch a phantom! I am talking of reality! Amber! Power! Chaos! Not daydreams made solid! Not second best!"

"If I had wanted more than I have, I knew what to do. I did not do it."

Brand laughed, began walking again. He had come a quarter of the way about the Pattern's periphery. The Jewel burned more brightly. His voice rang.

"You are a fool, to wear your chains willingly! But if things do not call out to you to possess them and if power holds no attraction, what of knowledge? I learned the last of Dworkin's lore. I have gone on since then and paid dark prices for greater insight into the workings of the universe. This you could have without that price tag."

"There would be a price," Benedict said, "one that I will not pay."

Brand shook his head and tossed his hair. The image of the Pattern wavered for a moment then, as a wisp of cloud crossed the moon. Tir-na Nog'th faded slightly, returned to normal focus.

"You mean it, you really mean it," Brand said, apparently not aware of the moment of fading. "I shan't test you further then. I had to try." He halted again, staring. "You are too good a man to waste yourself on that mess in Amber, defending something that is obviously falling apart. I am going to win, Benedict. I am going to erase Amber and build it anew. I am going to rub out the old Pattern and draw my own. You can be with me. I want you on my side. I am going to raise up a perfect world, one with more direct access to and from Shadow. I am going to merge Amber with the Courts of Chaos. I am going to extend this realm directly through all of Shadow. You will command our legions, the mightiest military forces ever assembled. You—"

"If your new world would be as perfect as you say, Brand, there would be no need for legions. If, on the other hand, it is to reflect the mind of its creator, then I see it as something less than an improvement over the present state of affairs. Thank you for your offer, but I hold with the Amber which already exists."

"You are a fool, Benedict. A well-meaning one, but a fool nevertheless."

He began to move again, casually. He was within forty feet of Benedict. Thirty. . . . He kept moving. He finally paused about twenty feet away, hooked his thumbs behind his belt, and simply stared. Benedict met his gaze. I checked the clouds again. A long mass of them continued a moonward slide. I could pull Benedict out at any time, though. It was hardly worth disturbing him at the moment.

"Why don't you come and cut me down then?" Brand finally said. "Unarmed as I am, it should not be difficult. The fact that the same blood flows in both our veins makes no difference, does it? What are you waiting for?"

"I already told you that I do not wish to hurt you," Benedict said.

"Yet you stand ready to, if I attempt to pass your way."

Benedict simply nodded.

"Admit that you fear me, Benedict. All of you are afraid of me. Even when I approach you weaponless like this, something must be twisting your guts. You see my confidence and you do not understand it. You must be afraid."

Benedict did not reply.

". . . And you fear my blood on your hands," Brand went on, "you fear my death curse."

"Did you fear Martin's blood on your own?" Benedict asked.

"That bastard puppy!" Brand said. "He was not truly one of us. He was only a tool."

"Brand, I have no desire to kill a brother. Give me that trinket you wear about your neck and come back with me now to Amber. It is not too late to set matters right."

Brand threw back his head and laughed.

"Oh, nobly spoken! Nobly spoken, Benedict! Like a true lord of the realm! You would shame me with your excessive virtue! And what is the sticking point of this all?" He reached down and stroked the Jewel of Judgment. "This?" He laughed again and strode forward. "This bauble? Would its surrender buy us peace, amity, order? Would it ransom my life?"

He halted once more, ten feet from Benedict now. He raised the Jewel between his fingers and looked down at it.

"Do you realize the full powers of this thing?" he asked.

"Enough of th—" Benedict began, and his voice cracked in his throat.

Brand hurriedly took another step forward. The Jewel was bright before him. Benedict's hand had begun to move toward his blade, but it did not reach it. He stood stiffly now, as if suddenly transformed into a statue. Then I began to understand, but by then it was too late.

Nothing that Brand had been saying had really mattered. It had simply been a running line of patter, a distraction thrown up before him while he sought cautiously after the proper range. He was indeed partly attuned to the Jewel, and the limited control this gave him was still sufficient to enable him to produce effects with it, effects which I was unaware it could produce, but of which he had known all along. Brand had carefully contrived his arrival a good distance from Benedict, tried the Jewel, moved a little nearer, tried again, kept up this movement, this testing, until he found the point where it could affect Benedict's nervous system.

"Benedict," I said, "you had better come to me now," and I exerted my will, but he did not budge nor did he reply. His Trump was still functioning, I felt his presence, I observed events because of it, but I could not reach him. The Jewel was obviously affecting more than his motor system.

I looked to the clouds again. They were still growing, they were reaching for the moon. It seemed they might come across it soon. If I could not pull Benedict out when it happened, he would fall to the sea as soon as the light was fully blocked, the city disrupted. Brand! If he became aware of it, he might be able to use the Jewel to dissipate the clouds. But to do that, he would probably have to release Benedict. I did not think he would do it. Still . . . The clouds seemed to be slowing now. This entire line of reasoning could become unnecessary. I thumbed out Brand's Trump though, and set it aside.

"Benedict, Benedict," said Brand, smiling, "of what use is the finest swordsman alive if he cannot move to take up his blade? I told you that you were a fool. Did you think I would walk willingly to my slaughter? You should have trusted the fear you must have felt. You should have known that I would not enter this place helpless. I meant it when I said that I was going to win. You were a good choice though, because you are the best. I really wish that you had accepted my offer. But it is not that important now. I cannot be stopped. None of the others has a chance, and with you gone things are going to be much easier."

He reached beneath his cloak and produced a dagger.

"Bring me through, Benedict!" I cried, but it was no use. There was no response, no strength to trump me up there.

I seized Brand's Trump. I recalled my Trump battle with Eric. If I could hit Brand through his Trump, I might be able to break his concentration sufficiently for Benedict to come free. I turned all of my faculties upon the card, preparing for a massive mental assault.

But nothing. The way was frozen and dark.

It had to be that his concentration on the task at hand, his mental involvement with the Jewel, was so complete that I simply could not reach him. I was blocked at every turn.

Suddenly, the stairway grew paler above me and I cast a quick glance at the moon. A limb of cumulus now covered a portion of its face. Damn!

I returned my attention to Benedict's Trump. It seemed slow, but I did recover the contact, indicating that somewhere, inside it all, Benedict was still conscious. Brand had moved a pace nearer and was still taunting him. The Jewel on its heavy chain burned with the light of its use. They stood perhaps three paces apart now. Brand toyed with the dagger.

". . . Yes, Benedict," he was saying, "you probably would have preferred to die in battle. On the other hand, you might look upon this as a kind of honor—a signal honor. In a way, your death will allow the birth of a new order . . ."

For a moment, the Pattern faded behind them. I could not tear my eyes from the scene to examine the moon, however. There, within the shadows and the flickering light, his back to the Pattern, Brand did not seem to notice. He took another step forward.

"But enough of this," he said. "There are things to be done, and the night grows no younger."

He stepped nearer and lowered the blade.

"Good night, sweet Prince," he said, and he moved to close with him.

At that instant, Benedict's strange mechanical right arm, torn from this place of shadow and silver and moonlight, moved with the speed of a striking snake. Thing of glinting, metallic planes like the facets of a gem, wrist a wondrous weave of silver cable, pinned with flecks of fire, stylized, skeletal, a Swiss toy, a mechanical insect, functional, deadly, beautiful in its way, it shot forward with a speed that I could not follow, while the rest of his body remained steady, a statue.

The mechanical fingers caught the Jewel's chain about Brand's neck. Immediately, the arm moved upward, raising Brand high above the floor. Brand dropped the dagger and clutched at his throat with both hands.

Behind him, the Pattern faded once again. It returned with a much paler glow. Brand's face in the lantern light was a ghastly, twisted apparition. Benedict remained frozen, holding him on high, unmoving, a human gallows.

The Pattern grew dimmer. Above me, the steps began to recede. The moon was half-occluded.

Writhing, Brand raised his arms above his head, catching at the chain on either side of the metal hand that held it. He was strong, as all of us are. I saw his muscles bunch and harden. By then, his face was dark and his neck a mass of straining cables. He bit his lip; the blood ran into his beard as he drew upon the chain.

With a sharp snap followed by a rattling, the chain parted and Brand fell to the floor gasping. He rolled over once, clutching at his throat with both hands.

Slowly, very slowly, Benedict lowered his strange arm. He still held the chain and the Jewel. He flexed his other arm. He sighed deeply.

The Pattern grew even dimmer. Above me, Tir-na Nog'th became transparent. The moon was almost gone.

"Benedict!" I cried. "Can you hear me?"

"Yes," he said, very softly, and he began to sink through the floor.

"The city is fading! You've got to come to me right away!"

I extended my hand.

"Brand . . ." he said, turning.

But Brand was sinking also, and I saw that Benedict could not reach him. I clasped Benedict's left hand and jerked. Both of us fell to the ground beside the high outcrop.

I helped him to his feet. Then we both seated ourselves on the stone. For a long while, we did not say anything. I looked again and Tir-na Nog'th was gone.

I thought back over everything that had happened, so fast, so sudden, that day. A great weight of weariness lay upon me now, and I felt that my energies must be at their end, that shortly I must sleep. I could scarcely think straight. Life had simply been too crowded recently. I leaned my head back against the stone once more, regarding cloud and star. The pieces . . . the pieces which it seemed should fit, if only the proper jiggle, twist or flip were applied. . . . They were jiggling, twisting, and flipping now, almost of their own accord. . . .

"Is he dead, do you think?" Benedict asked, pulling me back from a half-dream of emerging forms.

"Probably," I said. "He was in bad shape when things fell apart."

"It was a long way down. He might have had time to work some escape along the lines of his arrival."

"Right now it does not really matter," I said. "You've drawn his fangs."

Benedict grunted. He was still holding the Jewel, a much dimmer red than it had been so recently.

"True," he finally said. "The Pattern is safe now. I wish . . . I wish that some time, long ago, something had not been said that was said, or something done that was not done. Something, had we known, which might have let him grow differently, something which would have seen him become another man than the bitter, bent thing I saw up there. It is best now if he is dead. But it is a waste of something that might have been."

I did not answer him. What he had said might or might not be right. It did not matter. Brand might have been borderline psychotic, whatever that means, and then again maybe not. There is always a reason. Whenever anything has been mucked up, whenever anything outrageous happens, there is a reason for it. You still have a mucked-up, outrageous situation on your hands, however, and explaining it does not alleviate it one bit. If someone does something really rotten, there is a reason for it. Learn it, if you care, and you learn why he is a son of a bitch. The fact is the thing that remains, though. Brand had acted. It changed nothing to run a posthumous psychoanalysis. Acts and their consequences are the things by which our fellows judge us. Anything else, and all that you get is a cheap feeling of moral superiority by thinking how you would have done something nicer if it had been you. So as for the rest, leave it to heaven. I'm not qualified.

"We had best get back to Amber," Benedict said. "There are a great number of things that must be done."

"Wait," I said.

"Why?"

"I've been thinking."

When I did not elaborate, he finally said, "And. . . ?"

I riffled slowly through my Trumps, replacing his, replacing Brand's.

"Haven't you wondered yet about the new arm you wear?" I asked him.

"Of course. You brought it from Tir-na Nog'th, under unusual circumstances. It fits. It works. It proved itself tonight."

"Exactly. Isn't the last a lot of weight to dump on poor coincidence? The one weapon that gave you a chance up there, against the Jewel. And it just happened to be a part of you—and you just happened to be the person who was up there, to use it? Trace things back and trace them forward again. Isn't there an extraordinary—no, preposterous—chain of coincidences involved?"

"When you put it that way . . ." he said.

"I do. And you must realize as well as I do that there has to be more to it than that."

"All right. Say that. But how? How was it done?"

"I have no idea," I said, withdrawing the card I had not looked upon in a long, long while, feeling its coldness beneath my finger tips, "but the method is not important. You asked the wrong question."

"What should I have asked?"

"Not 'How?' but 'Who?' "

"You think that a human agency arranged that entire chain of events, up through the recovery of the Jewel?"

"I don't know about that. What's human? But I do think that someone we both know has returned and is behind it all."

"All right. Who?"

I showed him the Trump that I held.

"Dad? That *is* ridiculous! He must be dead. It's been so long."

"You know he could have engineered it. He's that devious. We never understood all of his powers."

Benedict rose to his feet. He stretched. He shook his head.

"I think you have been out in the cold too long, Corwin. Let's go home now."

"Without testing my guess? Come on! That is hardly sporting. Sit down and give me a minute. Let's try his Trump."

"He would have contacted someone by now."

"I don't think so. In fact— Come on. Humor me. What have we got to lose?"

"All right. Why not?"

He sat down beside me. I held the Trump where both of us could make it out. We stared at it. I relaxed my mind, I reached for contact. It came almost immediately.

He was smiling as he regarded us.

"Good evening. That was a fine piece of work," Ganelon said. "I am pleased that you brought back my trinket. I'll be needing it soon."

THE COURTS OF CHAOS

To Carl Yoke, First Reader——

From Lucetania to Euclid Park,
Sarcobatus Flats to Cygnus X-1——
May you live another ten thousand years.
May your liar be safe from trendeltiles.
May the diminutive deities
 break their collective leg.

I

Amber: high and bright atop Kolvir in the middle of the day. A black road: low and sinister through Garnath from Chaos to the south. Me: cursing, pacing and occasionally reading in the library of the palace in Amber. The door to that library: closed and barred.

The mad prince of Amber seated himself at the desk, returned his attention to the opened volume. There was a knock on the door.

"Go away!" I said.

"Corwin. It's me—Random. Open up, huh? I even brought lunch."

"Just a minute."

I got to my feet again, rounded the desk, crossed the room. Random nodded when I opened the door. He carried a tray, which he took to a small table near the desk.

"Plenty of food there," I said.

"I'm hungry, too."

"So do something about it."

He did. He carved. He passed me some meat on a slab of bread. He poured wine. We seated ourselves and ate.

"I know you are still mad . . ." he said, after a time.

"Aren't you?"

"Well, maybe I am more used to it. I don't know. Still . . . Yes. It was sort of abrupt, wasn't it?"

"Abrupt?" I took a large swallow of wine. "It is just like the old days. Worse even. I had actually come to like him when he was playing at being Ganelon. Now that he is back in control he is just as peremptory as ever, he has given us a set of orders he has not bothered to explain and he has disappeared again."

"He said he would be in touch soon."

"I imagine he intended that last time, too."

"I'm not so sure."

"And he explained nothing about his other absence. In fact, he has not really explained anything."

"He must have his reasons."

"I am beginning to wonder, Random. Do you think his mind might finally be going?"

"He was still sharp enough to fool you."

"That was a combination of low animal cunning and shapeshifting ability."

"It worked, didn't it?"

"Yes. It worked."

"Corwin, could it be that you do not want him to have a plan that might be effective, that you do not want him to be right?"

"That is ridiculous. I want this mess cleared up as much as any of us."

"Yes, but wouldn't you rather the answer came from another quarter?"

"What are you getting at?"

"You do not want to trust him."

"I will admit that. I have not seen him—as himself—in a hell of a long time, and . . ."

He shook his head.

"That is not what I mean. You are angry that he is back, aren't you? You hoped that we had seen the last of him."

I looked away.

"There is that," I finally said. "But not for a vacant throne, or not *just* for it. It is him, Random. Him. That's all."

"I know," he said. "But you have to admit he suckered Brand, which is not an easy thing to do. He pulled a stunt I still do not understand, getting you to bring that arm back from Tir-na Nog'th, somehow getting me to pass it along to Benedict, seeing to it that Benedict was in the right place at the proper moment, so that everything worked and he got the Jewel back. He is also still better than we are at Shadow play. He managed it right on Kolvir when he took us to the primal Pattern. I cannot do that. Neither can you. And he was able to whip Gérard. I do not believe that he is slowing down. I think he knows exactly what he is doing, and whether we like it or not, I think he is the only one who can deal with the present situation."

"You are trying to say that I should trust him?"

"I am trying to say that you have no choice."

I sighed.

"I guess you've put your finger on it," I said. "No sense in my being bitter. Still . . ."

"The attack order bothers you, doesn't it?"

"Yes, among other things. If we would wait longer, Benedict could field a greater force. Three days is not much time to get ready for something like this. Not when we are so uncertain about the enemy."

"But we may not be. He spoke in private with Benedict for a long while."

"And that is the other thing. These separate orders. This secrecy . . . He is not trusting us any more than he has to."

Random chuckled. So did I.

"All right," I said. "Maybe I would not either. But three days to launch a war." I shook my head. "He had better know something we don't."

"I get the impression that it is more a peremptory strike than a war."

"Only he did not bother to tell us what we are preempting."

Random shrugged, poured more wine.

"Perhaps he will say when he gets back. You did not get any special orders, did you?"

"Just to stand and wait. What about you?"

He shook his head.

"He said that when the time comes, I will know. At least with Julian, he told him to have his troops ready to move on a moment's notice."

"Oh? Aren't they staying in Arden?"

He nodded.

"When did he say this?"

"After you left. He trumped Julian up here to give him the message, and they rode off together. I heard Dad say that he would ride partway back with him."

"Did they take the eastern trail over Kolvir?"

"Yes. I saw them off."

"Interesting. What else did I miss?"

He shifted in his seat.

"The part that bothers me," he said. "After Dad had mounted and waved a good-bye, he looked back at me and said, 'And keep an eye on Martin.'"

"That is all?"

"That is all. But he was laughing as he said it."

"Just natural suspicion at a newcomer, I guess."

"Then why the laugh?"

"I give up."

I cut a piece of cheese and ate it.

"Might not be a bad idea, though. It might not be suspicion. Maybe he feels Martin needs to be protected from something. Or both. Or neither. You know how he sometimes is."

Random stood.

"I had not thought through to the alternative. Come with me now, huh?" he said. "You have been up here all morning."

"All right." I got to my feet, buckled on Grayswandir. "Where is Martin, anyway?"

"I left him down on the first floor. He was talking with Gérard."

"He is in good hands, then. Is Gérard going to be staying here, or will he be returning to the fleet?"

"I do not know. He would not discuss his orders."

We left the room. We headed for the stairway.

On the way down, I heard some small commotion from below and I quickened my pace.

I looked over the railing and saw a throng of guards at the entrance to the throne room, along with the massive figure of Gérard. All of them had their backs to us. I leaped down the final stairs. Random was not far behind me.

I pushed my way through.

"Gérard, what is happening?" I asked.

"Damned if I know," he said. "Look for yourself. But there is no getting in."

He moved aside and I took a step forward. Then another. And that was it. It was as if I were pushing against a slightly resilient, totally invisible wall. Beyond was a sight that tied my memory and feelings into a knot. I stiffened, as fear took hold of me by the neck, clasped my hands. No mean trick, that.

Martin, smiling, still held a Trump in his left hand, and Benedict —apparently recently summoned—stood before him. A girl was nearby, on the dais, beside the throne, facing away. Both men appeared to be speaking, but I could not hear the words.

Finally, Benedict turned and seemed to address the girl. After a time, she appeared to be answering him. Martin moved off to her left. Benedict mounted the dais as she spoke. I could see her face then. The exchange continued.

"That girl looks somewhat familiar," said Gérard, who had moved forward and now stood at my side.

"You might have gotten a glimpse of her as she rode past us," I told him, "the day Eric died. It's Dara."

I heard his sudden intake of breath.

"Dara!" he said. "Then you . . ." His voice faded.

"I was not lying," I said. "She is real."

"Martin!" cried Random, who had moved up on my right. "Martin! What's going on!"

There was no response.

"I don't think he can hear you," Gérard said. "This barrier seems to have cut us off completely."

Random strained forward, his hands pushing against something unseen.

"Let's all of us give it a shove," he said.

So I tried again. Gérard also threw his weight against the invisible wall.

After half a minute without success, I eased back.

"No good," I said. "We can't move it."

"What is the damned thing?" Random asked. "What is holding—"

I'd had a hunch—only that, though—as to what might be going on. And only because of the *déjà vu* character of the entire piece. Now, though . . . Now I clasped my hand to my scabbard, to assure myself that Grayswandir still hung at my side.

It did.

Then how could I explain the presence of my distinctive blade, its elaborate tracery gleaming for all to see, hanging where it had suddenly appeared, without support, in the air before the throne, its point barely touching Dara's throat?

I could not.

But it was too similar to what had happened that night in the dream city in the sky, Tir-na Nog'th, to be a coincidence. Here were none of the trappings—the darkness, the confusion, the heavy shadows, the tumultuous emotions I had known—and yet the piece was set much as it had been that night. It was very similar. But not precisely so. Benedict's stance seemed somewhat off—farther back, his body angled differently. While I could not read her lips, I wondered whether Dara was asking the same strange questions. I doubted it.

The tableau—like, yet unlike, that which I had experienced—had probably been colored at the other end—that is, if there were any connection at all—by the effects of Tir-na Nog'th's powers upon my mind at that time.

"Corwin," Random said, "that looks like Grayswandir hanging in front of her."

"It does, doesn't it?" I said. "But as you can see, I am wearing my blade."

"There can't be another just like it . . . can there? Do you know what is happening?"

"I am beginning to feel as if I may," I said. "Whatever, I am powerless to stop it."

Benedict's blade suddenly came free and engaged the other, so like my own. In a moment, he was fighting an invisible opponent.

"Give him hell, Benedict!" Random shouted.

"It is no use," I said. "He is about to be disarmed."

"How can you know?" Gérard asked.

"Somehow, that is me in there, fighting with him," I said. "This is the other end of my dream in Tir-na Nog'th. I do not know how he managed it, but this is the price for Dad's recovering the Jewel."

"I do not follow you," he said.

I shook my head.

"I do not pretend to understand how it is being done," I told him. "But we will not be able to enter until two things have vanished from that room."

"What two things?"

"Just watch."

Benedict's blade had changed hands, and his gleaming prosthesis shot forward and fixed itself upon some unseen target. The two blades parried one another, locked, pressed, their points moving toward the ceiling. Benedict's right hand continued to tighten.

Suddenly, the Grayswandir blade was free, and moving past the other. It struck a terrific blow to Benedict's right arm at the place where the metal portion joined it. Then Benedict turned and the action was blocked to our view for several moments.

Then the sight was clear again, as Benedict dropped to one knee, turning. He clutched at the stump of his arm. The mechanical hand/arm hung in the air near Grayswandir. It was moving away from Benedict and descending, as was the blade. When both reached the floor, they did not strike it but passed on through, vanishing from sight.

I lurched forward, recovered my balance, moved ahead. The barrier was gone.

Martin and Dara reached Benedict before we did. Dara had already torn a strip from her cloak and was binding Benedict's stump when Gérard, Random and I got there.

Random seized Martin by the shoulder and I turned him.

"What happened?" he asked.

"Dara . . . Dara told me she wanted to see Amber," he said. "Since I live here now, I agreed to bring her through and show her around. Then—"

"Bring her through? You mean on a Trump?"

"Well, yes."

"Yours or hers?"

Martin raked his lower lip with his teeth.

"Well, you see . . ."

"Give me those cards," said Random, and he snatched the case from Martin's belt. He opened it and began going through them.

"Then I thought to tell Benedict, since he was interested in her," Martin went on. "Then Benedict wanted to come and see—"

"What the hell!" Random said. "There is one of you, one of her, and one of a guy I've never even seen before! Where did you get these?"

"Let me see them," I said.

He passed me the three cards.

"Well?" he said. "Was it Brand? He is the only one I know who can make Trumps now."

"I would not have anything to do with Brand," Martin replied, "except to kill him."

But I already knew they were not from Brand. They were simply not in his style. Nor were they in the style of anyone whose work I knew. Style was not foremost in my mind at that moment, however. Rather, it was the features of the third person, the one whom Random had said he had never seen before. I had. I was looking at the face of the youth who had confronted me with a crossbow before the Courts of Chaos, recognized me and then declined to shoot.

I extended the card.

"Martin, who is this?" I asked.

"The man who made these extra Trumps," he said. "He drew one of himself while he was about it. I do not know his name. He is a friend of Dara's."

"You are lying," Random said.

"Then let Dara tell us," I said, and I turned to her.

She still knelt beside Benedict, though she had finished bandaging him and he was now sitting up.

"How about it?" I said, waving the card at her. "Who is this man?"

She glanced at the card, then up at me. She smiled.

"You really do not know?" she said.

"Would I be asking if I did?"

"Then look at it again and go look in a mirror. He is your son as much as mine. His name is Merlin."

I am not easily shocked, but this had nothing of ease about it. I felt dizzy. But my mind moved quickly. With the proper time differential the thing was possible.

"Dara," I said, "what is it that you want?"

"I told you when I walked the Pattern," she said, "that Amber must be destroyed. What I want is to have my rightful part in it."

"You will have my old cell," I said. "No, the one next to it. Guards!"

"Corwin, it is all right," Benedict said, getting to his feet. "It is not as bad as it sounds. She can explain everything."

"Then let her start now."

"No. In private. Just family."

I motioned back the guards who had come at my call.

"Very well. Let us adjourn to one of the rooms up the hall."

He nodded, and Dara took hold of his left arm. Random, Gérard, Martin and I followed them out. I looked back once to the empty place where my dream had come true. Such is the stuff.

II

I rode up over the crest of Kolvir and dismounted when I came to my tomb. I went inside and opened the casket. It was empty. Good. I was beginning to wonder. I had half-expected to see myself laid out before me, evidence that despite signs and intuitions I had somehow wandered into the wrong shadow.

I went back outside and rubbed Star's nose. The sun was shining and the breeze was chill. I had a sudden desire to go to sea. I seated myself on the bench instead and fumbled with my pipe.

We had talked. Seated with her legs beneath her on the brown sofa, Dara had smiled and repeated the story of her descent from Benedict and Lintra, the hellmaid, growing up in and about the Courts of Chaos, a grossly non-Euclidean realm where time itself presented strange distribution problems.

"The things you told me when we met were lies," I said. "Why should I believe you now?"

She had smiled and regarded her fingernails.

"I had to lie to you then," she explained, "to get what I wanted from you."

"That being . . . ?"

"Knowledge, of the family, the Pattern, the Trumps, of Amber. To gain your trust. To have your child."

"The truth would not have served as well?"

"Hardly. I come from the enemy. My reasons for wanting these things were not the sort of which you would approve."

"Your swordplay . . . ? You told me then that Benedict had trained you."

"I learned from the great Duke Borel himself, a High Lord of Chaos."

". . . and your appearance," I said. "It was altered on a number of occasions when I saw you walk the Pattern. How? Also, why?"

"All whose origins involve Chaos are shapeshifters," she replied.

I thought of Dworkin's performance the night he had impersonated me.

Benedict nodded.

"Dad fooled us with his Ganelon disguise."

"Oberon is a son of Chaos," Dara said, "a rebel son of a rebel father. But the power is still there."

"Then why is it we cannot do it?" Random asked.

She shrugged.

"Have you ever tried? Perhaps you can. On the other hand, it may have died out with your generation. I do not know. As to myself, however, I have certain favored shapes to which I revert in times of stress. I grew up where this was the rule, where the other shape was actually sometimes dominant. It is still a reflex with me. This is what you witnessed—that day."

"Dara," I said, "why did you want the things that you said you wanted—knowledge of the family, the Pattern, the Trumps, Amber? And a son?"

"All right." She sighed. "All right. You are by now aware of Brand's plans—the destruction and rebuilding of Amber . . . ?"

"Yes."

"This involved our consent and co-operation."

"Including the murder of Martin?" Random asked.

"No," she said. "We did not know who he intended to use as the —agent."

"Would it have stopped you had you known?"

"You are asking a hypothetical question," she said. "Answer it yourself. I am glad that Martin is still alive. That is all that I can say about it."

"All right," Random said. "What about Brand?"

"He was able to contact our leaders by methods he had learned from Dworkin. He had ambitions. He needed knowledge, power. He offered a deal."

"What sort of knowledge?"

"For one thing, he did not know how to destroy the Pattern—"

"Then you *were* responsible for what he did," Random said.

"If you choose to look at it that way."

"I do."

She shrugged, looked at me.

"Do you want to hear this story?"

"Go ahead." I glanced at Random and he nodded.

"Brand was given what he wanted," she said, "but he was not trusted. It was feared that once he possessed the power to shape the world as he would, he would not stop with ruling over a revised Amber. He would attempt to extend his dominion over Chaos as well. A weakened Amber was what was desired, so that Chaos would be stronger than it now is—the striking of a new balance, giving to us more of the shadowlands that lie between our realms. It was realized long ago that the two kingdoms can never be merged, or one destroyed, without also disrupting all the processes that lie in flux between us. Total stasis or complete chaos would be the result. Yet, though it was seen what Brand had in mind, our leaders came to terms with him. It was the best opportunity to present itself in ages. It had to be seized. It was felt that Brand could be dealt with, and finally replaced, when the time came."

"So you were also planning a double-cross," Random said.

"Not if he kept his word. But then, we knew that he would not. So we provided for the move against him."

"How?"

"He would be allowed to accomplish his end and then be destroyed. He would be succeeded by a member of the royal family of Amber who was also of the first family of the Courts, one who had been raised among us and trained for the position. Merlin even traces his connection with Amber on both sides, through my forebear Benedict and directly from yourself—the two most favored claimants to your throne."

"You are of the royal house of Chaos?"

She smiled.

I rose. Strode away. Stared at the ashes on the grate.

"I find it somewhat distressing to have been involved in a calculated breeding project," I said, at length. "But be that as it may, and accepting everything you have said as true—for the moment—why are you telling us all of these things now?"

"Because," she said, "I fear that the lords of my realm would go as far for their vision as Brand would for his. Farther, perhaps. That balance I spoke of. Few seem to appreciate what a delicate thing it is. I have traveled in the shadowlands near to Amber, and I have walked in Amber herself. I also have known the shadows that lie by Chaos' side. I have met many people and seen many things. Then, when I encountered Martin and spoke with him, I began to feel that the changes I had been told would be for the better would not simply result in a revision of Amber more along the lines of my elders' liking. They would, instead, turn Amber into a mere extension of the Courts, most of the shadows would boil away to join with Chaos. Amber would become an island. Some of my seniors who still smart at Dworkin's having created Amber in the first place are really seeking a return to the days before this happened. Total Chaos, from which all things arose. I see the present condition as superior and I wish to preserve it. My desire is that neither side emerge victorious in any conflict."

I turned in time to see Benedict shaking his head.

"Then you are on neither side," he stated.

"I like to think that I am on both."

"Martin," I said, "are you in this with her?"

He nodded.

Random laughed.

"The two of you? Against both Amber and the Courts of Chaos? What do you hope to achieve? How do you plan to further this notion of balance?"

"We are not alone," she said, "and the plan is not ours."

Her fingers dipped into her pocket. Something glittered when she withdrew them. She turned it in the light. It was our father's signet ring that she held.

"Where did you get that?" Random asked.

"Where else?"

Benedict stepped toward her and held out his hand. She gave it to him. He scrutinized it.

"It *is* his," he said. "It has the little markings on the back that I've seen before. Why do you have it?"

"First, to convince you that I am acting properly when I convey his orders," she said.

"How is it that you even know him?" I asked.

"I met him during his—difficulties—some time back," she told us. "In fact, you might say that I helped to deliver him from them. This was after I had met Martin, and I was inclined to be more sympathetic toward Amber. But then, your father is also a charming and persuasive man. I decided that I could not simply stand by and see him remain prisoner to my kin."

"Do you know how he was captured in the first place?"

She shook her head.

"I only know that Brand effected his presence in a shadow far enough from Amber that he could be taken there. I believe it involved a fake quest for a nonexistent magical tool which might heal the Pattern. He realizes now that only the Jewel can do it."

"Your helping him to get away . . . How did this affect your relations with your own people?"

"Not too damned well," she said. "I am temporarily without a home."

"And you want one here?"

She smiled again.

"It depends on how things turn out. If my people have their way, I would as soon go back—or stay with what shadows remain."

I withdrew a Trump, glanced at it.

"What of Merlin? Where is he now?"

"They have him," she said. "I fear he may be their man now. He knows his parentage, but they have had charge of his education for a long while. I do not know whether he could be gotten away."

I raised the Trump, stared at it.

"No good," she said. "It will not function between here and there."

I recalled how difficult Trump communication had been when I had been to the fringes of that place. I tried anyway.

The card grew cold in my hand and I reached out. There was the faintest flicker of a responding presence. I tried harder.

"Merlin, this is Corwin," I said. "Do you hear me?"

I seemed to hear a reply. It seemed to be, "I cannot—" And then there was nothing. The card lost its coldness.

"Did you reach him?" she asked.

"I am not sure," I said. "But I think so. Just for a moment."

"Better than I thought," she said. "Either conditions are good or your minds are very similar."

"When you began waving Dad's signet around you spoke of orders," Random said. "What orders?" And why is he sending them through you?"

"It is a matter of timing."

"Timing? Hell! He just left here this morning!"

"He had to finish one thing before he was ready for another. He had no idea how long it would take. But I was just in touch with him before I came here—though I was hardly prepared for the reception I walked into—and he is now ready to begin the next phase."

"Where did you speak with him?" I asked. "Where is he?"

"I have no idea where he is. He contacted me."

"And . . . ?"

"He wants Benedict to attack immediately."

Gérard finally stirred from the huge armchair in which he had sat listening. He rose to his feet, hooked his thumbs in his belt and looked down at her.

"An order like that would have to come directly from Dad."

"It did," she said.

He shook his head.

"It makes no sense. Why contact you—someone we have small reason to trust—rather than one of us?"

"I do not believe that he can reach you at the moment. On the other hand, he was able to reach me."

"Why?"

"He did not use a Trump. He does not have one for me. He used a reverberation effect of the black road, similar to the means by which Brand once escaped Corwin."

"You know a lot of what has been going on."

"I do. I still have sources in the Courts, and Brand transported himself there after your struggle. I hear things."

"Do you know where our father is right now?" Random asked.

"No, I do not know. But I believe that he has journeyed to the real Amber, to take counsel with Dworkin and to re-examine the damage to the primal Pattern."

"To what end?"

"I do not know. Probably to decide on the course of action he will take. The fact that he reached me and ordered the attack most likely means that he has decided."

"How long ago was this communication?"

"Just a few hours—my time. But I was far from here in Shadow. I do not know what the time differential is. I am too new at this."

"So it could be something extremely recent. Possibly only moments ago," Gérard mused. "Why did he talk with you rather than one of us? I do not believe that he could not reach us if he wished to."

"Perhaps to show that he looks upon me with favor," she said.

"All of this may be entirely true," Benedict stated. "But I am not moving without a confirmation of that order."

"Is Fiona still at the primal Pattern?" Random asked.

"Last I heard," I told him, "she had set up camp there. I see what you mean. . . ."

I shuffled out Fi's card.

"It took more than one of us to get through from there," he observed.

"True. So give me a hand."

He rose, came to my side. Benedict and Gérard also approached.

"This is not really necessary," Dara protested.

I ignored her and concentrated on the delicate features of my red-haired sister. Moments later, we had contact.

"Fiona," I asked, seeing from the background that she was still in residence at the heart of things, "is Dad there?"

"Yes," she said, smiling tightly. "He is inside with Dworkin."

"Listen, urgency prevails. I do not know whether or not you know Dara, but she is here—"

"I know who she is, but I have never met her."

"Well, she claims she has an attack order for Benedict, from Dad. She has his signet to back it up, but he did not speak of this earlier. Do you know anything about it?"

"No," she said. "All we did was exchange greetings when he and Dworkin were out here earlier to look at the Pattern. I had some suspicions then, though, and this confirms them."

"Suspicions? What do you mean?"

"I think Dad is going to try to repair the Pattern. He has the Jewel with him, and I overheard some of the things he said to Dworkin. If he makes the attempt, they will be aware of it in the Courts of Chaos the moment that he begins. They will try to stop him. He would want to strike first to keep them occupied. Only . . ."

"What?"

"It is going to kill him, Corwin. I know that much about it. Whether he succeeds or fails, he will be destroyed in the process."

"I find it hard to believe."

"That a king would give up his life for the realm?"

"That Dad would."

"Then either he has changed or you never really knew him. But I do believe he is going to try it."

"Then why send his latest order by someone he knows we do not really trust?"

"To show that he wants you to trust her, I would guess, once he has confirmed it."

"It seems a roundabout way of doing things, but I agree that we should not act without that confirmation. Can you get it for us?"

"I will try. I will get back to you as soon as I have spoken with him."

She broke the contact.

I turned toward Dara, who had heard only our side of the conversation.

"Do you know what Dad is going to do right now?" I asked her.

"Something involving the black road," she said. "He had indicated that much. What, though, or how, he did not say."

I turned away. I squared my cards and encased them. I did not like this turning of events. This entire day had started badly, and things had been going downhill ever since. It was only a little past lunchtime, too. I shook my head. When I had spoken with him, Dworkin had described the results of any attempt to repair the Pattern, and they had sounded pretty horrendous to me. Supposing Dad tried it, failed, and got himself killed in the attempt? Where would we be then? Right where we were now, only without a leader, on the eve of battle—and with the succession problem stirring again. That whole ghastly business would be in the back of our minds as we rode to the wars, and we would all begin our private arrangements to fight one another once more as soon as the current enemy was dealt with. There had to be another way of handling things. Better Dad alive and on the throne than a revival of the succession intrigues.

"What are we waiting for?" Dara asked. "Confirmation?"

"Yes," I replied.

Random began to pace. Benedict seated himself and tested the dressing on his arm. Gérard leaned against the mantelpiece. I stood and thought. An idea came to me just then. I pushed it away immediately, but it returned. I did not like it, but had nothing to do with practicalities. I would have to move quickly, though, before I had a chance to talk myself around to another viewpoint. No. I would stick with this one. Damn it!

There came a stirring of contact. I waited. Moments later, I regarded Fiona again. She stood in a familiar place that it took me several seconds to recognize: Dworkin's sitting room, on the other side of the heavy door at the back of the cave. Dad and Dworkin were both with her. Dad had dropped his Ganelon disguise and was his old self once again. I saw that he wore the Jewel.

"Corwin," Fiona said, "it is true. Dad did send the attack order with Dara, and he expected this call for confirmation. I—"

"Fiona, bring me through."

"What?"

"You heard me. Now!"

I extended my right hand. She reached forward and we touched.

"Corwin!" Random shouted. "What's happening!"

Benedict was on his feet, Gérard already moving toward me.

"You will hear about it shortly," I said, and I stepped forward.

I squeezed her hand before I released it and I smiled.

"Thanks, Fi. Hello, Dad. Hi, Dworkin. How's everything?"

I glanced once at the heavy door, saw that it stood open. Then I passed around Fiona and moved toward them. Dad's head was lowered, his eyes narrowed. I knew that look.

"What is this, Corwin? You are here without leave," he said. "I have confirmed that damned order, now I expect it to be carried out."

"It will be," I said, nodding. "I did not come here to argue about that."

"What, then?"

I moved nearer, calculating my words as well as the distance. I was glad that he had remained seated.

"For a time we rode as comrades," I said. "Damned if I did not come to like you then. I never had before, you know. Never had guts enough to say that before either, but you know it is true. I like to think that that is how things could have been, if we had not been what we are to each other." For the barest moment, his gaze seemed to soften as I positioned myself. Then, "At any rate," I went on, "I am going to believe in you that way rather than this way, because there is something I would never have done for you otherwise."

"What?" he asked.

"This."

I seized the Jewel with an upward sweeping motion and snapped the chain up over his head. I pivoted on my heel then and raced across the room and through the door. I drew it shut behind me and snapped it to. I could see no way to bar it from the outside, so I ran on, retracing the route through the cave from that night I had followed Dworkin along it. Behind me, I heard the expected bellow.

I followed the twistings. I stumbled only once. Wixer's smell still hung heavy in his lair. I pounded on and a final turning brought me a view of daylight ahead.

I raced toward it, slipping the Jewel's chain over my head as I went. I felt it fall to my breast, I reached down into it with my mind. There were echoes in the cave behind me.

Outside!

I sprinted toward the Pattern, feeling through the Jewel, turning it into an extra sense. I was the only person other than Dad or Dworkin fully attuned to it. Dworkin had told me that the Pattern's repair might be effected by a person's walking the Grand Pattern in such a state of attunement, burning out the smear at each crossing, replacing it with stock from the image of the Pattern that he bore within him, wiping out the black road in the process. Better me than Dad, then. I still felt that the black road owed something of its final form to the strength my curse against Amber had given it. I wanted to wipe that out, too. Dad would do a better job of putting things together after the war than I ever could, anyway. I realized, at that moment, that I no longer wanted the throne. Even if it were available, the prospect of administering to the kingdom down all the dull centuries that might lie before me was overwhelming. Maybe I would be taking the easy way out if I died in this effort. Eric was dead, and I no longer hated him. The other thing that had driven me—the throne—seemed now to have been desirable only because I'd thought he had wanted it so. I renounced both. What was left? I had laughed at Vialle, then wondered. But she had been right. The old soldier in me was strongest. It was a matter of duty. But not duty alone. There was more. . . .

I reached the edge of the Pattern, quickly made my way toward its beginning. I glanced back at the cavemouth. Dad, Dworkin, Fiona— none of them had yet emerged. Good. They could never make it in time to stop me. Once I set foot on the Pattern, it would be too late for them to do anything but wait and watch. I thought for a fleeting instant of Iago's dissolution, pushed that thought away, strove to calm my mind to the level necessary for the undertaking, recalled my battle with Brand in this place and his strange departure, pushed that away, too, slowed my breathing, prepared myself.

A certain lethargy came upon me. It was time to begin, but I held back for a moment, trying to fix my mind properly on the grand task that lay before me. The Pattern swam for a moment in my vision.

Now! Damn it! Now! No more preliminaries! Begin, I told myself. Walk!

Still, I stood, contemplating the Pattern as in a dream. I forgot about myself for long moments as I regarded it. The Pattern, with its long black smear to be removed . . .

It no longer seemed important that it might kill me. My mind drifted, considering the beauty of the thing. . . .

I heard a sound. It would be Dad, Dworkin, Fiona, coming. I had to do something before they reached me. I had to walk it, in a moment. . . .

I pulled my gaze away from the Pattern and glanced back toward the cavemouth. They had emerged, come partway down the slope and halted. Why? Why had they stopped?

What did it matter? I had the time I needed in which to begin. I began to raise my foot, to step forward.

I could barely move. I inched my foot ahead with a great effort of will. Taking this first step was proving worse than walking the Pattern itself, near to the end. But it did not seem so much an external resistance I fought against as it did the sluggishness of my own body. It was almost as if—

Then I had me an image of Benedict beside the Pattern in Tir-na Nog'th, Brand approaching, mocking, the Jewel burning upon his breast.

Before I looked down, I knew what I would see.

The red stone was pulsing in time with my heartbeat.

Damn them!

Either Dad or Dworkin—or both of them—reached through it at this instant, paralyzing me. I did not doubt that either of them could manage it alone. Still, at this distance, it was not worth surrendering without a fight.

I continued to push forward with my foot, sliding it slowly ahead toward the edge of the Pattern. Once I made it, I did not see how they . . .

Drowsing . . . I felt myself beginning to fall. I had been asleep for a moment. It happened again.

When I opened my eyes, I could see a portion of the Pattern. When I turned my head, I saw feet. When I looked up, I saw Dad holding the Jewel.

"Go away," he said to Dworkin and Fiona, without turning his head toward them.

They withdrew as he placed the Jewel about his own neck. He leaned forward then and extended his hand. I took it and he drew me to my feet.

"That was a damfool thing to do," he said.

"I almost made it."

He nodded.

"Of course, you would have killed yourself and not accomplished anything," he said. "But it was well done nevertheless. Come on, let's walk."

He took my arm, and we began to move about the periphery of the Pattern.

I watched that strange sky-sea, horizonless about us, as we went. I wondered what would have happened had I been able to begin the Pattern, what would be happening at that moment.

"You have changed," he finally said, "or else I never really knew you."

I shrugged.

"Something of both perhaps. I was about to say the same of you. Tell me something?"

"What?"

"How difficult was it for you, being Ganelon?"

He chuckled.

"Not hard at all," he said. "You may have had a glimpse of the real me."

"I liked him. Or rather, you being him. I wonder whatever became of the real Ganelon?"

"Long dead, Corwin. I met him after you had exiled him from Avalon, long ago. He wasn't a bad chap. Wouldn't have trusted him worth a damn, but then I never trust anyone I don't have to."

"It runs in the family."

"I regretted having to kill him. Not that he gave me much choice. All this was very long ago, but I remembered him clearly, so he must have impressed me."

"And Lorraine?"

"The country? A good job, I thought. I worked the proper shadow. It grew in strength by my very presence, as any will if one of us stays around for long—as with you in Avalon, and later that other place. And I saw that I had a long while there by exercising my will upon its time-stream."

"I did not know that could be done."

"You grow in strength slowly, beginning with your initiation into the Pattern. There are many things you have yet to learn. Yes, I strengthened Lorraine, and made it especially vulnerable to the growing force of the black road. I saw that it would lie in your path, no matter where you went. After your escape, all roads led to Lorraine."

"Why?"

"It was a trap I had set for you, and maybe a test. I wanted to be with you when you met the forces of Chaos. I also wanted to travel with you for a time."

"A test? What were you testing me for? And why travel with me?"

"Can you not guess? I have watched all of you over the years. I never named a successor. I purposely left the matter muddled. You are all enough like me for me to know that the moment I declared for one of you I would be signing his or her death warrant. No. I intentionally left things as they were until the very end. Now, though, I have decided. It is to be you."

"You communicated with me, as yourself, briefly, back in Lorraine. You told me then to take the throne. If you had made up your mind at that point why did you continue the masquerade?"

"But I had not decided then. That was merely a means to assure your continuing. I feared you might come to like that girl too much, and that land. When you emerged a hero from the Black Circle you might have decided to settle and stay there. I wanted to plant the notions that would cause you to continue your journey."

I was silent for a long while. We had moved a good distance about the Pattern.

Then, "There is something that I have to know," I said. "Before I came here I was speaking with Dara, who is in the process of trying to clear her name with us—"

"It *is* clear," he said. "I have cleared it."

I shook my head.

"I refrained from accusing her of something I have been thinking about for some time. There is a very good reason why I feel she cannot be trusted, despite her protests and your endorsement. Two reasons, in fact."

"I know, Corwin. But she did not kill Benedict's servants to manage her position at his house. I did it myself, to assure her getting to you as she did, at just the appropriate time."

"You? You were party to her whole plot? Why?"

"She will make you a good queen, son. I trust the blood of Chaos for strength. It was time for a fresh infusion. You will take the throne already provided with an heir. By the time he is ready for it, Merlin will long have been weaned from his upbringing."

We had come all the way around to the place of the black smear. I stopped. I squatted and studied it.

"You think this thing is going to kill you?" I finally asked.

"I know that it is."

"You are not above murdering innocent people to manipulate me. Yet you would sacrifice your life for the kingdom."

I looked up at him.

"My own hands are not clean," I said, "and I certainly do not presume to judge you. A while back, though, when I made ready to try the Pattern, I thought how my feelings had changed—toward Eric, toward the throne. You do what you do, I believe, as a duty. I, too, feel a duty now, toward Amber, toward the throne. More than that, actually. Much more, I realized, just then. But I realized something else, also, something that duty does not require of me. I do not know when or how it stopped and I changed, but I do not want the throne, Dad. I am sorry it messes up your plans, but I do not want to be king of Amber. I am sorry."

I looked away then, back down at the smear. I heard him sigh.

Then, "I am going to send you home now," he said. "Saddle your horse and take provisions. Ride to a place outside Amber—any place, fairly isolated."

"My tomb?"

He snorted and chuckled faintly.

"That will do. Go there and wait my pleasure. I have some thinking to do."

I stood. He reached out and placed his right hand on my shoulder. The Jewel was pulsing. He looked into my eyes.

"No man can have everything he wants the way that he wants it," he said.

And there was a distancing effect, as of the power of a Trump, only working in reverse. I heard voices, then about me I saw the room I had earlier departed. Benedict, Gérard, Random and Dara were still there. I felt Dad release my shoulder. Then he was gone and I was among them once again.

"What is the story?" Random said. "We saw Dad sending you back. By the way, how did he do that?"

"I do not know," I said. "But he confirms what Dara has told us. He gave her the signet and the message."

"Why?" Gérard asked.

"He wanted us to learn to trust her," I said.

Benedict rose to his feet. "Then I will go and do as I have been bid."

"He wants you to attack, then fall back," Dara said. "After that, it will only be necessary to contain them."

"For how long?"

"He said only that this will become apparent."

Benedict gave one of his rare smiles and nodded. He managed his card case with his one hand, removed the deck, thumbed out the special Trump I had given him for the Courts.

"Good luck," Random said.

"Yes," Gérard agreed.

I added my wishes and watched him fade. When his rainbow afterimage had vanished I looked away and noticed that Dara was crying silently. I did not remark on it.

"I, too, have orders now—of a sort," I said. "I had best be moving."

"And I will get back to the sea," said Gérard.

"No," I heard Dara say as I was moving toward the door.

I halted.

"You are to remain here, Gérard, and see to the safety of Amber herself. No attack will come by sea."

"But I thought Random was in charge of the local defense."

She shook her head.

"Random is to join Julian in Arden."

"Are you sure?" Random asked.

"I am certain."

"Good," he said. "It is nice to know he at least thought of me. Sorry, Gérard. That's the breaks."

Gérard simply looked puzzled. "I hope he knows what he is doing," he said.

"We have been through that already," I told him. "Good-bye."

I heard a footfall as I left the room. Dara was beside me.

"What now?" I asked her.

"I thought I would walk with you, wherever you are going."

"I am just going up the hill to get some supplies. Then I am heading for the stables."

"I will go with you."

"I am riding alone."

"I could not accompany you, anyway. I still have to speak with your sisters."

"They're included, huh?"

"Yes."

We walked in silence for a time, then she said, "The whole business was not so cold-blooded as it seemed, Corwin."

We entered the supply room.

"What business?"

"You know what I mean."

"Oh. That. Well, good."

"I like you. It could be more than that one day, if you feel anything."

My pride handed me a snappy reply, but I bit it back. One learns a few things over the centuries. She had used me, true, but then it seemed she had not been entirely a free agent at the time. The worst that might be said, I suppose, was that Dad wanted me to want her. But I did not let my resentment on this interfere with what my own feelings really were, or could become.

So, "I like you, too," I said, and I looked at her. She seemed as if she needed to be kissed just then, so I did. "I had better get ready now."

She smiled and squeezed my arm. Then she was gone. I decided not to examine my feelings just then. I got some things together.

I saddled Star and rode back up over the crest of Kolvir until I came to my tomb. Seated outside it, I smoked my pipe and watched the clouds. I felt I had had a very full day, and it was still early afternoon. Premonitions played tag in the grottoes of my mind, none of which I would have cared to take to lunch.

III

Contact came suddenly as I sat drowsing. I was on my feet in an instant. It was Dad.

"Corwin, I have made my decisions and the time has come," he said. "Bare your left arm."

I did this, as his form continued to grow in substantiality, looking more and more regal the while, a strange sadness on his face, of a sort I had never seen there before.

He took hold of my arm with his left hand and drew his dagger with his right.

I watched as he cut my arm, then resheathed his blade. The blood came forth, and he cupped his left hand and caught it. He released my arm, covered his left hand with his right and drew away from me. Raising his hands to his face, he blew his breath into them and drew them quickly apart.

A crested red bird the size of a raven, its feathers all the color of my blood, stood on his hand, moved to his wrist, looked at me. Even its eyes were red, and there was a look of familiarity as it cocked its head and regarded me.

"He is Corwin, the one you must follow," he told the bird. "Remember him."

Then he transferred it to his left shoulder, from whence it continued to stare at me, making no effort to depart.

"You must go now, Corwin," he said, "quickly. Mount your horse and ride south, passing into Shadow as soon as you can. Hellride. Get as far away from here as possible."

"Where am I going, Father?" I asked him.

"To the Courts of Chaos. You know the way?"

"In theory. I have never ridden the distance."

He nodded slowly.

"Then get moving," he said. "I want you to create as great a time differential as you can between this place and yourself."

"All right," I said, "but I do not understand."

"You will, when the time comes."

"But there is an easier way," I protested. "I can get there faster and with a lot less bother simply by getting in touch with Benedict with his Trump and having him take me through."

"No good," Dad said. "It will be necessary for you to take the longer route because you will be carrying something which will be conveyed to you along the way."

"Conveyed? How?"

He reached up and stroked the red bird's feathers.

"By your friend here. He could not fly all the way to the Courts—not in time, that is."

"What will he bring me?"

"The Jewel. I doubt that I will be able to effect the transfer myself when I have finished what I have to do with it. Its powers may be of some benefit to us in that place."

"I see," I said. "But I still need not ride the entire distance. I can Trump through after I receive it."

"I fear not. Once I have done what must be done here, the Trumps will all become inoperative for a period of time."

"Why?"

"Because the entire fabric of existence will be undergoing an alteration. Move now, damn it! Get on your horse and ride!"

I stood and stared a moment longer.

"Father, is there no other way?"

He simply shook his head and raised his hand. He began to fade.

"Good-bye."

I turned and mounted. There was more to say, but it was too late. I turned Star toward the trail that would take me southward.

While Dad was able to play with the stuff of Shadow atop Kolvir, I had never been able to. I required a greater distance from Amber in order to work the shifts.

Still, knowing that it could be done, I felt that I ought to try. So, working my way southward across bare stone and down rocky passes where the wind howled, I sought to warp the fabric or being about me as I headed toward the trail that led to Garnath.

. . . A small clump of blue flowers as I rounded a stony shoulder.

I grew excited at this, for they were a modest part of my working.

I continued to lay my will upon the world to come beyond each twisting of my way.

A shadow from a triangular stone, across my path . . . A shifting of the wind . . .

Some of the smaller ones were indeed working. A backward twist to the trail . . . A crevice . . . An ancient bird's nest, high on a rocky shelf . . . More of the blue flowers . . .

Why not? A tree . . . Another . . .

I felt the power moving within me I worked more changes.

A thought came to me then, concerning my newfound strength. It seemed possible that it might have been purely psychological reasons which had barred me from performing such manipulations earlier. Until very recently I had considered Amber herself the single, immutable reality from which all shadows took their form. Now I realized she was but first among shadows, and that the place where my father stood represented the higher reality. Thereofre, while the proximity made it difficult it did not make it impossible to effect changes in this place. Yet, under other circumstances I would have saved my strength until I had reached a point where it was easier to shift things about.

Now, now though, the need for haste lay upon me. I would have to exert myself, to rush, to do my father's bidding.

By the time I reached the trail leading down the southern face of Kolvir, the character of the land had already changed. I looked upon a series of gentle slopes, rather than the steep descent which normally marked the way. I was already entering the shadowlands.

The black road still lay like a dark scar to my left as I headed downward, but this Garnath through which it had been cut was in slightly better shape than that which I knew so well. Its lines were softer, from flocks of greenery which lay somewhat nearer the dead swath. It was as though my curse upon the land were slightly mitigated. Illusion of feeling, of course, for this was no longer exactly my Amber. But, *I am sorry for my part in this,* I addressed everything mentally, half-prayerlike. *I ride now to try to undo it. Forgive me, oh spirit of this place.* My eyes moved in the direction of the Grove of the Unicorn, but it was too far to the west, masked by too many trees, for me even to glimpse that sacred glade.

The slope grew more level as I descended, becoming a series of gentle foothills. I let Star move faster as we crossed them, bearing to the southwest, then finally the south. Lower, lower. At a great distance to my left the sea sparkled and shone. Soon the black road would come between us, for I was descending into Garnath in its direction. No matter what I did with Shadow, I would not be able to erase that ominous presence. In fact, the fastest course I could follow would be one that paralleled it.

We came at last to the floor of the valley. The Forest of Arden towered far to my right, sweeping westward, immense and venerable. I rode on, working what changes I could to bear me even farther from my home.

While keeping the black road on hand, I stayed a good distance from it. I had to, since it was the one thing I could not change. I kept shrubs, trees and low hills between us.

I reached out then, and the texture of the land changed.

Veins of agate . . . Heaps of schist . . . A darkening of the greenery . . .

Clouds swimming across the sky . . . The sun shimmering and dancing . . .

We increased our pace. The land sank lower still. Shadows lengthened, merged. The forest retreated. A rocky wall grew to my right, another to my left. . . . A cold wind pursued me down a rough canyon. Strata streaks—red, gold, yellow and brown—flashed by. The floor of the canyon grew sandy. Dust devils spun about us. I leaned farther forward as the way began to rise once again. The walls slanted inward, grew closer together.

The way narrowed, narrowed. I could almost touch either wall. . . .

Their tops came together. I rode through a shadowy tunnel, slowing as it darkened. . . . Phosphorescent designs burst into being. The wind made a moaning noise.

Out then!

The light from the walls was blinding, and giant crystals rose all about us. We plunged past, following an upward trail that led away from this region and through a series of mossy dells where small, perfectly circular pools lay still as green glass.

Tall ferns appeared before us and we made our way among them. I heard a distant trumpeting noise.

Turning, pacing . . . Red now the ferns, wider and lower . . . Beyond, a great plain, pinking into evening . . .

Forward, over pale grasses . . . The smell of fresh earth . . . Mountains or dark clouds far ahead . . . A rush of stars from my left . . . A quick spray of moisture . . . A blue moon leaps into the sky . . . Flickerings among the dark masses . . . Memories and a rumbling noise . . . Stormsmell and rushing air . . .

A strong wind . . . Clouds across the stars . . . A bright fork spearing a shattered tree to my right, turning it to flame . . . A tingling sensation . . . The smell of ozone . . . Sheets of water upon me . . . A row of lights to my left . . .

Clattering down a cobbled street . . . A strange vehicle approaching . . . Cylindrical, chugging . . . We avoid one another . . . A shout pursues me . . . Through a lighted window the face of a child . . .

Clattering . . . Splashing . . . Storefronts and homes . . . The rain lets up, dies down, is gone . . . A fog blows by, lingers, deepens, is pearled by a growing light to my left . . .

The terrain softens, grows red . . . The light within the mist brightens . . . A new wind, from behind, a growing warmth . . . The air breaks apart . . .

Sky of pale lemon . . . Orange sun rushing toward noon . . .

A shudder! A thing not of my doing, totally unanticipated . . . The ground moves beneath us, but there is more to it than that. The new sky, the new sun, the rusty desert I have just now entered—all of them expand and contract, fade and return. There comes a cracking sound, and with each fading I find Star and myself alone, amid a white nothingness—characters without a setting. We tread upon nothing. The light comes from everywhere and illuminates only ourselves. A steady cracking noise, as of the spring thaw come upon a Russian river I had once ridden beside, fills my ears. Star, who has paced many shadows, emits a frightened sound.

I look all about me. Blurred outlines appear, sharpen, grow clear. My environment is restored, though with a somewhat washed-out look to it. A bit of the pigment has been drained from the world.

We wheel to the left, racing for a low hill, mounting it, halting finally at its summit.

The black road. It too seems denatured—but even more so than the rest. It ripples beneath my gaze, almost seems to undulate as I watch. The cracking noise continues, grows louder. . . .

A wind comes out of the north, gentle at first but increasing in force. Looking in that direction, I see a mass of dark clouds building.

I know that I must move as I have never moved before. Ultimates of destruction and creation are occurring at the place I visited—

when? No matter. The waves move outward from Amber and this, too, may pass away—and me along with it. If Dad cannot put it all back together again.

I shake the reins. We race southward.

A plain . . . Trees . . . Some broken buildings . . . Faster . . .

The smoke of a forest afire . . . A wall of flame . . . Gone . . . Yellow sky, blue clouds . . . An armada of dirigibles crossing . . . Faster . . .

The sun drops like a piece of hot iron into a bucket of water, stars become streaks . . . A pale light upon a straight trail . . . Sounds dopplered from dark smears, the wailing . . . Brighter the light, fainter the prospect . . . Gray, to my right, my left . . . Brighter now . . . Nothing but the trail my eyes to ride . . . The wailing heightens to a shriek . . . Forms run together . . . We race through a tunnel of Shadow . . . It begins to revolve . . .

Turning, turning . . . Only the road is real . . . The worlds go by . . . I have released my control of the sets and ride now the thrust of the power itself, aimed only to remove me from Amber and hurl me toward Chaos . . . There is wind upon me and the cry in my ears . . . Never before have I pushed my power over Shadow to its limit . . . The tunnel grows as slick and seamless as glass . . . I feel I am riding down a vortex, a maelstrom, the heart of a tornado . . . Star and I are drenched with sweat . . . There is a wild feeling of flight upon me, as though I am pursued . . . The road is become an abstraction . . . My eyes sting as I try to blink away the perspiration . . . I cannot hold this ride much longer . . . There comes a throbbing at the base of my skull . . .

I draw back gently upon the reins and Star begins to slow . . .

The walls of my tunnel of light grow grainy . . . Blotches of gray, black, white, rather than a uniformity of shading . . . Brown . . . A hint of blue . . . Green . . . The wailing descends to a hum, a rumble, fading . . . Gentler the wind . . . Shapes come and go . . .

Slowing, slowing . . .

There is no path. I ride on mossy earth. The sky is blue, the clouds are white. I am very light-headed. I draw rein. I—

Tiny.

I was shocked as I lowered my eyes. I stood at the outskirts of a toy village. Houses I could hold in the palm of my hand, miniscule roads, tiny vehicles crawling along them. . . .

I looked back. We had crushed a number of these diminutive residences. I looked all around. There were fewer to the left. I guided Star carefully in that direction, kept moving until we had left that place. I felt bad about it—whatever it was—whoever dwelled there. But there was not a thing that I could do.

I moved again, passing through Shadow, until I came to what seemed a deserted quarry beneath a greenish sky. I felt heavier here. I dismounted, took a drink of water, walked around a bit.

I breathed deeply of the damp air that engulfed me. I was far from Amber now, about as far as one ever need go, and well on my way to Chaos. I had seldom come this far before. While I had chosen this place for a rest stop because it represented the nearest thing to normalcy I could catch hold of, the changes would soon be getting more and more radical.

I was stretching my cramped muscles when I heard the shriek, high in the air above me.

I looked up and saw the dark form descending, Grayswandir coming by reflex into my hand. But the light caught it at a proper angle as it came down, and the winged form took fire on its way.

My familiar bird circled, circled, descended to my outstretched arm. Those frightening eyes regarded me with a peculiar intelligence, but I did not spare them the attention I might have on another occasion. Instead, I sheathed Grayswandir and reached for the thing the bird bore.

The Jewel of Judgment.

I knew by this that Dad's effort, whatever it had amounted to, was finished. The Pattern had either been repaired or botched. He was either alive or dead. Choose a couple from either column. The effects of his act would be spreading outward from Amber through Shadow now, like the ripples in the proverbial pond. I would learn more of them soon enough. In the meantime, I had my orders.

I drew the chain over my head and let the Jewel fall upon my breast. I remounted Star. My bloodbird emitted a short cry and rose into the air.

We moved again.

. . . Over a landscape where the sky whitened as the ground darkened. Then the land flared and the sky grew black. Then the reverse. And again . . . With each stride the effect shifted, and as we moved faster it built to a stroboscopic series of still-shots about us, gradually growing to a jerky animation, then the hyperactive quality of a silent film. Finally, all was a blur.

Points of light flashed past, like meteors or comets. I began to feel a throbbing sensation, as of a cosmic heartbeat. Everything began to turn about me, as though I had been caught up in a whirlwind.

Something was going wrong. I seemed to be losing control. Could it be that the effects of Dad's doings had already reached the area of Shadow through which I passed? It seemed hardly likely. Still . . .

Star stumbled. I clung tightly as we went down, not wishing to be separated in Shadow. I struck my shoulder on a hard surface and lay there for a moment, stunned.

When the world came together about me again, I sat up and looked around.

A uniform twilight prevailed, but there were no stars. Instead, large rocks of various shapes and sizes drifted and hovered in the air. I got to my feet and looked all about.

It was possible, from what I could see of it, that the irregular stony surface on which I stood was itself but a mountain-sized boulder drifting with the others. Star rose and stood shivering at my side. An absolute silence contained us. The still air was cool. There was not another living thing in sight. I did not like this place. I would not have halted here of my own volition. I knelt to inspect Star's legs. I wanted to leave as soon as possible, preferably mounted.

As I was about this, I heard a soft chuckle which might have come from a human throat.

I paused, resting my hand upon Grayswandir's hilt and seeking the source of the sound.

Nothing. Nowhere.

Yet I had heard it. I turned slowly, looking in every direction. No . . .

Then it came again. Only this time, I realized that it had its source overhead.

I scanned the floating rocks. Shadow-draped, it was difficult to distinguish—

There!

Ten meters above the ground and thirty or so to my left, what appeared to be a human form stood atop a small island in the sky, regarding me. I considered it. Whatever it was, it seemed too far off to pose a threat. I was certain that I could be gone before it could reach me. I moved to mount Star.

"No good, Corwin," called the voice I least wanted to hear just then. "You are locked here. There is no way you can depart without my leave."

I smiled as I mounted, then drew Grayswandir.

"Let's find out," I said. "Come bar my way."

"Very well," he replied, and flames sprang from the bare rock, towering full circle about me, licking, sprawling, soundless.

Star went wild. I slammed Grayswandir back into the scabbard, whipped a corner of my cloak across Star's eyes, spoke soothing words. As I did this, the circle enlarged, the fires receding toward the edges of the great rock on which we stood.

"Convinced?" came the voice. "This place is too small. Ride in any direction. Your mount will panic again before you can shift into Shadow."

"Good-bye, Brand," I said, and I began to ride.

I rode in a large counterclockwise circle about the rocky surface, shielding Star's right eye from the flames about the periphery of things. I heard Brand chuckle again, not realizing what I was doing.

A pair of large rocks . . . Good. I rode on by, continuing the course. Now a jagged hedge of stone to my left, a rise, a dip . . . A mess of shadow the fires cast, across my path . . . There. Down . . . Up. A touch of green to that patch of light . . . I could feel the shifting begin.

The fact that it is easier for us to take a straight course does not make it the only way. We all pursue it so much of the time, though, that we tend to forget that one can also make progress by going around in circles. . . .

I could feel the shift more strongly as I neared the two large rocks again. Brand caught on about then, also.

"Hold it, Corwin!"

I threw him a finger and cut between the rocks, heading down into a narrow canyon speckled with points of yellow light. According to specifications.

I drew my cloak away from Star's head and shook the reins. The canyon cut abruptly to the right. We followed it into a better-lighted avenue which widened and brightened as we went.

. . . Beneath a jutting overhang, sky of milk shading to pearl on its other side.

Riding deeper, faster, farther . . . A jagged cliff crowned the upper talus to my left, greening in twisted sign of shrubbery beneath a pink-touched sky.

I rode until the greenery was bluery beneath a yellow sky, till the canyon rose to meet a lavender plain where orange rocks rolled as the ground was shaken beneath us in time with our hoofbeats. I crossed there under wheeling comets, coming to the shore of a blood-red sea in a place of heavy perfumes. I rode a large green sun and a small bronze one out of the sky as I paced that shore, while skeletal navies clashed and serpents of the deep circled their orange and blue-sailed vessels. The Jewel pulsed upon me and I drew strength from it. A wild wind came up and lofted us through a copper-clouded sky above a wailing chasm which seemed to extend forever, black-bottomed, spark-shot, fuming with heady scents. . . .

At my back, the sound of thunder, ceaseless . . . Fine lines, like the craqueleur of an old painting, abreast of us, advancing, everywhere . . . Cold, a fragrance-killing wind pursues . . .

Lines . . . The cracks widen, blackness flows to fill . . . Dark streaks race by, up, down, back upon themselves . . . The settling of a net, the labors of a giant, invisible spider, world-trapping . . .

Down, down and down . . . The ground again, wrinkled and leathery as a mummy's neck . . . Soundless, our throbbing passage . . . Softer the thunder, falling the wind . . . Dad's last gasp? Speed now and away . . .

A narrowing of lines, to the fineness of an etching, fading then in the three suns' heat . . . And faster yet . . .

A rider, approaching . . . Hand to hilt in time to my own . . . Me. Myself coming back? Simultaneous, our salutes . . . Through one another, somehow, the air like a sheet of water that one dry instant. . What Carroll mirror, what Remba, Tir-na Nog'th effect . . . Yet far, far to my left, a black thing writhing . . . We pace the road . . . It leads me on . . .

White sky, white ground and no horizon . . . Sunless and cloudless the prospect . . . Only that thread of black, far off, and gleaming pyramids everywhere, massive, disconcerting . . .

We tire. I do not like this place . . . But we have outrun whatever process pursues. Draw rein.

I was tired, but I felt a strange vitality within me. It seemed as though it arose from within my breast . . . The Jewel. Of course. I made an effort to draw upon this power again. I felt it flow outward through my limbs, barely halting at my extremities. It was almost as if—

Yes. I reached out and lay my will upon my blank and geometrical surroundings. They began to alter.

It was a movement. The pyramids shuffled by, darkening as they passed. The world turned upside down and I stood as on the underside of a cloud, watching landscapes flash by beneath/above.

Light streamed upward past me, from a golden sun beneath my feet. This, too, passed, and the fleecy ground darkened, firing waters upward to erode the passing land. Lightnings jumped up to strike the world overhead, to break it apart. In places it shattered and its pieces fell about me.

They began to swirl as a wave of darkness passed.

When the light came again, bluish this time, it held no point source and described no land.

. . . Golden bridges cross the void in great streamers, one of them flashing beneath us even now. We wind along its course, standing the while still as a statue . . . For an age, perhaps, this goes on. A phenomenon not unrelated to highway hypnosis enters through my eyes, lulls me dangerously.

I do what I can to accelerate our passage. Another age goes by.

Finally, far ahead, a dusky, misty blotch, our terminus, growing very slowly despite our velocity.

By the time we reach it, it is gigantic—an island in the void, forested over with golden, metallic trees. . . .

I stop the motion which has borne us thus far and we move forward under our own power, entering that wood. Grass like aluminum foil crunches beneath us as we pass among those trees. Strange fruit, pale and shiny, hangs about me. There are no animal sounds immediately apparent. Working our way inward, we come to a small clearing through which a quicksilver stream flows. There, I dismount.

"Brother Corwin," comes that voice again. "I have been waiting for you."

IV

I faced the wood, watched him emerge from it. I did not draw my weapon, as he had not drawn his. I reached down into the Jewel with my mind, though. After the excercise I had just completed, I realized that I could do a lot more than control weather with it. Whatever Brand's power, I felt I'd a weapon now with which to confront it directly. The Jewel pulsed more deeply as I did this.

"Truce," Brand said. "Okay? May we talk?"

"I do not see that we have anything more to say to one another," I told him.

"If you do not give me a chance you will never know for certain, will you?"

He came to a halt about seven meters away, flung his green cloak back over his left shoulder and smiled.

"All right. Say it, whatever it is," I said.

"I tried to stop you," he said, "back there, for the Jewel. It is obvious that you know what it is now, that you realize how important it is."

I said nothing.

"Dad has already used it," he continued, "and I am sorry to report that he has failed in what he set out to do with it."

"What? How could you know?"

"I can see through Shadow, Corwin. I would have thought our sister had filled you in more thoroughly on these matters. With a little mental effort, I can perceive whatever I choose now. Naturally, I was concerned with the outcome of this affair. So I watched. He is dead, Corwin. The effort was too much for him. He lost control of the forces he was manipulating and was blasted by them a little over halfway through the Pattern."

"You lie!" I said, touching the Jewel.

He shook his head.

"I admit that I am not above lying to gain my ends, but this time I am telling the truth. Dad is dead. I saw him fall. The bird brought you the Jewel then, as he had willed it. We are left in a universe without a Pattern."

I did not want to believe him. But it was possible that Dad had failed. I had the assurance of the only expert in the business, Dworkin, as to the difficulty of the task.

"Granting for the moment what you have said, what happens next?" I asked.

"Things fall apart," he replied. "Even now, Chaos wells up to fill the vacuum back at Amber. A great vortex has come into being, and it grows. It spreads ever outward, destroying the shadow worlds, and it will not stop until it meets with the Courts of Chaos, bringing all of creation full circle, with Chaos once more to reign over all."

I felt dazed. Had I struggled from Greenwood, through everything, to here, to have it end this way? Would I see everything stripped of meaning, form, content, life, when things had been pushed to a kind of completion?

"No!" I said. "It cannot be so."

"Unless . . ." Brand said softly.

"Unless what?"

"Unless a new Pattern is inscribed, a new order created to preserve form."

"You mean ride back into that mess and try to complete the job? You just said that the place no longer exists."

"No. Of course not. The location is unimportant. Wherever there is a Pattern there is a center. I can do it right here."

"You think that you can succeed where Dad failed?"

"I have to try. I am the only one who knows enough about it and has sufficient time before the waves of Chaos arrive. Listen, I admit to everything Fiona has doubtless told you about me. I have schemed and I have acted. I have dealt with the enemies of Amber. I have shed our blood. I tried to burn out your memory. But the world as we know it is being destroyed now, and I live here too. All of my plans—everything!—will come to nothing if some measure of order is not preserved. Perhaps I have been duped by the Lords of Chaos. It is difficult for me to admit that, but I see the possibility now. It is not too late to foil them, though. We can build the new bastion of order right here."

"How?"

"I need the Jewel—and your assistance. This will be the site of the new Amber."

"Supposing—*arguendo*—I give it to you. Would the new Pattern be exactly like the old one?"

He shook his head.

"It could not be, any more than the one Dad was attempting to create would have been like Dworkin's. No two authors can render the same story in the same fashion. Individual stylistic differences cannot be avoided. No matter how hard I might try to duplicate it, my version would be slightly different."

"How could you do this," I asked, "when you are not fully attuned to the Jewel? You would need a Pattern to complete the process of attunement—and, as you say, the Pattern has been destroyed. What gives?"

Then, "I said that I would need your help," he stated. "There is another way to attune a person to the Jewel. It requires the assistance of someone who is already attuned. You would have to project yourself through the Jewel once more, and take me with you—into and through the primary Pattern that lies beyond."

"And then?"

"Why, when the ordeal is past I will be attuned, you give me the Jewel, I inscribe a new Pattern and we are back in business. Things hold together. Life goes on."

"What of Chaos?"

"The new Pattern will be unmarred. They will no longer have the road giving them access to Amber."

"With Dad dead, how would the new Amber be run?"

He smiled crookedly.

"I ought to have something for my pains, oughtn't I? I will be risking my life with this, and the odds are not all that good."

I smiled back at him.

"Considering the payoff, what is to prevent me from taking the gamble myself?" I said.

"The same thing that prevented Dad from succeeding—all the forces of Chaos. They are summoned by a kind of cosmic reflex when such an act is begun. I have had more experience with them than you. You would not have a chance. I might."

"Now let us say that you are lying to me, Brand. Or let us be kind and say that you did not see clearly through all the turmoil. Supposing Dad did succeed? Supposing there is a new Pattern in existence right now? What would happen if you were to do another, here, now?"

"I . . . It has never been done before. How should I know?"

"I wonder?" I said. "Might you still get your own version of reality that way? Might it represent the splitting off of a new universe— Amber and Shadow—just for you? Might it negate ours? Or would it simply stand apart? Or would there be some overlapping? What do you think, given that situation?"

He shrugged his shoulders.

"I have already answered that. It has never been done before. How should I know?"

"But I think that you do know, or can make a very good guess at it. I think that that is what you are planning, that that is what you want to try—because that is all you have left now. I take this action on your part as an indication that Dad has succeeded and that you are down to your last card. But you need me and you need the Jewel for it. You cannot have either."

He sighed.

"I had expected more of you. But all right. You are wrong, but leave it at that. Listen, though. Rather than see everything lost, I will split the realm with you."

"Brand," I said, "get lost. You cannot have the Jewel, or my help. I have heard you out, and I think that you are lying."

"You are afraid," he said, "afraid of me. I do not blame you for not wanting to trust me. But you are making a mistake. You need me now."

"Nevertheless, I have made my choice."

He took a step toward me. Another . . .

"Anything you want, Corwin. I can give you anything you care to name."

"I was with Benedict in Tir-na Nog'th," I said, "looking through his eyes, listening with his ears, when you made him the same offer. Shove it, Brand. I am going on with my mission. If you think that you can stop me, now is as good a time as any."

I began walking toward him. I knew that I would kill him if I reached him. I also felt that I would not reach him.

He halted. He took a step backward.

"You are making a big mistake," he said.

"I do not think so. I think that I am doing exactly the right thing."

"I will not fight with you," he said hastily. "Not here, not above the abyss. You have had your chance, though. The next time that we meet, I will have to take the Jewel from you."

"What good will it be to you, unattuned?"

"There might still be a way for me to manage it—more difficult, but possible. You have had your chance. Goodbye."

He retreated into the wood. I followed after, but he had vanished.

I left that place and rode on, along a road over nothing. I did not like to consider the possibility that Brand might have been telling the truth, or at least a part of it. But the things he had said kept returning to plague me. Supposing Dad had failed? Then I was on a fool's errand. Everything was already over, and it was just a matter of time. I did not like looking back, just in case something was gaining on me. I passed into a moderately paced hellride. I wanted to get to the others before the waves of Chaos reached that far, just to let them know that I had kept faith, to let them see that in the end I had tried my best. I wondered then how the actual battle was going. Or had it even begun yet, within that time frame?

I swept along the bridge, which widened now beneath a brightening sky. As it assumed the aspect of a golden plain, I considered Brand's threat. Had he said what he had said simply to raise doubts, increase my discomfort and impair my efficiency? Possibly. Yet, if he required the Jewel he would have to ambush me. And I had a respect for that strange power he had acquired over Shadow. It seemed almost impossible to prepare for an attack by someone who could watch my every move and transport himself instantaneously to the most advantageous spot. How soon might it come? Not too soon, I guessed. First, he would want to frazzle my nerves—and I was already tired and more than a little punchy. I would have to rest, to sleep, sooner or later. It was impossible for me to go that great distance in a single stretch, no matter how accelerated the hellride.

Fogs of pink and orange and green fled past, swirled about me, filling up the world. The ground rang beneath us like metal. Occasional musical tones, as of rung crystal occurred overhead. My thoughts danced. Memories of many worlds came and went in random fashion. Ganelon, my friend-enemy, and my father, enemy-friend, merged and parted, parted and merged. Somewhere one of them asked me who had a right to the throne. I had thought it was Ganelon, wanting to know our several justifications. Now I knew that it had been Dad, wanting to know my feelings. He had judged. He had made his decision. And I was backing out. Whether it was arrested development, the desire to be free of such an encumbrance, or a matter of sudden enlightenment based on all that I had experienced in recent years, growing slowly within me, granting me a more mature view of the onerous role of monarch apart from its moments of glory, I do not know. I remembered my life on the shadow Earth, following orders, giving them. Faces swam before me—people I had known over the centuries—friends, enemies, wives, lovers, relatives. Lorraine seemed to be beckoning me on, Moire laughing, Deirdre weeping. I fought again with Eric. I recalled my first passage through the Pattern, as a boy, and the later one when, step by step, my memory was given back to me. Murders, thieveries, knaveries, seductions returned because, as Mallory said, they were there. I was unable, even, to place them all correctly in terms of time. There was no great anxiety because there was no great guilt. Time, time, and more time had softened the edges of harsher things, had worked its changes on me. I saw my earlier selves as different people, acquaintances I had outgrown. I wondered how I could ever have been some of them. As I rushed onward, scenes from my past seemed to solidify in the mists about me. No poetic license here. Battles in which I had taken part assumed tangible form, save for a total absence of sound—the flare of weapons, the colors of uniforms, banners and blood. And people —most of them now long dead—moved from my memory into silent animation about me. None of these were members of my family, but all of them were people who had once meant something to me. Yet there was no special pattern to it. There were noble deeds as well as shameful; enemies as well as friends—and none of the persons involved took note of my passage; all were caught up in some long-past sequence of actions. I wondered then at the nature of the place through which I rode. Was it some watered-down version of Tir-na Nog'th, with some mind-sensitive substance in the vicinity that drew from me and projected about me this "This Is Your Life" panorama? Or was I simply beginning to hallucinate? I was tired, anxious, troubled, distressed, and I passed along a way which provided a monotonous, gentle stimulation of the senses of the sort leading to reverie. . . . In fact, I realized that I had lost control over Shadow sometime back and was now simply proceeding in a linear fashion across this landscape, trapped in a kind of externalized narcissism by the spectacle. . . . I realized then that I had to stop and rest— probably even sleep a little—though I feared doing so in this place. I would have to break free and make my way to a more sedate, deserted spot. . . .

I wrenched at my surroundings. I twisted things about. I broke free.

Soon I was riding in a rough, mountainous area, and shortly thereafter I came to the cave that I desired.

We passed within, and I tended to Star. I ate and drank just enough to take the edge off my hunger. I built no fire. I wrapped myself in my cloak and in a blanket I had brought. I held Grayswandir in my right hand. I lay facing the darkness beyond the cavemouth.

I felt a little sick. I knew that Brand was a liar, but his words bothered me anyway.

But I had always been good at going to sleep. I closed my eyes and was gone.

V

I was awakened by a sense of presence. Or maybe it was a noise and a sense of presence. Whatever, I was awake and I was certain that I was not alone. I tightened my grip on Grayswandir and opened my eyes. Beyond that, I did not move.

A soft light, like moonlight, came in through the cavemouth. There was a figure, possibly human, standing just inside. The lighting was such that I could not tell whether it faced me or faced outward. But then it took a step toward me.

I was on my feet, the point of my blade toward its breast. It halted.

"Peace," said a man's voice, in Thari. "I have but taken refuge from the storm. May I share your cave?"

"What storm?" I asked.

As if in answer, there came a roll of thunder followed by a gust of wind with the smell of rain within it.

"Okay, that much is true," I said. "Make yourself comfortable."

He sat down, well inside, his back against the righthand wall of the cave. I folded my blanket for a pad and seated myself across from him. About four meters separated us. I located my pipe and filled it, then tried a match which had been with me from the shadow Earth. It lit, saving me a lot of trouble. The tobacco had a good smell, mixed with the damp breeze. I listened to the sounds of the rain and regarded the dark outline of my nameless companion. I thought over some possible dangers, but it had not been Brand's voice which had addressed me.

"This is no natural storm," the other said.

"Oh? How so?"

"For one thing, it is coming out of the north. They never come out of the north, here, this time of year."

"That's how records are made."

"For another, I have never seen a storm behave this way. I have been watching it advance all day—just a steady line, moving slowly, front like a sheet of glass. So much lightning, it looks like a monstrous insect with hundreds of shiny legs. Most unnatural. And behind it, things have grown very distorted."

"That happens in the rain."

"Not that way. Everything seems to be changing its shape. Flowing. As if it is melting the world—or stamping away its forms."

I shuddered. I had thought that I was far enough ahead of the dark waves that I could take a little rest. Still, he might be wrong, and it could just be an unusual storm. But I did not want to take the chance. I rose and turned to the rear of the cave. I whistled.

No response. I went back and groped around.

"Something the matter?"

"My horse is gone."

"Could it have wandered off?"

"Must have. I'd have thought Star'd have better sense, though."

I went to the cavemouth but could see nothing. I was half-drenched in the instant I was there. I returned to my position beside the left wall.

"It seems like an ordinary enough storm to me," I said. "They sometimes get pretty bad in the mountains."

"Perhaps you know this country better than I do?"

"No, I am just traveling through—a thing I had better be continuing soon, too."

I touched the Jewel. I reached into it, then through it, out and up, with my mind. I felt the storm about me and ordered it away, with red pulses of energy corresponding to my heartbeats. Then I leaned back, found another match and relit my pipe. It would still take a while for the forces I had manipulated to do their work, against a stormfront of this size.

"It will not last too long," I said.

"How can you tell?"

"Privileged information."

He chuckled.

"According to some versions, this is the way that the world ends—beginning with a strange storm from out of the north."

"That's right," I said, "and this is it. Nothing to worry about, though. It will be all over, one way or the other, before too long."

"That stone you are wearing . . . It is giving off light."

"Yes."

"You were joking about this being the end, though—were you not?"

"No."

"You make me think of that line from the Holy Book—*The Archangel Corwin shall pass before the storm, lightning upon his breast . . . .* You would not be named Corwin, would you?"

"How does the rest of it go?"

"*. . . When asked where he travels, he shall say, 'To the ends of the Earth,' where he goes not knowing what enemy will aid him against another enemy, nor whom the Horn will touch.*"

"That's all?"

"All there is about the Archangel Corwin."

"I have run into this difficulty with Scripture in the past. It tells you enough to get interested, but never enough to be of any immediate use. It is as though the author gets his kicks by tantalizing. One enemy against another? The Horn? Beats me."

"Where *do* you travel?"

"Not too far, unless I can find my horse."

I returned to the cavemouth. It was letting up now, with a glow like a moon behind some clouds to the west, another to the east. I looked both ways along the trail and down the slope to the valley. No horses anywhere in sight. I turned back to the cave. Just as I did, however, I heard Star's whinny far below me.

I called back to the stranger in the cave. "I have to go. You can have the blanket."

I do not know whether he replied, for I moved off into the drizzle then, picking my way down the slope. Again, I exerted myself through the Jewel, and the drizzle halted, to be replaced by a mist.

The rocks were slippery, but I made it halfway down without stumbling. I paused then, both to catch my breath and to get my bearings. From that point, I was not certain as to the exact direction from which Star's whinny had come. The moon's light was a little stronger, visibility a bit better, but I saw nothing as I studied the prospect before me. I listened for several minutes.

Then I heard the whinny once more—from below, to my left, near a dark boulder, cairn or rocky outcrop. There did seem to be some sort of turmoil in the shadows at its base. Moving as quickly as I dared, I laid my course in that direction.

As I reached level ground and hurried toward the place of the action, I passed pockets of ground mist, stirred slightly by a breeze from out of the west, snaking silvery, about my ankles. I heard a grating, crunching sound, as of something heavy being pushed or rolled over a rocky surface. Then I caught sight of a gleam of light, low on the dark mass I was approaching.

Drawing nearer, I saw small, manlike forms outlined in a rectangle of light, struggling to move a great rocky slab. Faint echoes of a clattering sound and another whinny came from their direction. Then the stone began to move, swinging like the door that it probably was. The lighted area diminished, narrowed to a sliver, vanished with a booming sound, all of the struggling figures having first passed within.

When I finally reached that rocky mass all was silent once again. I pressed my ear to the stone, but heard nothing. But, whoever they were, they had taken my horse. I had never liked horse thieves, and I had killed my share in the past. And right now, I needed Star as I had seldom needed a horse. So I groped about, seeking the edges of that stony gate.

It was not too difficult to describe its outlines with my fingertips. I probably located it sooner than I would have by daylight, when everything would have blended and merged more readily to baffle the eye. Knowing its situation, I sought further then after some handhold by which I might draw it. They had seemed to be little guys, so I looked low.

I finally discovered what might have been the proper place and seized hold of it. I pulled then, but it was stubborn. Either they were disproportionately strong or there was a trick to it that I was missing.

No matter. There is a time for subtlety and a time for brute force. I was both angry and in a hurry, so the decision was made.

I began to draw upon the slab once again, tightening the muscles in my arms, my shoulders, my back, wishing Gérard were nearby. The door creaked. I kept pulling. It moved slightly—an inch, perhaps—and stuck. I did not slacken, but increased my effort. It creaked again.

I leaned backward, shifted my weight and braced my left foot against the rocky wall at the side of the portal. I pushed with it as I drew back. There was more creaking and some grinding as it moved again—another inch or so. Then it stopped and I could not budge it.

I released my grip and stood, flexing my arms. Then I put my shoulder to it and pushed the door back to its fully closed position. I took a deep breath and seized it again.

I put my left foot back where it had been. No gradual pressure this time. I yanked and shoved simultaneously.

There was a snapping sound and a clattering from within, and the door came forward about half a foot, grinding as it moved. It seemed freer now, though, so I got to my feet, reversed my position—back to wall—and found sufficient purchase to push it outward.

It moved more easily this time, but I could not resist placing my foot against it as it began to swing and thrusting forward as hard as I could. It shot through a full hundred and eighty degrees, slammed back against the rock on the other side with a great booming noise, fractured in several places, swayed, fell and struck the ground with a crash that made it shudder, breaking off more fragments when it hit.

Grayswandir was back in my hand before it struck, and I had dropped into a crouch and stolen a quick look about the corner.

Light . . . There was illumination beyond . . . From little lamps depending from hooks along the wall . . . Beside the stairway . . . Going down . . . To a place of greater light and some sounds . . . Like music . . .

There was no one in sight. I would have thought that the godawful din I had raised would have caught someone's attention, but the music continued. Either the sound—somehow—had not carried, or they did not give a damn. Either way . . .

I rose and stepped over the threshold. My foot struck against a metal object. I picked it up and examined it. A twisted bolt. They had barred the door after themselves. I tossed it back over my shoulder and started down the stair.

The music—fiddles and pipes—grew louder as I advanced. From the breaking of the light, I could see that there was some sort of hall off to my right, from the foot of the stair. They were small steps and there were a lot of them. I did not bother with stealth, but hurried down to the landing.

When I turned and looked into the hall, I beheld a scene out of some drunken Irishman's dream. In a smoky, torchlit hall, hordes of meter-high people, red-faced and green clad, were dancing to the music or quaffing what appeared to be mugs of ale while stamping their feet, slapping tabletops and each other, grinning, laughing and shouting. Huge kegs lined one wall, and a number of the revelers were queued up before the one which had been tapped. An enormous fire blazed in a pit at the far end of the room, its smoke being sucked back through a crevice in the rock wall, above a pair of cavemouths running anywhere. Star was tethered to a ring in the wall beside that pit, and a husky little man in a leather apron was grinding and honing some suspicious-looking instruments.

Several faces turned in my direction, there were shouts and suddenly the music stopped. The silence was almost complete.

I raised my blade to an overhand, épée en garde position, pointed across the room toward Star. All faces were turned in my direction by then.

"I have come for my horse," I said. "Either you bring him to me or I come and get him. There will be a lot more blood the second way."

From off to my right, one of the men, larger and grayer than most of the others, cleared his throat.

"Begging your pardon," he began, "but how did you get in here?"

"You will be needing a new door," I said. "Go and look if you care to, if it makes any difference—and it may. I will wait."

I stepped aside and put the wall to my back.

He nodded.

"I will do that."

And he darted by.

I could feel my anger-born strength flowing into and back out of the Jewel. One part of me wanted to cut and slash and stab my way across the room, another wanted a more humane settlement with people so much smaller than myself; and a third and perhaps wiser part suggested that the little guys might not be such pushovers. So I waited to see how my door-opening feat impressed their spokesman.

Moments later, he returned, giving me wide berth.

"Bring the man his horse," he said.

A sudden flurry of conversation occurred within the hall. I lowered my blade.

"My apologies," said the one who had given the order. "We desire no trouble with the like of you. We will be foraging elsewhere. No hard feelings, I hope?"

The man in the leather apron had untethered Star and started in my direction. The revelers drew back to make way as he led my mount through the hall.

I sighed.

"I will just call it a day and forgive and forget," I said.

The little man seized a flagon from a nearby table and passed it to me. Seeing my expression, he sipped from it himself.

"Join us in a drink, then?"

"Why not?" I said, and I took it and quaffed it as he did the same with the second one.

He gave a gentle belch and grinned.

" 'Tis a mighty small draught for a man of your size," he said then. "Let me fetch you another, for the trail."

It was a pleasant ale, and I was thirsty after my efforts.

"All right," I said.

He called for more as Star was delivered to me.

"You can wrap the reins around this hook here," he said, indicating a low projection near the doorway, "and he will be safe out of the way."

I nodded and did that as the butcher withdrew. No one was staring at me any longer. A pitcher of the brew arrived and the little man refilled our flagons from it. One of the fiddlers struck up a fresh tune. Moments later, another joined him.

"Sit a spell," said my host, pushing a bench in my direction with his foot. "Keep your back to the wall as you would. There will be no funny business."

I did, and he rounded the table and seated himself across from me, the pitcher between us. It was good to sit for a few moments, to take my mind from my journey for just a little while, to drink the dark ale and listen to a lively tune.

"I will not be apologizing again," said my companion, "nor explaining either. We both know it was no misunderstanding. But you have got the right on your side, it is plain to see." He grinned and winked. "So I am for calling it a day, too. We will not starve. We will just not feast tonight. 'Tis a lovely jewel you are wearing. Tell me about it?"

"Just a stone," I said.

The dancing resumed. The voices grew louder. I finished my drink and he refilled the flagon. The fire undulated. The night's cold went out of my bones.

"Cozy place you've got here," I said.

"Oh, that it is. Served us for time out of mind, it has. Would you be liking the grand tour?"

"Thank you, no."

"I did not think so, but 'twas my hostly duty to offer. You are welcome to join in the dancing, too, if you wish."

I shook my head and laughed. The thought of my cavorting in this place brought me images out of Swift.

"Thanks anyway."

He produced a clay pipe and proceeded to fill it. I cleaned my own and did the same. Somehow all danger seemed past. He was a genial enough little fellow, and the others seemed harmless now with their music and their stepping.

Yet . . . I knew the stories from another place, far, so far from here . . . To awaken in the morning, naked, in some field, all traces of this spot vanished . . . I knew, yet . . .

A few drinks seemed small peril. They were warming me now, and the keening of the pipes and the wailings of the fiddles were pleasant after the brain-numbing twistings of the hellride. I leaned back and puffed smoke. I watched the dancers.

The little man was talking, talking. Everyone else was ignoring me. Good. I was hearing some fantastic yarn of knights and wars and treasures. Though I gave it less than half an ear, it lulled me, even drew a few chuckles.

Inside, though, my nastier, wiser self was warning me: All right, Corwin, you have had enough. Time to take your leave . . .

But, magically it seemed, my glass had been refilled, and I took it and sipped from it. One more, one more is all right.

No, said my other self, he is laying a spell on you. Can't you feel it?

I did not feel that any dwarf could drink me under the table. But I was tired, and I had not eaten much. Perhaps it would be prudent . . .

I felt myself nodding. I placed my pipe on the table. Each time that I blinked it seemed to take longer to reopen my eyes. I was pleasantly warm now, with just the least bit of delicious numbness in my tired muscles.

I caught myself nodding, twice. I tried to think of my mission, of my personal safety, of Star. . . . I mumbled something, still vaguely awake behind closed eyelids. It would be so good, just to remain this way for half a minute more. . . .

The little man's voice, musical, grew monotonous, dropped to a drone. It did not really matter what he was say—

Star whinnied.

I sat bolt upright, eyes wide, and the tableau before me swept all sleep from my mind.

The musicians continued their performance, but now no one was dancing. All of the revelers were advancing quietly upon me. Each held something in his hand—a flask, a cudgel, a blade. The one in the leather apron brandished his cleaver. My companion had just fetched a stout stick from where it had leaned against the wall. Several of them lofted small pieces of furniture. More of them had emerged from the caves near the fire pit, and they bore stones and clubs. All traces of gaiety had vanished, and their faces were now either expressionless, twisted into grimaces of hate or smiling very nasty smiles.

My anger returned, but it was not the white-heat thing I had left earlier. Looking at the horde before me, I had no wish to tackle it. Prudence had come to temper my feelings. I had a mission. I should not risk my neck here if I could think of another way of handling things. But I was certain that I could not talk my way out of this one.

I took a deep breath. I saw that they were getting ready to rush me, and I thought suddenly of Brand and Benedict in Tir-na Nog'th, Brand not even fully attuned to the Jewel. I drew strength from that fiery stone once again, growing alert and ready to lay about me if it came to that. But first, I would have a go at their nervous systems.

I was not certain how Brand had managed it, so I simply reached out through the Jewel as I did when influencing the weather. Strangely, the music was still playing, as though this action of the little people was but some grisly continuation of their dance.

"Stand still." I said it aloud and I willed it, rising to my feet. "Freeze. Turn to statues. All of you."

I felt a heavy throbbing within/upon my breast. I felt the red forces move outward, exactly as on those other occasions when I had employed the Jewel.

My diminutive assailants were poised. The nearest ones stood stock-still, but there were still some movements among those to the rear. Then the pipes let out a crazy squeal and the fiddles fell silent. Still, I did not know whether I had reached them or whether they had halted of their own accord on seeing me stand.

Then I felt the great waves of force which flowed out from me, embedding the entire assembly in a tightening matrix. I felt them all trapped within this expression of my will, and I reached out and untethered Star.

Holding them with a concentration as pure as anything I used when passing through Shadow, I led Star to the doorway. I turned then for a final look at the frozen assembly and pushed Star on ahead of me up the stair. As I followed, I listened, but there were no sounds of renewed activity from below.

When we emerged, dawn was already paling the east. Strangely, as I mounted, I heard the distant sounds of fiddles. Moments later, the pipes came in on the tune. It seemed as though it mattered not at all whether they succeeded or failed in their designs against me; the party was going to go on.

As I headed us south, a small figure hailed me from the doorway I had so recently quitted. It was their leader with whom I had been drinking. I drew rein, to better catch his words.

"And where do you travel?" he called after me.

Why not?

"To the ends of the Earth!" I shouted back.

He broke into a jig atop his shattered door.

"Fare thee well, Corwin!" he cried.

I waved to him. Why not, indeed? Sometimes it's damned hard to tell the dancer from the dance.

VI

I rode fewer than a thousand meters to what had been the south, and everything stopped—ground, sky, mountains. I faced a sheet of white light. I thought then of the stranger in the cave and his words. He had felt that the world was being blotted by that storm, that it corresponded to something out of a local apocalyptic legend. Perhaps it had. Perhaps it had been the wave of Chaos of which Brand had spoken, moving this way, passing over, destroying, disrupting. But this end of the valley was untouched. Why should it remain?

Then I recalled my actions on rushing out into the storm. I had used the Jewel, the power of the Pattern within it, to halt the storm over this area. And if it had been more than an ordinary storm? The Pattern had prevailed over Chaos before. Could this valley where I had stopped the rainfall be but a small island in a sea of Chaos now? If so, how was I to continue?

I looked to the east, from whence the day brightened. No sun stood new-risen in the heavens, but rather a great, blindingly burnished crown, a gleaming sword hanging through it. From somewhere I heard a bird singing, notes almost like laughter. I leaned forward and covered my face with my hands. Madness . . .

No! I had been in weird shadows before. The farther one traveled, the stranger they sometimes grew. Until . . . What was it I'd thought that night in Tir-na Nog'th?

Two lines from a story of Isak Dinesen's returned to me, lines which had troubled me sufficiently to cause me to memorize them, despite the fact that I had been Carl Corey at the time: ". . . Few people can say of themselves that they are free of the belief that this world which they see around them is in reality the work of their own imagination. Are we pleased with it, proud of it, then?" A summation of the family's favorite philosophical pastime. Do we make the Shadow worlds? Or are they there, independent of us, awaiting our footfalls? Or is there an unfairly excluded middle? Is it a matter of more or less, rather than either-or? A dry chuckle arose suddenly as I realized that I might never know the answer for certain. Yet, as I had thought that night, there is a place, a place where there comes an end to Self, a place where solipsism is no longer the plausible answer to the locales we visit, the things that we find. The existence of this place, these things, says that here, at least, there is a difference, and if here, perhaps it runs back through our shadows, too, informing them with the not-self, moving our egos back to a smaller stage. For this, I felt, was such a place, a place where the "Are we pleased with it, proud of it, then?" need not apply, as the rent vale of Garnath and my curse might have nearer home. Whatever I ultimately believed, I felt that I was about to enter the land of the completely not-I. My powers over Shadow might well be canceled beyond this point.

I sat up straight and squinted against the glare. I spoke a word to Star and shook the reins. We moved ahead.

For a moment, it was like riding into a fog. Only it was enormously brighter, and there was absolutely no sound. Then we were falling.

Falling, or drifting. After the initial shock, it was difficult to say. At first, there was a feeling of descent—perhaps intensified by the fact that Star panicked when it began. But there was nothing to kick against, and after a time Star ceased all movement save for shivering and heavy breathing.

I held the reins with my right hand and clutched the Jewel with my left. I do not know what I willed or how I reached with it, exactly, but that I wanted passage through this place of bright nothingness, to find my way once more and move on to the journey's end.

I lost track of time. The feeling of descent had vanished. Was I moving, or merely hovering? No way to say. Was the brightness really brightness, still? And that deadly silence . . . I shuddered. Here was even greater sensory deprivation than in the days of my blindness, in my old cell. Here was nothing—not the sound of a scuttling rat nor the grinding of my spoon against the door; no dampness, no chill, no textures. I continued to reach . . .

Flicker.

It seemed there had been some momentary breaking of the visual field to my right, near subliminal in its brevity. I reached out and felt nothing.

It had been so brief a thing that I was uncertain whether it had really occurred. It could easily have been an hallucination.

But it seemed to happen again, this time to my left. How long the interval between, I could not say.

Then I heard something like a groan, directionless. This, too, was very brief.

Next—and for the first time, I was certain—there came a gray and white landscape like the surface of the moon. There and gone, perhaps a second's worth, in a small area of my visual field, off to my left. Star snorted.

To my right appeared a forest—gray and white—tumbling, as though we passed one another at some impossible angle. A small-screen fragment, less than two seconds' worth.

Then pieces of a burning building beneath me . . . Colorless . . .

Snatches of wailing, from overhead . . .

A ghostly mountain, a torchlit procession ascending a switchback trail up its nearest face . . .

A woman hanging from a tree limb, taut rope about her neck, head twisted to the side, hands tied behind her back . . .

Mountains, upside down, white; black clouds beneath . . .

Click. A tiny thrill of vibration, as if we had momentarily touched something solid—Star's hoof on stone, perhaps. Then gone . . .

Flicker.

Heads, rolling, dripping black gore . . . A chuckle from nowhere . . . A man nailed to a wall, upside down . . .

The white light again, rolling and heaving, wavelike . . .

Click. Flicker.

For one pulsebeat, we trod a trail beneath a stippled sky. The moment it was gone, I reached for it again, through the Jewel.

Click. Flicker. Click. Rumble.

A rocky trail, approaching a high mountain pass . . . Still monochrome, the world . . . At my back, a crashing like thunder . . .

I twisted the Jewel like a focus knob as the world began to fade. It came back again. . . . Two, three, four . . . I counted hoofbeats, heartbeats against the growling background. . . . Seven, eight, nine . . . The world grew brighter. I took a deep breath and sighed heavily. The air was cold.

Between the thunder and its echoes, I heard the sound of rain. None fell upon me, though.

I glanced back.

A great wall of rain stood perhaps a hundred meters to the rear. I could distinguish only the dimmest of mountain outlines through it. I

clucked to Star and we moved a little faster, climbing to an almost
level stretch that led between a pair of peaks like turrets. The world
ahead was still a study in black and white and gray, the sky before
me divided by alternate bands of darkness and light. We entered the
pass.

I began to tremble. I wanted to draw rein, to rest, eat, smoke, dismount and walk around. Yet, I was still too close to that stormscreen
to so indulge myself.

Star's hoofbeats echoed within the pass, where rock walls rose
sheer on either hand beneath that zebra sky. I hoped these mountains would break this stormfront, though I felt that they could not.
This was no ordinary storm, and I had a sick feeling that it stretched
all the way back to Amber, and that I would have been trapped and
lost forever within it but for the Jewel.

As I watched that strange sky, a blizzard of pale flowers began to
fall about me, brightening my way. A pleasant odor filled the air.
The thunder at my back softened. The rocks at my sides were shot
with silver streaks. The world was possessed of a twilight feeling to
match the illumination, and as I emerged from the pass, I saw down
into a valley of quirked perspective, distances impossible to gauge,
filled with natural-seeming spires and minarets reflecting the moon-
like light of the sky-streaks, reminiscent of a night in Tir-na Nog'th,
interspersed with silvery trees, spotted with mirror-like pools, traversed by drifting wraiths, almost terraced-seeming in places, natural
and rolling in others, cut by what appeared to be an extension of the
line of trail I followed, rising and falling, hung over by an elegiac
quality, sparked with inexplicable points of glitter and shine, devoid
of any signs of habitation.

I did not hesitate, but began my descent. The ground about me
here was chalky and pale as bone—and was that the faintest line of a
black road far off to my left? I could just about make it out.

I did not hurry now, as I could see that Star was tiring. If the
storm did not come on too quickly, I felt that we might take a rest
beside one of the pools in the valley below. I was tired and hungry
myself.

I kept a lookout on the way down, but saw no people, no animals.
The wind made a soft, sighing noise. White flowers stirred on vines
beside the trail when I reached the lower levels where regular foliage
began. Looking back, I saw that the stormfront still had not passed
the mountain crest, though the clouds continued to pile behind it.

I made my way on down into that strange place. The flowers had long before ceased to fall about me, but a delicate perfume hung in the air. There were no sounds other than our own and that of the constant breeze from my right. Oddly shaped rock formations stood all about me, seeming almost sculpted in their purity of line. The mists still drifted. The pale grasses sparkled damply.

As I followed the trail toward the valley's wooded center, the perspectives continued to shift about me, skewing distances, bending prospects. In fact, I turned off the trail to the left to approach what appeared to be a nearby lake and it seemed to recede as I advanced. When I finally came upon it, however, dismounted and dipped a finger to taste, the water was icy but sweet.

Tired, I sprawled after drinking my fill, to watch Star graze while I began a cold meal from my bag. The storm was still fighting to cross the mountains. I looked for a long while, wondering about it. If Dad had failed, then those were the growls of Armageddon and this whole trip was meaningless. It did me no good to think that way, for I knew that I had to go on, whatever. But I could not help it. I might arrive at my destination, I might see the battle won, and then see it all swept away. Pointless . . . No. Not pointless. I would have tried, and I would keep on trying to the end. That was enough, even if everything was lost. Damn Brand, anyway! For starting—

A footfall.

I was into a crouch and I was turned in that direction with my hand on my blade in an instant.

It was a woman that I faced, small, clad in white. She had long, dark hair and wild, dark eyes, and she was smiling. She carried a wicker basket, which she placed on the ground between us.

"You must be hungry, Knight at arms," she said in strangely accented Thari. "I saw you come. I brought you this."

I smiled and assumed a more normal stance.

"Thank you," I said. "I am. I am called Corwin. Yourself?"

"Lady," she said.

I quirked an eybrow. "Thank you—Lady. You make your home in this place?"

She nodded and knelt to uncover the basket.

"Yes, my pavilion is farther back, along the lake." She gestured with her head, eastward—in the direction of the black road.

"I see," I said.

The food and the wine in the basket looked real, fresh, appetizing,

better than my traveler's fare. Suspicion was with me, of course.
"You will share it with me?" I asked.

"If you wish."

"I wish."

"Very well."

She spread a cloth, seated herself across from me, removed the
food from the basket and arranged it between us. She served it then,
and quickly sampled each item herself. I felt a trifle ignoble at this,
but only a trifle. It was a peculiar location for a woman to be resid-
ing, apparently alone, just waiting around to succor the first stranger
who happened along. Dara had fed me on our first meeting, also;
and as I might be nearing the end of my journey, I was closer to the
enemy's places of power. The black road was too near at hand, and I
caught Lady eying the Jewel on several occasions.

But it was an enjoyable time, and we grew more familiar as we
dined. She was an ideal audience, laughing at all my jokes, making
me talk about myself. She maintained eye contact much of the time,
and somehow our fingers met whenever anything was passed. If I
were being taken in in some way, she was being very pleasant about
it.

As we had dined and talked, I had also kept an eye on the progress of that inexorable-seeming stormfront. It had finally breasted the
mountain crest and crossed over. It had begun its slow descent of the
high slope. As she cleared the cloth, Lady saw the direction of my
gaze and nodded.

"Yes, it is coming," she said, placing the last of the utensils in the
basket and seating herself beside me, bringing the bottle and our
cups. "Shall we drink to it?"

"I will drink with you, but not to that."

She poured.

"It does not matter," she said. "Not now," and she placed her
hand on my arm and passed me my cup.

I held it and looked down at her. She smiled. She touched the rim
of my cup with her own. We drank.

"Come to my pavilion now," she said, taking my hand, "where
we will wile pleasurably the hours that remain."

"Thanks," I said. "Another time and that wiling would have been
a fine dessert to a grand meal. Unfortunately, I must be on my way.
Duty nags, time rushes, I've a mission."

"All right," she said. "It is not that important. And I know all about your mission. It is not all that important either, now."

"Oh? I must confess that I fully expected you to invite me to a private party which would result in me alone and palely loitering on the cold side of some hill sometime hence if I were to accept."

She laughed.

"And I must confess that it was my intention to so use you, Corwin. No longer, though."

"Why not?"

She gestured toward the advancing line of disruption.

"There is no need to delay you now. I see by this that the Courts have won. There is nothing anyone can do to halt the advance of the Chaos."

I shuddered briefly and she refilled our cups.

"But I would rather you did not leave me at this time," she went on. "It will reach us here in a matter of hours. What better way to spend this final time than in one another's company? There is no need even to go as far as my pavilion."

I bowed my head, and she drew up close against me. What the hell. A woman and a bottle—that was how I had always said I wanted to end my days. I took a sip of the wine. She was probably right. Yet, I thought of the woman-thing which had trapped me on the black road as I was leaving Avalon. I had gone at first to aid her, succumbed quickly to her unnatural charms—then, when her mask was removed, saw that there was nothing at all behind it. Damned frightening, at the time. But, not to get too philosophical, everybody has a whole rack of masks for different occasions. I have heard pop psychologists inveigh against them for years. Still, I have met people who impressed me favorably at first, people whom I came to hate when I learned what they were like underneath. And sometimes they were like that woman-thing—with nothing much really there. I have found that the mask is often far more acceptable than its alternative. So . . . This girl I held to me might really be a monster inside. Probably was. Aren't most of us? I could think of worse ways to go if I wanted to give up at this point. I liked her.

I finished my wine. She moved to pour me more and I stayed her hand.

She looked up at me. I smiled.

"You almost persuaded me," I said.

Then I closed her eyes with kisses four, so as not to break the charm, and I went and mounted Star. The sedge was not withered, but he was right about the no birds. Hell of a way to run a railroad, though.

"Good-bye, Lady."

I headed south as the storm boiled its way down into the valley. There were more mountains before me, and the trail led toward them. The sky was still streaked, black and white, and these lines seemed to move about a bit; the over-all effect was still that of twilight, though no stars shone within the black areas. Still the breeze, still the perfume about me—and the silence, and the twisted monoliths and the silvery foliage, still dew-damp and glistening. Rag ends of mist blew before me. I tried to work with the stuff of Shadow, but it was difficult and I was tired. Nothing happened. I drew strength from the Jewel, trying to transmit some of it to Star, also. We moved at a steady pace until finally the land tilted upward before us, and we were climbing toward another pass, a more jagged thing than the one by which we had entered. I halted to look back, and perhaps a third of the valley now lay behind the shimmering screen of that advancing storm-thing. I wondered about Lady and her lake, her pavilion. I shook my head and continued.

The way steepened as we neared the pass, and we were slowed. Overhead, the white rivers in the sky took on a reddish cast which deepened as we rode. By the time I reached the entrance, the whole world seemed tinged with blood. Passing within that wide, rocky avenue, I was struck by a heavy wind. Pushing on against it, the ground grew more level beneath us, though we continued to climb and I still could not see beyond the pass.

As I rode, something rattled in the rocks to my left. I glanced that way, but saw nothing. I dismissed it as a falling stone. Half a minute later, Star jerked beneath me, let out a terrible neigh, turned sharply to the right, then began to topple, leftward.

I leaped clear, and as we both fell I saw that an arrow protruded from behind Star's right shoulder, low. I hit the ground rolling, and when I halted I looked up in the direction from which it must have come.

A figure with a crossbow stood atop the ridge to my right, about ten meters above me. He was already cranking the weapon back to prepare for another shot.

I knew that I could not reach him in time to stop him. So I cast about for a stone the size of a baseball, found one at the foot of the escarpment to my rear, hefted it and tried not to let my rage interfere with the accuracy of my throw. It did not, but it may have contributed some extra force.

The blow caught him on the left arm, and he let out a cry, dropping the crossbow. The weapon clattered down the rocks and landed on the other side of the trail, almost directly across from me.

"You son of a bitch!" I cried. "You killed my horse! I'm going to have your head for it!"

As I crossed the trail, I looked for the fastest way up to him and saw it off to my left. I hurried to it and commenced climbing. An instant later, the light and the angle were proper and I had a better view of the man, bent nearly double, massaging his arm. It was Brand, his hair even redder in the sanguine light.

"This is it, Brand," I said. "I only wish someone had done it a long time ago."

He straightened and watched me climb for a moment. He did not reach for his blade. Just as I got to the top, perhaps seven meters away from him, he crossed his arms on his breast and lowered his head.

I drew Grayswandir and advanced. I admit that I was prepared to kill him in that or any other position. The red light had deepened until we seemed bathed in blood. The wind howled about us, and from the valley below came a rumble of thunder.

He simply faded before me. His outline grew less distinct, and by the time I reached the place where he had been standing he had vanished entirely.

I stood for a moment, cursing, remembering the story that he had somehow been transformed into a living Trump, capable of transporting himself anywhere in a very brief time.

I heard a noise from below. . . .

I rushed to the edge and looked down. Star was still kicking and blowing blood, and it tore my heart to see it. But that was not the only distressing sight.

Brand was below. He had picked up the crossbow and begun preparing it once more.

I looked about for another stone, but there was nothing at hand. Then I spotted one farther back, in the direction from which I had come. I hurried to it, resheathed my blade and raised the thing. It was about the size of a watermelon. I returned with it to the edge and sought Brand.

He was nowhere in sight.

Suddenly, I felt very exposed. He could have transported himself to any vantage and be sighting in on me at that instant. I dropped to the ground, falling across my rock. A moment later, I heard the bolt strike to my right. The sound was followed by Brand's chuckle.

I stood again, knowing it would take him at least a little while to recock his weapon. Looking in the direction of the laughter, I saw him, atop the ledge across the pass from me—about five meters higher than I was, and about twenty meters distant.

"Sorry about the horse," he said. "I was aiming for you. But those damned winds . . ."

By then I had spotted a niche and I made for it, taking the rock with me for a shield. From that wedge-shaped fissure, I watched him fit the bolt.

"A difficult shot," he called out, raising the weapon, "a challenge to my marksmanship. But certainly worth the effort. I've plenty more quarrels."

He chuckled, sighted and fired.

I bent low, holding the rock before my middle, but the bolt struck about two feet to my right.

"I had sort of guessed that might happen," he said, beginning to prepare his weapon once again. "Had to learn the windage, though."

I looked about for smaller stones to use for ammunition as I had earlier. There were none nearby. I wondered about the Jewel then. It was supposed to act to save me in the presence of immediate peril. But I had a funny feeling that this involved close proximity, and that Brand was aware of this and was taking advantage of the phenomenon. Still, mightn't there be something else I could do with the Jewel to thwart him? He seemed too far away for the paralysis trick, but I had beaten him once before by controlling the weather. I wondered how far off the storm was. I reached for it. I saw that it would take minutes I did not possess in order to set up the conditions necessary to draw lightning upon him. But the winds were another matter. I reached out for them, felt them. . . .

Brand was almost ready to shoot again. The wind began to scream through the pass.

I do not know where his next shot landed. Nowhere near me,

though. He fell to readying his weapon again. I began setting up the factors for a lightningstroke. . . .

When he was ready, when he raised the weapon this time, I raised the winds once more. I saw him sight, I saw him draw a breath and hold it. Then he lowered the bow and stared at me.

"It just occurred to me," he called out, "you've got that wind in your pocket, haven't you? That is cheating, Corwin." He looked all about. "I should be able to find a footing where it will not matter, though. Aha!"

I kept working to set things up to blast him, but conditions were not ready yet. I looked up at that red- and black-streaked sky, something cloud-like forming above us. Soon, but not yet . . .

Brand faded and vanished again. Wildly, I sought him everywhere.

Then he faced me. He had come over to my side of the pass. He stood about ten meters to the south of me, with the wind at his back. I knew that I could not shift it in time. I wondered about throwing my rock. He would probably duck and I would be throwing away my shield. On the other hand . . .

He raised the weapon to his shoulder.

Stall! cried my own voice within my mind, while I continued to tamper with the heavens.

"Before you shoot, Brand, tell me one thing. All right?"

He hesitated, then lowered the weapon a few inches.

"What?"

"Were you telling me the truth about what happened—with Dad, the Pattern, the coming of Chaos?"

He threw back his head and laughed, a series of short barks.

"Corwin," he stated then, "it pleases me more than I can say to see you die not knowing something that means that much to you."

He laughed again and began to raise the weapon. I had just moved to hurl my rock and rush him. But neither of us completed either action.

There came a great shriek from overhead, and a piece of the sky seemed to detach itself and fall upon Brand's head. He screamed and dropped the crossbow. He raised his hands to tear at the thing that assailed him. The red bird, the Jewel bearer, born of my blood from my father's hand, had returned, to defend me.

I get go the rock and advanced upon him, drawing my blade as I went. Brand struck the bird and it flapped away, gaining altitude, circling for another dive. He raised both arms to cover his face and head, but not before I saw the blood that flowed from his left eye socket.

He began to fade again even as I rushed toward him. But the bird descended like a bomb and its talons struck Brand about the head once again. Then the bird, too, began to fade. Brand was reaching for his ruddy assailant and being slashed by it as they both disappeared.

When I reached the place of the action the only thing that remained was the fallen crossbow, and I smashed it with my boot.

Not yet, not yet the end, damn it! How long will you plague me, brother? How far must I go to bring it to an end between us?

I climbed back down to the trail. Star was not yet dead and I had to finish the job. Sometimes I think I'm in the wrong business.

VII

A bowl of cotton candy.

Having traversed the pass, I regarded the valley that lay before me. At least, I assumed that it was a valley. I could see nothing below its cover of cloud/mist/fog.

In the sky, one of the red streaks was turning yellow; another, green. I was slightly heartened by this, as the sky had behaved in a somewhat similar fashion when I had visited the edge of things, across from the Courts of Chaos.

I hitched up my pack and began down the trail. The winds diminished as I went. Distantly, I heard some thunder from the storm I was fleeing. I wondered where Brand had gone. I had a feeling that I would not be seeing him again for a time.

Partway down, with the fog just beginning to creep and curl about me, I spotted an ancient tree and cut myself a staff. The tree seemed to shriek as I severed its limb.

"Damn you!" came something like a voice from within it.

"You're sentient?" "I'm sorry . . ."

"I spent a long time growing that branch. I suppose you are going to burn it now?"

"No," I said. "I needed a staff. I've a long walk before me."

"Through this valley?"

"That's right."

"Come closer, that I may better sense your presence. There is something about you that glows."

I took a step forward.

"Oberon!" it said. "I know thy Jewel."

"Not Oberon," I said. "I am his son. I wear it on his mission, though."

"Then take my limb, and have my blessing with it. I've sheltered your father on many a strange day. He planted me, you see."

"Really? Planting a tree is one of the few things I never saw Dad do."

"I am no ordinary tree. He placed me here to mark a boundary."

"Of what sort?"

"I am the end of Chaos and of Order, depending upon how you view me. I mark a division. Beyond me other rules apply."

"What rules?"

"Who can say? Not I. I am only a growing tower of sentient lumber. My staff may comfort you, however. Planted, it may blossom in strange climes. Then again, it may not. Who can say? Bear it with you, however, son of Oberon, into the place where you journey now. I feel a storm approaching. Good-bye."

"Good-bye," I said. "Thank you."

I turned and walked on down the trail into the deepening fog. The pinkness was drained from it as I went. I shook my head as I thought about the tree, but its staff proved useful for the next several hundred meters, where the going was particularly rough.

Then things cleared a bit. Rocks, a stagnant pool, some small, dreary trees festooned with ropes of moss, a smell of decay . . . I hurried by. A dark bird was watching me from one of the trees.

It took wing as I regarded it, flapping in a leisurely fashion in my direction. Recent events having left me a little bird-shy, I drew back as it circled my head. But then it fluttered to rest on the trail before me, cocked its head and viewed me with its left eye.

"Yes," it announced then. "You are the one."

"The one what?" I said.

"The one I will accompany. You've no objection to a bird of ill omen following you, have you, Corwin?"

It chuckled then, and executed a little dance.

"Offhand, I do not see how I can stop you. How is it that you know my name?"

"I've been waiting for you since the beginning of Time, Corwin."

"Must have been a bit tiresome."

"It has not been all that long, in this place. Time is what you make of it."

I resumed walking. I passed the bird and kept going. Moments later, it flashed by me and landed atop a rock off to my right.

"My name is Hugi," he stated. "You are carrying a piece of old Ygg, I see."

"Ygg?"

"The stuffy old tree who waits at the entrance to this place and won't let anyone rest on his branches. I'll bet he yelled when you whacked it off." He emitted peals of laughter then.

"He was quite decent about it."

"I'll bet. But then, he hadn't much choice once you'd done it. Fat lot of good it will do you."

"It's doing me fine," I said, swinging it lightly in his direction.

He fluttered away from it.

"Hey! That was not funny!"

I laughed.

"I thought it was."

I walked on by.

For a long while, I made my way through a marshy area. An occasional gust of wind would clear the way nearby. Then I would pass it, or the fogs would shift over it once again. Occasionally, I seemed to hear a snatch of music—from what direction, I could not tell—slow, and somewhat stately, produced by a steel-stringed instrument.

As I slogged along, I was hailed from somewhere to my left:

"Stranger! Halt and regard me!"

Wary, I halted. Couldn't see a damned thing through that fog, though.

"Hello," I said. "Where are you?"

Just then, the fogs broke for a moment and I beheld a huge head, eyes on a level with my own. They belonged to what seemed a giant body, sunk up to the shoulders in a quag. The head was bald, the skin pale as milk, with a stony texture to it. The dark eyes probably seemed even darker than they really were by way of contrast.

"I see," I said then. "You are in a bit of a fix. Can you free your arms?"

"If I strain mightily," came the reply.

"Well, let me check about for something stable you can grab onto. You ought to have a pretty good reach there."

"No. That is not necessary."

"Don't you want to get out? I thought that was why you hollered."

"Oh, no. I simply wanted you to regard me."

I moved nearer and stared, for the fog was beginning to shift again.

"All right," I said. "I have seen you."

"Do you feel my plight?"

"Not particularly, if you will not help yourself or accept help."

"What good would it do me to free myself?"

"It is your question. You answer it."

I turned to go.

"Wait! Where do you travel?"

"South, to appear in a morality play."

Just then, Hugi flew out of the fog and landed atop the head. He pecked at it and laughed.

"Don't waste your time, Corwin. There is much less here than meets the eye," he said.

The giant lips shaped my name. Then: "He is indeed the one?"

"That's him, all right," Hugi replied.

"Listen, Corwin," said the sunken giant. "You are going to try to stop the Chaos, aren't you?"

"Yes."

"Do not do it. It is not worth it. I want things to end. I desire a release from this condition."

"I already offered to help you out. You turned me down."

"Not that sort of release. An end to the whole works."

"That is easily done," I said. "Just duck your head and take a deep breath."

"It is not only personal termination that I desire, but an end to the whole foolish game."

"I believe there are a few other folks around who would rather make their own decisions on the matter."

"Let it end for them, too. There will come a time when they are in my position and will feel the same way."

"Then they will possess the same option. Good day."

I turned and walked on.

"You will, too!" he called after me.

As I hiked along, Hugi caught up with me and perched on the end of my staff.

"It's neat to sit on old Ygg's limb now he can't—Yikes!"

Hugi sprang into the air and circled.

"Burned my foot! How'd he do that?" he cried.

I laughed.

"Beats me."

He fluttered for a few moments, then made for my right shoulder.

"Okay if I rest here?"

"Go ahead."

"Thanks." He settled. "The Head is really a mental basket case, you know."

I shrugged my shoulders and he spread his wings for balance.

"He is groping after something," he went on, "but proceeding incorrectly by holding the world responsible for his own failings."

"No. He would not even grope to get out of the mud," I said.

"I meant philosophically."

"Oh, that sort of mud. Too bad."

"The whole problem lies with the self, the ego, and its involvement with the world on the one hand and the Absolute on the other."

"Oh, is that so?"

"Yes. You see, we are hatched and we drift on the surface of events. Sometimes, we feel that we actually influence things, and this gives rise to striving. This is a big mistake, because it creates desires and builds up a false ego when just being should be enough. That leads to more desires and more striving and there you are, trapped."

"In the mud?"

"So to speak. One needs to fix one's vision firmly on the Absolute and learn to ignore the mirages, the illusions, the fake sense of identity which sets one apart as a false island of consciousness."

"I had a fake identity once. It helped me a lot in becoming the absolute that I am now—me."

"No, that's fake, too."

"Then the me that may exist tomorrow will thank me for it, as I do that other."

"You are missing the point. That you will be fake, too."

"Why?"

"Because it will still be full of those desires and strivings that set you apart from the Absolute."

"What is wrong with that?"

"You remain alone in a world of strangers, the world of phenomena."

"I like being alone. I am quite fond of myself. I like phenomena, too."

"Yet the Absolute will always be there, calling to you, causing unrest."

"Good, then there is no need to hurry. But yes, I see what you mean. It takes the form of ideals. Everyone has a few. If you are saying that I should pursue them, I agree with you."

"No, they are distortions of the Absolute, and what you are talking about is more striving."

"That is correct."

"I can see that you have a lot to unlearn."

"If you are talking about my vulgar instinct for survival, forget it."

The trail had been leading upward, and we came now to a smooth, level place, almost paved-seeming, though strewn lightly with sand. The music had grown louder and continued to do so as I advanced. Then, through the fog, I saw dim shapes moving, slowly, rhythmically. It took several moments for me to realize that they were dancing to the music.

I kept moving until I could view the figures—human-seeming, handsome folk, garbed in courtly attire—treading to the slow measures of invisible musicians. It was an intricate and lovely dance that they executed, and I halted to watch some of it.

"What is the occasion," I asked Hugi, "for a party out here in the middle of nowhere?"

"They dance," he said, "to celebrate your passage. They are not mortals, but the spirits of Time. They began this foolish show when you entered the valley."

"Spirits?"

"Yes. Observe."

He left my shoulder, flew above them and defecated. The dropping passed through several dancers as if they were holograms, without staining a brocaded sleeve or a silken shirt, without causing any of the smiling figures to miss a measure. Hugi cawed several times then and flew back to me.

"That was hardly necessary," I said. "It is a fine performance."

"Decadent," he said, "and you should hardly take it as a compliment, for they anticipate your failure. They but wish to get in a final celebration before the show is closed."

I watched for a time anyway, leaning upon my staff, resting. The figure described by the dancers slowly shifted, until one of the women—an auburn-haired beauty—was quite near to me. Now, none of the dancers' eyes at any time met my own. It was as if I were not present. But that woman, in a perfectly timed gesture, cast with her right hand something which landed at my feet.

I stooped and found it substantial. It was a silver rose—my own emblem—that I held. I straightened and fixed it at the collar of my cloak. Hugi looked the other way and said nothing. I had no hat to doff, but I did bow to the lady. There might have been a slight twitch at her right eye as I turned to go.

The ground lost its smoothness as I walked, and finally the music faded. The trail grew rougher, and whenever the fogs cleared the only views were of rocks or barren plains. I drew strength from the Jewel when I would otherwise have collapsed, and I noted that each such fix was of shorter duration now.

After a time, I grew hungry and I halted to eat what rations I had left.

Hugi stood on the ground nearby and watched me eat.

"I will admit to a certain small admiration for your persistence," he said, "and even for what you implied when you spoke of ideals. But that is about it. Earlier, we were talking about the futility of desire and of striving—"

"You were. It is not a major concern in my life."

"It should be."

"I have had a long life, Hugi. You insult me by assuming I have never considered these footnotes to sophomore philosophy. The fact that you find consensus reality barren tells me more about you than it does about that state of affairs. To wit, if you believe what you say I feel sorry for you, in that you must for some inexplicable reason be here desiring and striving to influence this false ego of mine rather than free of such nonsense and on your way to your Absolute. If you do not believe it, then it tells me that you have been sent to hinder and discourage me, in which case you are wasting your time."

Hugi made a gargling noise. Then: "You are not so blind that you deny the Absolute, the beginning and end of everything?"

"It is not indispensable to a liberal education."

"You admit the possibility?"

"Perhaps I know it better than you, bird. The ego, as I see it, exists at an intermediate stage between rationality and reflex existence. Blotting it out is a retreat, though. If you come from that Absolute— of a self-canceling All—why do you wish to go back home? Do you so despise yourself that you fear mirrors? Why not make the trip worthwhile? Develop. Learn. Live. If you have been sent on a journey why do you wish to cop out and run back to your point of departure? Or did your Absolute make a mistake in sending something of your caliber? Admit that possibility and that is the end of the news."

Hugi glared at me, then sprang into the air and flew off. Going to consult his manual, perhaps. . . .

I heard a peal of thunder as I rose to my feet. I began walking. I had to try to keep ahead of things.

The trail narrowed and widened a number of times before it vanished completely, leaving me to wander across a gravelly plain. I felt more and more depressed as I traveled, trying to keep my mental compass set in the proper direction. I almost came to welcome the sounds of the storm, for they at least gave me a rough idea as to which way was north. Of course, things were a bit confusing in the fog, so that I could not be absolutely certain. And they were growing louder. . . . Damn.

. . . And I had been grieved by the loss of Star, troubled by Hugi's futilitarianism. This was definitely not a good day. I began to doubt that I was going to complete my journey. If some nameless denizen of this dark place did not ambush me before too long, there was a strong possibility that I would wander here until my strength failed or the storm caught me. I did not know whether I would be able to beat back that canceling storm another time. I began to doubt it.

I tried using the Jewel to disperse the fog, but its effects seemed blunted. By my own sluggishness, perhaps. I could clear a small area, but my rate of travel quickly bore me through it. My sense of Shadow was dulled in this place which seemed in some way the essence of Shadow.

Sad. It would have been nice to go out with opera—in a big Wagnerian finale beneath strange skies, against worthy opponents—not scrabbling about in a foggy wasteland.

I passed a familiar-seeming outcrop of stone. Could I have been moving in a circle? There is a tendency to do that when completely lost. I listened for the thunder, to take my bearings again. Perversely, all was silent. I moved to the outcrop and seated myself on the ground, resting my back against it. No sense to merely wandering. I would wait a time for the thunder's signal. I withdrew my Trumps as I sat there. Dad had said that they would be out of commission for a time, but I had nothing better to do.

One by one, I went through them all, trying to reach everyone, save for Brand and Caine. Nothing. Dad had been right. The cards lacked the familiar coldness. I shuffled the entire deck then and cast my fortune, there on the sand. I got an impossible reading and put them all away again. I leaned back and wished I had some water left. For a long while, I listened for the storm. There were a few growls, but they were directionless. The Trumps made me think of my family. They were up ahead—wherever that might be—waiting for me. Waiting for what? I was transporting the Jewel. To what end? At first, I had assumed that its powers might be necessary in the conflict. If so, and if I were indeed the only one who could employ them, then we were in bad shape. I thought of Amber then, and I was shaken with remorse and a kind of dread. Things must not end for Amber, ever. There had to be a way to roll back the Chaos. . . .

I threw away a small stone I had been toying with. Once I released it, it moved very slowly.

The Jewel. Its slowdown effect again . . .

I drew more energy and the stone shot away. It seemed that I had just taken strength from the Jewel a little while ago. While this treatment energized my body, my mind still felt fogged up. I needed sleep —with lots of rapid eye movements. This place might seem a lot less unusual if I were rested.

How close was I to my destination? Was it just beyond the next mountain range, or an enormous distance farther? And what chance had I of staying ahead of that storm, no matter what the distance? And the others? Supposing the battle was already concluded and we had lost? I had visions of arriving too late, to serve only as gravedigger. . . . Bones and soliloquies, Chaos . . .

And where was that damned black road now that I finally had a use for it? If I could locate it, I could follow it. I had a feeling that it was somewhere off to my left. . . .

I reached out once again, parting the fogs, rolling them back. . . . Nothing . . .

A shape? Something moving?

It was an animal, a large dog perhaps, moving to remain within the fog. Was it stalking me?

The Jewel began to pulse as I moved the fog even farther back. Exposed, the animal seemed to shrug itself. Then it moved straight toward me.

VIII

I stood as it came near. I could see then that it was a jackal, a big one, its eyes fixed on my own.

"You are a little early," I said. "I was only resting."

It chuckled.

"I have come merely to regard a Prince of Amber," the beast said. "Anything else would be a bonus."

It chuckled again. So did I.

"Then feast your eyes. Anything else, and you will find that I have rested sufficiently."

"Nay, nay," said the jackal. "I am a fan of the House of Amber. And that of Chaos. Royal blood appeals to me, Prince of Chaos. And conflict."

"You have awarded me an unfamiliar title. My connection with the Courts of Chaos is mainly a matter of genealogy."

"I think of the images of Amber passing through the shadows of Chaos. I think of the waves of Chaos washing over the images of Amber. Yet at the heart of the order Amber represents moves a family most chaotic, just as the House of Chaos is serene and placid. Yet you have your ties, as well as your conflicts."

"At the moment," I said, "I am not interested in paradox hunting and terminology games. I am trying to get to the Courts of Chaos. Do you know the way?"

"Yes," said the jackal. "It is not far, as the carrion bird flies. Come, I will set you in the proper direction."

It turned and began walking away. I followed.

"Do I move too fast? You seem tired."

"No. Keep going. It is beyond this valley certainly, is it not?"

"Yes. There is a tunnel."

I followed it, out across sand and gravel and dry, hard ground. There was nothing growing at either hand. As we walked, the fogs thinned and took on a greenish cast—another trick of that stippled sky, I assumed.

After a time, I called out, "How much farther is it?"

"Not too far now," it said. "Do you grow tired? Do you wish to rest?"

It looked back as it spoke. The greenish light gave to its ugly features an even more ghastly cast. Still, I needed a guide; and we were heading uphill, which seemed to be proper.

"Is there water anywhere near about?" I asked.

"No. We would have to backtrack a considerable distance."

"Forget it. I haven't the time."

It shrugged and chuckled and walked on. The fog cleared a little more as we went, and I could see that we were entering a low range of hills. I leaned on my staff and kept up the pace.

We climbed steadily for perhaps half an hour, the ground growing stonier, the angle of ascent steeper. I found myself beginning to breathe heavily.

"Wait," I called to him. "I do want to rest now. I thought you said that it was not far."

"Forgive me," it said, halting, "for jackalocentrism. I was judging in terms of my own natural pace. I erred in this, but we *are* almost there now. It lies among the rocks just ahead. Why not rest there?"

"All right," I replied, and I resumed walking.

Soon we reached a stony wall which I realized was the foot of a mountain. We picked our way among the rocky debris which lined it and came at last to an opening which led back into darkness.

"There you have it," said the jackal. "The way is straight, and there are no troublesome side branches. Take your passage through, and good speed to you."

"Thank you," I said, giving up thoughts of rest for the moment and stepping inside. "I appreciate this."

"My pleasure," he said from behind me.

I took several more steps and something crunched beneath my feet and rattled when kicked aside. It was a sound one does not readily forget. The floor was strewn with bones.

There came a soft, quick sound from behind me, and I knew that I did not have time to draw Grayswandir. So I spun, raising my staff before me and thrusting with it.

This maneuver blocked the beast's leap, striking it on the shoulder.

But it also knocked me over backward, to roll among the bones. The staff was torn from my hands by the impact, and in the split second of decision allowed me by my opponent's own fall I chose to draw Grayswandir rather than grope after it.

I managed to get my blade unsheathed, but that was all. I was still on my back with the point of my weapon to my left when the jackal recovered and leaped again. I swung the pommel with all of my strength into its face.

The shock ran down my arm and up into my shoulder. The jackal's head snapped back and its body twisted to my left. I brought the point into line immediately, gripping the hilt with both hands, and I was able to rise to my right knee before it snarled and lunged once more.

As soon as I saw that I had it on target, I threw my weight behind it, driving the blade deep into the jackal's body. I released it quickly and rolled away from those snapping jaws.

The jackal shrieked, struggled to rise, dropped back. I lay panting where I had fallen. I felt the staff beneath me and seized it. I brought it around to guard and drew myself back against the cave wall. The beast did not rise again, however, but lay there thrashing. In the dim light, I could see that it was vomiting. The smell was overpowering.

Then it turned its eyes in my direction and lay still.

"It would have been so fine," it said softly, "to eat a Prince of Amber. I always wondered—about royal blood."

Then the eyes closed and the breathing stopped and I was left with the stink.

I rose, back still against the wall, staff still before me, and regarded it. It was a long while before I could bring myself to retrieve my blade.

A quick exploration showed me that I was in no tunnel, but only a cave. When I made my way out, the fog had grown yellow, and it was stirred now by a breeze from the lower reaches of the valley.

I leaned against the rock and tried to decide which way to take. There was no real trail here.

Finally, I struck off to my left. That way seemed somewhat steeper, and I wanted to get above the fog and into the mountains as soon as I could. The staff continued to serve me well. I kept listening for the sound of running water, but there was none about.

I struggled along, always continuing upward, and the fogs thinned and changed color. Finally, I could see that I was climbing toward a wide plateau. Above it, I began to catch glimpses of the sky, many-colored and churning.

There were several sharp claps of thunder at my back, but I still could not see the disposition of the storm. I increased my pace then, but began to grow dizzy after a few minutes. I stopped and seated myself on the ground, panting. I was overwhelmed with a sense of failure. Even if I made it up to the plateau, I had a feeling that the storm would roar right across it. I rubbed my eyes with the heels of my hands. What was the use of going on if there was no way I could make it?

A shadow moved through the pistachio mists, dropped toward me. I raised my staff, then saw that it was only Hugi. He braked himself and landed at my feet.

"Corwin," he said, "you have come a good distance."

"But maybe not good enough," I said. "The storm seems to be getting nearer."

"I believe that it is. I have been meditating and would like to give you the benefit of—"

"If you want to benefit me at all," I said, "I could tell you what to do."

"What is that?"

"Fly back and see how far off the storm really is, and how fast it seems to be moving. Then come and tell me."

Hugi hopped from one foot to the other. Then, "All right," he said, and leaped into the air and batted his way toward what I felt to be the northwest.

I leaned on the staff and rose. I might as well keep climbing at the best pace I could manage. I drew upon the Jewel again, and strength came into me like a red lightning flash.

As I mounted the slope, a damp breeze sprang up from the direction in which Hugi had departed. There came another thunderclap. No more growls and rumbles.

I made the most of the influx of energy, climbing quickly and efficiently for several hundred meters. If I were going to lose, I might as well make it to the top first. I might as well see where I was and learn whether there was anything at all left for me to try.

My view of the sky grew more and more clear as I climbed. It had changed considerably since last I had regarded it. Half of it was of uninterrupted blackness and the other half those masses of swimming colors. And the entire heavenly bowl seemed to be rotating about a point directly overhead. I began to grow excited. This was the sky I was seeking, the sky which had covered me that time I had journeyed to Chaos. I struggled higher. I wanted to utter something heartening, but my throat was too dry.

As I neared the rim of the plateau, I heard a flapping sound and Hugi was suddenly on my shoulder.

"The storm is about ready to crawl up your arse," he said. "Be here any minute."

I continued climbing, reached level ground and hauled myself up to it. I stood for a moment then, breathing heavily. The wind must have kept the area clear of fog, for it was a high, smooth plain, and I could see the sky for a great distance ahead. I advanced, to find a point from which I could see beyond the farther edge. As I moved, the sounds of the storm came to me more clearly.

"I do not believe you will make it across," Hugi said, "without getting wet."

"You know that is no ordinary storm," I croaked. "If it were, I'd be thankful for the chance of getting a drink."

"I know. I was speaking figuratively."

I growled something vulgar and kept going.

Gradually, the vista before me enlarged. The sky still did its crazy veil dance, but the illumination was more than sufficient. When I reached a position where I was positive what lay before me, I halted and sagged against my staff.

"What is the matter?" Hugi asked.

But I could not speak. I simply gestured at the great wasteland which commerced somewhere below the farther lip of the plateau to sweep on for at least forty miles before butting up against another range of mountains. And far off to the left and still running strong went the black road.

"The waste?" he said. "I could have told you it was there. Why didn't you ask me?"

I made a noise halfway between a groan and a sob and sank slowly to the ground.

How long I remained so, I am not certain. I felt more than a little delirious. In the midst of it I seemed to see a possible answer, though something within me rebelled against it. I was finally roused by the noises of the storm and Hugi's chattering.

"I can't beat it across that place," I whispered. "There is no way."

"You say you have failed," Hugi said. "But this is not so. There is neither failure nor victory in striving. It is all but an illusion of the ego."

I rose slowly to my knees.

"I did not say that I had failed."

"You said that you cannot go on to your destination."

I looked back, to where lightnings now flashed as the storm climbed toward me.

"That's right, I cannot do it that way. But if Dad failed, I have got to attempt something that Brand tried to convince me only he could do. I have to create a new Pattern, and I have to do it right here."

"You? Create a new Pattern? If Oberon failed, how could a man who can barely stay on his feet do it? No, Corwin. Resignation is the greatest virtue you might cultivate."

I raised my head and lowered the staff to the ground. Hugi fluttered down to stand beside it and I regarded him.

"You do not want to believe any of the things that I said, do you?" I told him. "It does not matter, though. The conflict between our views is irreducible. I see desire as hidden identity and striving as its growth. You do not." I moved my hands forward and rested them on my knees. "If for you the greatest good is union with the Absolute, then why do you not fly to join it now, in the form of the all-pervading Chaos which approaches? If I fail here, it will become Absolute. As for me, I must try, for so long as there is breath within me, to raise up a Pattern against it. I do this because I am what I am, and I am the man who could have been king in Amber."

Hugi lowered his head.

"I'll see you eat crow first," he said, and he chuckled.

I reached out quickly and twisted his head off, wishing that I had time to build a fire. Though he made it look like a sacrifice, it is difficult to say to whom the moral victory belonged, since I was planning on doing it anyway.

IX

. . . Cassis, and the smell of the chestnut blossoms. All along the Champs-Elysées the chestnuts were foaming white. . . .

I remembered the play of the fountains in the Place de la Concorde. . . . And down the Rue de la Seine and along the quais, the smell of the old books, the smell of the river. . . . The smell of chestnut blossoms . . .

Why should I suddenly remember 1905 and Paris on the shadow Earth, save that I was very happy that year and I might, reflexively, have sought an antidote for the present? Yes . . .

White absinthe, Amer Picon, grenadine . . . Wild strawberries, with Crème d'Isigny . . . Chess at the Café de la Régence with actors from the Comédie Française, just across the way . . . The races at Chantilly . . . Evenings at the Boîte à Fursy on the Rue Pigalle . . .

I placed my left foot firmly before my right, my right before my left. In my left hand, I held the chain from which the Jewel depended —and I carried it high, so that I could stare into the stone's depths, seeing and feeling there the emergence of the new Pattern which I described with each step. I had screwed my staff into the ground and left it to stand near the Pattern's beginning. Left . . .

The wind sang about me and there was thunder near at hand. I did not meet with the physical resistance that I did on the old Pattern. There was no resistance at all. Instead—and in many ways worse—a peculiar deliberation had come over all my movements, slowing them, ritualizing them. I seemed to expend more energy in preparing for each step—perceiving it, realizing it and ordering my mind for its execution—than I did in the physical performance of the act. Yet the slowness seemed to require itself, was exacted of me by some unknown agency which determined precision and an adagio tempo for all my movements. Right . . .

. . . And, as the Pattern in Rebma had helped to restore my faded memories, so this one I was now striving to create stirred and elicited the smell of the chestnut trees, of the wagonloads of vegetables moving through the dawn toward the Halles. . . . I was not in love with anyone in particular at the time, though there were many girls— Yvettes and Mimis and Simones, their faces merge—and it was spring in Paris, with Gipsy bands and cocktails at Louis'. . . . I remembered, and my heart leaped with a kind of Proustian joy while Time tolled about me like a bell. . . . And perhaps this was the reason for the recollection, for this joy seemed transmitted to my movements, informed my perceptions, empowered my will. . . .

I saw the next step and I took it. . . . I had been around once now, creating the perimeter of my Pattern. At my back, I could feel the storm. It must have mounted to the plateau's rim. The sky was darkening, the storm blotting the swinging, swimming, colored lights. Flashes of lightning splayed about, and I could not spare the energy and the attention to try to control things.

Having gone completely around, I could see that as much of the new Pattern as I had walked was now inscribed in the rock and glowing palely, bluely. Yet, there were no sparks, no tingles in my feet, no hair-raising currents—only the steady law of deliberation, upon me like a great weight. . . . Left . . .

. . . Poppies, poppies and cornflowers and tall poplars along country roads, the taste of Normandy cider . . . And in town again, the smell of the chestnut blossoms . . . The Seine full of stars . . . The smell of the old brick houses in the Place des Vosges after a morning's rain . . . The bar under the Olympia Music Hall . . . A fight there . . . Bloodied knuckles, bandaged by a girl who took me home . . . What was her name? Chestnut blossoms . . . A white rose. . .

I sniffed then. The odor was all but gone from the remains of the rose at my collar. Surprising that any of it had survived this far. It heartened me. I pushed ahead, curving gently to my right. From the corner of my eye, I saw the advancing wall of the storm, slick as glass, obliterating everything it passed. The roar of its thunder was deafening now.

Right, left . . .

The advance of the armies of the night . . . Would my Pattern hold against it? I wished that I might hurry, but if anything I was moving with increasing slowness as I went on. I felt a curious sense of bilocation, almost as if I were within the Jewel tracing the Pattern there myself while I moved out here, regarding it and mimicking its progress. Left . . . Turn . . . Right . . . The storm was indeed advancing. Soon it would reach old Hugi's bones. I smelled the moisture and the ozone and wondered about the strange dark bird who had said he'd been waiting for me since the beginning of Time. Waiting to argue with me or be eaten by me in this place without history? Whatever, considering the exaggeration usual in moralists, it was fitting that, having failed to leave me with my heart all laden with rue over my spiritual condition, he be consumed to the accompaniment of theatrical thunder. . . . There was distant thunder, near thunder and more thunder now. As I turned in that direction once more, the lightning flashes were nearly blinding. I clutched my chain and took another step. . . .

The storm pushed right up to the edge of my Pattern, and then it parted. It began to creep around me. Not a drop fell upon me or the Pattern. But slowly, gradually, we came to be totally engulfed within it.

It seemed as if I were in a bubble at the bottom of a stormy sea. Walls of water encircled me and dark shapes darted by. It seemed as if the entire universe were pressing in to crush me. I concentrated on the red world of the Jewel. Left . . .

The chestnut blossoms . . . A cup of hot chocolate at a sidewalk café . . . A band concert in the Tuileries Gardens, the sounds climbing through the sunbright air . . . Berlin in the twenties, the Pacific in the thirties—there had been pleasures there, but of a different order. It may not be the true past, but images of the past that rush to comfort or torment us later, man or nation. No matter. Across the Pont Neuf and down the Rue Rivoli, buses and fiacres . . . Painters at their easels in the Luxembourg Gardens . . . If all were to fall well, I might seek a shadow like this again one day . . . It ranked with my Avalon. I had forgotten . . . The details . . . The touches that make for life . . . The smell of the chestnuts . . .

Walking . . . I completed another circuit. The wind screamed and the storm roared on, but I was untouched. So long as I did not permit it to distract me, so long as I kept moving and maintained my focus on the Jewel. . . . I had to hold up, had to keep taking these slow, careful steps, never to stop, slower and slower but constantly moving. . . . Faces . . . It seemed that rows of faces regarded me from beyond the Pattern's edge. . . . Large, like the Head, but twisted—grinning, jeering, mocking me, waiting for me to stop or step wrongly . . . Waiting for the whole thing to come apart around me. . . . There was lightning behind their eyes and in their mouths, their laughter was the thunder. . . . Shadows crawled among them. . . . Now they spoke to me, with words like a gale from off a dark ocean . . . I would fail, they told me, fail and be swept away, this fragment of a Pattern dashed to pieces behind me and consumed. . . . They cursed me, they spat and vomited toward me, though none of it reached. . . . Perhaps they were not really there. . . . Perhaps my mind had been broken by the strain. . . . Then what good were my efforts? A new Pattern to be shaped by a madman? I wavered, and they took up the chorus, "Mad! Mad! Mad!" in the voices of the elements.

I drew a deep breath and smelled what was left of the rose and thought of chestnuts once again, and days filled with the joys of life and organic order. The voices seemed to soften as my mind raced back through the events of that happy year. . . . And I took another step. . . . And another. . . . They had been playing on my weaknesses, they could feel my doubts, my anxiety, my fatigue. . . . Whatever they were, they seized what they saw and tried to use it against me. . . . Left . . . Right . . . Now let them feel my confidence and wither, I told myself. I have come this far. I will continue. Left . . .

They swirled and swelled about me, still mouthing discouragements. But some of the force seemed gone out of them. I made my way through another section of arc, seeing it grow before me in my mind's red eye.

I thought back to my escape from Greenwood, to my tricking Flora out of information, to my encounter with Random, our fight with his pursuers, our journey back to Amber. . . . I thought of our flight to Rebma and my walking of the reversed Pattern there for a restoration of much of my memory. . . . Of Random's shotgun wedding and my sojourn to Amber, where I fought with Eric and fled to Bleys. . . . Of the battles that followed, my blinding, my recovery, my escape, my journey to Lorraine and then to Avalon. . . .

Moving into even higher gear, my mind skimmed the surface of subsequent events. . . . Ganelon and Lorraine . . . The creatures of the Black Circle . . . Benedict's arm . . . Dara . . . The return of Brand and his stabbing . . . My stabbing . . . Bill Roth . . . hospital records . . . My accident . . .

. . . Now, from the very beginning at Greenwood, through it all, to this moment of my struggle to assure each perfect maneuver as it appeared to me, I felt the growing sense of anticipation I had known —whether my actions were directed toward the throne, vengeance, or my conception of duty—felt it, was aware of its continuous existence across those years up until this moment, when it was finally accompanied by something else . . . I felt that the waiting was just about over, that whatever I had been anticipating and struggling toward was soon to occur.

Left . . . Very, very slowly . . . Nothing else was important. I threw all of my will into the movements now. My concentration became total. Whatever lay beyond the Pattern, I was now oblivious to it. Lightnings, faces, winds . . . It did not matter. There was only the Jewel, the growing Pattern and myself—and I was barely aware of myself. Perhaps this was the closest I would ever come to Hugi's ideal of merging with the Absolute. Turn . . . Right foot . . . Turn again . . .

Time ceased to have meaning. Space was restricted to the design I was creating. I drew strength from the Jewel without summoning it now, as part of the process in which I was engaged. In a sense, I suppose, I was obliterated. I became a moving point, programmed by the Jewel, performing an operation which absorbed me so totally that I had no attention available for self-consciousness. Yet, at some level, I realized that I was a part of the process, also. For I knew, somehow, that if anyone else were doing it, it would be a different Pattern emerging.

I was vaguely aware that I had passed the halfway point. The way had become trickier, my movements even slower. Despite the matter of velocity, I was somehow reminded of my experiences on originally becoming attuned to the Jewel, in that strange, many-dimensional matrix which seemed to be the source of the Pattern itself.

Right . . . Left . . .

There was no drag. I felt very light, despite the deliberation. A boundless energy seemed to wash constantly through me. All of the sounds about me had merged into a white noise and vanished.

Suddenly then, I no longer seemed to be moving slowly. It did not seem as if I had passed a Veil or barrier, but rather that I had undergone some internal adjustment.

It felt as if I were moving at a more normal pace now, winding my way through tighter and tighter coils, approaching what would soon be the design's terminus. Mainly, I was still emotionless, though I knew intellectually that at some level a sense of elation was growing and would soon burst through. Another step . . . Another . . . Perhaps half a dozen more paces . . .

Suddenly, the world went dark. It seemed that I stood within a great void, with only the faint light of the Jewel before me and the glow of the Pattern like a spiral nebula through which I was striding. I wavered, but only for an instant. This must be the last trial, the final assault. I would have to be sufficient to the distraction.

The Jewel showed me what to do and the Pattern showed me where to do it. The only thing missing was a view of myself. Left . . .

I continued, executing each move with all of my attention. An opposing force began to rise against me finally, as on the old Pattern. But for this, I was prepared by years of experience. I struggled for two more steps against the mounting barrier.

Then, within the Jewel, I saw the ending of the Pattern. I would have gasped at the sudden realization of its beauty, but at this point even my breath was regulated by my efforts. I threw all of my strength into the next step, and the void seemed to shake about me. I completed it, and the next was even more difficult. I felt as if I were at the center of the universe, treading on stars, struggling to impart some essential motion by what was basically an act of will.

My foot slowly advanced, though I could not see it. The Pattern began to brighten. Soon its blaze was almost blinding.

Just a little farther . . . I strove harder than I ever had on the old Pattern, for now the resistance seemed absolute. I had to oppose it with a firmness and constancy of will that excluded everything else, though I seemed not to be moving at all now, though all of my energies seemed diverted into the brightening of the design. At least, I would go out with a splendid backdrop. . . .

Minutes, days, years . . . I do not know how long this went on. It felt like forever, as if I had been engaged in this single act for all of eternity. . . .

Then I moved, and how long that took I do not know. But I completed the step and began another. Then another . . .

The universe seemed to reel about me. I was through.

The pressure was gone. The blackness was gone. . . .

For an instant, I stood at the center of my Pattern. Without even regarding it, I fell forward onto my knees and bent double, my blood pounding in my ears. Head swimming, I panted. I began to shake, all over. I had done it, I realized dimly. Come whatever may, there was a Pattern. And it would endure. . . .

I heard a sound where there should have been none, but my jaded muscles refused to respond, even reflexively, until it was too late. Not until the Jewel was jerked from my limp fingers did I raise my head and roll back onto my haunches. No one had been following me through the Pattern—I was certain that I would have been aware of it. Therefore . . .

The light was almost normal, and blinking against it, I looked up into Brand's smiling face. He wore a black eyepatch now, and he held the Jewel in his hand. He must have teleported himself in.

He struck me just as I raised my head, and I fell onto my left side. He kicked me in the stomach then, hard.

"Well, you've done it," he said. "I did not think you could. Now I have another Pattern to destroy before I set things right. I need this to turn the battle at the Courts first, though." He waved the Jewel. "Good-bye for now."

And he vanished.

I lay there gasping and clutching at my stomach. Waves of blackness rose and fell, like a surf, within me, though I did not completely succumb to unconsciousness. A feeling of enormous despair washed over me, and I closed my eyes and moaned. There was no Jewel for me to draw upon now, either.

The chestnut trees . . .

X

As I lay there hurting, I had visions of Brand appearing on the battlefield where the forces of Amber and Chaos fought, the Jewel pulsing about his neck. Apparently his control over it was sufficient, as he saw it, to enable him to turn things against us. I saw him lashing out with lightning bolts among our troops. I saw him summoning great winds and hailstorms to strike at us. I almost wept. All of this, when he could still redeem himself by coming in on our side. Just winning was not enough for him now, though. He had to win for himself, and on his own terms. And I? I had failed. I had thrown up a Pattern against the Chaos, a thing I had never thought I could do. Yet, this would be as nothing if the battle was lost and Brand returned and wiped out my work. To have come this close, passing through everything that I had, and then to fail here. . . . It made me want to cry "Injustice!" though I knew the universe did not run in accordance with my notions of equity. I gnashed my teeth and spat some dirt I had mouthed. I had been charged by our father to take the Jewel to the place of battle. I had almost made it.

A sense of strangeness came over me then. Something was calling for my attention. What?

The silence.

The raging winds and the thunder had ceased. The air was still. In fact, the air felt cool and fresh. And on the other side of my eyelids, I knew that there was light.

I opened my eyes. I saw a sky of a bright, uniform white. I blinked, I turned my head. There was something off to my right. . . .

A tree. A tree stood where I had planted the staff I had cut from old Ygg. It was already far taller than the staff itself had been. I could almost see it growing. And it was green with leaves and white with a sprinkling of buds; a few blossoms had opened. From that direction, the breeze brought me a faint and delicate scent which offered me some comfort.

I felt along my sides. I did not seem to have any broken ribs, though my guts still felt knotted from the kick I had taken. I rubbed my eyes with my knuckles and ran my hands through my hair. I sighed heavily then and rose to one knee.

Turning my head, I regarded the prospect. The plateau was the same, yet somehow not the same. It was still bare but was no longer harsh. Likely an effect of the new illumination. No, there was more to it than that. . . .

I had continued to turn, completing my scanning of the horizon. It was not the same place where I had commenced my walk. There were differences both subtle and gross: altered rock formations, a dip where there had been a rise, a new texture to the stone beneath and near me, in the distance what appeared to be soil. I stood and it seemed that now, from somewhere, I caught the scent of the sea. This place had an entirely different feeling to it than the one to which I had mounted—so long ago, it seemed. It was too much of a change for that storm to have wrought. It reminded me of something.

I sighed again, there at the Pattern's center, and continued to consider my surroundings. Somehow, in spite of myself, my despair was slipping away and a feeling of—"refreshment"—seems somehow the best word—was rising within me. The air was so clean and sweet, and the place had a new, unused feeling about it. I—

Of course. It was like the place of the primal Pattern. I turned back to the tree and regarded it again, higher already. Like, yet unlike . . . There was something new in the air, the ground, the sky. This was a new place. A new primal Pattern. Everything about me then was a result of the Pattern in which I stood.

I suddenly realized that I was feeling more than refreshment. It was now a sense of elation, a kind of joy that was moving through me. This was a clean, fresh place and I was somehow responsible for it.

Time passed. I just stood there watching the trees, looking around me, enjoying the euphoria that had come over me. Here was some kind of victory, anyway—until Brand came back to wipe it out.

Suddenly, I was sober again. I had to stop Brand, I had to protect this place. I was at the center of a Pattern. If this one behaved like the other, I could use its power to project me anywhere I desired. I could use it to go and join the others now.

I dusted myself off. I loosened my blade in the scabbard. Things might not be as hopeless as they had seemed earlier. I had been told to convey the Jewel to the place of battle. So Brand had done it for me; it would still be there. I would simply have to go and take it back from him, somehow, to make things turn the way they were supposed to have fallen.

I looked all around me. I would have to return here, to investigate this new situation at another time, if I survived what was to come. There was mystery here. It hung in the air and drifted on the breeze. It could take ages to unravel what had occurred when I had drawn the new Pattern.

I saluted the tree. It seemed to stir as I did so. I adjusted my rose and pushed it back into shape. It was time to move again. There was a thing I had yet to do.

I lowered my head and closed my eyes. I tried to recall the lay of the land before the final abyss at the Courts of Chaos. I saw it then, beneath that wild sky, and I peopled it with my relatives, with troops. I seemed to hear the sounds of a distant battle as I did this. The scene adjusted itself, came clearer. I held the vision an instant longer, then charged the Pattern to take me there.

. . . A moment later, it seemed, I stood upon a hilltop beside a plain, a cold wind whipping my cloak about me. The sky was that crazy, turning, stippled thing I remembered from last time—half-black, half-psychedelic rainbows. There were unpleasant fumes in the air. The black road was off to the right now, crossing that plain and passing beyond it over the abyss toward that nighted citadel, firefly gleams flickering about it. Gauzy bridges drifted in the air, extending from far in that darkness, and strange forms traveled upon them as well as upon the black road. Below me on the field was what seemed to be the main concentration of troops. At my back, I heard something other than Time's winged chariot.

Turning toward what must have been north by a succession of previous reckonings regarding its course, I beheld the advance of that devil-storm through distant mountains, flashing and growling, coming on like a sky-high glacier.

So I had not stopped it with the creation of a new Pattern. It seemed that it had simply passed by my protected area and would continue until it got to wherever it was going. Hopefully then, the thing would be succeeded by whatever constructive impulses were now spreading outward from the new Pattern, with the reimposition of order throughout the places of Shadow. I wondered how long it would take for the storm to get here.

I heard the sound of hoofs and turned, drawing my blade. . . .

A horned rider on a great black horse was bearing down upon me, something like firelight glowing in his eyes.

I adjusted my position and waited. He seemed to have descended from one of the gauzy roadways which had drifted in this direction. We were both fairly far removed from the main scene of action. I watched as he mounted the hill. Odd horse, that. Nice chest. Where the hell was Brand? I wasn't looking for just any fight.

I watched the rider as he came on, and the crooked blade in his right hand. I repositioned myself as he moved in to cut me down. When he swung, I was ready with a parry that pulled his arm within reach. I caught hold of it and dragged him from his mount.

"That rose . . ." he said as he fell to the ground. I do not know what else he might have said, because I cut his throat, and his words and everything else about him were lost with the fiery slash.

I whirled then, drawing Grayswandir away, sprinted several paces and had hold of the black charger's bridle. I spoke with the horse to calm him and led him away from the flames. After a couple of minutes we were on better terms, and I mounted.

He was skittish at first, but I just had him pace the hill top lightly while I continued to observe. The forces of Amber appeared to be on the offense. Smoldering corpses were all over the field. The main force of our enemies was drawn back onto a height near the lip of the abyss. Lines of them, not yet broken but hard pressed, were falling backing slowly toward it. On the other hand, more troops were crossing that abyss and joining the others who held the heights. Estimating their growing numbers and their position quickly, I judged that these might be readying an offense of their own. Brand was nowhere in sight.

Even if I had been rested and wearing armor I would have had second thoughts about riding down and joining in the fray. My job right now was to locate Brand. I doubted that he would be directly involved in the fighting. I looked off to the sides of the battle proper, seeking a lone figure. No . . . Perhaps the far side of the field. I would have to circle to the north. There was too much that I could not see to the west.

I turned my mount and made my way down the hill. It would be so pleasant to collapse, I decided. Just to fall down in a heap and sleep. I sighed. Where the hell was Brand?

I reached the bottom of the hill and turned to cut through a culvert. I needed a better view—

"Lord Corwin of Amber!"

He was waiting for me as I rounded a bend in the depression, a big, corpse-colored guy with red hair and a horse to match. He wore coppery armor with greenish tracings, and he sat facing me, still as a statue.

"I saw you on the hilltop," he said. "You are not mailed, are you?"

I slapped my chest.

He nodded sharply. Then he reached up, first to his left shoulder, then to his right, then to his sides, opening fastenings upon his breastplate. When he had them undone, he removed it, lowered it toward the ground on his left side and let it fall. He did the same with his greaves.

"I have long wanted to meet you," he said. "I am Borel. I do not want it said that I took unfair advantage of you when I killed you."

Borel . . . The name was familiar. Then I remembered. He had Dara's respect and affection. He had been her fencing teacher, a master of the blade. Stupid, though, I saw. He had forfeited my respect by removing his armor. Battle is not a game, and I had no desire to make myself available to any presumptuous ass who thought otherwise. Especially a skilled ass, when I was feeling beat. If nothing else, he could probably wear me down.

"Now we shall resolve a matter which has long troubled me," he said.

I replied with a quaint vulgarism, wheeled my black and raced back the way I had come. He gave chase immediately.

As I passed back along the culvert, I realized that I did not have a sufficient lead. He would be upon me in a matter of moments with my back all exposed, to cut me down or force me to fight. However, while limited, my choices included a little more than that.

"Coward!" he cried. "You flee combat! Is this the great warrior of whom I have heard so much?"

I reached up and unfastened my cloak. At either hand, the culvert's lip was level with my shoulders, then my waist.

I rolled out of the saddle to my left, stumbled once and found my footing. The black went on. I moved to my right, facing the draw.

Catching my cloak in both hands, I swung it in a reverse-veronica maneuver a second or two before Borel's head and shoulders came abreast of me. It swept over him, drawn blade and all, muffling his head and slowing his arms.

I kicked then, hard. I was aiming for his head, but I caught him on the left shoulder. He was spilled from his saddle, and his horse, too, went by.

Drawing Grayswandir, I leaped after him. I caught him just as he had brushed my cloak aside and was struggling to rise. I skewered him where he sat and saw the startled expression on his face as the wound began to flame.

"Oh, basely done!" he cried. "I had hoped for better of thee!"

"This isn't exactly the Olympic Games," I said, brushing some sparks from my cloak.

I chased down my horse then and mounted. This took me several minutes. As I continued northward, I achieved higher ground. From there, I spotted Benedict directing the battle, and in a draw far to the rear, I caught a glimpse of Julian at the head of his troops from Arden. Benedict was apparently holding them in reserve.

I kept going, toward the advancing storm, beneath the half-dark, half-painted, revolving sky. I soon reached my goal, the highest hill in sight, and began to mount it. I halted several times on the way up, to look back.

I saw Deirdre in black armor, swinging an ax; Llewella and Flora were among the archers, Fiona was nowhere in sight. Gérard was not there either. Then I saw Random on horseback, swinging a heavy blade, leading an assault toward the enemy's high ground. Near him was a knight clad in green whom I did not recognize. The man swung a mace with deadly efficiency. He wore a bow upon his back, and he'd a quiver of gleaming arrows at his hip.

The sounds of the storm came louder as I reached the summit of my hill. The lightning flickered with the regularity of a neon tube and the rain sizzled down, a fiberglass curtain that had now passed over the mountains.

Below me, both beasts and men—and more that a few beast-men —were woven in knots and strands of battle. A cloud of dust hung over the field. Assessing the distribution of forces, however, it did not appear to me that the growing forces of the enemy could be pushed much farther. In fact, it seemed that it was just about time for the counterattack. They appeared to be ready up in their craggy places, and just waiting for the order.

I was about a minute and a half off. They advanced, sweeping down the slope, reinforcing their lines, pushing our troops back, driving ahead. And more were arriving from beyond the dark abyss. Our own troops began a reasonably orderly retreat. The enemy pressed harder, and when things seemed about ready to be turned into a rout an order must have been given.

I heard the sound of Julian's horn, and shortly thereafter I saw him astride Morgenstern leading the men of Arden onto the field. This balanced the opposing forces almost exactly and the noise level rose and rose while the sky turned above us.

I watched the conflict for perhaps a quarter of an hour, as our own forces slowly withdrew across the field. Then I saw a one-armed figure on a fiery striped horse suddenly appear atop a distant hill. He bore a raised blade in his hand and he was faced away from me, toward the west. He stood unmoving for several long moments. Then he lowered the blade.

I heard trumpets in the west, and at first I saw nothing. Then a line of cavalry came into view. I started. For a moment, I thought Brand was there. Then I realized it was Bleys leading his troops to strike at the enemy's exposed flank.

And suddenly, our troops in the field were no longer retreating. They were holding their line. Then, they were pressing forward.

Bleys and his riders came on, and I realized that Benedict had the day again. The enemy was about to be ground to pieces.

Then a cold wind swept over me from out of the north, and I looked that way again.

The storm had advanced considerably. It must have started moving faster just recently. And it was darker now than it had been, with brighter flashes and louder roars. And this cold, wet wind was increasing in intensity.

I wondered then . . . would it simply sweep over the field like an annihilating wave and that be that? What of the effects of the new Pattern? Would these follow, to restore everything? Somehow, I doubted this. If this storm smashed us, I'd a feeling we would stay smashed. It would require the force of the Jewel to permit us to ride it out until order was restored. And what would be left if we survived it? I simply could not guess.

So what was Brand's plan? What was he waiting for? What was he going to do?

I looked out over the battlefield once more. . . .

Something.

In a shadowy place on the heights where the enemy had regrouped, been reinforced, and down which it had stormed . . . something.

A tiny flash of red . . . I was sure I had seen it.

I kept watching, waiting. I had to see it again, to pinpoint it. . . .

A minute passed. Two, perhaps . . .

There! And again.

I wheeled the black charger. It looked possible to make it around the enemy's near flank and up to that supposedly vacant height. I raced down the hill and began that course.

It had to be Brand with the Jewel. He had chosen a good, safe spot, from which he commanded a view of the entire battlefield as well as the approaching storm. From there, he could direct its lightning into our troops as the front advanced. He would signal a retreat at the proper moment, hit us with the storm's strange furies, then sidetrack the thing to bypass the side he was backing. It seemed the simplest and most effective use of the Jewel under the circumstances.

I would have to get close fast. My control of the stone was greater than his, but it diminished with distance, and he would have the Jewel on his person. My best bet would be to charge right into him, to get within control range at all costs, take over command of the stone and use it against him. But he might have a bodyguard up there with him. That troubled me, because dealing with it could slow me disastrously. And if he did not, what was to prevent him from teleporting himself away if the going got too rough? Then what could I do? I would have to start all over, hunting him again. I wondered whether I could use the Jewel to keep him from transporting himself. I did not know. I resolved to try.

It might not have been the best of plans, but it was the only one I had. There was no longer time to plot.

As I rode, I saw that there were others headed for that height, also. Random, Deirdre and Fiona, mounted and accompanied by eight horsemen, had made their way through the enemy lines, with a few other troops—friends or foes, I could not tell—maybe both—riding hard behind them. The knight clad in green seemed to be moving the fastest, gaining on them. I did not recognize him—or her, as the case might be. I did not doubt the objective of the van-guard, however—not with Fiona there. She must have detected Brand's presence and be leading the others to him. A few drops of hope fell upon my heart. She might be able to neutralize Brand's powers, or minimize them. I leaned forward, still bearing to my left, hurrying my horse along. The sky kept turning. The wind whistled about me. A terrific clap of thunder rolled by. I did not look back.

I was racing them. I did not want them to get there before me, but I feared that they would. The distance was just too great.

If only they would turn and see me coming, they would probably wait. I wished there had been some way of giving them a sign of my presence earlier. I cursed the fact that the Trumps no longer worked.

I began shouting. I screamed after them, but the wind blew my words away and the thunder rolled over them.

"Wait for me! Damn it! It's Corwin!"

Not even a glance in my direction.

I passed the nearest engagements and rode along the enemy's flank out of range of missiles and arrows. They seemed to be retreating faster now and our troops were spreading out over a larger area. Brand must be getting ready to strike. Part of the rotating sky was covered by a dark cloud which had not been above the field minutes before.

I turned toward my right, behind the retreating forces, racing on toward those hills the others were already mounting.

The sky continued to darken as I neared the foot of the hills, and I feared for my kinsmen. They were getting too close to him. He would have to do something. Unless Fiona was strong enough to stop him. . . .

The horse reared and I was thrown to the ground at the blinding flash which had occurred before me. The thunder cracked before I hit the earth.

I lay there for several moments, dazed. The horse had run off, was perhaps fifty meters away, before he halted and began to move about uncertainly. I rolled onto my stomach and looked up the long slope. The other riders were also down. Their group had apparently been struck by the discharge. Several were moving, more were not. None had yet risen. Above them, I saw the red glow of the Jewel, back be-neath an underhang, brighter and steadier now, and the shadowy outline of the figure who wore it.

I began crawling forward, upward and to my left. I wanted to get out of line of sight with that figure before I risked rising. It would take too long to reach him crawling, and I was going to have to skirt the others now, because his attention would be with them.

I made my way carefully, slowly, using every bit of cover in sight, wondering whether the lightning would be striking in the same place again soon—and if not, when he would begin pulling disaster down upon our troops. Any minute now, I judged. A glance back showed me our forces spread over the far end of the field, with the enemy pulled back and coming this way. Before too long, in fact, it seemed I might have them to worry about, too.

I made it into a narrow ditch and wormed my way south for perhaps ten meters. Out again then on the far side, to take advantage of a rise, then some rocks.

When I raised my head to take stock of the situation, I could no longer see the glow of the Jewel. The cleft from which it had shone was blocked by its own eastern shoulder of stone.

I kept crawling, though, near to the lip of the great abyss itself, before I bore to my right once more. I reached a point where it seemed safe to rise, and I did so. I kept expecting another flash, another thunderclap—nearby or on the field—but none came. I began to wonder . . . why not? I reached out, trying to sense the presence of the Jewel, but I could not. I hurried toward the place where I had seen the glow.

I glanced back over the abyss to be sure that no new menaces were approaching from that direction. I drew my blade. When I reached my goal, I stayed close to the escarpment and worked my way northward. I dropped low when I came to its edge and peered around.

There was no red glow. No shadowy figure either. The stony recess appeared to be empty. There was nothing suspicious anywhere in the vicinity. Could he have teleported again? And if so, why?

I rose and passed about the rocky rise. I continued moving in that direction. I tried once more to feel the Jewel, and this time I made a faint contact with it—somewhere off to my right and above, it seemed.

Silent, wary, I moved that way. Why had he left his shelter? He had been perfectly situated for what he had been about. Unless . . .

I heard a scream and a curse. Two different voices. I began to run.

XI

I passed the niche and kept going. Beyond it, there was a natural trail winding upward. I mounted this.

I could see no one as yet, but my sense of the Jewel's presence grew stronger as I moved. I thought that I heard a single footfall from off to my right and I whirled in that direction, but there was no one in sight. The Jewel did not feel that near either, so I continued.

As I neared the top of the rise, the black drop of Chaos hanging behind, I heard voices. I could not distinguish what was being said, but the words were agitated.

I slowed as I neared the crest, lowered myself and peered around the side of a rock.

Random was a small distance ahead of me and Fiona was with him, as were Lords Chantris and Feldane. All, save Fiona, held weapons as if ready to use them, but they stood perfectly still. They were staring toward the edge of things—a shelf of rock slightly above their level and perhaps fifteen meters distant—the place where the abyss began.

Brand stood in that place, and he was holding Deirdre before him. She was unhelmed, her hair blowing wild, and he had a dagger at her throat. It appeared that he had already cut her slightly. I dropped back.

I heard Random say softly, "Is there nothing more you can do, Fi?"

"I can hold him here," she said, "and at this range, I can slow his efforts at weather control. But that is all. He's got some attunement with it and I do not. He also has proximity going for him. Anything else I might try, he can counter."

Random gnawed his lower lip.

"Put down your weapons," Brand called out. "Do it now, or Deirdre's dead."

"Kill her," Random said, "and you lose the only thing that's keeping you alive. Do it, and I'll show you where I'll put my weapon."

Brand muttered something under his breath. Then: "Okay. I will start by mutilating her."

Random spat.

"Come on!" he said. "She can regenerate as well as the rest of us. Find a threat that means something, or shut up and fight it out!"

Brand was still. I thought it better not to reveal my presence. There must be something I could do. I ventured another look, mentally photographing the terrain before I dropped back. There were some rocks way off to the left, but they did not extend far enough. I saw no way that I might sneak up on him.

"I think we are going to have to rush him and chance it," I heard Random say. "I don't see anything else. Do you?"

Before anyone answered him, a strange thing occurred. The day began to grow brighter.

I looked all about me for the source of the illumination, then sought it overhead.

The clouds were still there, the crazy sky doing its tricks beyond them. The brightness was in the clouds, however. They had paled and were now glowing, as if they masked a sun. Even as I watched, there was a perceptible brightening.

"What is he up to now?" Chantris asked.

"Nothing that I can tell," Fiona said. "I do not believe it is his doing."

"Whose then?"

There was no answer that I could overhear.

I watched the clouds grow brighter. The largest and brightest of them seemed to swirl then, as if stirred. Forms tossed within it, settled. An outline began to take shape.

Below me, on the field, the sounds of battle lessened. The storm itself was muted as the vision grew. Something was definitely forming in the bright place above our heads—the lines of an enormous face.

"I do not know, I tell you," I heard Fiona say in response to something mumbled.

Before it finished taking form, I realized that it was my father's face in the sky. Neat trick, that. And I had no idea what it represented either.

The face moved, as if he were regarding us all. There were lines of strain there, and something of concern to his expression. The brightness grew a little further. His lips moved.

When his voice came down to me it was somehow at an ordinary conversational level, rather than the vast booming I had expected:

"I send you this message," he said, "before undertaking the repair of the Pattern. By the time you receive it, I will already have succeeded or failed. It will precede the wave of Chaos which must accompany my endeavor. I have reason to believe the effort will prove fatal to me."

His eyes seemed to sweep across the field.

"Rejoice or mourn, as you would," he went on, "for this is either the beginning or the end. I will send the Jewel of Judgment to Corwin as soon as I have finished with it. I have charged him to bear it to the place of conflict. All of your efforts there will be as nothing if the wave of Chaos cannot be averted. But with the Jewel, in that place, Corwin should be able to preserve you until it passes."

I heard Brand's laugh. He sounded quite mad now.

"With my passing," the voice continued, "The problem of the succession will be upon you. I had wishes in this regard, but I see now that these were futile. Therefore, I have no choice but to leave this on the horn of the Unicorn.

"My children, I cannot say that I am entirely pleased with you, but I suppose this works both ways. Let it be. I leave you with my blessing, which is more than a formality. I go now to walk the Pattern. Good-bye."

Then his face began to fade and the brightness drained out of the cloudbank. A little while, and it was gone. A stillness lay upon the field.

". . . and, as you can see," I heard Brand saying, "Corwin does not have the Jewel. Throw down your weapons and get the hell out of here. Or keep them and get out. I do not care. Leave me alone. I have things to do."

"Brand," Fiona said, "can you do what he wanted of Corwin? Can you use it to make that thing miss us?"

"I could if I would," he said. "Yes, I could turn it aside."

"You will be a hero if you do," she said gently. "You will earn our gratitude. All past wrongs will be forgiven. Forgiven and forgotten. We—"

He began to laugh wildly.

"*You* forgive *me?*" he said. You, who left me in that tower, who put the knife into my side? Thank you, sister. It is very kind of you to offer to forgive me, but excuse me if I decline."

"All right," Random said, "what *do* you want? An apology? Riches and treasure? An important appointment? All of these? They are yours. But this is a stupid game you are playing. Let us end it and go home, pretend it was all a bad dream."

"Yes, let us end it," Brand replied. "You do that by throwing down your weapons first. Then Fiona releases me from her spell, you all do an about-face and march north. You do it or I kill Deirdre."

"Then I think you had better go ahead and kill her and be ready to fight it out with me," he said, "because she will be dead in a little while anyway, if we let you have your way. All of us will."

I heard Brand's chuckle.

"Do you honestly think I am going to let you die? I need you—as many of you as I can save. Hopefully Deirdre, too. You are the only ones who can appreciate my triumph. I will preserve you through the holocaust that is about to begin."

"I do not believe you," Random said.

"Then take a moment and think about it. You know me well enough to know that I will want to rub your noses in it. I want you as witnesses to what I do. In this sense, I require your presence in my new world. Now, get out of here."

"You will have everything you want plus our gratitude," Fiona began, "if you will just—"

"Go!"

I knew that I could delay no longer. I had to make my move. I also knew that I could not reach him in time. I had no choice but to try using the Jewel as a weapon against him.

I reached out and felt its presence. I closed my eyes and summoned my powers.

Hot. Hot, I thought. It is burning you, Brand. It is causing every molecule in your body to vibrate faster and faster. You are about to become a human torch—

I heard him scream.

"Corwin!" he bellowed. "Stop it! Wherever you are! I'll kill her! Look!"

Still willing the Jewel to burn him, I rose to my feet. I glared at him across the distance that separated us. His clothing was beginning to smolder.

"Stop it!" he cried, and he raised the knife and slashed Deirdre's face.

I screamed and my eyes swam. I lost control of the Jewel. But Deirdre, her left cheek bloody, sank her teeth into his hand as he moved to cut her again. Then her arm was free, and she jabbed her elbow into his ribs and tried to pull away.

As soon as she moved, as soon as her head dropped, there was a silver flash. Brand gasped and let go the dagger. An arrow had pierced his throat. Another followed an instant later and stood out from his breast, a little to the right of the Jewel.

He stepped backward and made a gurgling noise. Only there was no place to which he might step, from the edge of the abyss.

His eye went wide as he began to topple. Then his right hand shot forward and caught hold of Deirdre's hair. I was running by then, shouting, but I knew that I could not reach them in time.

Deirdre howled, a look of terror on her bloodstreaked face, and she reached out to me. . . .

Then Brand, Deirdre and the Jewel were over the edge and falling, vanished from sight, gone. . . .

I believe that I tried to throw myself after them, but Random caught hold of me. Finally, he had to hit me, and it all went away.

When I came around, I lay upon the stony earth farther back from the edge of that place where I had fallen. Someone had folded my cloak into a pillow for me. My first vision was of the turning sky, reminding me somehow of my dream of the wheel the day I had met Dara. I could feel the others about me, hear their voices, but I did not at first turn my head. I just lay there and regarded the mandala in the heavens and thought upon my loss. Deirdre . . . she had meant more to me than all the rest of the family put together. I cannot help it. That is how it was. How many times had I wished she were not my sister. Yet, I had reconciled myself to the realities of our situation. My feelings would never change, but . . . now she was gone, and this thought meant more to me than the impending destruction of the world.

Yet, I had to see what was happening now. With the Jewel gone, everything was over. Yet . . . I reached out, trying to feel its presence, wherever it might be, but there was nothing. I began to rise then, to see how far the wave had advanced, but a sudden arm pushed me back.

"Rest, Corwin." It was Random's voice. "You're beat. You look as if you have crawled through hell. There is nothing you can do now. Take it easy."

"What difference does the state of my health make?" I replied. "In a little while, it will not matter."

I made to rise again, and this time the arm moved to support me.

"All right, then," he said. "Not that much worth seeing, though."

I suppose that he was right. The fighting appeared to be over except for a few isolated pockets of resistance by the enemy, and these were rapidly being enveloped, their combatants slain or captured, everyone moving in this direction, withdrawing before the advancing wave which had reached the far end of the field. Soon our height would be crowded with all of the survivors from both sides. I looked behind us. No new forces were approaching from the dark citadel. Could we retreat to that place when the wave finally reached us here? Then what? The abyss seemed the ultimate answer. "Soon," I muttered, thinking of Deirdre. "Soon . . ." Why not?

I watched the stormfront, flashing, masking, transforming. Yes, soon. With the Jewel gone along with Brand—

"Brand . . ." I said. "Who was it finally got him?"

"I claim that distinction," said a familiar voice which I could not place.

I turned my head and stared. The man in green was seated on a rock. His bow and quiver lay beside him on the ground. He flashed an evil smile in my direction.

It was Caine.

"I'll be damned," I said, rubbing my jaw. "A funny thing happened to me on the way to your funeral."

"Yes. I heard about it." He laughed. "You ever kill yourself, Corwin?"

"Not recently. How'd you manage it?"

"Walked to the proper shadow," he said, "waylaid the shadow of myself there. He provided the corpse." He shuddered. "An eerie feeling, that. Not one I'd care to repeat."

"But why?" I said. "Why fake your death and try to frame me for it?"

"I wanted to get to the root of the trouble in Amber," he said, "and destroy it. I thought it best to go underground for that. What better way than by convincing everyone that I was dead? I finally succeeded, too, as you saw." He paused. "I'm sorry about Deirdre, though. But I had no choice. It was our last chance. I did not really think he would take her with him."

I looked away.

"I had no choice," he repeated. "I hope you can see that."

I nodded.

"But why did you try to make it look as if I had killed you?" I asked.

Just then Fiona approached with Bleys. I greeted them both and turned back to Caine for my answer. There were things I wanted to ask Bleys, too, but they could wait.

"Well?" I said.

"I wanted you out of the way," he said. "I still thought you might be behind the whole thing. You or Brand. I had it narrowed down that far. I thought it might even be the two of you in it together— especially with him struggling to bring you back."

"You have that wrong," said Bleys. "Brand was trying to keep him away. He had learned that his memory was returning and—"

"I gather," Caine replied, "but at the time it looked that way. So I wanted Corwin back in a dungeon while I searched for Brand. I lay low then and listened in on the Trumps to everything everyone said, hoping for a clue as to Brand's whereabouts."

"That's what Dad meant," I said.

"What?" Caine asked.

"He implied there was an eavesdropper on the Trumps."

"I do not see how he could have known. I had learned to be completely passive about it. I had taught myself to deal them all out and touch all of them lightly at the same time, waiting for a stirring. When it came, I would shift my attention to the speakers. Taking you one at a time, I even found I could sometimes get into your minds when you were not using the Trumps yourselves—if you were sufficiently distracted and I allowed myself no reaction."

"Yet he knew," I said.

"It is entirely possible. Likely, even," said Fiona, and Bleys nodded.

Random drew nearer.

"What did you mean when you asked about Corwin's side?" he inquired. "How could you even know about it unless—"

Caine merely nodded. I saw Benedict and Julian together in the distance, addressing their troops. At Caine's silent movement, I forgot them.

"You?" I croaked. "You stabbed me?"

"Have a drink, Corwin," Random said, passing me his flask. It was a dilute wine. I gulped it. My thirst was immense, but I stopped after several good swigs.

"Tell me about it," I said.

"All right. I owe you that," he said. "When I learned from Julian's mind that you had brought Brand back to Amber, I decided that an earlier guess had been correct—that you and Brand were in it together. That meant you both had to be destroyed. I used the Pattern to project myself into your chambers that night. There, I tried to kill you, but you moved too fast and you somehow managed to Trump out before I got a second chance."

"Well, damn your eyes," I said. "If you could touch our minds couldn't you have seen that I was not the man you were looking for?"

He shook his head.

"I could pick up only surface thoughts and reactions to your immediate environment. Not always that, even. And I had heard your curse, Corwin. And it was coming true. I could see it all around us. I felt that we would all be a lot safer with you and Brand both out of the way. I knew what he could do, from his actions back before your return. I could not get at him just then, though, because of Gérard. Then he began to grow stronger. I made one effort later, but it failed."

"When was that?" Random asked.

"That was the one Corwin got blamed for. I masked myself. In case he managed to get away as Corwin had, I did not want him knowing I was still around. I used the Pattern to project myself into his chambers and tried to finish him off. We were both hurt—there was a lot of blood around—but he managed to Trump away, too. Then I got in touch with Julian a while back and joined him for this battle, because Brand just had to show up here. I had some silver-tipped arrows made because I was more than half convinced that he was no longer like the rest of us. I wanted to kill him fast and do it from a distance. I practiced my archery and came looking for him. I finally found him. Now everyone tells me I was wrong about you, so I guess your arrow will go unused."

"Thanks a lot."

"I might even owe you an apology."

"That would be nice."

"On the other hand, I thought that I was right. I was doing it to save the rest—"

I never did get Caine's apology, because just then a trumpet blast seemed to shake the entire world—directionless, loud, prolonged. We cast about, seeking its source.

Caine stood and pointed.

"There!" he said.

My eyes followed his gesture. The curtain of the stormfront was broken off to the northwest, at the point where the black road emerged from it. There, a ghostly rider on a black horse had appeared and was winding his horn. It was a while before more of its notes reached us. Moments later, two more trumpeters—also pale, and mounted on black steeds—joined him. They raised their horns and added to the sound.

"What can it be?" Random asked.

"I think I know," Bleys said, and Fiona nodded.

"What, then?" I asked.

But they did not answer me. The horsemen were beginning to move again, passing along the black road, and more were emerging behind them.

I watched. There was a great silence on the heights about me. All of the troops had halted and were regarding the procession. Even the prisoners from the Courts, hemmed by steel, turned their attention that way.

Led by the pale trumpeters came a mass of horsemen mounted on white steeds, bearing banners, some of which I did not recognize, behind a man-thing who bore the Unicorn standard of Amber. These were followed by more musicians, some of them playing upon instruments of a sort I had never seen before.

Behind the musicians marched horned man-shaped things in light armor, long columns of them, and every twentieth or so bore a great torch before him, reaching high above his head. A deep noise came to us then—slow, rhythmic, rolling beneath the notes of the trumpets and the sounds of the musicians—and I realized that the foot soldiers were singing. A great deal of time seemed to pass as this body advanced along that black way across the distant track below us, yet none of us stirred and none of us spoke. They passed, with the torches and the banners and the music and the singing, and they finally came to the edge of the abyss and continued over the near-invisible extension of that dark highway, their torches flaring against the blackness now, lighting their way. The music grew stronger, despite the distance, with more and more voices added to that chorus, as the guard continued to emerge from that flashing stormcurtain. An occasional roll of thunder passed by, but this could not drown it; nor did the winds which assailed the torches extinguish any so far as I could see. The movement had a hypnotic effect. It seemed that I had been watching the procession for countless days, years perhaps, listening to the tune I now recognized.

Suddenly, a dragon sailed through the stormfront, and another, and another. Green and golden and black as old iron, I watched them soar on the winds, turning their heads to trail pennons of fire.

The lightning flashed behind them and they were awesome and magnificent and of incalculable size. Beneath them came a small herd of white cattle, tossing their heads and blowing, beating the ground with their hoofs. Riders passed beside and among these, cracking long black whips.

Then came a procession of truly bestial troops from a shadow with which Amber sometimes has commerce—heavy, scaled, taloned—playing upon instruments like bagpipes, whose skirling notes came to us with vibrance and pathos.

These marched on, and there were more torch bearers and more troops with their colors—from shadows both distant and near. We watched them pass and wind their way into the far sky, like a migration of fireflies, their destination that black citadel called the Courts of Chaos.

There seemed no end to it. I had lost all track of time. But the stormfront, strangely, was not advancing as all this went on. I had even lost something of my sense of person, to be caught up in the procession which passed us. This, I knew, was an event which could never be repeated. Bright flying things darted above the columns and dark ones floated, higher.

There were ghostly drummers, beings of pure light and a flock of floating machines; I saw horsemen, clad all in black, mounted on a variety of beasts; a wyvern seemed to hang in the sky for a moment, like part of a fireworks display. And the sounds—of hoofbeats and footfalls, of singing and skirling, of drumming and trumpeting—mounted to a mighty wave that washed over us. And on, on, on out over the bridge of darkness, wound the procession, its lights lining the great span for a vast distance now.

Then, as my eyes drifted back along those lines, another shape emerged from the glistening curtain. It was a cart draped all in black and drawn by a team of black horses. At each corner rose a staff which glowed with blue fire, and atop it rested what could only be a casket, draped with our Unicorn flag. The driver was a hunchback clad in purple and orange garments, and I knew even at that distance that it was Dworkin.

It is thus, then, I thought. *I do not know why, but somehow it is fitting, fitting that it be the Old Country to which you travel now. There were many things that I might have said while you lived. Some of them I did say, but few of the right words were ever spoken. Now it is over, for you are dead. As dead as all of those who have gone before you into that place where the rest of us soon may follow. I am sorry. It was only after all these years, on your assuming another face and form, that I finally knew you, respected you, even came to like you—though you were a crochety old bastard in that form, too. Was the Ganelon self the real you all along, or was it only another form adopted for convenience's sake, Old Shape-shifter? I will never know, but I like to think that I finally saw you as you were, that I met someone I liked, someone I could trust, and that it was you. I wish that I might have known you even better, but I am grateful for this much. . . .*

"Dad. . . .?" Julian said softly.

"He wanted to be taken beyond the Courts of Chaos and into the final darkness when his time came at last," Bleys said. "So Dworkin once told me. Beyond Chaos and Amber, to a place where none reigned."

"And so it is," Fiona said. "But is there order somewhere beyond that wall they come through? Or does the storm go on forever? If he succeeded, it is but a passing matter and we are in no danger. But if he did not . . ."

"It does not matter," I said, "whether or not he succeeded, because I did."

"What do you mean?" she asked.

"I believe that he failed," I said, "that he was destroyed before he could repair the old Pattern. When I saw this storm coming—actually, I experienced a part of it—I realized that I could not possibly make it here in time with the Jewel, which he had sent to me after his efforts. Brand had been trying to get it from me all along the way—to create a new Pattern, he said. Later, that gave me the idea. When I saw that all else was failing, I used the Jewel to create a new Pattern. It was the most difficult thing I ever did, but I succeeded. Things should hold together after this wave passes, whether we survive it or not. Brand stole the Jewel from me just as I completed it. When I recovered from his attack I was able to use the new Pattern to project me here. So there is still a Pattern, no matter what else happens."

"But Corwin," she said, "what if Dad succeeded?"

"I do not know."

"It is my understanding," Bleys said, "from things that Dworkin told me, that two distinct Patterns could not exist in the same universe. Those in Rebma and Tir-na Nog'th do not count, being but reflections of our own. . . ."

"What would happen?" I said.

"I think there would be a splitting off, the founding of a new exist-ence—somewhere."

"Then what would its effect be upon our own?"

"Either total catastrophe or no effect whatsoever," Fiona said. "I can make a case for its going either way."

"Then we are right back where we started," I said. "Either things are going to fall apart shortly or they are going to hold."

"So it would seem," Bleys said.

"It does not matter, if we are not going to be around after that wave gets to us," I said. "And it will."

I turned my attention back to the funeral cortege. More horsemen had emerged behind the wagon, followed by marching drummers. Then pennons and torches and a long line of foot soldiers. The sing-ing still came to us, and far, far out over the abyss it seemed the pro-cession might finally have reached that dark citadel.

. . . *I hated you for so long, blamed you for so many things. Now it is over, and none of these feelings remain. Instead, you had even wanted me to be king, a job for which—I see now—I am not fitted. I see that I must have meant something to you after all. I will never tell the others. It is enough to know it myself. But I can never think of you in the same fashion again. Already your image blurs. I see Ganelon's face where yours should be. He was my companion. He risked his neck for me. He was you, but a different you—a you that I had not known. How many wives and enemies had you outlived? Were there many friends? I think not. But there were so many things about you of which we knew nothing. I never thought that I would see your passing. Ganelon—Father—old friend and enemy, I bid you farewell. You join Deirdre, whom I have loved. You have preserved your mystery. Rest in peace, if that be your will. I give you this withered rose I have borne through hell, casting it into the abyss. I leave you the rose and the twisted colors in the sky. I will miss you. . . .*

Finally, the long line came to an end. The last marchers emerged from the curtain and moved away. The lightning still flared, the rain still poured and the thunder rumbled. No member of the procession that I could recall had seemed wet, however. I had been standing at the edge of the abyss, watching them pass. There was a hand on my arm. How long it had been there, I could not tell. Now that the passage was complete, I realized that the stormfront was advancing again.

The rotation of the sky seemed to be bringing more darkness upon us. There were voices off to my left. It seemed they had been talking for a long while, but I had not been hearing their words. I realized that I was shaking, that I ached all over, that I could barely stand.

"Come and lie down," Fiona said. "The family has shrunken enough for one day."

I let her lead me away from the edge.

"Would it really make any difference?" I asked. "How much longer do you think we have?"

"We do not have to stay here and wait for it," she said. "We will cross the dark bridge into the Courts. We have already broken their defense. The storm may not reach that far. It may be stopped here by the abyss. We ought to see Dad off, anyway."

I nodded.

"It would seem we have small choice but to be dutiful unto the end."

I eased myself down and sighed. If anything, I felt even weaker now.

"Your boots . . ." she said.

"Yes."

She pulled them off. My feet throbbed.

"Thanks."

"I'll get you some rations."

I closed my eyes. I dozed. Too many images played within my head to make for a coherent dream. How long this lasted, I do not know, but an old reflex drew me to wakefulness at the sound of an approaching horse. Then a shadow passed over my eyelids.

I looked up and beheld a muffled rider, silent, still. I was regarded.

I looked back. No threatening gesture had been made, but there was a feeling of antipathy in that cold gaze.

"There lies the hero," said a soft voice.

I said nothing.

"I could slay you easily now."

I recognized the voice then, though I had no idea as to the reason behind the sentiment.

"I came upon Borel before he died," she said. "He told me how ignobly you had bested him."

I could not help it, I could not control it. A dry chuckle rose in my throat. Of all the stupid things to get upset about. I might have told her that Borel had been far better equipped and far fresher than I, and that he had come to me looking for a fight. I might have told her that I do not recognize rules when my life is at stake, or that I do not consider war a game. I could have said a great number of things, but if she did not know them already or did not choose to understand them, they would not have made a bit of difference. Besides, her feelings were already plain.

So I simply said one of the great rite truths: "There is generally more than one side to a story."

"I will settle for the one I have," she told me.

I thought about shrugging, but my shoulders were too sore.

"You have cost me two of the most important persons in my life," she said then.

"Oh?" I said. "I'm sorry, for you."

"You are not what I was led to believe. I had seen you as a truly noble figure—strong, yet understanding and sometimes gentle. Honorable . . ."

The storm, much closer now, was flaring at her back. I thought of something vulgar and said it. She let it pass as if she had not heard me.

"I am going now," she said, "back to my own people. You have won the day thus far—but that way lay Amber." She gestured toward the storm. I could only stare. Not at the raging elements. At her. "I doubt there is anything of my new allegiance left for me to renounce," she continued.

"What about Benedict?" I asked softly.

"Don't . . ." she said, and she turned away .There was a silence. Then, "I do not believe that we will ever meet again," she said, and her horse carried her off to my left, in the direction of the black road.

A cynic might have decided that she had simply chosen to toss in her lot with what she now saw as the winning side, as the Courts of Chaos would likely survive. I simply did not know. I could think only of what I had seen when she had gestured. The cowling had slipped away and I had gotten a glimpse of what she had become. It had not been a human face, there within the shadows. But I turned my head and watched until she was gone. With Deirdre, Brand and

Dad gone, and now a parting with Dara on these terms, the world was much emptier—whatever was left of it.

I lay back and sighed. Why not just remain here when the others departed, wait for the storm to wash over me, and sleep . . . dissolve? I thought of Hugi. Had I digested his flight from life as well as his flesh? I was so tired that it seemed the easiest course. . . .

"Here, Corwin."

I had been dozing again, though only for a moment. Fiona was beside me once more, with rations and a flask. Someone was with her.

"I did not wish to interrupt your audience," she said. "So I waited."

"You heard?" I asked.

"No, but I can guess," she said, "since she is gone. Here."

I swallowed some wine, turned my attention to the meat, the bread. Despite my state of mind, they tasted good to me.

"We will be moving soon," Fiona said, casting a glance at the raging stormfront. "Can you ride?"

"I think so," I said.

I took another drink of the wine.

"But too much has happened, Fi," I told her. "I have gone numb emotionally. I broke out of a sanitarium on a shadow world. I have tricked people and I've killed people. I have calculated and I have fought. I won back my memory and I have been trying to straighten out my life. I have found my family, and found that I love it. I have been reconciled with Dad. I have fought for the kingdom. I have tried everything I know to hold things together. Now it appears that it has all come to nothing, and I have not enough spirit left to mourn further. I have gone numb. Forgive me."

She kissed me.

"We are not yet beaten. You will be yourself again," she said.

I shook my head.

"It is like the last chapter of *Alice*," I said. "If I shout, 'You are only a pack of cards!' I feel we will all fly into the air, a hand of painted pasteboards. I am not going with you. Leave me here. I am only the Joker, anyway."

"Right now, I am stronger than you are," she said. "You are coming."

"It is not fair," I said softly.

"Finish eating," she said. "There is still some time."

As I did, she went on, "Your son Merlin is waiting to see you. I would like to call him up here now."

"Prisoner?"

"Not exactly. He was not a combatant. He just arrived a little while ago, asking to see you."

I nodded and she went away. I abandoned my rations and took another swig of wine. I had just become nervous. What do you say to a grown son you only recently learned existed? I wondered about his feelings toward me. I wondered whether he knew of Dara's decision. How should I act with him?

I watched him approach from a place where my relatives were clustered, far off to my left. I had wondered why they had left me by myself this way. The more visitors I received the more apparent it became. I wondered whether they were holding up the withdrawal because of me. The storm's moist winds were growing stronger. He was staring at me as he advanced, no special expression on that face so much like my own. I wondered how Dara felt now that her prophecy of the destruction seemed to have been fulfilled. I wondered how her relationship with the boy actually stood. I wondered . . . many things.

He leaned forward to clasp my hand.

"Father . . ." he said.

"Merlin." I looked into his eyes. I rose to my feet, still holding his hand.

"Do not get up."

"It is all right." I clasped him to me, then released him. "I am glad," I said. Then: "Drink with me." I offered him the wine, partly to cover my lack of words.

"Thank you."

He took it, drank some and passed it back.

"Your health," I said and took a sip myself. "Sorry I cannot offer you a chair."

I lowered myself to the ground. He did the same.

"None of the others seemed to know exactly what you have been doing," he said, "except for Fiona, who said only that it had been very difficult."

"No matter," I said. "I am glad to have made it this far, if for no other reason than this. Tell me of yourself, son. What are you like? How has life treated you?"

He looked away.

"I have not lived long enough to have done too much," he said.

I was curious whether he possessed the shapeshifting ability, but restrained myself from asking at this point. No sense in looking for our differences when I had just met him.

"I have no idea what it was like," I said, "growing up in the Courts."

He smiled for the first time.

"And I have no idea what it would have been like anywhere else," he responded. "I was different enough to be left to myself a lot. I was taught the usual things a gentleman should know—magic, weapons, poisons, riding, dancing. I was told that I would one day rule in Amber. This is not true anymore, is it?"

"It does not seem too likely in the foreseeable future," I said.

"Good," he replied. "This is the one thing I did not want to do."

"What do you want to do?"

"I want to walk the Pattern in Amber as Mother did and gain power over Shadow, so that I might walk there and see strange sights and do different things. Do you think I might?"

I took another sip and I passed him the wine.

"It is quite possible," I said, "that Amber no longer exists. It all depends on whether your grandfather succeeded in something he attempted—and he is no longer around to tell us what happened. However, one way or the other, there is a Pattern. If we live through this demon storm, I promise you that I will find you a Pattern, instruct you and see you walking it."

"Thanks," he said. "Now will you tell me of your journey here?"

"Later," I told him. "What did they tell you of me?"

He looked away.

"I was taught to dislike many of the things about Amber," he finally said. Then, after a pause: "You, I was taught to respect, as my father. But I was reminded that you were of the party of the enemy." Another pause. "I remember that time on patrol, when you had come to this place and I found you, after your fight with Kwan. My feelings were mixed. You had just slain someone I had known, yet—I had to admire the stance you took. I saw my face in your own. It was strange. I wanted to know you better."

The sky had rotated completely and the darkness was now above us, the colors passing over the Courts. The steady advance of the flashing stormfront was emphasized by this. I leaned forward and reached for my boots, began pulling them on. Soon it would be time to begin our retreat.

"We will have to continue our conversation on your home ground," I said. "It is about time to fly the storm."

He turned and considered the elements, then looked back out over the abyss.

"I can summon a filmy if you wish."

"One of those drifting bridges such as you rode on the day we met?"

"Yes," he answered. "They are most convenient. I—"

There had been a shout from the direction of my assembled relatives. Nothing threatening seemed to be about when I regarded them. So I got to my feet and took a few steps toward them, Merlin rising to follow me.

Then I saw her. A white form, pawing air it seemed, and rising out of the abyss. Her front hoofs finally struck its brink, and she came forward and then stood still, regarding us all: our Unicorn.

XIII

For a moment, my aches and my fatigue fell away. I felt a tiny twinge of something like hope as I considered the dainty white form which stood before us. A part of me wanted to rush forward, but something much stronger kept me motionless, waiting.

How long we stood thus, I could not tell. Below, on the slopes, the troops had been readying themselves for travel. The prisoners had been bound, horses loaded, equipment secured. But this vast army in the process of march ordering its gear had suddenly halted. It was not natural that they should have become aware so quickly, but every head that I could see was turned in this direction, toward the Unicorn on the brink, limned against that wild sky.

I was suddenly aware that the wind at my back had grown still, though the thunder continued to rumble and explode and the lightning flares threw dancing shadows before me.

I thought of the other time I had seen the Unicorn—at the recovery of the Shadow-Caine's body, the day I had lost a fight with Gérard. I thought of the stories I had heard. . . . Could she really help us?

The Unicorn took a step forward and halted.

She was such a lovely thing that somehow I was heartened just by looking upon her. It was a kind of aching feeling that she aroused, though; hers was a beauty of the sort to be taken in small doses. And I could somehow sense the unnatural intelligence within that snowy head. I wanted very badly to touch her, but knew that I could not.

She cast her gaze all about. Her eyes lighted upon me, and I would have looked away if I had been able. This was not possible, however, and I returned that gaze in which I read an understanding beyond my own. It was as if she knew everything about me, and in this instant had comprehended all of my recent trials—seeing, understanding, possibly sympathizing. For a moment, I felt that I saw something of pity and a strong love reflected there—and perhaps a touch of humor.

Then her head turned and the gaze was broken. I sighed involuntarily. At that moment, in the lightning's glare, I thought I caught a glimpse of something shining at the side of her neck.

She advanced another step, and now she was looking upon the crowd of my kinsmen toward which I had been moving. She lowered her head and made a small whickering noise. She tapped at the earth with her right front hoof.

I felt Merlin at my side. I thought upon things I would be losing if it all ended here.

She took several dancing steps forward. She tossed her head and lowered it. It seemed that she did not like the notion of approaching so large a group of people.

At her next step, I saw the glitter again, and more. A tiny spark of red shone through her fur farther down on her neck. She was wearing the Jewel of Judgment. How she had retrieved it, I had no idea. And it did not matter. If she would just deliver it, I felt that I could break the storm—or at least shield us from this section of it until it had passed.

But that one glance had been enough. She paid me no more heed. Slowly, carefully, as if ready to bolt at the slightest disturbance, she advanced upon the spot where Julian, Random, Bleys, Fiona, Llewella, Benedict and several nobles stood.

I should have realized then what was occurring, but I did not. I simply watched the sleek beast's movements as she picked her way forward, passing about the periphery of the group.

She halted once again and lowered her head. Then she shook her mane and dropped to her front knees. The Jewel of Judgment hung suspended from her twisted, golden horn. The tip of her horn was almost touching the person before whom she knelt.

Suddenly, in my mind's eye, I saw our father's face in the heavens, and his words came back to me: "With my passing, the problem of the succession will be upon you. . . . I have no choice but to leave this on the horn of the Unicorn."

A murmur moved through the group, as I realized this same thought must be occurring to the others. The Unicorn did not stir at this disturbance, however, but remained a soft, white statue, not even seeming to breathe.

Slowly, Random reached forward and removed the Jewel from her horn. His whisper carried to me.

"Thank you," he said.

Julian unsheathed his blade and placed it at Random's feet as he knelt. Then Bleys and Benedict and Caine, Fiona and Llewella. I went and joined them. So did my son.

Random stood silent for a long while. Then, "I accept your allegiance," he said. "Now get up, all of you."

As we did, the Unicorn turned and bolted. She raced down the slope and was out of sight in a matter of moments.

"I had never expected anything like this to happen," Random said, still holding the Jewel at eye level. "Corwin, can you take this thing and stop that storm?"

"It is yours now," I said, "and I do not know how extensive the disturbance is. It occurs to me that in my present condition I might not be able to hold up long enough to keep us all safe. I think it is going to have to be your first regal act."

"Then you are going to have to show me how to work it. I thought we needed a Pattern to perform the attunement."

"I think not. Brand indicated that a person who was already attuned could attune another. I have given it some thought since then, and I believe I know how to go about it. Let's get off to one side somewhere."

"Okay. Come on."

Already, something new had come into his voice and posture. The sudden role had begun working its change immediately, it seemed. I wondered what sort of king and queen he and Vialle would become. Too much. My mind felt disassociated. Too much had happened too recently. I could not contain all of the latest events in one big piece of thinking. I just wanted to crawl off somewhere and sleep around the clock. Instead, I followed him to a place where a small cooking fire still smoldered.

He poked at the fire and tossed a handful of sticks onto it. Then he seated himself close to it and nodded to me. I went over and sat down beside him.

"About this king business," he said. "What am I going to do, Corwin? It caught me totally unprepared."

"Do? Probably a very good job," I replied.

"Do you think there were many hard feelings?"

"If there were, they did not show," I said. "You were a good choice, Random. So much has happened recently . . . Dad sheltered us actually, maybe more than was good for us. The throne is obviously no plum. You have a lot of hard work ahead of you. I think the others have come to realize this."

"And yourself?"

"I wanted it only because Eric did. I did not realize it at the time, but it is true. It was the winning counter in a game we had been playing across the years. The end of a vendetta, really. And I would have killed him for it. I am glad now that he found another way to die. We were more alike than we were different, he and I. I did not realize that until much later either. But after his death, I kept finding reasons for not taking the throne. Finally, it dawned on me that it was not really what I wanted. No. You are welcome to it. Rule well, brother. I am sure that you will."

"If Amber still exists," he said after a time, "I will try. Come, let us be about this business with the Jewel. That storm is getting uncomfortably near."

I nodded and took the stone from his fingers. I held it by its chain with the fire behind it. The light came through; its insides seemed clear.

"Lean closer and stare into the Jewel with me," I directed.

He did this, and while we both regarded the stone, I told him, "Think of the Pattern," and I commenced thinking of it myself, trying to summon to mind its loops and swirls, its palely glowing lines.

I seemed to detect a slight flaw near to the stone's center. I considered it as I thought upon the twistings, the turns, the Veils. . . . I imagined the current which swept through me every time I essayed that complex way.

The imperfection in the stone grew more distinct.

I lay my will upon it, summoning it into fullness, clarity. A familiar feeling came over me as this occurred. It was that which had taken me on the day I had attuned myself to the Jewel. I only hoped that I was strong enough now to go through the experience once again.

I reached out and clasped Random by the shoulder.

"What do you see?" I asked him.

"Something like the Pattern," he said, "only it seems to be three dimensional. It lies at the bottom of a red sea. . . ."

"Come with me then," I said. "We must go to it."

Again, that feeling of movement, drifting at first, then falling with increasing velocity toward the never fully seen sinuosities of the Pattern within the Jewel. I willed us ahead, feeling my brother's presence beside me, and the ruby glow which surrounded us darkened, becoming the blackness of a clean night sky. This special Pattern grew with each thudding heartbeat. Somehow, the process seemed easier than it had before—perhaps because I was already attuned.

Feeling Random beside me, I drew him along as that familiar shape grew and its starting point became apparent. As we were moved in that direction, I once again tried to encompass the totality of this Pattern and was lost once more in what seemed its extra-dimensional convolutions. Great curves and spirals and knotted-seeming traceries wound before us. The sense of awe I had felt earlier swept over me, and from somewhere nearby I was aware of this in Random, also.

We progressed to the section of the beginning and were swept into it. There was a shimmering brightness all about us flashed through with sparks as we were woven into the matrix of light. This time, my mind was entirely absorbed by the process and Paris seemed far away. . . .

A subconscious memory reminded me of the more difficult sections, and here I employed my desire—my will, if you like—to hurry us along the dazzling route, recklessly drawing strength from Random to accelerate the process.

It was as if we negotiated the luminous interior of an enormous and elaborately convoluted seashell. Only our passage was soundless, and we ourselves disembodied points of sentience.

Our velocity seemed to increase constantly, as did a mental aching I did not recall from the previous traversal of the design. Perhaps it was related to my fatigue, or to my efforts to hurry things so. We crashed through the barriers; we were surrounded by steady, flowing walls of brightness. I felt myself growing faint, dizzy, now. But I could not afford the luxury of unconsciousness, nor could I permit us to move more slowly with the storm as near as I remembered it. Again, regretfully, I drew strength from Random—this time just to keep us in the game. We sped ahead.

This time, I did not experience the tingling, fiery sensation of somehow being shaped. It must have been an effect of my attunement. My previous passage through it might have rendered me some small immunity in this regard.

After a timeless interval, it seemed that I felt Random falter. Perhaps I represented too great a drain upon his energies. I began to wonder whether I would leave him with sufficient strength to manipulate the storm if I leaned upon him any further. I resolved not to draw upon his resources any more than I already had. We were well along the way. He should be able to continue without me, if it came to that. I would simply have to hang on as best I could now. Better for me to be lost here than both of us.

We swept on, my senses rebelling, the dizziness recurring. I set my will to our progress and forced everything else from my mind. It seemed we were nearing the terminus when a darkening began which I knew was not a part of the experience. I fought down panic.

It was no good. I felt myself slipping away. So close! I was certain we were almost finished. It would be so easy to—

Everything swam away from me. My last sensation was a knowledge of Random's concern.

It was flickering orange and red between my feet. Was I trapped in some astral hell? I continued to stare as my mind slowly cleared. The light was surrounded by darkness and . . .

There were voices, familiar . . .

Things cleared. I was lying on my back, feet toward a campfire.

"It is all right, Corwin. It is all right."

It was Fiona who had spoken. I turned my head. She was seated on the ground above me.

"Random . . . ?" I said.

"He is all right, also—Father."

Merlin was seated off to the right.

"What happened?"

"Random bore you back," Fiona said.

"Did the attunement work?"

"He thinks so."

I struggled to sit up. She tried to push me back, but I sat up anyway.

"Where is he?"

She gestured with her eyes.

I looked and I saw Random. He was standing with his back to us about thirty meters away, on a shelf of rock, facing the storm. It was very close now, and a wind whipped his garments. Lightning trails crissed and crossed before him. The thunder boomed almost constantly.

"How long—has he been there?" I asked.

"Only a few minutes," Fiona replied.

"That is how long it has been—since our return?"

"No," she said. "You have been out for a fairly long while. Random talked with the others first, then ordered a troop withdrawal. Benedict has taken them all to the black road. They are crossing over."

I turned my head.

There was movement along the black road, a dark column heading out toward the citadel. Gossamer strands drifted between us; there were a few sparks at the far end, about the nighted hulk. Overhead, the sky had completely reversed itself, with us beneath the darkened half. Again, I felt the strange feeling of having been here long, long ago, to see that this, rather than Amber, was the true center of creation. I grasped after the ghost of a memory. It vanished.

I searched the lightning-shot gloom about me.

"All of them—gone?" I said to her. "You, me, Merlin, Random—we're the only ones left here?"

"Yes," Fiona said. "Do you wish to follow them now?"

I shook my head.

"I am staying here with Random."

"I knew you would say that."

I got to my feet as she did. So did Merlin. She clapped her hands and a white horse came ambling up to her.

"You have no further need for my ministrations," she said. "So I will go and join the others in the Courts of Chaos. There are horses for you tethered by those rocks." She gestured. "Are you coming, Merlin?"

"I will stay with my father, and the king."

"So be it. I hope to see you there soon."

"Thanks, Fi," I said.

I helped her to mount and watched her ride off.

I went over and sat down by the fire again. I watched Random, who stood unmoving, facing the storm.

"There are plenty of rations and wine," Merlin said. "May I fetch you some?"

"Good idea."

The storm was so close that I could have walked down to it in a couple of minutes. I could not tell yet whether Random's efforts were having any effect. I sighed heavily and let my mind drift.

Over. One way or another, all of my efforts since Greenwood were over. No need for revenge any longer. No. We had an intact Pattern, maybe even two. The cause of all our troubles, Brand, was dead. Any residuum of my curse was bound to be wiped out by the massive convulsions sweeping through Shadow. And I had done my best to make up for it. I had found a friend in my father and come to terms with him as himself before his death. We had a new king, with the apparent blessing of the Unicorn, and we had pledged him our loyalty. It seemed sincere to me. I was reconciled with my entire family. I felt that I had done my duty. Nothing drove me now. I had run out of causes and was as close as I might ever be to peace. With all this behind me, I felt that if I had to die now, it was all right. I would not protest quite so loudly as I would have at any other time.

"You are far from here, Father."

I nodded, then smiled. I accepted some food and began eating. As I did, I watched the storm. Still too early to be certain, but it seemed that it was no longer advancing.

I was too tired to sleep. Or something like that. My aches had all subsided and a wondrous numbness had come over me. I felt as if I were embedded in warm cotton. Events and reminiscences kept the mental clockwork turning within me. It was, in many ways, a delicious feeling.

I finished eating and built up the fire. I sipped the wine and watched the storm, like a frosted window set before a fireworks display. Life felt good. If Random succeeded in pulling this one off, I would be riding into the Courts of Chaos tomorrow. What might await me there, I could not tell. Perhaps it might be a gigantic trap. An ambush. A trick. I dismissed the thought. Somehow, right now, it did not matter.

"You had begun telling me of yourself, Father."

"Had I? I do not recall what I said."

"I would like to get to know you better. Tell me more."

I made a popping noise with my lips and shrugged.

"Then this." He gestured. "This whole conflict. How did it get started? What was your part in it? Fiona told me that you had dwelled in Shadow for many years without your memory. How did you get it back and locate the others, and return to Amber?"

I chuckled. I regarded Random and the storm once more. I took a drink of wine and drew up my cloak against the wind.

"Why not?" I said then. "If you've a stomach for long stories, that is. . . . I suppose that the best place to begin is at Greenwood Private Hospital, on the shadow Earth of my exile. Yes . . ."

XIV

The sky turned, and turned again as I spoke. Standing against the storm, Random prevailed. It broke before us, parting as if cloven by a giant's axblade. It rolled back at either hand, finally sweeping off to the north and the south, fading, diminishing, gone. The landscape it had masked endured, and with it went the black road. Merlin tells me that this is no problem, though, for he will summon a strand of gossamer when the time comes for us to cross over.

Random is gone now. The strain upon him was immense. In repose, he no longer looked as once he did—the brash younger brother we delighted in tormenting—for there were lines upon his face which I had never noticed before, signs of some depth to which I had paid no heed. Perhaps my vision has been colored by recent events, but he seemed somehow nobler and stronger. Does a new role work some alchemy? Appointed by the Unicorn, anointed by the storm, it seems that he had indeed assumed a kingly mien, even in slumber.

I have slept—even as Merlin now dozes—and it pleased me to be, for this brief while before his awakening, the only spot of sentience on this crag at the rim of Chaos, looking back upon a surviving world, a world that has been scoured, a world which endures. . . .

We may have missed Dad's funeral, his drifting into some nameless place beyond the Courts. Sad, but I lacked the strength to move. And yet, I have seen the pageant of his passing, and I bear much of his life within me. I have said my good-byes. He would understand. And good-bye, Eric. After all this time I say it, in this way. Had you lived so long, it would have been over between us. We might even one day have become friends, all our causes for strife passed. Of them all, you and I were more alike than any other pair within the family. Save, in some ways, Deirdre and myself. . . . But tears on this count were shed long ago. Good-bye again, though, dearest sister, you will always live somewhere in my heart.

And you Brand . . . With bitterness do I regard your memory, mad brother. You almost destroyed us. You nearly toppled Amber from her lofty perch on the breast of Kolvir. You would have shattered all of Shadow. You almost broke the Pattern and redesigned the universe in your own image. You were mad and evil, and you came so close to realizing your desires that I tremble even now. I am glad that you are gone, that the arrow and the abyss have claimed you, that you sully no more the places of men with your presence nor walk in the sweet airs of Amber. I wish that you had never been born and, failing that, that you had died sooner. Enough! It diminishes me to reflect so. Be dead and trouble my thinking no more.

I deal you out like a hand of cards, my brothers and sisters. It is painful as well as self-indulgent to generalize like this, but you—I—we—seem to have changed, and before I move into the traffic again I require a final look.

Caine, I never liked you and I still do not trust you. You have insulted me, betrayed me and even stabbed me. Forget that. I do not like your methods, though I cannot fault your loyalty this time around. Peace, then. Let the new reign begin with a clean slate between us.

Llewella, you possess reserves of character the recent situation did not call upon you to exercise. For this, I am grateful. It is sometimes pleasant to emerge from a conflict untested.

Bleys, you are still a figure clad in light to me—valiant, exuberant and rash. For the first, my respect, for the second, my smile. And the last seems to have at least been tempered in recent times. Good. Stay away from conspiracies in the future. They do not suit you well.

Fiona, you have changed the most. I must substitute a new feeling for an old one, princess, as we have become for the first time friends. Take my fondness, sorceress. I owe you.

Gérard, slow, faithful brother, perhaps we have not all changed. You stood rock-like and held to what you believed. May you be less easily gulled. May I never wrestle you again. Go down to your sea in your ships and breathe the clean salt air.

Julian, Julian, Julian . . . Is it that I never really knew you? No. Arden's green magic must have softened that old vanity during my long absence, leaving a juster pride and something I would fain call fairness—a thing apart from mercy, to be sure, but an addition to your armory of traits I'll not disparage.

And Benedict, the gods know you grow wiser as time burns its way to entropy, yet you still neglect single examples of the species in your knowledge of people. Perhaps I'll see you smile now this battle's done. Rest, warrior.

Flora . . . Charity, they say, begins at home. You seem no worse now than when I knew you long ago. It is but a sentimental dream to regard you and the others as I do, totting up by balance sheets, looking for credits. We are not enemies, any of us, now, and that should be sufficient.

And the man clad in black and silver with a silver rose upon him? He would like to think that he has learned something of trust, that he has washed his eyes in some clear spring, that he has polished an ideal or two. Never mind. He may still be only a smart-mouthed meddler, skilled mainly in the minor art of survival, blind as ever the dungeons knew him to the finer shades of irony. Never mind, let it go, let it be. I may never be pleased with him.

Carmen, *voulez-vous venir avec moi?* No? Then good-bye to you too, Princess of Chaos. It might have been fun.

The sky is turning once more, and who can say what deeds its stained-glass light might shine upon? The solitaire has been dealt and played. Where there had been nine of us now there are seven and one a king. Yet Merlin and Martin are with us, new players in the ongoing game.

My strength returns as I stare into the ashes and consider the path I have taken. The way ahead intrigues me, from hell to hallelujah. I have back my eyes, my memories, my family. And Corwin will always be Corwin, even on Judgment Day.

Merlin is stirring now, and this is good. It is time to be about. There are things to do.

Random's last act after defeating the storm was to join with me. drawing power from the Jewel, to reach Gérard through his Trump. They are cold once more, the cards, and the shadows are themselves again. Amber stands. Years have passed since we departed it, and more may elapse before I return. The others may already have Trumped home, as Random has done, to take up his duties. But I must visit the Courts of Chaos now, because I said that I would, because I may even be needed there.

We ready our gear now, Merlin and I, and soon he will summon a wispy roadway.

When all is done in that place, and when Merlin has walked his

Pattern and gone to claim his worlds, there is a journey that I must make. I must ride to the place where I planted the limb of old Ygg, visit the tree it has grown to. I must see what has become of the Pattern I drew to the sound of pigeons on the Champs-Elysées. If it leads me to another universe, as I now believe it will, I must go there, to see how I have wrought.

The roadway drifts before us, rising to the Courts in the distance. The time has come. We mount and move forward.

We are riding now across the blackness on a road that looks like cheesecloth. Enemy citadel, conquered nation, trap, ancestral home . . . We shall see. There is a faint flickering from battlement and balcony. We may even be in time for a funeral. I straighten my back and I loosen my blade. We will be there before much longer.

Good-bye and hello, as always.